Phoenix on Fire©

Written By:
Skye Falcon

Publisher's Thoughts:

We hope that you enjoy the newest novel by
Skye Falcon. Please know that the names,
characters, places, or situations within this
book are fictitious, or a product of the
Author's imagination, or experience. Any
resemblance found to any current situations,
or person's living is entirely in the reader's
mind. The publisher of this book does not
control what other's post, or what is on third
party web sites regarding this book.

"This book is dedicated to my Grandmothers, who in completely different ways, had to fight for their own personal rights to live peacefully. Their strength, fight, and drive will always push me to do better. To be better. I am so thankful to have them both in my life. Whether it was Monday-Tuesdays, or Thursday-Fridays...My life will be forever warmed by their constant love and support."

This book is dedicated to Barbara, and Nancy.

~1~

I backed out of the garage, running later that I'd like to admit. For whatever reason, I had the vibes all night long. I didn't sleep very well. Not to mention the hot water heater breaking, and making my shower take entirely too long. *Oh, come on! You know why you had the vibes...* I shook my head, and pulled up next to the mailbox. I pulled the pile of mail into my lap, and started to flip through.

"Bills, bills, Oh!" I couldn't help but squeal. My new business decals had arrived, and I couldn't wait to show Gabe. Carefully setting them aside, I finished looking through the pile. My heart stopped when I saw the small white envelope. The eeriest feeling came over me, and drew goose bumps throughout my body. Sliding my finger through the seal made me count the years. *7 years now...but yet it still feels like yesterday.* I pulled out the paper, and opened it carefully. His hand writing was still the same rushed, angry style. Swallowing, I read the first few lines.

> *"Dearest Janie, Writing you from the yard today, hoping that this month finds you well. I think about you daily, and still dream of your forgiveness..."*

It continued on, but I had to stop and collect myself. Reading his words made them extremely real in my head, tripping memories from long ago. Over the years the letters were always angry, and hate filled. Many I just simply refused to read. *Although, not reading them took you a while to learn, too.* Skimming through it, I could tell this was one of the newer, more apologetic ones. I quickly picked up my cell, and dialed as fast as I could. "Hey! Sorry, I'm running late. I got another letter. Yeah, I'll bring it with me. Ok, be there soon." I dropped my cell into my bag, and headed for my lunch date.

No sooner did I pull up outside the Plex, Sean was there to greet me. Smiling huge, as always. My radio was blaring *Mazzy Star*, so I took my time climbing out of the car. He motioned for me, and I held up a finger while I finished singing the song. *So impatient to see you, he is.* I smiled at his antics through the windshield. *Ah, his childlike behavior, and inability to act like an adult…the only reasons you managed to avoid him all these years.* I giggled, and opened the car door.

"Hey Janes!!" I waved, and he motioned me over. My large sunglasses hid the fact that I was watching him look me up and down. I couldn't help but smirk. *Some things never change…* Sean had married a few years before, and although I had never been able to figure out the why's or how's of it, he seemed happy. His arms were around me quickly. "It's so good to see you! And I love your choice of song. *Fade into You* has always been one of my favorites." I slid my hands in between us, and broke the hug. I think I may have blushed. "Come on," he took my hand. "Delaney is inside getting a table."

"Oh good! I'm glad she came! I wanted to get you guys hooked up with some services before the baby comes." I smiled widely at him, and winked. Walking into the Plex, I saw Delaney right away. She had jet black hair, and a beautiful smile. She waved us over, and I patted her on the shoulder when I sat down. "Hey girl! How are you feeling? Sean's told me how rough it's been."

"Aw, thanks for asking. I'm doing okay, this

is all just so much. So tiring." She paused, and rubbed her forehead. I squeezed her other hand reassuringly. "Geez, Janes…how'd you make it through two babies??" She looked so sad, and powerless.

"This too shall pass! I know it is hard now, but I promise you it gets better! By the sixteenth week in both of my pregnancies things started to calm down. With Lilah's pregnancy, I was under so much stress until that half way mark that everyone was surprised I didn't have more problems than I did." I patted her arm again. "Just know you're not alone, and you can call me anytime. Ok?" I smiled gently, and reached in my bag. "Better read this one, Sean." I handed the letter towards him. He sighed, and shook his head. His expression reminded me how he truly felt about things from our past.

"How many years has it been? And he's still at it?"

"It's been seven. Seven years since his sentencing next Tuesday." I shuttered to myself, remembering receiving the news that he had been sentenced. And learning he wouldn't be a bother any longer. *Obviously the courts didn't believe you then. Him not bother you? Oh how funny…* Sean took the envelope, and opened it up. As he began, his face scrunched up reading parts about Michael's hopes for me. Once he hit the middle of the letter, his face was pained, and he shook his head.

"There's so much blame on you, still, even in his apologies." He folded the note and stuck it back in the envelope. "There's just no excuse. I'm glad I haven't gotten any letters for a while. I don't like to have to relive it, and I can't imagine you do either." I shook my head, and slid the envelope

6

back into my bag.

"Not especially. Tends to be a bit of a damper on things!" I chuckled idly, hoping the subject would be changed.

"The things I've heard you all talking about with Mike…was that his name?" She turned toward her husband for clarification. Sean nodded.

"He was Mike to me. Michael to Janie. Now he's just "shit fucker" to us both." He smiled at me, and winked. *His winking is going to get him in trouble one of these days…* Delaney & I both giggled.

"Well, he sounds like a terrible sonofabitch. I'm glad that he was before my time." We all agreed on that one, and finished our lunch outing. I was glad that Sean and I had remained friends over the years. It was so refreshing to be able to still have parts of my past around that weren't so tainted. *Not tainted, but don't deny the strain…*

"Well you two, it's been wonderful to see you. I'm glad you've moved back, and are in the city again. We'll have you over for a cookout, soon, I'm sure. Once we get the new schedules figured out." I smiled and hugged Delaney gently. I turned towards Sean, who engulfed me with his giant hug. *He always smells so good.*

"Sounds great, Janes. Please pass along my hellos to everyone." His hands were on my back still, one low and one high. His fingers began to push into my flesh, and I swear I heard his breath hitch. *No!! Not in front of your wife!!* I pulled back, and looked in his eyes. It was still that same long, river of what used to come off as pity…but now I was beginning to wonder if there was more.

"Bye, guys!" I jumped back into my Jeep, cranked up the radio, and headed back home. It was time to pick the kids up from the sitter, and get the evening routine going.

~ ~ ~ ~ ~ ~

Opening the front door of the house, I was almost run over by my children. *Still feels strange saying that, doesn't it Janie?* I closed the front door, and smiled. I patted my belly while I put my bags on the bench. Thinking back to Lilah's birth, and having her tiny little face completely change my world. Who would have ever thought she'd turn out to be such a spitfire? And Galen a few years later, my little cuddle bug. Two of the things I'd do anything for in this world. *Who are now screaming, running through the house in search of their father...*

My thoughts suddenly twisted, and as I turned around, I felt my eyebrow raise. The hairs on the back of my neck stood up, and suddenly his arms were around me.

"Welcome home, baby." He said in a whisper. Quickly spinning me around to face him, and pushing us back into the foyer. "I've missed you today." His lips were fierce on my own, and his tongue was hungry in my mouth. His hands wandered up and down my rib cage, and his thumbs gently pushed on my nipples. Looking in these baby blues has never gotten old. My hands held to his shoulders, and gripped into his ripped muscles. I broke the kiss to bury my head into his neck. These arms were still my solace after all this time...*and falling into them later is just what the doctor ordered.* Suddenly, we weren't alone. His hands brushed my cheeks, and he whispered into my ear. "Soon. Let's get these things fed, and put in bed." I smiled into his lips as I kissed him.

"I told you Daddy was here, Galen!" Lilah yelled in his face. "Daddy!! Daddy! I missed you today!! Mommy said she saw Uncle Sean and Laney today. And I made this picture for you!" She was very proud of her work. Gabe took it from her, and gave her a big hug. I loved watching their interactions. Lilah was a little Gabriel. The bluest eyes and darkest hair, and her face was the feminine version of her Dad's. When she was little, I would get lost in her eyes just like Gabe's. I sighed out loud.

"Thank you, Lilah. I'll hang it on the wall with your other masterpieces." He smiled and turned to Galen. He reached his arms up, and Gabe picked him up. "How're you today, buddy?" Tickling his belly, he made the funniest laugh. Galen's always been my observer. Super smart, and thinks everything out. Even at 4. "It looks like your day was good then?" He put Galen back on the floor, and waited for his answer.

"Yes Daddy," he shifted while he gathered his thoughts. "I pwayed outside today, and I caught a wightning bug!" He motioned with his hands through his story of how he caught this magnificent bug. I headed into the kitchen to make dinner, while Gabe cleaned up, and got the kids into their pajamas.

~2~

After dinner, when the kids were soundly in their beds, we were still able to slip away into passion filled darkness, together. I was always eager to reach the bedroom, and close the door. I could finally shed my stressors, my clothes, and my inhibitions. I loved my kids more than anything, but I surely loved my husband even more. I turned the corner into the bedroom, to find that the comforter had been smoothed out, and the pillows strewn about on the floor. *What on earth is he up to?* Gabe was in the closet, so I could not see what he was doing. I turned into the bathroom to brush my teeth, and pee. When I returned, the blindfold and cuffs were on the bed. My heart instantly sped up. *Oh, yes...please...*

I slowly walked to the bed, staring into Gabe's eyes. I dropped my robe, and sat waiting for him on the bed. He stood before me in only warm up pants. *These pants will surely be the death of you...* His hands dove into my hair, and massaged my scalp. My eyes closed, as if automatically, to his touch. I loved the way his fingers felt circling, rubbing, and swirling my long hair around. My hands instinctively reached out towards his waist, and I clutched on to him. Pulling him into me, so my cheek was resting on his belly. I inhaled deeply. *MMMmmm... he smells soo good.*

I thumbed the tops of his warm up pants, and began to shimmy them down, all while gently kissing his abdomen. Once I pulled them over his hardening length, they fell to the floor. Now his stiff, soft skin was dancing around underneath my chin. I slowly tipped my head down, as to not disturb the head massage that was now making my muscles relax, and my panties drenched. I slowly rubbed my lips across the soft skin of his cock, and lost my breath. *The passion and desire burns so brightly between you...* I inhaled him into my mouth. Sucking him deeply into the back of my throat. To the place where the deepest, darkest moans escaped his lips, and I felt more powerful than ever. Bringing this amazing man to the brink…over, and over again.

After a few moments, I came up for air, and wiped off my lips. Gabe's mouth came crashing down on mine, and the passion exploded. His tongue thrust into my mouth, and a low, carnal moan escaped his lips. He flipped me face down on the bed, and quickly slid my pants off. Climbing up my back, he took his position sitting on my rear. I could feel his body heat pouring out of him, and that made me needy. He eased each wrist into the handcuffs. *MMMmmm… cold metal… more…* I tightly closed my eyes, and hoped he would continue. I tried to control my moans, because if it was too loud… our fun would end.

I pulled at the restraints, and they were secure. I glanced over my shoulder in time to catch Gabe handling his length, with his eyes glued to my ass. After a few moments, he noticed I was watching. He abruptly stopped, and spanked me hard. I gasped. *Perfect. More…* His hot hands came around my face, and then he pulled my hair into a pony tail. Grasping it tightly, he pulled my head back to meet his mouth. His tongue probed inside, showing me just how hungry he was. Holding up the blindfold, I was enthralled with his next plans, and wiggled in the restraints. His flash of a huge smile told me this was going to be very worth my time.

"What do you think, love?" He spun it on his finger. I smiled, and nodded. He kissed my cheeks as he slid it on. I felt him leave the bed, and I could feel his movements around the room. I was instantly on edge. "I'm coming back to take your panties." His hands were quick, and yanked them down my legs. My breathing was erratic, and shaking with each body quiver. *Thanks for the warning...* His hand came down hard, and fast. The crack of skin on skin could have shattered glass. The electric waves that coursed through my body with each spank were indescribable. They were the freedom I desperately sought. *Yes, more...* His relentless spankings ceased, and he moved away from the bed again.

Laying by myself, blindfolded, always left me anticipating…and thinking. In my mind, Gabe was all over me. My thoughts were so vivid, I could feel his hands on me. And it was making me hot. I was ready. Handcuffed to the bedposts, and desperate. I pulled myself up on my knees, and dangled my ass in the air. *Hoping for something there, Janes??* God, yes. The moan escaped my lips before I could quiet it. In a split second, I felt close movement, and froze.

His breath was hot in my ear, and on my neck. Chills over took my willing body. He tickled his hands all over my body, but touched me with no other part. I could hear the clicking of what sounded like lids, or bottles, maybe. He stopped touching me suddenly, and I slumped in surrender. *Well, damn! What the hell?* Now this was teasing, and that wasn't very nice at all. Without notice, he was entirely inside me, and I was crying out to God. The shock of his full entrance, and my high hormones had me clenching around him seconds in. I tried to focus my thoughts on how exquisite he felt driving in and out of me. How I could feel each throb of pleasure, at the same time I could see it on his face.

"Ohh, Gabe!!" I screamed. There was no stopping this one. I could feel myself squeezing the life out of him, or so I thought. *Untrue.* His hands tightened on my hips, and he changed his rhythm.

Oh my... I turned my hands to hold on to the cuffs so my head wouldn't ram into the wall. *It's no longer in question. Walking tomorrow will be an issue.* He gave a few forceful, claiming thrusts. His fingers dug into my skin now, but the pain evened out with the pleasure. I could feel him pulsating inside me, and I relaxed my head back onto the mattress.

After a few minutes, he eased out of me, and cleaned us both off. I lay sprawled out on the bed. Still handcuffed, and blindfolded. Just enjoying the quiet, and the low electric hum coursing through my body from the multiple orgasms I just had. He turned on some low music, and I could smell the joint. The bed shifted, and he gently touched my forehead and slid the blindfold off. His face was relaxed, and happy.

"Hello again, beautiful." He leaned in, and kissed me deeply.

"Hi yourself," I said in my raspy after sex voice. I rattled my chains, hoping my suitor would set me free. He held the lit joint up to my lips, and I couldn't help but inhale.
"Please?" I added, as I exhaled. He nodded, and emptied his hands. He unlocked the cuffs, and I flipped over, and sat back against the headboard.
"Thank you," I said as I leaned in for a kiss.

"You're very welcome. And thank you, my love." He reached for my breasts, and squeezed them a bit. He moaned in his throat, and I blushed. "I love taking you from behind, but I miss playing with these..." I shook my head, and reached for my water. It was these nights that Gabe and I had always shared, even eight years ago when we first met. *It's a deep love, Janes. Forever connected.* The silly things that always keep things exciting. These "trivial" things that draw us together more. We decided long ago that it was us in the beginning, and should be us in the end. I smiled at my thoughts.

"Can I have some more?" I pointed towards the ashtray. He re-lit our midnight secret, and we passed it a few more times. This was my favorite time of the day…the night. And sitting with my love.

~3~

Morning light brought giggles and snuggly cuddles. I loved sleeping in, but I loved waking up next to my babies even more. I left them in bed with Gabe, watching cartoons. *Isn't that what Saturday mornings were about?* Today would be a big day for us. A year ago, when Gabe's dad passed away, we began adding on to our house. The mother-in-law suite was completed, and Jean Lazarus would be living at our new half address as of this weekend. Although I had some worries about this move, it was also going to allow me to expand my business freely, without having to worry about the kids.

"Mommy!!" Lilah suddenly screamed. I ran out of the bathroom to find Gabe holding Galen upside down in bed. I giggled.

"I see nothing wrong here." I said, as I tickled his little belly.

"Noo mama!! Noo!!!" He laughed uncontrollably. I took him out of Gabe's arms, and pulled Lilah out of bed.

"Time to get up! Grandma will be here soon! You guys get to help her move into the new guest house today!" Their squeals were unstoppable. I turned towards Gabe, who just reemerged from the bathroom. "She's bringing the last loads over today with her. Then we're done with all of this." I walked towards him, and quickly hugged his bare chest. I inhaled deeply. *MMmm.... Delectable. As always.*

"Thanks for doing all this, Janes. She really appreciates it. And so do I." He smiled, and kissed my neck.

"I don't mind doing it. It's going to help all of us out. And I think your dad is resting easier knowing she's okay now." His hug tightened, and then we went about our morning. Prepping the kids, moving boxes for Jean. Her boxes seemed endless. *That's what happens after you hit 70 Janie. You realize you've saved the most ridiculous things...*

"Oh you kids," Jean paused. "I'm exhausted. You've already done so much. I almost can't stand to watch you do anymore!" She rifled through her purse, and pulled out some coupons. "How about if I take the kids to dinner, and you guys can finish and have a break?" She smiled widely, and held my hand. For a 70 year old, she was in great shape. But her eyes showed her age, and her life.

"Jean, that's the best idea you've had all day!" I exclaimed. We all laughed aloud. I went in the house, and readied the kids. They were more than excited to go out with Grandma, and were both looking forward to spending time with her every day after school.

"We be good mama! We pwomise!" Galen said as he hugged me tightly. Lilah's hug was fast. She loved her Grandma, and couldn't wait to go out. They all waved as they left the driveway. Just then, I heard the 'pop' of a bottle. I knew exactly what that sound was. I turned to see Gabe pouring my glass of wine.

"Thought you might want a break, super mom." He smiled, and kissed me lightly. I took the glass willingly, tipped it towards my lips, and drank every drop in one drink. "Oh, a refill for my lady?" He joked, while he poured.

"Yes, please. It's delicious." I took my glass back, and sat at the bar. "Do you want to see the new decals I got for work today?" I smiled, hoping he did. He smiled, and came to the bar with me.

"Absolutely. I'm so glad that, now that mom's here, you'll be able to get out a bit more. I think it's going to be great for business." He smiled again. *He sure is smiley...he must be having some good thoughts.* I pulled the decals out of the box. They were silver and purple in color. *Perfect!*

"They look great!" I exclaimed. The logos were a perfect artistic swirl, with a clean, bold typeface announcing the company name. It was pretty official now. At Your Service, LLC was now a licensed maid and party planning service. I checked Gabe's reaction to the decals, and he was already off the stool and headed towards me. I laid the decal on the bar, and smiled at his advance. He took my face in his hands.

"This is why I loved you the instant I met you. Your drive for everything you do..." he kissed me deeply. His tongue everywhere in my mouth. "These decals are great. You're going to get a lot of new business. I'm so proud of you." He pulled me towards the back deck, and our hot tub. *Ahh, yes... the renovations paid off for this mommy, too.* The private deck and hot tub area were my requests for add-ons when we built Jean's suite on to the house. Lucky for us, a few years ago our landlords decided to sell us the property. We thought it appropriate to put our roots right where it all started. And I loved the house. *Well, three remodels later...* Stepping on to the dimly light deck in the moonlight sure was a sight. We hadn't gotten to spend much time together out here yet. He pulled me out of my thoughts, and over to the hot tub. He quickly dropped his pants, and slid right in.

Looking him over, and the ornery grin on his face, I knew just what my love needed. Slowly, I kicked off one sandal at a time. Thankfully, I had shaved the day before, so as I was running my hands up my legs as sensually as I could, I wasn't getting poked. My hands came to my shorts, and I ran my fingers around the insides of my waistband. Undid the button with a quick flip, and they dropped to the ground, revealing the tiny white panties that I had on. Smirking, I grabbed the bottom hem of my shirt, and slowly pulled it off over my head. Watching him move in anticipation, and his expression was enough to make my nipples hard. I thumbed my panties, and slowly bent and pulled them down my legs. Stepped out of them gingerly, and slowly crawled towards the hot tub. And Gabe.

"Oh, quit teasing me baby... get in here!" He smacked the water with his hand, and put on a bit of a pout. I barely had both legs in when his hands began creeping up my legs. I knew where he was headed, and he wasn't going fast enough! *Please touch me...* His hands lurked around the tops of my thighs, and always headed back down. His lips began teasing my neck, gently nibbling away. The throbbing I felt was growing more intense by the second. This time his hand extended upward, and I quickly moved downward to create a bit of friction. He grabbed on to my labia, and pulled, just enough to make me moan. I sunk into the water as he pulled me down to him.

His hands were hot on my skin, and I could feel him feeling around my body with his fingers. Entering into any area where he thought appropriate, and this time, I was along for the ride. *He's like fine alcohol…aging perfectly with time.* I tried to control my thoughts, and relish this moment of climax. His fingers were always fast to find the way. Suddenly he shifted, and set me onto his lap. I slid straight down, and took him all in. He propped his elbows on the sides of the hot tub, and we rocked in a steady pace until I could feel the throbbing intensify again. I pushed my chest against his as I screamed out his name again.

"Gabe—riel!" I managed to get out. At that moment, his fingers dug into my flesh, and he pulled me as far down into him as he could. His head fell back, and a huge moan escaped his lips. I could feel him pulsating inside me, and I laid my head onto his chest. Our silence was heavy like the sex in the air. These were our recharging moments. Sitting, completely connected together, basking in the sexual intimacy of the moments. Pleasing our inner, carnal beasts, together.

After a few minutes, I lifted myself off of him, and sat in the seat next to him. I pushed the music button, and *At Last* came onto the radio. Such a good song. I just laid my head back on the rest, and lost myself in the music and hot waves. *And maybe lost yourself in that sexy man next to you? Yeah, I think I'm right.* Our toes intermingled by the drain, and our legs floated around each other.

"You know, you'd better get all of me while you can. I'm sure your mom will tire quickly, and they'll be back soon." I smiled at him, and patted his chest. He wrapped an arm around me, and pulled me into an embrace.

"You're right. Maybe we should have a movie night with the kids before you start to work more on Monday?" I nodded in agreement. "I'll pick the movie." I laughed out loud.

"Naturally you *would* pick. Choose something that's PG or less. Please." I grabbed his face with my hands, and kissed his face as I got out of the hot tub. "Don't stay in there too long…you'll wrinkle." I made a silly face, and walked my naked-self back through the yard, and into the house. I could feel the look on his face as I walked away, and that made me blush.

Once the kids were back home, we invited Jean to watch a movie with us. Gabe picked Toy Story, which was his favorite of all time. We had popcorn, and treats. The kids took the talk about Mommy going back to work pretty well. *Better than you thought, you mean?* The cuddles meant more tonight for some odd reason. I loved my people, and had gone through so much to get to this point.

~4~

Monday morning came too quickly, and the sunlight seemed to burn my eyes. I felt so scattered brained, even with just dressing myself. In my flurry, I did check in on the kids, who had gotten themselves up, and were already in the kitchen making their demands at Grandma. Jean waved and smiled widely at me.

"Good luck today, honey!" I waved, and smiled back. But I think she could tell I was a tad bit anxious.

"Bye Mom!" Lilah shouted as I ran out the

door.

"Goodbye my lady! I'll see you this afternoon! Have a good day at school!" As I turned to the door, I also turned into Gabe.

"You're not getting away without giving me a hug, silly." He was gentle, but strong. *Aww.* He knows that I need the support. We've always been good at reading each other.

"I'm sorry," I leaned in and squeezed tighter. "I'm just nervous." I rested my head on his shoulder, and stayed very still.

"What's first on your agenda?" He stroked my back as he spoke.

"I'm meeting them at the park to divvy up the workload to the girls I hired on last week. Getting all of their contact info, giving them the supplies.... I think that's it." I looked up at him, and sighed. His finger lifted my chin, and his lips met mine.

"Well, get going then, love. You've got a big day." He leaned in for one more kiss. "I sure love you." I pulled away, and got into my Jeep.

"And I you," I said as I turned her on, and left the driveway. Heading to the park, my head was swirling with business ideas, and how I was going to approach these ladies. I needed this to work, as I had wanted so badly to be a party planner. I was so thankful to my friend for suggesting adding the maid and cleaning aspect, too.

~

I waited in the pavilion and set up my "welcome" baskets for them. There were three ladies I was beginning with in the start-up, and I already had enough clients booked to keep these

20

ladies busy all week. This was working out just how I had hoped. I was going to be able to focus on party planning, and I was meeting with my first party client this afternoon. I was distracted from my thoughts when I saw the bright yellow car pull in. Catherine Patton was first to arrive. She seemed to be the most ambitious of the group, to say the least.

"Hi, Janie!" She smiled very big, and looking down at my cleaning basket creations, she smiled even bigger.

"Good morning, Caty. How are you today?" I kept telling myself to be overly nice. *Keep those management skills flowing, and with a quality that you would want.*

"I'm doing pretty well. I'm really excited to get this started!" She sat beside me at the picnic table.

"Well, for starters, pick a basket. It will be your basket while you're working here at At Your Service. They're colored coded, so no one can take someone else's things." I saw her make a face out of the corner of my eye. "I know it seems silly, but trust me. I'm just heading off disasters before they ever have a chance to begin." I smiled at her. I reached into my bag, and pulled out some paperwork. "Here's your weeks' worth of clients, information, and the liability form I'll need you to sign." I stopped momentarily to see that another car had pulled in. "Hopefully that's them."

"Ok, I'll fill out my part while you fill the girls in." I smiled at her, and I noted how easy rolling she was. I appreciated that more than she could know. I watched the two girls are they walked up together. Both dressed decently, but the skinny, paler girl looked like she had been out all night before.

"Hey Janie, we made it!" Kiara said. "Sorry we're a little late." I smiled at them, and motioned for them to have a seat.

"First, one of these welcome baskets is all yours. These will be your cleaning supplies while you're working for me. You stick with your color, and that's how we'll track what you're going through, keep stock on equipment, and such. Make sense?" They all nodded at me. "In the packet of paperwork, please fill out the liability and contact forms for me. I'll need those before I release you to the clients." I watched as they fished around for pens and such. "While you're writing, I'll talk. Basically, we'll meet up a few times a month, and I'll go over schedules, how you're doing, and all the other fun manager type things that come up. You'll have roughly three clients a day, and based around the schedules that we discussed last week. We will stay in touch through the week via email, text, or phone." I turned to Caty, "You'll be my business cleaner, since you preferred to have evening hours." I smiled, hoping she was okay with that.

"Absolutely. Sounds great to me!" She nodded and smiled.

"Do any of you have questions?" I paused. "Oh! I must introduce you...This is Caty Patton. Caty, this is Kiara Grimes and Mylah Bush. For now, it will just be us. And you'll be pleased to know it's a full time position right now. Ok, questions?" I waited to hear what they had to say. Caty shook her head no. Mylah looked pleased enough, but still a bit hammered from earlier that morning. Kiara looked like she was thinking.

"Janie, what do you want us to wear to this job?" I liked that she was comfortable speaking up, and asking me questions. Communication was one of my favorite things.

"In your welcome kit, you'll find the shirts we talked about. With the shirt, wear decent shorts or pants. If you're cold, a cardigan. Okay?" Kiara smiled, and nodded. "Alright!" This was it. Handing out the job assignments solidified our first day of business. "Here's your clients Caty. And yours, Kiara. And lastly, Mylah. If any trouble arises, call my cell. If you run into trouble with a client, call myself, or our security team." Mylah looked confused. "Mylah, remember we talked about security? There's a company that checks our clients for us, and if there's trouble, we can call them. However, if the trouble is too much, or dangerous, call 911. Understand?" They all nodded again. *Should this be this easy? God, cross your fingers that you hired all the ones with brains..*

As I watched them drive away to their prospective job sites, I couldn't stop smiling. I shot off a quick text to Gabe.

> *Day off to a good start. The girls seemed to catch on quick. Cross your fingers. XXXO*

~

As I drove to my first potential party planning client, my nerves went into my throat again. I just needed to get through this one meeting to get my bearings in all of this. I was listening loudly to oldies on my way to the clients' house, and Pat Benetar was signing louder than ever. Half-way there it dawned on me that leaving my windows down, like I had just done for fifteen miles, really makes a girls hair jacked up. Taking a second to pull my hair into a pony tail, I twisted the mess up into a bun, double checking it in the mirror. *Oh, that's much better!*

"Damn it!" I mumbled as I looked in my rearview mirror. I turned onto the driveway. It was gated, and lined with trees. I couldn't help but smirk at myself a little bit. This was going to bring in big money for my newly opened business. And possibly give me some recognition within the local cities, as this party would be for a local advertising company's fundraiser. I pushed the red button on the box at the gate.

"Welcome to Tribex Estate. How may I help you?" said a man's voice on the other end of the line.

"Hi. I'm here to meet with Liz. Liz Malloy." I waited for the response.

"Yes, Mrs. Lazarus, is it? Mrs. Malloy is waiting for you. Please drive to the front doors, and I will see you in." I smiled at his politeness. As I pulled through the front gates, the estate and buildings looked huge. Liz and I had gone to high school together back in the day. She had really done well for herself, courtesy of her family, of course. That aside, I hoped she would be impressed. The sinking feeling was back in my gut. I parked on the curb by the front door. I was a few feet away when the doors instantly opened to a butler, with the nicest old man smile ever.

"Hello, madam. I am Ernest. Please follow me to Mrs. Malloy's office." He nodded, and I smiled back. He was quite fast for a man of his age and stature. He opened the door, and motioned me into her office. She was walking towards me, hands extended, beaming radiantly.

"Hello Janie! It's been a long time! Tell me about the past few years!" As I sat down with her, I suddenly relaxed, and felt the friendly businesswoman slide right out of me. This was easier than I had thought. *This is perfect, Janie. You're doing it!!*

As I climbed back into the car, I had to just sit and take it all in. 4 text messages told me that Kiara and Caty had both completed their days, and Mylah was almost done herself. The radio came on, and *Wild Horses* was playing. I rested my head on the headrest, and closed my eyes for a moment. I had one last meeting for today. Hopefully one last client to book. The address was close to where I already was, so the drive was only about ten minutes.

This house was large, as well, but much more homey than the others. I pulled up to the security gate, and noticed a keypad. I had to code, so I waited momentarily, until a security guard appeared. He asked my name, and nodded me on through the gates. I pulled into the parking area, and parked. I climbed out, taking in the whole house, and all the surroundings. It looked older, but also renovated with much newer parts. I liked the gable updates in the front. Suddenly, the door opened.

"Uh, Hello. Mrs. Lazarus?" He questioned. As he took steps towards me, I couldn't help but take him all in. He was in his 40s, wasn't much taller than myself, and had dark hair. His features were very prominent, and his smile was the brightest white I had ever seen. He extended his hand to me, and I took it in a cautious hand shake.

"Hi," he smiled again. "I'm Donovan James." I smiled back at him. Donovan James was one of our local millionaires. He had made it big with a new design of a boat called *The Hammerhead*, which he had crafted about ten years before. From all of the rumors around town, he was in a loveless marriage to his trophy wife- who relished in pool boys over charity work any day.

"Hi, Mr. James. I'm Janie Lazarus." We shook, and he released the hand shake. "I'm here to discuss the arrangements you had called me about. Is there a place that we can sit and chat?"

"Absolutely. Right this way, please." His hand fell onto the middle of my back, and I immediately got the chills. *Whoa, buddy. Personal space is always a good way to start a relationship.* I stepped ahead of him, and thankfully just out of reach.

Walking through the house, I noticed the multitude of rooms. There were wall hangings and paintings everywhere. They were dark, and passion filled. I loved them.

"I love your artwork, Mr. James." I pointed at a few as we walked down the hall.

"Janie," he paused at a doorway. "Can I call you Janie?" I nodded, and smiled. "Ok, please call me Donovan. Mr. James is too formal for me."

"Ok, Donovan." I took a seat on the chair he had motioned to. "So tell me, you said that there were multiple services you were looking for from my company. Which ones were you thinking about?" I watched him at his bar, pouring himself a drink, very slowly. Scotch wasn't my favorite, but I knew it lead to interesting possibilities during meetings. As he picked up his glass, he started slinking back to the meeting area where I was.

"First things first. Would you like a drink, Janie?" He paused, and set his own drink down at his seat.

"Maybe just some water, or iced tea if you've got any." I smiled, trying desperately to gauge this intense man. He grabbed a bottle of ice tea out of the bar fridge, and handed it to me.

"Well," he shifted in his chair so we were facing each other. "I'd like to have a large party to announce a new product that will be going onto our line of customizable boats. I want vendors, my advertising reps, just everyone I can think of to attend." He smiled, and took a large swig of scotch.

"When would you like to plan for this big event, Donovan?" I finished jotting down the details on my paper, and awaited his response.

"I think I'd like it in November. That way I can plan the release to have pre-orders for the holidays." He was staring intently at me. Watching my hands...*and the rest of you?* I shook the thought out of my head.

"November is no problem. That gives me just about two months to get it handled." I leaned forward to grab my iced tea, and take a drink. I could feel his eyes on me at every turn. "So, was there something else you wanted to set up? Or are we done for today? All the party details I'll email you confirmations for-"He interrupted me.

"Yes, Janie. There is more..." He shifted in his chair, and sat on the edge of his seat. "I've followed you over the past few years because I use to work with Sean Westing." The connections were being made in my head, and I felt myself relax a bit. Friend of a friend. Excellent, always makes for good business. "I've got kind of an odd request for your company." I raised an eyebrow at that statement.

"I'm afraid to ask...but go ahead. What exactly are you wanting?" I sat ready to hear whatever he was going to say, expecting him at this point to ask me to commit a felony for him, with the look he had on his face.

"Ok, please keep an open mind, Janie." He smiled, but this time it was ornery. Deceitful. Sneaky. "I would like to enroll my house in your weekly cleaning program." I wrinkled my nose, waiting to hear the rest of the circumstance. "I would like to hire YOU, specifically. And I would like you to clean my house in the nude." I felt my jaw shift, drop, and then my cheeks flushed slightly. I opened my mouth to speak, but only a nervous giggle came out.

"I'm really not sure that, I-" He cut me off again.

"Understand, I do not mean sex, prostituting, touching, etc. Just cleaning. Dusting, moping, hell, whatever you do normally. Just…" he smiled, and looked me up and down. "Naked." He began rubbing his hands together, like the prize was his to win. My thoughts were spinning. "Of course, I would be willing to pay whatever your asking price for this special service." I caught him wink in the corner of my eye.

For some reason, there wasn't an instant "No" on the tip of my tongue. I was considering his request, and all the ramifications that would come from it. *If people knew.* The money would be outstanding, but what about the kids? *They wouldn't know. They wouldn't need to know. Who does?* No one. My smile grew, and turned as devious as Donovan's.

"I'll need to think about this, and come up with a figure for you." I raised my eyebrow at him. "This would be a confidential contract, and neither of us would be able to tell anyone outside of our contract about this, for obvious reasons." He nodded in agreement. "This isn't something I've

28

ever considered before, but I can see the market in this area, and how it would be appealing to you. To all men, for that matter." I stood, and watched his eyes undress me from my ankles to my shoulder blades. *Oh my, look at him eating you with his eyes! He wants you bad, Janie.* I shuddered at my thoughts. He stood to see me out.

"Oh Janie," he opened the door as we walked out. "You've made this man very happy, and looking forward to next week. Rest assured, this is our deal only. I'm not sure this would look great on my resume, either." He winked. "I'll be looking for your email, Mrs. Lazarus." He waved in my direction, and wolf whistled as he went in the house.

I climbed in my car quickly, and headed towards home.

So many thoughts I was having on this drive. I needed to make sure that no one found out about this, or I could only imagine the trouble that I would be in. I couldn't help but wonder to myself if any of my employees would be up for such a venture. *Mylah...the wild one.* I nodded at my own devious thoughts. If this went well with Donovan, maybe we could quietly expand into the naked side of things...and she would be the first one I approached. Just then, I turned into my driveway, and could see Gabe out on our deck, busily working away.

~5~

I hadn't realized how late it had gotten when I was at Donovan's house. *Lost in the new business already, Janes?* I pulled into the garage, and walked around the side of the house to the deck. His eyes came up from his laptop, he smiled at me, and reached out for me. After all these years, I still couldn't help falling into those arms every chance I got.

"Hello, baby." He said, sniffing me in. "How was your first day? I didn't expect you so late! So I'm hoping it was a good day!" He released me a bit, and I sat in the chair next to him.

"It was fabulous, and went better than I thought it would. The girls showed up on time today at the park, and they all finished their clients before I was even home! No issues!!" I kicked my sandals off under the table, and leaned back in the chair. "And even better?" I looked at him, and smiled. He was genuinely on pins and needles to hear about everything. *You're so lucky.* "I signed two huge clients today. One advertising company party, and another large client for personal cleaning service, and a massive company party in November." My smile was huge.

"Oh, baby! I'm so proud of you!!" His mouth covered mine, and a deep, quick kiss followed. "I think we should celebrate a little." He started moving around, packing up his work stuff.

"Ok, honey… but how're the kids? I missed them today." He smiled at me, almost endearingly.

"They had a busy day with my Mom, and they were already in bed. Galen was already asleep, but he did wake to give me an extra kiss for you." Just then he leaned into me, and planted another kiss on my lips. This one was passionate, but yearned for something more.

"MMmm…" I moaned. He backed up, and headed to take his stuff in. "THAT was not a Galen-kiss." I winked at him. "Could you grab my sweatshirt then?" He smiled, and nodded. The yard was quiet, and the pond was shimmering. The locusts were loud, and singing. Gabe returned and tossed my sweatshirt to me, and a blanket. I decided for a full ensemble change, and quickly whipped off my work shirt, and slid on the sweatshirt. My skirt fell next, and I wrapped the blanket around myself. I caught Gabe's wide mouthed smile as I fell back into my chair. He was busily fumbling with some smoke, and prepping my joint for me. I laughed to myself while I waited.

"I love that after all these years…here," I looked around and pointed at "our" world. "Some of it doesn't change. That we can still hold on to ourselves here." He scooted his chair closer to mine, and rubbed my thigh.

"This will always be our place." He handed me a perfectly rolled joint, and a lighter. He nudged my arm with his elbow, and motioned me to pick it up. His lit with little assistance, so I was sure mine would be fine. I drew in slowly, because sometimes my lungs seemed to reject anything, even air these days. *Ever since you were stabbed before, it's like your lungs just never healed right. Another "Thanks, Michael!" moment.* It was smooth, and brought on zero coughs. Three hits in all my worries had floated away, and I was now in the crook of the arm of my love, and toasty warm.

We relaxed together on the deck for hours. Gabe eventually let the fire he made die down, and there was an orange glow across the entire yard. We were in the shadows of privacy fences, and smoke from the fire. My eye lids were heavy, but suddenly became light as feathers as I felt his hand brush over my nipple, and his breath suddenly ended in my ear.

I immediately turned myself towards him on this giant, outdoor lounger couch. I unwrapped

31

myself from my blanket, exposing the magenta frilly undies that I had been hiding all day. He slid his shirt off, and climbed under the blanket with me. Now we lay chest to chest. Struggling a bit, I managed to remove my sweatshirt, so our bare chests could touch.

Within moments, hands were everywhere. Touching. Pulling. Grabbing. Squeezing. Pleading. I could feel hardened parts of him pushing into me, while his fingers pushed deep into my core. I wrapped my hand around his rock hard erection, and began to squeeze gently around him. His moans became more intense, and his teeth clasped around my ear. Between the biting and the moans, it was hopeless for me to try to hold back. He made sure to bring me over the edge with his hands, way before he moved on to the real excitement.

He flipped me over, and held me on to the cushion firmly. He began rubbing his length along my rear, back and forth slowly. I could feel every detail, every vein of him, rubbing on the flesh of my ass. He squeezed the skin on my back repeatedly, which was bringing me right back to the edge. And very quickly. I could feel myself clenching, and I was grinding my teeth together. In the midst of it all, somehow he managed to get my legs spread, and slid himself right in. *Oh, my! Perfect!* A massive moan escaped my lips.

"MMmm…." He squeezed my skin again, and drove himself in deeper. I closed my eyes tightly, and buried my face in the cushion. His fingers tightened around my hips, and I could feel him throbbing harder and harder inside of me. The moans escaping his lips were keeping me on the brink. It rolled on, over, and through me continuously, like waves in the ocean. He pushed deeper each time he felt me throb around him, and tiny moans left my throat.

Suddenly, he pulled out of me, and flipped me over. *God, I love this couch thingy...* Looking up, he was shimmery with sweat. His hair was roughed up, and his blue eyes burned with desire. He spread my knees apart, and scooted his hips into me. He pulled me onto his lap, and began to tease my burning hot core with his own. Slipping only the tip in sent me over the edge, and I clawed at the cushion. Staying on his knees, he slid into me, holding onto my shoulders. He was probing my soul, and I opened up to let him in. I couldn't control my body, and rode each wave of pleasure out to its end.

His hands moved around my body, and around my breasts. He squeezed my nipples, and rounded them with the tips of his fingers. His fingers lingered around my shoulder, before closing around my neck. His hand tightened slightly, taking my breath away, as he drove into me with full force. His eyes burned, and stared straight into my own. His hand tightened again, cutting off my breath completely. *Yes, the panic...* My eyes closed, my head fell back, and I was lost in the moment. I could feel him start to climax, and I relaxed in the moment, and clamped around his rod. He shot into me, and collapsed on top of me.

We lay still for a little while, but once the thunder began, we started to pick up our things, to move into the house. I rolled off of the lounger, and slid my clothes back on. I leaned over and kissed Gabe's bare shoulder.

"I'm going to go kiss my babies goodnight. Can you clean up please?" I nuzzled his back, waiting for his response. Which at this point, was no more than a moan, and slight head nod. "Ok, I'll see you in bed in ten." I patted his back, and headed inside. The house was all locked up, and pretty dark. I could hear Galen's night radio playing songs quietly. My boy needed a bit of noise to be comfortable at night. I opened his door slowly, and had to hold my giggle in. His little body had fallen half off of his bed, and it looked so uncomfortable. I cautiously put him back in bed, and tucked him in. "Goodnight, little man," I whispered in his ear. I closed the door quietly, and headed towards Lilah's room.

All was quiet there, too. She looked like such an angel when she was asleep. *A little mouthy, these days, when awake...don't you think?* I smiled at my thoughts. I kissed her forehead, and tip toed out of the room. Heading back to my room, I saw Gabe sliding into bed. I glanced at my pile of paperwork and contracts to prep in the morning. And I lost my breath. *Donovan.* I'd have to get to his contract then, too. *It's all in the name of business profit, right Janie?* I raised an eyebrow. *And...slight curiosity?*

"Come to bed, Janes. It's late." Brought back to reality, thankfully. I smiled, and turned off the light. I climbed into bed next to my love, and relaxed next to his warmth.

~6~

The next morning, I woke up to the kids jumping on my bed. I tried to hide my face in the pillows, but the next thing I knew, I was nose to nose with my miniature Gabe. Once Galen saw my eyes open, he squealed with joy.

"Mmoommmmyyy!!!!" He yelled. "I see

34

you, Mommy!" He tugged at the covers, and I could feel Lilah climbing up next to him. "Come on, Li! Mom's ober here!" He giggled at himself tugging, with no progress.

"Come on, Mmmoommm!" Lilah's impatience rang out. "I'm starrrrving!" *Oh she's just like you! So dramatic!* Ok, now the thought of food sort of made me hungry, too. I sat up quickly, yelling like a monster to scare the pants off of the kids. Lilah screamed, and went running out of the room. And Galen just laughed and laughed.

"Ok, buddy. Give me a minute, and I'll make you some breakfast before your day with Grandma." He smiled, and ran back out to play. I stretched, and hit the bathroom. I put on my robe, as part of my work day today was from home. It didn't take me long to whip up breakfast for everyone, including Jean. She was thankful for the extra time she got to spend with us. So far, this was working out great for us all.

"Thanks, Janie. This is delicious," Jean said, and she put her plate in the dishwasher. She turned towards the kids, "Are you ready for school today? And learning in the park?" The kids both squealed with excitement. "We'll make dinner for mom and dad tonight, too, okay?" She winked at me, and I smiled back. The kids couldn't wait. I patted Jean's shoulder, and kissed the tops of each of their heads.

"Have a good day today guys! I'll see you at dinner. I'm going to work now!" I grabbed my herbal tea, a banana, and headed back to my office. Gabe added the office on for me a few years after Lilah was born. It's directly off of my bedroom, next to our back patio. Great view for work, and hidden away from the rest of the house. I sat down at my grand desk, and opened my laptop.

Flipping through the contracts from the previous day, I was putting all the dates and info for the clients. I shot off a few emails on the Tribex party I was planning. Everything was set up, and ready to go for that one. I smiled at myself, very proudly. *Day two, and you're kicking ass! An entire party, set up, in one day? You're amazing, Janes.* I nodded in agreement. And then I came across Donovan James' folder.

I opened it hesitantly, replaying our entire conversation in my head. It was like it was only five minutes ago that it happened…especially when the hair on my neck stood up from thinking about it too long. I shuddered. I tried to logically think about how much the service that Mr. James desired would cost. *Double the normal rate? Triple? More?* I tapped my pen on the paper, and thought of all of the situations that he would get to watch me in. *Think of all the ways you'll have to stretch to reach those dusty corners, get under those tables, and into those bathtubs… Remember how his eyes burned into you the first time he saw you?*

Finally, it came to me. I quickly typed out the email that confirmed his large event party details, times, and everything that I had set up for it already. He was quick to respond to my first email.

"To: Janie Lazarus
From: Donovan James, Owner
September 29, 2008 10:03am

That looks amazing, Janie! Thank you so much for being so prompt with this. It truly shows your work ethic.

Now, how about the other contract deal? Any news there yet?

D. James"

I quickly responded, and I noted the fury in my fingers. *Wow, Janie. Think of how much work you would get done if you typed that fast all of the time!* Pounding the words out faster and faster as the thoughts flowed.

"To: Donovan James, Owner
From: Janie Lazarus
September 29, 2008 10:08am

Yes, I have come up with a schedule, and a price. It will cost you, but I think you will approve. See the attached contract, and let me know.

Janie"

I sat back, and waited for his response. *You're being a bit ridiculous Janie. It shouldn't matter this much!* I shook the thought out. To suffice my achy brain, I closed the email, and went back to setting up the last caterers for Mr. James's large party. Yes, I'd be productive. *Stay focused.* Half an hour later, I had the entire party completed, but for a few minor details to be done the week of the party. I was again impressed with myself. I flipped back over to check my email one last time before I wrapped up to do some house cleaning. *Wouldn't you know, there it is...* I double clicked the email, and it opened up.

"To: Janie Lazarus
From: Donovan James, Owner

September 29, 2008 10:23am

I am more than ready. Let's start tomorrow, instead of next week. I will pay upfront. Don't say no. See you at 10am. If there's issues, use 556.8764.

Donovan"

As I finished reading it, I realized I was smiling. *Why are you so excited about this? What am I missing? Or...what don't I know yet?* I couldn't even respond to that. I sighed loudly, and closed my laptop. Time to kick business is gear! I decided to get the house cleaning done, as my days were looking busier, and I didn't want Jean to do it.

By the time I finished cleaning, and taking a quick shower, Jean and the kids had dinner on the table. They made an Italian feast, with giant meatballs and spaghetti. The kids were starving, and exhausted. After they stuffed their faces, they scooted off to bed quickly. Jean cleaned up, and left Gabe and I together at the table.

"I'm really thankful your Mom is here, and this is going so well." I smiled at him, and put my hand over his. He beamed back.

"Thanks, Janes. That means a lot. I'm really glad it's working out, too. That reminds me," he paused and took a bite. "This is really good." I nodded. "I talked to your mom today." I could feel my mouth drop open.

"What?! Oh, I see how it is…. She calls you now, not me!" I made a pouty face, and Gabe punched me in the shoulder gently.

"Oh stop!" He laughed. "You know you were crazy busy yesterday. You probably didn't even see she called you!" He laughed loudly, and drank his merlot. "I smacked his arm, and shook my head. "Anyway, they'll be in town in a week or so, and wanted to stay a few nights. I already okayed it, of course." He winked at me, as he always loved my parents.

"That's awesome! I can't wait to see them, and fill them in on all my new business stuff! Oh, and guess what?!" I held his forearm.

"Uh oh," he paused. "If you're this excited, it can't be good." He smirked, and waited for my answer.

"Oh, it's nothing bad! Tomorrow should be my first big payday! I'm really excited!" He leaned towards me, and held my face with his hands.

"I'm so proud of you, baby." He kissed me gently. He took his last bite, and picked up both of our plates to put in the dishwasher. I collected the wine glasses, and carefully set them in the rack. "We should head to bed early…take the kids lead, you know?" He smiled, and wrapped me in his arms. "I've got a busy day tomorrow, too. Possibly getting a new vendor at the Phoenix. Long and boring…" he sighed loudly.
We walked together into the bedroom.

"Well, here's to long days." Climbing under the covers always felt good, but tonight it seemed extra soft. "And snuggly nights." I curled up around him once he settled, and we both snoozed off faster than I knew possible.

~7~

Morning was busy, and everyone was out of the house early. Gabe had long meetings, and Jean had

39

a full day planned with the kids. They were extra lovey this morning, and doused me with numerous hugs and kisses. A perfect way to start my day. I decided to shower again, and officially do my makeup. *Hopefully you haven't forgotten how..* I smiled, and tried to steady my hand for the eye makeup. I hadn't yet mastered the "smokey-eye," but thought this was good enough.

I curled my hair, and left it down, falling onto my shoulders. The bra I picked was black lace, and had a matching black thong. *Way to give him the full order, girl.* I wore a bustier over the undies, and a black skirt with it. My tight white blouse, with ruffle front, was low cut, and button up. *Ahh yes, very appropriate for quick removal. Yeah, Janes?* I found my black heels to wear with it. I stepped in front of the mirror, and even shocked myself a bit. I nodded in the mirror, grabbed my bags and paperwork, and headed to the car.

The drive to the James' residence was only about twenty minutes from my own house. Barely enough time to get my fill of loud music before work. My head was starting to spin slightly, and starting to question what I was doing. I shook my head at the thoughts. *It's money, and that's why you're doing it. Technically, you're only cleaning, so what rules are you breaking?* None. *Yet, anyway...* I was breaking no rules, and that made me smile. When I pulled in to park, I noticed there was a bright red car next to Donovan's black BMW. As I climbed out of the car, with an arm full of paperwork, I made sure my coat was snugly fastened. Steps away from the door, it opened for me, and there was his bright smile.

"Welcome, Janie. How are you doing today?" His smile was warm, and friendly. He waved me into the house, and into his office. "Please, come in here for a moment, and we can go over the final paperwork." I smirked at him, and raised my eyebrow. I couldn't see that anyone else was around, but he was acting odd, so I went with it.

"Yes, here are the contracts, and event info for your November party, Mr. James." I handed him a giant stack of paperwork, and on top I placed our cleaning contract. I smiled at him widely as he took the stack. He glanced at the stacks, and smirked to himself at the cleaning contract. He quickly signed the copy, and handed it back to me.

"Well, that one looks fabulous. I can't wait to see more…" He looked at me over the bridge of his nose, and winked. "As for these others, these are all confirmations, right?"

I nodded. "Yes, sure are. There are two copies that need your signature to state that you're good to go for the party." I leaned over the desk, and rifled through the paperwork in his hand. He patiently held the papers until I found what I was looking for. "Ah, here it is." As I looked up, and met his eyes, I noticed his eyes were not on my own. They were hungrily staring down my blouse, and my black lace was showing. He refocused, and quickly signed the documents.

"Ok, Mrs. Lazarus… it will just be a moment until my wife, Alli leaves for her day." Just then, as if timed and on cue, she appeared. I smiled at her as she walked across the room. Her face remained very blank, to both of us. *Ugh, bitch.*

"Is *this* the new cleaning lady?" She looked me up and down, and once again. He tried hard to hold his laugh in. I could taste her judgment, and was it ever bitter. It was as if she had been here before, faced with the woman who would be pleasuring her husband, because she obviously wouldn't. *Oh, Janie...what a statement. Very telling, too... of your true plans, maybe?* I squelched that thought quickly.

"Yes, dear. She is my new event planner, and her business has a cleaning service, too..." He stepped around his desk towards me. "This is Janie Lazarus. She's a dear friend of our friends' the Westings. Remember them? It has been awhile since you've seen them." She nodded, and barely smiled. "Well Alli, don't let us keep you. Off to the country club for now. I hope your day is well. Let me walk you out." He patted her on the shoulder, and she turned and walked out.

I sucked in my breath, and hoped that the awkward moment was over. I sat down in a chair at Donovan's desk, and waited for him to return from walking her out. Which only took mere seconds, it seemed. *Is it just me, or did they seem to really not like each other much? Hmm...*

"Sorry about that, Janie. At least you got to meet her, I suppose." He shuddered at his own words, and physically shook his head at his own comment.

"Well, she seemed..." I was at a loss, and couldn't hold in my giggle. "Really great." There was that awkward silence again. He sat at his desk, and rubbed his head with his hands, and cleared his throat.

"Yeah, well..." he sighed heavily. "Money doesn't buy me love, I guess." He smiled again, and shrugged. "What do you need from me to get started? Anything?" I smiled at him, and could tell he was getting nervous.

"I really don't need much...but I do have a

small favor." I cautiously looked at him.

"Name it." He smiled, as if waiting on pins and needles.

"Could you put this CD in somewhere, and crank it up?" He took the CD from me, and nodded with a semi-perplexed look on his face. "Don't worry, just music. Some of my favorites. Will help me keep track of my time, too." I winked at him, and stood from my chair. He darted off into the hall, and moments later, the music was on. I left the room, and walked by him in the hall. I made sure to pass a little too closely to get his attention, and headed towards the kitchen. *It's now, or never, Janes. Go for it.*

As I idly pranced into the kitchen, I unbuttoned my coat, and slid it off. I hung it nicely on the coat rack I found in the kitchen. I sat at the table, as one of my favorite songs came on the CD. I fell into the song, and let it completely take over. The words fell from my mouth, and I couldn't help singing out loud, as finding my comfort in this new, and very awkward situation was very important. Closing my eyes, my head fell back, and the buttons on my blouse started coming undone. *The most expensive strip tease you've ever done... get it, girl!* I smiled at the thoughts, while my fingers did the work.

I rounded the table, and let my skirt drop to the floor as well. Cleaning in a heels was over rated, but it was making me feel hotter than ever. I knew he was lingering from somewhere in this giant house. I could feel his eyes on me, but I wasn't connected enough to feel where it was coming from. I began to clean the kitchen, wiping off counter tops, and mopping the floors.

I moved from room to room, lost in the

music. I pulled my phone out of my bustier to check the time. *45 minutes already?!* The time was passing quickly, and I wasn't as embarrassed, or as unsure as I thought I would be. I walked back into the kitchen, and put my phone into my purse. I had to clean the upstairs next, and I thought it was time to spice things up a bit more. *He is paying you for this, you know.* I did know, and with that, I slowly started unhooking the corset. Half way unbuttoned, just past my belly button, I heard his breath hitch. He was close. That made me smile.

I nonchalantly just kept going, unhooking each hook slowly. Purposefully. In the middle of the unhooking, my chest was free, and my breasts retook their unclasped shape. He moaned, and I felt myself blush. *Janie!* Finally, I could take a full breath again, and I stood in my heels, and black lingerie. I picked up my cleaning supplies, and headed towards the stairs. Suddenly, I wasn't alone.

"Can I help you carry anything up, Janie?" He smiled at me, closing the distance between us a bit.

"No Sir," I continued up the stair case. I could feel his eyes burning into my ass as I climbed each stair. "I'm fully capable, and on the job." I turned to face him on the top stair. His face was inches from my own, and his body was closer than I expected. His breathing was heavy, and his pupils were dilated. *You know what that means...watch yourself...* His mere closeness in my bubble triggered memories from my past that would surely ruin this moment, and this job. *Relax, it's not him, Janes. This man won't do that to you.* I quickly refocused, and backed up a few steps. "Let me finish this for you, Donovan." I smiled at him, and spun on my heel.

"Yes, and I'm sorry." He cleared his throat. "Please continue. You are doing an amazing job. And you're so... perfect." I turned to smirk at him, and noticed he was leaning on the wall, with his hand down his pants. My eyes met his, and his smile became devious, and hungry. My head turned back swiftly to hide my blushing cheeks. *Is he really doing what I think he's doing?!* A few slow, deep breaths later, and I was back to cleaning. It was sort of hot.

My mind was racing about the man masturbating in the corner, while I cleaned half-naked. Was I making the right decision? Was it really worth the thousands he'd be paying me each month? I turned and looked towards him again. His face was darker, extremely focused, but he still held that grin. As the sweat beads swelled up on his forehead, little moans escaped his lips. *Let's make it worse. Let's make him want what he can't have.* It was happening. I was having more fun than I imagined with all of this. When I walked in the bathroom to clean, I slid my panties off. Now I was down to heels, and my cleaning supplies.

"Oh my God..." and a loud thump later, I turned to see Donovan had fallen into the chair to get a better view. Raising my eyebrow at him, he nodded, as if pleading for more. I bent over to reach into the tub, making sure my ass was aimed directly at him. I spread my legs a bit wider, and went deep to clean the basin floor. I heard his breathing pick up, and a moan escaped his lips. I finished cleaning the bathroom, and picked up my supplies. As I walked out of the bathroom, slowly slinking, completely naked and extremely geared up, I couldn't help check out what he was working with as I got closer. *Oh my... this one's got some sizeable assets!* I smiled at my own lusty thoughts, and brushed one of my nipples with my hand. Suddenly, he stiffened, and started to twitch.

"Mr. James," I smiled and bent over to his ear. "Your house is clean," I whispered, needy, but in control to him. I stood, and proceeded back to the kitchen to put the supplies away, and begin dressing. He emerged a few moments later, and I was re-hooking my bustier closed.

"Janie," he began, as he rifled through his pockets. "This was amazing. Here's the first of many, many paychecks from me." He paused, and looked cautiously at me. "I hope you're going to stick with this. I could look at you every minute of every day for the rest of my life." He stuck his hand out for a quick shake, and I took it firmly.

"This has been very enlightening, Donovan. And," I couldn't help look down at his still partially hardened crotch. "The pleasure was all mine." I winked, and headed for the front door. "See you in a few days!" I yelled, and tossed my hand in the air for a wave.

This client would be trouble, and I could tell already. Keeping a clear head would do me best. I was desperately trying to burn the images out of my head of Donovan rubbing himself all over, before I got home. The trouble was, being watched so intently... so lustfully, filled me with more hormones and sexual energy than I was ready for. I needed relief, and fast. I unlocked the car with my key fob, and climbed in the backseat to change. The thong was so tightly pressed against my swelling parts, that simply moving them around to take them off had me close to climax. *Who knew that would be so hot?!* I slowed my breathing, and tried to relax before I got out, to get back in the front seat. The mere amount of rubbing of my undies helped ease my pain enough. *But barely.*

As I shifted to the front seat of my car, I saw a note on the windshield, and pulled it out to read. I opened up the half fold, but didn't really understand the message. "Good to see you again," was all it said. *What???* I looked around, but saw no one, or nothing out of place. I shrugged it off, and climbed in to drive home.

~

Tonight we planned a movie night with the kids, and Jean. Once Gabe was home from work, we popped the popcorn, and snuggled in to watch the movie. Galen giggled through the whole movie, barely stopping long enough to breathe. Lilah fell asleep half-way through, and Gabe carried her off to bed. Jean was exhausted after her long day with my babies, and she scooted off as well. Now we cleaned up the living room, and listened to Galen sing his bedtime songs.

"Ok Mommy, I'm ready for bed now." He yawned so big, I couldn't resist scooping him up and carrying him off to bed.

"Come here, mister." I took him to Gabe first. "Give Daddy a big kiss, and tell him goodnight." I smiled, while hanging on to my little man, and watching him reach out to Gabe, whose hands suddenly slid around Galen's body, and were on my own.

"Goodnight, little man. I love you." He kissed Galen, and patted his head.

"See you in the morning, Daddy!" He waved as I carried him away. I heard Gabe's cell phone ring as I walked away, but didn't think much of it. I

47

laid Galen down in his bed, and tucked him in tightly.

"There!" I patted his belly. "Snug as a bug, in a rug, you are!" I kissed his forehead, and turned on his night light, and white noise radio.

"Mommy?" I turned towards him.

"Yes, honey?" I bent by his bed in the dimmed light.

"Do you love your new job?" I nodded, and smiled. "Can I come with you someday?" I smiled again.

"Absolutely! What a great idea! Let's make it one of our date days, and you can come meet all of my friends!" His face was beaming, and he was nodding like he had accidentally done some lines of sugar immediately before bed. "Okay, let's shake on it." I stuck my hand out to him, and he quickly pulled my hand to his heart.

"Deal, Mommy." Then he quickly let go. "Now, go. I need to sleep." *So abrupt!* My internal monologue was laughing hysterically. *Oh, Galen...* I left his room, still shaking my head at him as I closed the door. Walking back through the house, I picked up a few toys, and threw them back into the toy room.

As I reentered the living room, Gabe's face was ashen, and he still had his cell phone in his hand. I sat next to him on the couch, tidying up the tables, waiting to see if he would speak.

"Dare I ask what's going on?" I hesitantly pushed. His head shook for a moment, and then he came around.

"Well," he started. "I don't really know what the hell it's about. It was a text message, from a number I don't recognize. See?" He handed me his phone, and the number did not look familiar to me, either. But the message did, and I felt my face change. *Good to see you again.* "Janie," he lifted my chin. "This means something to you?" I shook my head a bit.

"Yes, and No. Today, leaving my cleaning job, there was a piece of paper on my windshield with this same message." His face lost all color. "OH, silly. Don't worry! It's probably someone playing a dumb prank. Surely it's nothing…" I paused, and thought. "Who would do that? Not Michael…the jail monitors his mail." He shook his head.

"Do you still have the paper? I'd like to keep it all together." I nodded, and stood up. As I did, he grabbed my hand, and his eyes met mine. "I'll keep you safe, always. You know that, right?" My other hand instinctively came up, and caressed his cheek. I bent down, and kissed him gently.

"Of course I know that. Honey," I sat beside him again. "I'm not worried. Someone's just being dumb. It's happened before, you know?" I stood again, and headed to get the paper for him. "I'll meet you in bed in five. Okay?" I looked over my shoulder to see him nodding, and turning the lights off in the living room.

We climbed into bed, and his warm body was quickly, directly next to mine. I hugged him into me, and breathed him in. My thoughts were everywhere. *Who's leaving the messages? Why the both of you? What about Donovan? Could it be him? Is it Michael? His family again?* I tried to slow my thoughts, but they were creeping in faster and faster. I closed my eyes tighter, and focused on Lilah and Galen. I thought of all of the giggling during our evening, and the millions of kisses I had from them in the last few hours. Then I thought of

Gabe, and doing so made me squeeze into him even more. I fell into his warmth…and closed my eyes to fall into dreamland soon after.

~8~

I knew what had made me sick. Worrying constantly about those damn notes, had worn me out more than I had realized. As the morning sun shone through the window, the light hit my face, and I wrinkled my nose. *Ugh.* I had missed three days of work, stuck in bed with the flu. I was happy that the kids and Gabe did not catch it, but it was hard to be away from work. Thankfully, my staff had all stepped up to help, and kept everything going strong. I rolled over in bed, to find a glass of OJ and a note from Gabe.

> "Drink this. You had color this morning. Congrats! Hopefully I'll see you in the living room soon. PS. Phone's been blowing up. Check it."

I smiled at his words, and sat up in bed. I waited for the head rush to follow, but it finally didn't come. I sighed, and checked my messages. Multiple from Kiara, and Mylah, but everything was going great. I quickly texted them back, and answered my mom's few texts about the kids' sizes and such. One left unread message, and it's Donovan. *Uh oh…* I cautiously open the message…

Janie, are we on for today?

Instant palm to forehead moment, and my fingers fumbled to shoot off the text message quickly.

D- Let's do tomorrow. I've been under the weather. So sorry. Is this okay? J

I sent the message, and headed in to the bathroom to get clean. I turned on the shower as hot as I could stand it, and let it warm as I undressed. My thoughts were scattered everywhere. My work, Gabe, the kids, and now a bit of Donovan. The water fell down on my shoulders, and I could almost feel the energy coming back into my tired body. I pictured him in his balcony, handling himself not so gently, while looking at me as if he was going to devour me whole. *It was nice, wasn't it?* I knew why this was so appealing to me.

I loved my husband more than anything in the world. Life has this way of keeping two people so busy, then adding kids, and everything else… the closeness just drifts sometimes. I was momentarily lost in my thoughts. I missed being Gabe's focus and attention, and I know when the kids were infants, he missed mine. *Voyeurism is something you love…you always have! Just admit it! You love being looked at, wanted, and lusted for. And that's okay.* It was true, I did love it. *I just think you'd love it more if it were Gabe.* Maybe that's why I was so comfortable with this set-up. It's filling a need that I… Suddenly, my thoughts were interrupted, and I heard the door open.

"Janes?" He cleared his throat. "I just wanted to check on you. I saw you moved," he laughed. "So, I figured that was probably a good thing." I smiled at his comment. Regardless of things I missed, like his lusting at me constantly, I still absolutely loved this man. I opened the shower door to give him a full view, his jaw dropped, and eyebrow raised. "Guess it's good that my mom and the kids are gone, huh?"

"Open invite, if you have time." I smiled, and hoped for the best. Without much pressure, he walked towards the shower slowly. First his shirt came off, and then he dropped the rest. He was exquisite, as always. Before he stepped in the shower, he grabbed the remote for the bedroom's sound system, and turned it on. With Adele now blaring in the background, when his warm body pressed into my back and his arms around my front, there was nothing else in my mind but him.

"Oh yes, I've got time." His lips began a line of kisses on my neck, and onto my shoulders. I leaned into him, and his hands consumed my breasts. His now rock hard length was pressing into my backside, begging to come in. I put my hands into his hair, and scratched into his scalp. His teeth sank into my shoulder, and my entire body clenched, and fell into him. He spun me to face him, and my mouth met his with hunger. *Oh, I need this...* His tongue was hot and needy, and dancing with my own. The need for air broke our kiss, and hands began wandering everywhere.

Grasping him in my hands, I put one foot on the stair in the tub, and bent over to inhale him. His voice went hoarse, and he gasped for air. *Ahh, yes...unhinging you. My favorite.* While I looked at him in his eyes, taking him deeply inside, I smiled through the job. My tongue danced around his tip, and he shook from the delight and sensory

52

overload. Standing again, he turned me around. I looked back over my shoulder to see his cunningly hungered smile.

"Hold on to the bar, Janie. Now." I bent over willingly, quite possibly overly excited for what was to come. *It's been too long..* He steadied my wiggling backside with his hands, and very purposely began touching closer, and closer to my sweet spot. With each brushing of his fingers, my body reacted intensely. I needed him inside me. *Now.* Something deep inside me was begging to be filled. He spread me apart, and teased me with his hard head, before plunging deep inside.

"OOoohh!" I moaned, and steadied myself to take the pounding. His fingertips squeezed into my hips, while he drove into me. I could feel myself tantric-ally squeezing him to death inside me, but my body pressed on for more. *More... I need more.* My thoughts went dark, and suddenly, the plea just fell out. "Harder!"

Without hesitation, my wishes were granted. His hands adjusted, so he wouldn't lose his grip on me as he pulled out farther, and dove in even deeper than before. Each thrust ended with moans escaping my lips. I clung to the bar in the shower, readjusting my feet, as I was starting to slip. He could feel my tension growing, getting ready to completely burst all over him. I watched him in the shower mirror, and slyly smiled at his actions. He nodded at me in the mirror, and wrinkled his nose, while he drove into me hard as ever. That was all I needed, and my muscles relaxed, and throbbed at the same time. Everywhere. *Wonderful. Blissful.* He held me for the moments I needed to come back from oblivion. I smiled when I returned, and spun him to sit on the shower step.

"Are you sure you've got it in you??" He put down a towel, and adjust himself on the seat. It was hard not to stare at his package, because like him, that was extraordinary, too. I quickly re-rinsed in the shower, never breaking my eye contact with him, and came back to face him. I clutched his cock, and slid onto his lap, taking him into me entirely. I covered my mouth with his, and my tongue probed inside. His hands fumbled with my nipples, while I slid up and down his hard shaft. His breathing quickened, and his length hardened even more. Continuing my fast rhythm, I could feel myself clenching around him.

His hands dug into my shoulders to pull me even father onto him. His eyes closed, and shut tightly, and he stayed deep inside me while he climaxed. I could feel him pulsating over and over, coming down from his peak. I laid on his chest in the water, as we both came back down together. My mouth was close to his ear, and I couldn't help whispering to him.

"Yeah, I've got it in me." A breathless laugh escaped my lips, and he laughed out loud.

"Oh, baby, you more than had it in you." He kissed my cheek. "That was amazing. Now I need a shower." He laughed again. I shifted off of him, and fell on to the shower seat. My legs were like jelly, and standing was out of the question. Everlong was now blaring on the radio, and it was sort of a perfect fit for watching my love wash me off of him in the shower. His small, but very pleased smile, was permanent. I couldn't help let the lyrics sink in a bit… *"Breathe out, so I can breathe you in… and I wonder… if everything could ever feel this good forever? If anything could ever be this good again, the only thing I'd ever ask of you, you've got to*

promise not to stop when I say you win..."
He could tell I was lost in the song, and in the moment.

"Hey," I turned and smiled at him. He pulled me up to him, and held me tightly. He kissed me deeply, and slowly. His hands cradled my face, and calmed my soul. "I love you." He smiled again, but now it was full of love, and fulfillment. I rested my head on his chest.

"I love you, too, Gabe." I couldn't help but relish in this moment. We finally had time to spend with each other, and it was so badly needed. I could've stayed with him in our shower all day. Checking my fingers, I noticed I was extra wrinkly and water logged. I squeezed the water out of my hair, and started to dry off. "Guess that means we have to get back to the real world again, huh?" I

"Yeah, for now." He smacked my ass when he climbed out of the shower. "But there's always tonight, right?" His eyes told me he was still hungry. And that pleased me beyond measure. *Weren't you just talking about this Janie?* We both proceeded to dress for our day, still catching each other's glimpses, and smiles from across the room.

"Well babe, I'm out for the day. Do you have a lot of work to do?" I shook my head.

"Not really. Just working from home today, and playing with the kids later. OH! And Heather and Greg might come over this evening, so maybe you could try to get off early? Even just a little." He leaned in to kiss me goodbye on his way out.

"Ok, I'll try, and let you know later. Love you." As the words left his lips, he was already pulling down the driveway. I guess our shower time may have made him a bit late. *Oops. So worth it.*

The day rolled on quickly, and evening fell upon us. The kids and I had played outside in the crisp fall air after school. Jean was thankful for the break, but still stayed close on her patio, reading a book, never far from us. I took note at all of the ways my babies were growing up in front of me, and I was in awe. Lilah's stubbornly fierce personality was starting to really show, and even though it drove me mad, I knew deep down it was what she needed to protect herself in this world. Galen had such a gentle heart, and he hated to see anyone upset. I loved his cuddles, and wondered how long they would last.

Our date with the Hartley's fell through, as Heather wasn't feeling very well. I was getting dinner on the table, when my phone rang. I quickly picked it up to answer.

"Hello?" There was a silent pause. "Hello??" This time I was a bit more impatient.

"Hello! Janie!" The connection was terrible, so I listened hard. "Just a second..." On and off through the static. "Okay, how's that? Can you hear me now?" He laughed. *Sean.*

"Oh! Hey! I couldn't hear you through the static! How are you?!" I finished getting the kid's dinner on their plates while we chatted. Galen wrinkled his nose that I was on the phone. "Just a second," I said to Sean. I turned towards Galen. "Listen, it's just Sean. Here's your food, eat up." I patted his head, and turned to see Lilah carrying her own plate to sit down with. She smiled at me very big, and I couldn't help smile back. "Ok, all good. Had to get the kids settled." He laughed.

"Understand that. I've been good, very busy though. I'm finally coming back into town to stay for a while!"

"Oh that's wonderful! Poor Delaney, home alone all this time!" I paused, as it seemed too silent. "How's she doing anyway? It's been almost a month since I've seen you guys."

"Ehh, she's alright, I guess." I heard him sigh into the phone.

"What's wrong, Sean?" Now I was just plain curious. *Curiosity killed the cat...* He sighed again.

"I don't know. She's just no fun right now. Tired all the time, so super bitchy..." he trailed off.

"Oh, come on. She's growing your kid, give her a break!" I shook my head in disbelief, as I moved on the dishes. "It's a hard job you know."

"Yeah, it's not just that. Listen, no worries. Everything's good. I just wanted to hear your voice, needed a good ole phone dose of your happy." He chuckled. I had missed him a bit, but that made it sound like he missed me much more. *Don't go there with this one, Janes. You know better.*

"Well, good. I'm glad you called. We'll need to set something up soon. Maybe a hot tub party with cookout. How's that sound?" In my own head, it sounded lovely. Something I needed to talk to Gabe about to plan a bit.

"Perfect Janes! Aim for about 3 weeks from now, okay? That way I can take off the entire weekend. Alright, I'm going to be trapped in another tunnel, so I'd better go."

"Alright, I'll text you party details soon. Be safe." I was sort of excited for this upcoming party, and my thoughts were running wild.

"Tell Gabe I said Hey, and I'll talk to you soon, babe." And with that, he hung up. *Babe? He's lost his damn mind.* When I hung up, I noticed an unanswered text on my phone. I opened it quickly, to find that it was Donovan.

> *Janie, I hope you're feeling better. Tomorrow it is. Anticipation is killer. D*

I could feel the redness come across my cheeks, and I was thankful no one was home to notice. The kids ate their dinner peacefully, and got into bed all by themselves. We read a story before bed, *the Pink Elephant with Golden Spots,* and off to dreamland they went. Now I sat in bed, waiting for Gabe to get home, working on a bit of work.

I was emailing the new schedules to the girls, when I heard a knock at the front door. It was dark outside, but I noticed it was only 7:26pm. I threw my robe on over my scandalous pajamas, and headed through the living room to see who it was. I couldn't see any shadows through the window, or in the porch light. *What the hell?* My breaths slowed down, and my extreme focus sprung to life. There was complete silence on my front porch, and all around the house, for that matter. I cautiously approached the door, and looked through the peep hole. *No one.* The living room was dimly lit, and all the shades were drawn. I skimmed the room, and saw no movement. The kids' room door was left propped, as I had left it. Nothing was out of place, except for the knocking. Which I knew I had heard. *You did, it was loud.*

There again! I heard something outside. A rustling, of some sort. Living in the woods made it hard to tell where such noises were coming from. Panic was setting in. I hastily got my cell phone,

58

and shot off a text to Gabe.

Something's going on. Home, NOW.

I tried to calm myself, and did some slow breathing, the entire time listening for any other noise to detect where this was coming from. I headed towards the windows that line our front porch, and peeked carefully out one of the blinds. There was a box on the sidewalk, steps off of the porch. *No, Janie. Just no. It's not worth risking those babies.* And again, rustling. But now it sounded farther away. I heard a car's motor rev to start, and heard it take off in the distance. *Was that the knocker?* I pulled out my phone to text him again.

Box on porch, heard car leave. Meet me there.

I paced back and forth for what seemed like hours, but was only about five minutes. He pulled into the driveway quickly, and did not open the garage door as normal. Seconds later, another car pulled into the drive. It looked to be Greg's Mustang. They both hopped out of their cars quickly, and began running a perimeter check. Watching them was bringing back horrible memories, and I was breathing heavily. I could hear them talking in the quiet evening air, and I tried to listen in.

"Ten minutes already? He's probably gone." Greg was running, and out of breath. "But you're right, I think they went this way, and parked over there." Two people running now. I could hear all of their footsteps in the brush.

"This is nuts, man. First the notes, and now this." They were getting closer, so I stepped out onto the porch. I was still a good distance from the box, but knew they'd both be angry that I stepped outside. "Let's go check out the box, and my wife." I heard Gabe say. As they turned the corner, both of their faces changed to anger, and their speed picked up.

"Janie! Shit!" Gabe was angry. "You know better." He shook his head, and stopped at the box. Greg scowled at me, but turned his focused attention to the box. "Since you're here already, tell us what happened." Their eyes were piercing on me. And it happened.

My head hurt again, and I was bleeding. I knew he was close, and I needed to find safety. Suddenly his hands were all over me. Pulling and tugging me farther...

"Janie! Honey! Please open your eyes." Gabe was talking loudly, and shaking me. "Come on, calm your breathing back to normal again. You're okay, baby. I'm here." His voice was stern, and calming. I opened my eyes to see his panicked face, stricken with grief and fear. He sat me up a bit as he saw me come around. "You passed out, honey. How are you feeling?" *Passed out? What the fuck?* I pulled myself up, and shook my head.

"I feel okay now, just confused." I stood up slowly, and he stayed close to steady me.

"Can you tell me about what happened? You tried before, and then collapsed." He looked so worried. Greg's face was pale, and he was very quiet.

"Yes, I, ah..." I paused to remember, and the overwhelming feeling came back. "I was up in bed,

60

working on emails and stuff. There was a knock on the door, so I came out to see. I remember I noticed that there was no shadow on this window," I pointed to the side. "There was also no movement on the porch itself, which told me something was off. There was rustling outside, but I couldn't pin point where. And then I heard a car start, and take off. Then saw the box on the sidewalk." I nodded at them both. Greg was turned, scanning the tree line again.

"Do you feel okay now, love?" He sighed, and rubbed his forehead. "I can't be worried about you, and this. I about had a heart attack." I smiled at him.

"I'm okay now." I paused, "I think a lot of the past just overwhelmed me for a moment. Let's check out that box." I stepped forward, and was stopped by his hand.

"Yeah, WE will do that. Thanks. Stay here." He smiled sternly, and walked back to the box. Greg was on the ground with the box, moving it gently.

"This doesn't feel like anything dangerous. No odors, no noises. But then," he paused, and turned the box around slowly. "Also, no mailing labels. So, it's safe to say it wasn't FedEx." He chuckled to himself. "Trying to find the humor here, friends. Help me out, G." Gabe went to him, and together they opened the box slowly.

"What the fuck?!" Gabe exclaimed when he opened the box. Now I was curious. "Oh, Jesus. Seems like we've got another one." That told me what I needed to know. Greg's head fell down, and Gabe picked up the box to bring to me.

Inside the box was a picture of our house, our cars, and our work places. One picture was of my car at Donovan James' house. Although these pictures were only of places, and not people, our experience in the past with stalker types has not been great. Of course there was Michael, and then when his family retaliated. That enabled some of them to take on the "stalker roll" frequently through the years. It had been a quiet two years, and we were hopeful that everything was done with that. *Apparently not.*

"At least we're good at handling these people after all of these years." I shook my head as I pushed the box back to Gabe. My thoughts were running wild. *Michael, still winning after all these years.* Greg shuffled towards us.

"Guys," he paused. He looked pained. "What if it isn't his family? I mean," he trailed off again. Gabe shifted on his feet, and listened harder to Greg. "This wasn't ever their style. I just don't want you to be only open to that, you know?" Without warning, I couldn't breathe.

"You're right, Greg." He was still nodding his head, taking it all in. "I'm going to go write all this down, and email our friends at the station." He freed a hand, and stuck it out to Greg. "Thank you, sir. For coming to assist me, yet again. I am forever in your debt." They both laughed loudly.

"It's no problem, man. We're family." They shook, and Greg turned to leave. I yelled, as he walked away.

"Tell Heather I miss her!" He smiled, and waved as he drove away. Gabe was collecting the box, his briefcase, and all of his stuff to head in the house. It was getting late, and he seemed edgy. *Understandably so.* I headed in to check on the kids, who were still sleeping like little angels. I checked the window back to Jean's guest house, and all seemed fine. Bed was now calling my name, and I was hopeful that sleep would help calm my nerves.

Gabe wasn't far behind me, climbing into bed. He curled around me perfectly, and I could feel his breath ending on my neck. His hand gently cupped my breast, before coming to rest on my belly. My eyes closed in the silence, and eventually, my brain turned off.

~10~

The ringing was obnoxious, and entirely too loud. The angry, grumpy, woken up too early man was also not fun to deal with.

"Hello?!" I heard him say angrily in the dark. "What the fuck does that mean? Are you kidding me right now?!" He took a drink of the water on his bedside table. "Oh he's going to hear all about this one. I'll be there as soon as I can." He slammed his phone down, and sighed angrily. I carefully put my hand onto his back, and he slumped back over. "Morning, baby." He turned and kissed my cheek. "I've got to go into work now. Someone screwed something up with a delivery. Someone's getting fired."

"I'm sorry. I hope it's not too difficult." My eyes wouldn't stay open. "What time is it?" I squinted the best I could to try and see.

"It's only 6am, so go back to sleep a bit. I'll text you a bit after lunch. I'll be home early today since I'm going in early." I nodded, and he patted my forehead. "Back to sleep, love." And I was out again.

~

When my cell phone buzzed, I sat straight up. I wasn't sure what time it was, or how long Gabe had been gone. I yawned, as I picked up my phone to check. It was Kiara, clocking in her completion of her two jobs for today. I yawned again, and responded quickly.

Great job so far, Kiara! Your customers have left great feedback so far! Keep it up!

You need to get up, too, Janie! It's another pay day!! I smiled, and stretched as far as I could. I stood, and headed to shower. I turned on the radio, so I could get some energy from my music, too. While I shaved, I couldn't help but think about what had happened last week with Donovan, and I wondered if it would be the same this week. I had planned my actions for this week, and thought maybe I should give him a bit more of a show. Only if the situation permitted, of course. I finished in the shower, and headed to the closet to find something appropriate to wear.

Let's keep it simple today. Simple, yet elegant. Perfect. I had some black lace thigh highs, and a French cut thong. I chose a black see-through camisole top. *You call it a "top," I call it "tiny."* I left my hair down, and curled it with large rollers. I liked the way that the hair felt as it fell onto my bare breasts. I slid on my skirt, and put on a blouse over the top. Last week's black heels worked well, so I grabbed those on my way out of the house.

I had little fear as I drove to Donovan's this week. I knew more of what he was thinking, and more of what he expected. *Excited, are you?* I was even looking forward to it this time. I pulled into the driveway, and keyed in the code. The red car was nowhere in sight. *Relief on that front.* I fixed my makeup in my mirror, and reapplied my lipstick. I climbed out of the car, and took a deep breath of air. They had a beautiful side flower garden, and somehow this late in October, is was still very fragrant. Out of the blue, there was music in the background. I giggled a bit when I heard it was my CD. The door opened, as I grew closer.

"I've been waiting for you," he said as I entered the premises. He locked the door behind me. "No worries. Just us. Wifey's out of the state, currently." His smile grew larger, and I could feel my own turning into something devious. *Whoa, Janie. Keep it together. Nothing like that now.* I strolled through the doors, and began stripping immediately. Four steps in, I had lost my jacket, and hand bag. At ten steps, I spun around to face him with my blouse unbuttoned completely. His face was beaming, and yearning for more. Perfect timing for Bon Jovi's *Lay Your Hands on Me* to come on the radio, blaring. I took off my blouse, and threw it over my bag. I grabbed my broom and cleaning stuff, and headed up the stairs. He followed closely behind.

Stopping at the bottom of the stairs, I let my skirt slide off of my hips. My thigh highs took his breath away.

"Janie," he jumped up a few steps ahead of me. "Do you know how beautiful you are?" I blushed. He rubbed the hardening lump at his crotch. My eyes were uncontrollably drawn in to look. "Oh, don't do that. You should just get to work." He sounded rough, and needy.

"Ok, I'll clean." I stepped up the stairs,

doing my best model walk I had. I began sweeping the balcony, and he took his place in "the chair" that he frequented last time. I swept out the bedrooms, making sure to bend to use my dust pan. I could feel his eyes burning into me. "Donovan," I began. "I love it when you watch me." I winked at him, as I bent over right next to his chair. His breath hitched immediately. I stood up to find him unzipped, palming himself, intently looking at me. There were two chairs where he sat, and I moved to sit in the other. "Mind if I sit down, boss?" I smiled at him.

"Please do," he said, while slowly rubbing his shaft up and down. I sat slowly, and raised my hands slowly to my chest. I pulled the ties at my top, and it fell into the chair around me. His head rolled around, and he closed his eyes briefly, inhaling sharply. "God, I'd take you if I could. You know that, right?" His gazes was very intense. I nodded, and smiled.

"I've gathered that over our past few interactions." I blushed. He watched me, and adjusted his position in the chair. Now he was sitting directly facing me, cock in hand.

"You like it too, don't you, Janie?" He asked, longing for any type of contact. I could feel the heat rise into my face, and my crotch throbbed. *Keep control of this. Don't let him take over.* I nodded again. His head fell back again, and he moaned. "What would it take? Anything… I… once." His eyes opened to find me rolling my nipples between my fingers. *That's it. Keep him going. You're good at that.* I shook my head at him.

"I'm sure I can help you out from over here." I turned my chair directly in front of his. I leaned back into my chair, and opened my legs completely to him. My thigh highs withheld, and left and nice path straight to the good spots. His eyes followed the lengths of my legs, and his eyes locked in on my core. His pumping was faster, and my own body was starting to react. *If you're only touching yourself, I suppose you're safe, and in control. Continue... this is fun to watch.*

I let my fingers wander around my body, again pinching my nipples. Going lower, further south, and into the waistband of my panties. I swung my knee over the side of the chair, and fully slid my panties to the side for a full view. I dipped my finger into myself, and closed my eyes. I could hear his breath quicken, and his leg bumped into mine. I was entirely too geared up not to get off myself, so I got lost in the moment for a brief minute or so.

In my mind's eye, Gabe was pounding me away on the couch at home. With closed eyes, I could picture him tearing me apart. That's exactly what I needed, as my fingers were only going so far. In and out, up to knuckle, and back. When I opened my eyes, he was sitting up, pants around his ankles, leaning in mere inches from me. I blushed, and instantly came around my fingers. While my legs trembled, his hand settled on my knee. My nerves kicked in, but he wasn't pushing. At closer glance, he was steadying himself, while he got off.

"Can I see that again? Just one last time?" I smiled, and sat up to meet him the middle.

"I suppose..." I whispered. I pushed my knee to his knee, for stabilization. I pulled my panties over to the side fully, and began rubbing my clit. I was soaking wet, and that was obvious. "You can see this is beneficial for us both." He smiled, and gazed at my wet, swelling pussy. I sunk two fingers in, and he froze. Spasms running through his body,

67

while he shot his load all over the arm of the chair.

"Oh my fucking God Janie…" He relaxed in his chair, letting his length soften on his belly. I had repositioned in my chair, and replaced my top. "I'm going to dream about that later, and when I do, it's going to be even messier." He motioned to his pants, and the chair. I couldn't help my smile.

"No worries, I'll re-clean that area for you before I go for today. I, ahh, do have a favor though." He smiled, and nodded. "Could I have a drink of water? That was, uhh, a good workout." He smiled, and headed down the stairs.

"I'll be back with drinks. Don't feel like you have to rush." I shook my head, and started cleaning up the area we were just in. There went my thoughts again. Things went a bit farther than I had imagined, but I can't say I hated it. *It was mutual, right?* I nodded. Donovan reappeared with a bottle of water, and what appeared to be scotch. "Here's your beverage, skirt, and your payment. But I wanted to ask… Can I just set up a transfer for business stuff? That way we can nix this cash hand-off…" He looked at the check. "Sort of makes me feel bad handing you money after you're done." He smiled, sheepishly.

"Yes, that would be great. And less to keep track of." He nodded again.

"I'll set it up today, and will be active as of our next meeting." He wrote something down on his phone, and stuff it back into his pocket. "I really trust this, you know. I love your company, and you're really beautiful. And I really appreciate the safety factors with you." I smiled, and slid my skirt on.

"Oddly, it's a deal that's working out for me, as well. As long as boundaries are respected, we'll be just fine Donovan. When next week are you thinking?" I headed down stairs, and pulled out my date book.

"Well, it's a crazy week," he pulled out his phone again. He scrolled through a few things, and I looked at my phone and noticed a missed text. It was already 2pm, and Gabe was apparently heading home. "How about next Thursday, same time?"

"That works for me. I'll be going then," I said as I pulled on my jacket. Donovan stepped over to assist, and held my coat sleeve so I could get it on easier. Once it was on, he leaned down, and kissed my cheek. I leaned back a bit, and looked him in the eye.

"Thank you, truly." He smiled, and opened the front door. I slowly walked back to my Jeep, tossing my equipment into the back. I waved at him as I pulled out of the driveway, still a bit speechless from the interaction. I composed myself as I drove, and pulled into our driveway not long after. I sat in the car for a moment, and shot off a few emails to new potential clients. When I looked up, the first thing I saw was the hot tub, and I went straight for it.

I quickly stripped, and made a pile of my clothes on the ground. I climbed in, and kicked on the jets for the hour cycle. I knew Gabe would be home soon, and I hoped that he wouldn't be too exhausted to give me a little before the kids and Jean got home.

~11~

Moments later, I heard tires on our driveway. I couldn't even bring myself to open my eyes, but by the walk that exited the car, I knew it was Gabe. I threw my arm in the air, and waved, hoping he would see where I was, and come straight over. *It worked.*

"Are you drowning in there, my love?" He approached, and his eyes widened to see my nakedness floating around. I reached for him, and after looking me over, he knew exactly what was going on. He gave me his hand, and I instantly pushed it into my crotch. He smiled, and pulled his hand back. "Well, you're all sorts of worked up, aren't you?" The deviousness came across his face. "I'll be right back." He headed in the house, and I hoped it wouldn't be for long.

He returned in his towel, and with a smoke in hand. He raised it to show me, and I smiled at him. I watched him lurk around the hot tub, placing the smoke down in a dry spot for later. He walked all the way around the tub, and hung his towel over the hook. When he faced me, the deviousness had turned hungry. He climbed into the hot tub with me, and sat back on the jets. He rested his head on the pillow, completely oblivious to my need for him jumping out of my body. There was no more resisting.

I crawled over to him, and up on top of him. The water dripped off of my nipples, and onto him as I straddled him on the seat. The cool air was a nice offset to the hot water we were in. My hips instinctively started grinding him, and I could feel him stiffening under me. I couldn't wait any longer, I needed him inside me. I lifted myself, and him, and slid down his thick shaft. I dug my fingers into his slippery shoulders, clinging to him for support. I was up and down him faster than ever, keeping up with a crazy rhythm.

I slowed to go deep, and rock on him a bit. The fullness of him drove me wild, and I wanted all I could get. I felt it start, and my muscles started to tense. Gabe felt it too, and met my eyes with a sly smile. He held my shoulders down so I couldn't move off of his massive cock. Thusly making me feel each and every pulsation of my orgasm. *So fucking intense.*

After the first ceased, he motioned me off of him, and to turn over. As I got on my knees, his hands spread me apart. I felt him slide back into me, and start drumming away. I felt the pressure of his thumb on my ass, and I knew exactly what was next. Sure enough, in he went. The combined pressure from the anal play was driving me over any edge I ever had, and screaming seemed to be the only option. I clung to the pillow on the hot tub chair, and hoped for some little bits of control. He was driving me wild. I could feel myself clench around him everywhere, and just as it tightened, he pulled his thumb back out, and I squirted all over his fat dick.

Gabe's dick throbbed, and once I heard his breath hitch, I knew he was going to come. I reached around, and tightly squeezed his balls, strengthening his own explosion. I felt every pulsation flow into me, and it made me feel so relaxed. We rolled off of each other, and back into the hot tub seats. He caught his breath, and reached for the big smoke he brought out. Drying off his hands, he picked it up.

"Oh Gabe," I leaned into him, and nibbled on his neck. He inhaled the first hit, and rested his head back on the pillow again.

"I know, baby. I wish everyday home from work was like that." I inhaled, and it went down relatively smoothly. He toweled off his hands again, and turned back to me to take the joint. "I don't tell you enough…but…" he inhaled. "You're absolutely fucking beautiful. The hottest mom I know." He smiled wide, and nudged me with his shoulder. I blushed. "Janie! Blushing?!" He grabbed his chest as if in shock. "I haven't seen those rosy cheeks for a while." He reached up, and caressed my face. "That just makes you even more desirable." I inhaled again, and shook my head. *Ah, there's the lusting that you've missed from him. See, he's still right with you.*

"I love you, G." Is all I could manage, blissed out, and trying not to be too heavy in the moment. We relaxed together for a little while longer, and noticed the kids would be home soon with Jean. "Today was a good day. I got paid, too. Someone's birthday is coming up, and he's been an awfully good boy." I handed him the joint, and kissed him deeply. He smiled very big.

"I don't know how good I've been, but I'm glad it's another birthday spent with my love." I kissed him again, and got lost all over again.

~

After our hot tub excursion, I found the energy to make a Mexican feast for dinner. The kids loved taco night, and I loved the giggles that came along with it. I heard Jean and the kids come in the back room door. Their little voices sounded cranky, and tired. *Oh lovely, my favorite.*

"Hey guys!" I said with open arms, and a smile. To my surprise, they both seemed to perk up, and jumped straight into my arms. "How was your day?!" These days I had spent away from them had truly made me love them both, and appreciate them both even more than I already did.

"Hi Mom!!" Galen hugged me quickly, and dashed away into the kitchen. "I smell tacos!" He excitedly threw his stuff on the bench, and hopped in his chair. I turned to see Lilah's smile, and sleepy eyes. I motioned her into my hug.

"How was your day, princess?" I tilted her head towards my face. "How was gymnastics? You look tired." I patted her head, and hugged her again.

"I'm good, but ready for bed." She said as she walked away, yawning. "Where's Dad?" she asked, impatiently.

"Oh, he's coming. Was just showering, I think." I turned to Jean, who tried escaping out of the back door before I could catch her. "Jean! Wait!" I caught her as she was closing the door. "Hey, please come and eat with us tonight. I made plenty." I opened the door for her, and she smiled very big.

"Thank you, Janie. That does smell absolutely delicious! A salad sounds wonderful." I watched her as she scooted right back over by the kids. *How lucky are you that your kids have her?* Extremely lucky, and I knew it.

"Gramma, come sit by me!" Galen exclaimed loudly. Lilah shifted her seat, so they could both sit by Jean without argument. She saw that I was watching her, smiling, and she smiled back and winked at me. I couldn't help but shake my head. I heard his footsteps coming into the room before I saw him.

"Hey kids!! I missed you today!!!" He scooped them up, with his poor mother in the middle. "How was school? And gymnastics, princess?" He sat back a bit, and selected his own chair. "Galen! Did you grow?!" He winked at him, and Galen was beaming.

"Yes Daddy! I did!! This much!" He put his fingers about two inches apart, and waited for Gabe's reaction. Gabe's mouth fell open, and he put his "extremely shocked" face on.

"I learned the triple back handspring today in gymnastics. They made me do it twenty times…" she yawned, while she explained. I loved watching their interactions while they chatted, and stuffed their faces. I couldn't help but interject, as it was getting quite late.

"Ok, guys, finish up so you can have your cookies. And then get ready for bed!" I loaded the dishwasher with the dirty plates and such, and the phone rang. Gabe was bringing his plate to me, set it on the counter, and headed to answer the phone. The kids were eating their cookies, making Oreo smiles, and Jean was laughing. I could slightly hear Gabe in the other room on the phone, and the tone sounded angry. I finished what I was doing, and closed the dishwasher. Turning the corner, his face told me what I had missed.

"Who IS this?!" he demanded in to the phone. Pacing quickly back and forth in the spare room. I could hear noise on the phone, but otherwise, was left in the dark. His eyes met mine a few times, and each time he would purposely look away. "No, you're not listening. I'm going to figure out who you are, and when I do, you're dead." He slammed the phone into the cradle.

"Gabe?" I hesitantly asked. "What's going on? What was that about?" He was silent, still, and leaning against the wall. I decided to back out, and give him some space. I headed back in to the kitchen, to see Jean helping the kids clean up. I smiled at her, and hugged her. "Thank you, sweet lady. Something has come up," I broke the hug so she could see my face, and worry. "Could you please put the kids to bed for me tonight? I need to be with Gabe." She nodded immediately.

"Yes dear, of course." She turned away, and then quickly back. "Dinner was delicious, thank you so much." She turned back towards the kids. "Okay fellas, let's hit the hay!" The kids giggled, and I was again reassured that this was a great decision. I turned off the lights in the kitchen, and headed back into our room where Gabe had gone.

"Hey," I said, casually, as I entered the room. He looked up at me, and smiled. He reached his hand out, and I took it.

"I'm sorry, I just didn't know what to say." He put his head on my hand, and sighed. "That was whoever has been leaving us presents. It's a man, for sure." He looked back up at me, just in time to see the blood drain from my face. "It's not Michael, and doesn't sound like anyone of his people. This voice is familiar, but I can't place it." He shook his head, in disappointment with himself. I squinted my eyes, as if trying to pull up memories of distant men in our lives. *Nothing. Who the hell is doing this?*

"How are we going to figure this one out?" I squeezed his hand, and pulled him out of his chair. "Everything's going to be fine. We're prepared for this, right?" I smiled at him, hoping for the best.

"God, I hope so." He hugged me, and knocked us both down into the bed. "Either way," he kissed my face. "I'm protecting my people without logic, and beyond measure. I'm contacting the department tomorrow. We'll get our options, and go from there." He pulled the blankets over us, and turned on some quiet music.

Lying next to him was the only comfort I needed sometimes…and this was one of those times. Whoever was trying to hurt us now was going to get a shock. I just hoped we can catch them. The radio station turned to Led Zeppelin, and *Thank You* had come on. *Ugh, the things this damn song drudges up…*

~12~

I was up early, made breakfast for everyone, and ready to go before 10am today. *Ah! Something to be happy about!* I gathered my binders together, as I would be out client prospecting this afternoon. Gabe entered the kitchen, and gave my ass a good smack. I instantly pushed back into his hand, which made his breath catch.

"Whoa, I forget about you sometimes, my love…" he slid his hand further into my crotch, via my skirt. "Always so ready and willing." He kissed me deeply, and continued to his breakfast.

"Oh yes, always for you…" I winked, and refilled his coffee. "I've got a few meetings today with the girls. And I'm hoping to sign a few new clients, too." He smiled at me, and shook his head.

"My girl, the businesswoman. I just love how you're doing with all of this, and I love how it's brightened your spirit even more." He was beaming. *And so are you.* He grabbed his planner, and packed his briefcase. "Oh, by the way, I'm meeting with the new detective assigned to your case this afternoon. I wanted to fill them in on this new stuff, and see what they want us to do about it all." He smiled, and sighed when he saw my look of despair. *What a way to kill the morning buzz, honey.*

"Okay, will you fill me in later?" He nodded from across the room, while he finished getting his things ready for work. I couldn't help that my mind began to wander. *A new detective? A voice that sounded familiar?* It was hard to wrap my head around it all, and still focus on my daily tasks. But I did, because it had to be done. "I need to get going, too. I'm meeting with Kiara and Mylah today about helping with the events I've got coming up." I quickly got my purse, satchel, and work planner. His hands wrapped around me before I could turn around, and he smelled delicious.

"I hope you have a good day today. Please be safe out there, ok?" He tipped my chin to his mouth for a quick kiss. I nodded at him, and hugged him once more. His embrace was solid today, and unfaltering. Just what I needed.

"You too, Gabe. I love you." I smiled, and we walked out to the garage together. We followed each other in to town, and then turned in different directions. I watched his car drive farther, and farther away from me. I couldn't help feel a bit more alone than I had before. My mind was racing, still, from the phone call last night. I tried to crank up the radio, and focus on the meeting I was headed to.

When I pulled up to the pavilion, Mylah and Kiara were already there, waiting for me. I smiled as I got out of the car, and headed towards the smiling beauties.

"Hey Janie!" Mylah said, looking quite nice all made up, and dressed. *Guess she wasn't out late last night then.*

"Hi Girls," I sat down. "How are you doing? Tell me about your first few weeks!" I took out my notebook, ready to hear their issues, needs and all the rest. To my surprise, they both just smiled.

"Our weeks have gone extremely well Janie! I don't think either of us have any complaints!" They both look at each other, and nodded in agreement. "Our clients are super nice, and they tip *very* well." They giggled.

"Oh, I'm so glad to hear this!" I took notes on the things she said, as quickly as I could. "Would both of you like more clientele? I wasn't sure if your schedules permitted it, or not, but the offer is yours before I hire another person." I waited patiently, and could tell Mylah wasn't too keen on the idea.

"I'd love a few more clients. Could it be on specific days, around my school schedule?" I nodded.

"Absolutely! What days would you like me to add to?" She flipped through her planner, and decided on her needs.

"I could add some to Monday and Wednesday." I turned towards Mylah.

"How about you, Mylah?" I waited patiently. She fumbled around with her phone, with her planner, and her fingernails. *Ugh, I wonder if she bites those...*

"I'm not sure yet. Can I let you know? I mean, I'd like to, but..." she trailed off. I could tell there was more to the story then she let on, so I put my hand up, and smiled.

"No problem. Just let me know when you know, okay?" I scribbled she'd call me on the deal. "And Mylah... If you ever need to talk something through, I'm more than happy to listen. Okay?" She smiled idly, and wrote herself a note to call me.

"I'm just so glad this is working for you

Janie! For all of us! The money is great, and I love the flexibility." She giggled, and poked Mylah. "And the new girls are starting to grow on me." They both laughed out loud.

"I'm really thankful for you two, and Caty, too. This is all going so smoothly, and I couldn't be happier about it all!! Kiara, I'll text you your new clients, and their info once I get them, okay? Other than that, you're done here for today!"

"Awesome! Thanks again, Janie! I'll be in touch!!" She turned towards Mylah before she left. "Another party Friday? You better blow me up!" She winked, laughed, and ran to her car. Mylah was lingering around, and I imagined it was to talk.

"Okay, you're right. I need to talk. Have time?" She smiled, and scooted closer to me.

"Of course, I can make my own schedule, you know." I winked at her. "What's up?"

"Well, I've got a new night job…" there was a pause. A very distinctive, heavy pause. I felt my eyes get bigger, waiting for her to finish the thought. "Stripping." She said plain as day. She was gauging my reaction, trying to see how I felt about it already.

"Well, it's great money. Where are you doing it at? A safe place, I hope." She was stunned, and her mouth fell open. Her face, and open mouth, made me laugh out loud. "Honey, you're a big girl. And it's not my judgment! Do what you have to do!" *Maybe you should approach her on the other deals?*

"I'm so glad you don't mind. I was really worried you may fire me." I shook my head in disbelief. "I'll never let it interfere with my clients, and work for you. I promise." She smiled hesitantly.

"Sounds good to me." I paused, and raised

79

an eyebrow. "Who knows, maybe soon I'll find a client you could strip-clean for." I giggled, and she laughed hard.

"Are there really services like that?" I wrinkled my nose, and shook my head yes. "Wow, I guess it's not really different though, now that I think about it." I smiled, and agreed again. "Alright Janes, I won't keep you. I feel soo much better now that I told you that!" My brain was starting to lose focus on Mylah, and focus more on my cleaning job. *Oh, the one where you're strip-cleaning for him?* I smirked at myself.

"Mylah! One last thing," I caught her as she got up. "Please, please be safe. Use the security service we use if you should ever have a problem. Even at that job, okay?" Before I knew what was happening, her arms were around me.

"Thank you for caring Janie, and looking out for me." I patted her back, and looked off, through the fields of the playground. There weren't a lot of kids out today, just a few sets, and their moms. Past the playground was the forest, and the colors on the trees were amazing. Wait. *What the hell was that? A person?* I squinted, and saw nothing. I pulled away from Mylah, and sent her on her way.

"You're welcome, Mylah. Keep in touch about your schedule, and I'll see you soon." She smiled, and waved as she walked away. And I found myself spinning around on my heel, rechecking the tree line. *Nothing? It can't be nothing.* I could've sworn I saw a person lingering in the trees.

I pulled my papers around me, and grabbed my cell phone. There were a few businesses I needed to call to secure accounts with, and this seemed like as good of a place as any. I dove in quickly, hoping that the phone side of this day would be over soon. I was tired of talking to people already.

The third business ended up being my third new contract. *Awesome job signing all three!* I was pretty excited. These big business moments, for me, were huge. I put my cell phone down on the table, and opened up my planner to schedule the new clients in. Something kept triggering my nerves, and I kept turning to check the trees. I shook off the thoughts, and chalked it up to nerves with everything going on, yet again.

I picked up my bags, and headed towards the parking lot. As I was walking out to my car, I heard what sounded like a person walking behind me. *Quickly. Very quickly.* I grabbed my keys, and situated them in between each of my fingers. I stopped at the back of my car, and turned quickly. As I did, the figure of the man turned quickly behind another vehicle. *Get out of here. Now, Janie.* I got into my car faster than ever, locked the doors as I was giving it gas, and speeding away. Looking in my rearview mirror as I drove away, I saw nothing.

My heart was beating out of control. *What just happened? Anything?* My whole body was shaking, like it knew something that I didn't. I wasn't sure what to do with all of this, so I headed home. Relaxing is what I needed. I turned on the radio, and tried to forget my worry. I blared *Possession* and sang the whole way home, more than ready to hug my kids, and my handsome husband after this long day.

~**13**~

After I put the kids to bed, Jean and I cleaned up the kitchen. I couldn't help but think about how much this lady had changed my life. She stepped in to help me when Lilah was born, as I was still recovering mentally so much from the ordeal with Michael. She never judged me, only loved, and encouraged. I caught myself smiling at her in thought.

"Jean," I started. "Are you happy with us?" I couldn't help myself, and she was a bit taken aback by the question. "I mean, do you have what you need? Want days off? Anything?" I put my hand on her shoulder, and rubbed her arm. Her smile told me everything I ever needed to know.

"You have made my life amazing, again. I missed Gabe's father so much, but being around my angels every day keeps me going. Keeps me happy." She held my hand. "Things are great as they are. I wouldn't change a thing. I sure love you kids, all my angels." I hugged her.

"We love you, too, Jean." My cell phone buzzed, and I reached for it. "Have a good evening tonight, Jean." I said as she was leaving.

"Oh, I will. Friends are coming over for bridge tonight. So, don't mind the extra cars." She smiled, and closed the door behind her. Looking down at my phone, I saw Gabe had texted.

Home in 3 shakes of a donkey. Love you.

I laughed out loud. Sometimes I had no idea what that man was talking about, but at least he was almost home. *At least he's really sexy, too. That helps, you know.* True. I checked in on the kids, one asleep, and one reading. I decided to take the quiet opportunity to pick up the house a bit, as it had been days. I turned on some music quietly, and dimmed the lights a bit.

I started walking around and closing the blinds. I was on the third window, and I heard a noise come out of Lilah's room. I turned my head to see her wave at me, and close her door behind her. *Ah, potty break.* When I turned back around, and reached for the blind cord to pull the shades, I saw the face on the other side of the glass peering in at me. I couldn't contain my scream, and as I did, the figure disappeared from the window. I fumbled for my cell phone, and stumbled into the couch.

After unlocking my screen, and beginning to dial, I looked up for a split second to see the man, standing on my porch, looking squarely in the window at me. *Oh my God.* My body was frozen, and I couldn't move. I tried to take in the moment, and remember every detail I could. He was taller than me, but not as tall as... *Michael.* He had a black winter mask over his face, and his eyes were dark. He wore jeans, and a dark shirt. He had on black boots. I heard noise in Lilah's room. *What if there are more of them?! Focus, Janie! NOW!*

Without moving my arms, I unlocked my phone with one hand. I hit the emergency dial button, and 911 came to screen. I glanced down with my eyes only to make sure that no movement triggered my visitor. When it was ringing, I hit the speakerphone button. *Stay calm, you can do this.* I knew I was behind a locked door, but it was only glass. *And glass can shatter.*

Suddenly, I heard the operator answer. "911, what is your emergency?" I took a big breath, and if to distract the visitor, lifted my right hand and held it out to the visitor in a "stop" motion, while covering up his line of sight to my mouth.

"I need police, fast. Someone is trying to break in my house! They're staring at me through my front door right now!! Yes, that's the address. *Please hurry!!"* I took a step back, and heard Lilah's door creek open. "Lilah!" I whispered. "Go into Galen's room, and lock the door. Don't open it until I come and get you. NOW." She looked terrified, and that alone made the lump rise in my throat.

"Ok, mam," the operator paused, and I could hear her dispatching police to me. "Stay calm, honey. They'll be there in no time." Even though I was conscious of our talking, I couldn't take my eyes off the visitor. Something so familiar about his eyes, but I couldn't place him. Just then, the visitor raised his hand, and pointed directly at me. I swallowed hard, and wanted to run and hide.

"Oh my God," I whisper screamed into the phone. "He's pointing at me through my glass door! I need them here NOW! How long??" My whole body began to tremble. "I need someone to call my husband now." My thoughts were quickening, and I was losing it. I swallowed the tears, and breakdown, and thought of my loves just rooms away. "Oh my God.. My mother-in-law lives in our back guest house, and she was having friends over. Oh Jesus.." I almost lost it again.

"Janie, you can do this. I'm right here, and my dispatcher is calling your husband. I have one car less than a mile away. Has he moved? Tell me about him." I could hear her frantically typing, and I knew the description would be needed.

"He's about the same size as my husband in height. Wearing black boots, jeans, and a black sweatshirt or hoodie. He has dark eyes, and a black winter face mask hat thing on. And black leather gloves. He's standing in my porch light, a foot away from my front door knob." My breathing was labored and heavy. I could feel the vibration of another call coming in through my phone. I glanced down to see it was Gabe. Tears welded up in my eyes, because I couldn't disconnect with the 911 operator.

"Ok, Janie, you should see lights and hear sirens any minute." More loud typing. "Is he still there?" I turned my head to look towards the tree line, and when I did, my visitor did, too. I could see the reds and blues flashing through the trees, and I sighed a little. Looking back towards my visitor, our eyes met one last time. He stepped towards the door, and I stepped back.

"I'll see you soon, Janie." He yelled through the door, and took off to the right side of the house.

"He just took off to the right side of my house, towards the pond. Did you hear what he said?" I was out of breath, and the tears were streaming down my cheeks.

"Yes, Janie. I've recorded it, as well." There was a silent pause. "They've radioed me that they are in your driveway. Would you like me to stay on the line with you? OR would you like to wait for the police officer to come to your door?" She waited.

"I'll stay inside, and wait for them." She typed fast.

"Ok, mam. Don't go outside until they come to the front door. Good job, Janie." As I hung up the phone, I saw headlights pull into the driveway quickly. *Gabe.* I watched him be detained by the police, until they completed their perimeter search. I headed towards Galen's room, and knocked gently on the door.

"Hey princess, it's mommy. Open up." After a second, she cautiously opened the door. Galen was soundly sleeping in his bed, oblivious. Lilah smiled at me, and reached out for a hug.

"Mommy, you looked scared. Are we okay?" She looked in my eyes, and held my cheeks. I nodded, and tried to smile through my worry.

"Yes baby," I picked her up. "Let's go back to bed, okay?" She nodded, and yawned. Carrying her through the house, I couldn't help cling to her a bit tighter. *Here comes your past again, now stepping on your children.* I felt my eyes fill with tears, knowing I had no instant fix for this. I laid her down gently, sucking my own tears back inside, and tucked her in tightly. At this moment, I was glad she hadn't seen what I thought she had seen. *The Visitor.* I patted her head, and sang her a song before I closed her door to deal with the current issues.

I emerged from her room moments later, to Gabe rushing into the house with the police officers. I motioned them all to be quiet, and step out onto the porch. Gabe's arms were around me before anything, and that triggered the emotions once again. I sobbed into his coat, not knowing which way was up or down. He put my coat around me, and helped me out into a chair on the porch. The officers surrounded me, and I could see just how many had responded to my call for help. 6 cars, and 10 officers. One officer approached Gabe and I, and tipped his hat to us.

"Good evening, Mam," he extended his hand. "I'm Detective Brian Gustovson, and I'm in charge of your case nowadays. I just spoke with your husband this afternoon, so I am freshly updated on the issues." I nodded, and listened. "We've got the description you gave the dispatcher, and are still searching for the suspect. Any notes, calls, or anything that we haven't been informed of at this point?" I shook my head no. The detective's walkie-talkie buzzed a loud alarm, and he reached down to answer it.

"Ah, yeah, Lt." there was a break in communication. "House full of ladies in the back are all alright, and oblivious." I sighed in relief, knowing that no one else had been affected. Detective Gustovson smiled at me, and responded.

"Great, thank you. Out." He put his radio down on the table. He handed me a card, and it had multiple phone numbers on it. "Here's my phone numbers. Use one, use all. I'll always be around one of them." He rifled through some paperwork, and read some things to himself. "Okay, Mr. and Mrs. Lazarus," he began. "I don't want to take any chances considering the history, and that we don't know who this..." he paused.

"Visitor." I said disdainfully.

"Yes, visitor. We don't know who this is. Now, I need you to think about anyone that this may be. Even if it seems far-fetched, let me know." Suddenly, as if on cue, my memories of the park incident today resurfaced.

"Today I had a meeting at the park with my employees. I felt like someone was watching me, over and over." I shook my head. "I just shrugged it off as paranoia with everything else going on." I looked towards Gabe, and his face was ashen. I hadn't seen his face like this in so long, and it was torture. I looked towards the officer who was writing things down in this book, ever so fast. "Do you think it was him?" The officer nodded.

87

"Most likely. But don't worry. We're going to do our best with this. Remember," he leaned down towards me. "None of this is your fault, and we'll do our best to find whoever this is. You'll be on security detail for the next three days." I felt Gabe's hand squeeze mine. "Any questions?" I shook my head. Unfortunately, I remember how all of this went down before. Gabe stood, and shook his hand.

"Thank you, Brian, for your continued help with all of this. I'll be in touch." They nodded at each other, and the police began pulling out of the driveway, and one stopped and stayed in the middle of the drive. Gabe took note of the police car staying, and waved at the officers in the car. They waved back. He took me by the hands, and pulled me into a hug. "I know it's hard not to worry," he paused. "And it's probably bringing up all sorts of crazy shit." I felt the tears start to flow again. "I'll protect you here, and make you as safe as I can." I hugged him hard.

"Let's go relax a bit." I wandered back towards the bedroom.

"Have any green? Are the kids out for the night?" I nodded, and nodded again.

"Lilah woke up, and came out while the visitor was out there. I thought she saw him, but then it turned out she didn't. Galen never woke up. They were both back to sleep when you came in the house before." I plopped down on the bed, and reached for the tin of green. *Score! Already rolled!* I took the first hit, slowly, and with purpose. I watched Gabe stalk around the room, changing his clothes for bed, and trying to figure out what to do next. "Hey." I interrupted his thought. "Want?" I held my hand out, with the lit joint burning away.

He couldn't say no, and took a long, slow hit just as I had. He smiled at me, and shook his head.

"I fully expected you to be way more upset than you are, Janes." He sat back, and wrinkled his forehead. "Oh, I hope that came out the right way. I just mean that, with all this, again... I'm just..." He stopped, shaking his head. I inhaled again.

"I've had a bit-o-bullshit in my life already, so I guess I'm just better at keeping it together. Maybe?" I giggled, and drew off of the joint again. "Really, I think I'm just nuts, and a nervous wreck." I smiled at him, and handed him the doobie. He took a few more hits, and snuffed it out.

"I think you're superwoman." He poked my side, laid down, and spooned my back. "But I may be a little biased." He kissed my cheek, and snuggled in to my hair. I couldn't help but smirk at the last conversation, as I knew he was proud of me. *Who is doing this to us? Why do I always attract the crazy people?* I tried to clear my head, and just listen to the sounds of the finally quiet of the outdoors. *I'm sure the visitor will be back soon enough.*

~14~

Sleep was hard to come by last night. I didn't get much of it, and decided to get ahead on invoices, and contracts for the business. The clock said it was 7am, but it still felt like the middle of the night, to me. I heard the back door open, and lock re-lock, after. *Jean.* When she turned the corner in the kitchen, she was surprised to see that I was sitting at the bar, with all of my work laid out everywhere. She scanned the counter, and her eyes opened wider.

"Good Morning, Sweetie," she found a bare place to set her purse down. "Is everyone okay today? What on earth happened last night?" She looked puzzled, and I sighed at her question.

"There was someone here, trying to break in." I paused, and started piling up my paperwork. *Don't be late to Donovan's today.* "The police will be around here for a few days, making sure that everything is okay." She stepped towards me, and without real thought, I stepped back. She frowned at me.

"Aww, honey…" she slowly, and purposefully put both hands on my shoulders. "It's going to be okay. It was okay before, and will be again." She patted my shoulder, and I tried to smile a little. "And anyway," she paused with her eyebrows high. "You sure do have crazy bastards in your life, don't you honey?" She winked at me, and I couldn't help but giggle.

"Oh, Jean," I shook my head. "You have no idea." We both smiled, and I finished packing up my briefcases, just as Gabe walked in.

"Good morning, to two of my best ladies." He hugged us both. "Everyone doing okay this morning?" He smacked my ass as I pulled away, and I shot him the *look*.

"Yes, G. It's a new day today," I said through a yawn.

"Yeah, you didn't sleep, did you?" He rubbed his thumb across my cheeks. It was pointless to lie to him. He just knew me too well.

"Not so much. I need to get ready for work though…OH!" I suddenly remembered the hot tub party I was supposed to plan. *Damn it.* "Gabe, I talked to Sean the other day, and he'll be available and in town next weekend." I pulled out my planner to verify dates. "Yes. Next weekend. So, do you want to do a cookout and tub party?" He smiled.

"Absolutely. Inviting everyone?" I nodded, and he nodded back. "Sounds great. Mom," he turned towards Jean, who was already smiling, and shaking her head. "Mind having the kids over for a sleepover next weekend?"

"Of course I will, son. I'd love to!" She was busily readying the kids breakfasts, and I noticed ours too. Gabe turned back towards me, and we smiled at each other.

"Okay then. Party Set. I need to get ready for work now, or I'm going to be late!" I scurried around, piling up my brief cases, and new contracts. I wrapped my arms backwards around my already ready husband, and hugged him tightly. He turned in my arms, and planted a large, wet kiss on my neck.

"I'm getting off early the next few days, so you guys won't be home alone in the evenings anymore." I hugged him tighter, as I knew how hard that was to pull off at the Phoenix, these days. "Bill's in town finally, and we're having a meeting today. I plan on filling him in, too."

"Okay, well, I suppose I'll see you later this afternoon then." I kissed him again. It was just so addicting. He patted Jean, and headed out the door fast as lightning. I headed back to get ready for my big day with Donovan. I hadn't had much time to focus on my plan with him this time, considering how crazy last time was. *Crazy? Seemed like you liked it then, Janes. Are you really sure this is a good idea considering everything that's going on?* I shook the ridiculous thoughts out of my head, and pictured my bank account balance instead. Yes, right now it was indeed worth it.

I showered quickly, and checked the time. Almost 8:30am now. I opened my lingerie drawer, and searched through the options. I found my old full body lace suit, and checked it over. There were no obvious holes in this crotch-less, black lace piece. I slid it on, pulling every inch on carefully, and threw on some khaki's over it. I headed back into the bathroom to curl my hair, and put on my makeup. I couldn't help but notice how enticing this outfit was, glancing down at myself in the mirror. *Yes, he'll approve. Jesus, Janie.* The smirk was impossible to hide, so instead I focused on finishing the package for work. I threw on a big sweatshirt, and my running shoes.

When I got in the car to head to the James' residence, I couldn't help but look around the car, and make sure everything was as it should be. The backseat of my Jeep was filled with car seats, and kid junk. The back seemed to be filled with cleaning supplies, and work kits. I sighed. *Nothing. You have got to relax if you want all of this to go smoothly today. You know it.* I pulled out of the driveway, and headed to get the job done.

~

Pulling into his residence, I'd always gotten butterflies. They were worse than ever now, and I was shaking a little. I checked around the front of his huge estate, noticed no red car, and no movement which was more than reassuring to me right now. I parked, and got out of the car. The door didn't open this time, and I wondered why. I rang the bell, and waited outside patiently. I could hear sounds coming from inside, but I could not identify what they were.

"Just a second!" I heard him yell from somewhere deep inside the mansion. "Almost there!" I could hear his footsteps running down the stairs. When he opened the door, I noticed that he was in his black, silk robe. I swallowed hard, and my eyebrow raised. *Uhh, you're blushing, too.* "Janie?!" he sounded puzzled.

~15~

"Hi, Donovan. How're you?" I asked cheerfully, and pushed my way into the mansion. I turned around to see his face strained, and puzzled. "What's wrong?"

"Well, Uhh," he ran his hands through his hair. "You're dressed...oddly...today." At that moment, I couldn't hold in my laughter, and it flowed out loudly all over the room. He smiled, hesitantly, at my outburst, and his face grew even more confused. "What's so funny?" I put down my supplies on the table, and shook my head. I bypassed him in the foyer, and entered into his office, where the stereo system was. I found my CD, still in rotation. *Whoa! He listens to it when you're not working, too!* I hit play, and cranked it up.

I walked back into the hall, by the table where I had just put all of my things. I turned off my cell phone, put it in my purse, and zipped it closed. I sat down on a chair that was close by, threw a leg over the other, and started to take off my shoes.

"You know, Donovan," I began, as my shoe hit the floor. I lifted the other, and slid it off as well. "I've had an extremely bad last 24 hours, and your...worry on my clothing choice has almost angered me!" I glanced up at his face, and watched it change through a myriad of emotions. He just was not sure how to take anything I was saying. "So, I guess that leaves me no choice but to just…" I stood up abruptly. "Get to work." I said smiling big as ever. I took two steps into his personal space, so we were too close for comfort. "Unless you don't want me to clean for you today." I raised an eyebrow, and waited for his response.

"Oh no, please go right ahead Janie." He cautiously said, watching me very closely. I smiled, and took a few steps to head into the kitchen to clean, and closed the door behind me.

While I was in there mopping and scrubbing away, I couldn't help but wonder what he was up to, or if he was waiting to see what I was going to do next. While I was finishing up, and putting the dishes away, he appeared in the kitchen. He still had on that black silk robe, and I had to admit, he was a treat to look at. Middle aged or not, the years had been gentle on his baby face, and solid body. *Solid, large body, if you remember from last time, girl.*

"Hey Donovan," I said nonchalantly. He sat at the table a few feet away from me, and sipped on his drink. *Scotch on the rocks.* "I'm going to head up to clean upstairs now." I turned and winked at him, and pulled my sweatshirt over my head. When I opened my eyes again, I was met with his shock and awe facial expression. Pretending like I wasn't sure what he was looking at, I looked down, and checked myself out. *Pretty perfect, if I do say so myself. I especially like the perky, turned on a bit nipples…that adds in the extra whorish flair, kid.* I said nothing, but turned and headed out of the kitchen.

Walking down the hall, I could feel his eyes

on me. I stopped by the table with my purse, and unzipped it slowly. The burning feeling of his eyes staring at me, body part by body part, was almost too intense. I reached into my purse for my lipstick, and applied it to my lips. *Slowly.* I recapped the lipstick, and pursed my lips together. I made one kissing noise, and idly turned my head enough to see him, intently gazing at me. I put the lip refresher back into my purse, and re-zipped it closed. I took a few steps towards the stairs, and undid my pants button secretly as I went. When I was close enough, I leaned on the banister. My loose khaki's slid down very quickly over the lace body suit. The feeling of them falling made my internal drive heat up. They felt like silk being pulled over my legs, and over again. In my deep thought and focus, I heard his breath hitch. I turned to see him on the far wall from me, with his devious, devilish grin.

"Well, Donovan," I stepped up a few stairs. "I should really get to work!" I hopped up the rest of the stairs quickly, and headed for the vacuum cleaner. I began vacuuming the rugs, and watched him slowly slink up the stairs. Our eyes were locked on each other's every movement. I shook my head, and refocused on the rug. *Whoa, a little too intense there. Don't be like that Janie.*

"Janie," he asked. "Don't forget to get under that end table over there." He pointed to the far table, and I headed over to it. I nodded at him, and I turned to reach the vacuum underneath the table. It was indeed a stretch, and now I knew what he wanted. *Order delivered, boss.* I stepped toward the table, keeping my legs shoulder length apart, and bent with the vacuum. I knew his eyes were locked on my pussy, and I could feel it getting hotter. *And wetter.* "Oh, Janie," he said adoringly. "Don't forget

95

this one."

I headed across the room to a table that was directly across from the wall he was leaning against. I pulled the hose extension from the vacuum, and fell to the floor to climb under the table. I almost couldn't hold in my laughter. I turned so I could see him from under the table, and he raised an eyebrow at me. He hoisted himself from the wall, and headed over to take a seat in the chair. As he walked across the room, his robe opened, and I saw the naked flesh probing out of the silky cloth.

I climbed out from underneath the table, and put the vacuum cleaner back together again. As I put the vacuum in the upstairs cleaning closet, I pulled out the step stool, and feather duster. I slowly moved to the center of the open area, underneath the chandelier. I climbed up slowly, making sure to widen my steps, to deepen his stare. My body was a raging inferno, and I needed relief. I backed off of the stool, and noticed he had shifted the chairs as they were the last time we were there. *Facing each other. He must like the front row seats.* I smiled, cautiously headed for the chair, and sat down.

There were no words spoken. The sexual stench was heavy in the air, and it was more than obvious what we were both after. *Release.* I laid back in my chair, looking him directly in the eye, and began feather dusting my chest. Slowly at first, with a quickening pace. My nipples reacted to the touch, and through the lace, began to protrude into the openings of the lace. He laid back as well, watching me intently. The grin was coming and going, as if it came with each dirty thought I triggered.

I slowly opened my legs, exposing myself completely. My hands began to wander, and my eyes fell closed. *Freshmen* came on the CD, and I found myself lost in distant thought of my past sexual experiences. *Remember those times that Michael let his minions watch? After you relaxed, you really got into it. Paid for it, too.* My fingers were met with soaking wet lace, more than ready to take my willing participant. *NO! You're not taking anybody, Miss. Come on, just rub one off with him like last time. Easy-peasy.* Oh how I tried to focus on my thoughts, because they were so correct. But when I opened my eyes, I was met with an open-robed Donovan, harder than ever.

"You do this to me, Janie." He said breathlessly, as his hand came up and firmly palmed his length. His eyes bore into me, and I couldn't help but let my hands wander. I found my throbbing, swollen clit quickly, and began rubbing it fiercely. I sunk my right hand into my crotch, rubbing myself to climax. I held my hair out of my face by sinking my left hand into the long locks of curls. My eyes closed, and my head rolled around the back of the chair. I could feel my muscles tensing everywhere, and the tightness was holding. I held my breath to help push me over the edge, and opened my eyes again.

He was sitting on the edge of his chair, aiming his cock right at me, stroking it harder than I had ever witnessed in my life. His eyes were still locked in with mine, and his breathing was heavy. I pushed my fingers farther in, and pushed squarely on my g-spot. My body went tightly, and I could feel myself coming everywhere. Moments later, I opened my eyes, and Donovan was on his knees on the floor, between my legs. I heard his breath hitch, and seconds later his hot fluids pumped all over the floor, and that fine silk robe.

I took a moment to adjust in my chair, and swung my legs over the edge of the side. He picked himself up off of the floor, and plopped back down into the chair. We both smiled, still breathing heavy. *Well, now that you're more relaxed...*

"The whole voyeur thing.." I sighed, and stood up quickly. "I like it way too much." I smiled, and headed downstairs. I didn't find the need of sitting there and staring at each other. This wasn't like that. *Couldn't be like that.* Picking up my khaki's at the bottom of the stairs, I hit the bathroom on the way to my purse, and peed. I slid my pants back on, and they again enticed the same nerves as before. *MMMmmm...* I went out into the hallway, and grabbed my sweatshirt. I slid it on, and went to the laundry room to put the clean towels in the bin, completing my jobs for today. When I came back out of the laundry room, Donovan greeted me in the entrance way, smiling, holding an envelope. I felt my forehead instantly wrinkle.

"This is for you." Noticing my expression, he frowned, and held it out further. "It's a bonus. I'm very grateful." His smile was genuine, and he handed it towards me. I grabbed my purse as I walked towards him, and I was pretty sure I was blushing again. "Let me walk you out." He opened the front door, and walked out on the front patio with me. He held the door open for me, and I stepped out. Simultaneously, we both gasped.

~16~

"What the fuck?!!" was all that escaped my lips. Looking at my jeep, the back window had been shattered, and there was an obvious note stuffed in the side of my door. I could feel my temper boiling

98

over, and I ran out to my Jeep. Donovan ran with me, fumbling with his cell phone along the way. Before going too close to the car, I bent down, and checked underneath the car first. *Nothing. Just the underbody.* I checked around both sides of the car, and Donovan's BMW, too. I looked back at Donovan, who was now on the phone, and looked very angry.

He was deep in conversation with what sounded like his security, trying to find out who had gotten into the gates. I cautiously approached the driver's side window, and carefully pulled the paper out from the window. I turned it over, and read the message.

"Is this soon enough? Soon. XO"

Instinctively, I pulled out my cell phone and first called Gabe. As I waited for it to ring, Donovan came back to stand next to me. I smiled at him, awkwardly, and Gabe answered.

"Hello Love." He said calmly as ever.

"Hey, bad news.. My back window is shattered, and there's a note." He interrupted me instantly.

"Are you safe? Where are you?" I could hear him typing quickly in the background.

"I'm still at the James' Estate. I just finished working. Mr. James," I paused, and looked at him out of the corner of my eye. "He's here, waiting with me. I'll call Detective Gustovson now." I sighed loudly, and put my hand on my forehead.

"Okay, I'm coming there to follow you home." He cleared his throat. "Greg's installed a new security system at home today, too. Just so you know. God damnit!"

"What?!" he sounded distressed.

"I'm sorry, I'm just so angry and sick of all of this bullshit! I thought we were done with the crazy fuckers, Janie." I didn't know what to say. It was true. *What have I done to this poor man? What have I put him through?* "I'll be there in twenty. Don't leave until I'm there, please." He sounded so mad. I wasn't going to poke at him.

"Okay, see you soon." I hung up the phone, and sat on the cement bench close to the cars. I pulled my purse onto my lap, and started looking for the Detective's card. Donovan came and sat next to me.

"Janie, I've got to ask," he questioned. "What's going on? Are you okay?" I kept digging through my purse, and sighed heavily. I nodded.

"Yeah, I'm fine." I cleared my throat. "Someone's stalking me. Last night they were at my house, and for the past few weeks, they've left clues and signs. Weird shit everywhere." I found the card. "Just one second, and I'll explain more." I smiled, and dialed the Detective's number.

"Detective Gustovson here." I tried to remember to talk slowly, and not go into freak out mode. Although, I did feel much better knowing that someone was here with me. And it was day light.

"Detective, this is Janie Lazarus. I've got a problem." I waited, in hoped that he would remember who I was.

"Janie! What's happening?" I could hear typing.

"I'm at the James' Estate. They are clients of mine, and I was just getting ready to leave after working, and my Jeep windows are smashed, and

100

there was a note left in the door." I waited for directions, fully knowing there would be many.

"Okay. Don't leave. Don't touch anything. Are you safe? Can you go back inside?" There was a pause in his typing.

"Mr. James is here with me, and we seem to be alone here. We won't touch anything." My thoughts were starting to run wild, and I shook my head to regain a bit of focus.

"Stay where you are. I'll be there as soon as I can." He hung up, as did I. I turned back towards Donovan, who now looked so worried.

"At this point, we don't know who it is." I looked down at my shaking hands. "Look, I feel terrible that this happened on your property." He shook his head, and stopped me with his hand on my mouth. I felt my eyebrow raise. *That's too close for comfort. But... it's so oddly comforting right now.*

"Don't you dare apologize. It's not your fault. We all have a history..." he trailed off, and shook his head. "I'm just a bit confused how they got inside my gates in the first place. My security team is pulling the videos, and will absolutely help as they can." He patted my knee. "Don't worry, I'll help you with this however I can. I don't want you stressed. I want you..." he raised his eyebrows at that comment, as if in agreement. *Oh shit.* "I want you to be ready for work! ALL. THE. TIME." I blushed at his blunt comment.

"Thanks, Donovan." I sighed. "Had a good time today." I elbowed him while we sat and waited for everyone to show up. He leaned into my elbow, and made a moaning noise in his throat. Just then, both our heads snapped up when 4 police cars appeared with lights and sirens.

"Oh, wow, Janie..." he elbowed me this time.

"I'm apparently addictive. You should note that." Our eyes met after my semi-inappropriate comment, and his look was very telling. The small smirk, and the excited squint in his eyes... *He wants you soo bad. The feelings are almost palpable.* I winked, as I stood up to greet Detective Gustovson. "Hello, Detective."

"Please call me Brian. Okay, give it to me." He smiled, as if knowing I knew the drill better than anyone.

"I arrived about 10am, went in to do my cleaning and such. Finished up about 30 minutes ago, and Mr. James walked me out to find this." I pointed at the disaster of my back window. "I called Gabriel first, and then immediately called you. Mr. James security team was pulling video footage for you. Oh," I paused, and bent down to get the note off of the ground. "And this." I handed him the note, he read it quickly, and rolled his eyes when he finished.

"Okay, thank you Janie. Please just have a seat for a moment. Is your husband on his way?" I nodded. "Okay, I'm going to go get a statement from Mr. James." I smiled at him, and hugged my cell phone. Suddenly, my phone buzzed. It was a text from my mom.

Love you Sweetheart! Will be visiting this weekend! Set it all up with G! So excited to see you and the babies!!

Oh, God. I had forgotten about my parents coming into town. Their timing for the drama was impeccable. I guess we would have to fill them in anyway, regardless of if they were here or not. I shot her back a quick text.

Can't wait. What a week it's been. Love you.

I noticed that the police, and Donovan's security team were going over notes, and footage on a tablet. Pens were going frantically, and Donovan was pointing out things on the video. I wasn't sure if I really wanted to know what was going on, or not. Just then, Gabe pulled into the driveway. I saw him rushing over to me, and I opened my arms to him. I instantly sank into his warmth as it engulfed me. He buried his nose in my hair.

"Hey, baby," he pulled me back a bit, to check me over. "Are you okay?" I nodded.

"Of course. Whoever it was, wasn't here when we came out. It's just a big mess." I pointed at the Jeep. Gabe walked around the vehicle, and noted that my front tires had also been slashed. He walked over to the group of police, and security, and pointed out the tires to them. As if they were lemmings, they all instantly moved over to the Jeep. Gabe, shaking his head, walked back to me, and sat down with me on the cement bench. He was looking around at the scenery of the huge mansion, and landscape.

"Wow, my girl's got the big time clientele!!" He nudged me, and laughed.

"You know it!" I gave him a thumbs up, and laughed a bit myself. We sat and watched the multitude of finger prints taken, footage gone over, and over again...and everyone mull around looking for "clues." I was exhausted again, and I suddenly felt like I had been awake for days. "I'm tired." I mumbled to myself, knowing that my knight-in-shining armor would save me.

"I heard that, Janes. Just a minute." And like that, he was off back into the group of police, getting us the clearance to leave. I saw him motion to the group, and get his cell phone out to make a call. He shook hands with the Detective, and with Donovan. After, he turned back to me, and began walking towards me. Over his shoulder, I could see Donovan's gaze landing squarely in my eyes. It seemed to be of genuine concern. *So you think.* "Alright babe, you're riding shotgun with me. Jeep's getting towed to get fixed, and returned in a few days." He smiled, and extended his hand to help me up. I grasped it, and stood.

"Good. Let's go home. I'm tired." I checked the clock in Gabe's Pontiac G8, and it was already 7:30pm. *This fucking Visitor is getting on my last nerve!* "Do you know if the kids are fed or not?" He reached across the divider, and squeezed my hand.

"Yeah, my mom's got them taken care of. They're at her house tonight, too." He smiled, and pulled my hand up for a kiss. That relieved me a little bit knowing I could just relax tonight, and try to find some sense in all of this.

"Your mom is pretty great. And I am more than ready to relax a bit." I pulled my hand from his, and rested my hands in my lap. I noticed Gabe watching my body language, just as all of the therapists had taught him to do with me years and years before.

"Then relax you shall. We could turn on some music, and relax... Yes. That's the plan." As if he read my mind, suddenly the car was going a bit faster down all of our old country roads. When we pulled into our driveway, I could see the lights in the guest house on in the living room. I couldn't help but smile.

"Look." I pointed. "That means it's a slumber party." I laughed out loud, and headed in the house. Gabe followed close behind me, and locked the door. He grabbed the note on the counter, and typed in a code on the new alarm box on the wall. The small box spoke back, and said, "Alarmed." Gabe's eyebrows raised, and he nodded in approval. He saw me watching him, and his face softened.

"My mom's got one now, too. Hopefully this will help us all relax a little bit. Oh and remember," he spun around with the freezer bag of green. "We've still got police detail out front. Brian says probably for the week. I'm happy about that though." I nodded.

"Me too. Makes me feel like I can breathe." His head snapped around quickly, almost as if he couldn't believe what I had just said.

~17~

He pulled me onto the couch, and hugged me with his entire self. My head fit perfectly under his chin, and in his neck. He smelled so delicious, that one inhale was all I needed to get all revved up inside. His body was hard against mine, and he shifted so he could get back up. *Damnit.*

"I'm going to close the windows, and grab us some beverages. Want some iced tea?" He smiled, and I nodded. I adjusted the pillows on the couch so we could sit more comfortably together. I reached over the couch, and got the remote for the music. He reappeared with our drinks, and a freshly lit joint, that he handed to me. I took it more than willingly, and relaxed to inhale. The *Grateful Dead* came on the radio, and I giggled out loud.

"I love this." I motioned to the smoke, and the music. This was perfect. The lights were dim, the blinds were closed. Sinking into the couch cushions, I finally felt my body start to relax a little. The alarm was on. The music was awesome, and I was getting mellow, and fast. Gabe climbed onto the couch next to me, and took a deep hit of smoke. He motioned me over for a kiss, which I indeed took greedily. He repositioned himself so our shoulders were touching, while we lay together smoking our cares away. A few minutes later, we were both silent, and a cloud of smoke hung in the air.

"I'm really proud of you," he began. I could feel my body tense. I wasn't sure I was ready for this right now. "I mean, all of this constant drama, all these years. And it hasn't held you back." *Held me back? No. Fucked me up? Yes.* His fingers stroked my forehead, carefully pulling the hair out of my eyes, and putting it back behind my ears. He inhaled again, and passed it back to me. I smiled at him, and took it carefully in between my fingers.

My brain was now spinning. Wondering. Panicking, almost. *If he finds out about my job, he's going to be so angry. So, so angry.* I fought the thoughts, and focused on inhaling and exhaling only. He nudged me, and turned to face me.

"What's going on in there, baby? You look upset." I could feel my forehead wrinkle, and a sigh escaped my lips.

"I'm alright," I paused. "My nerves are just shot from said constant drama." He relaxed a bit, and leaned back into the couch. As we sat on the couch, the song changed on the radio, I couldn't help but sing. I could feel Gabe's fingers tapping the beat to *Picture* when it came on, and I was taken back to that night in the barn. *It's been a long, long time since those days. Hard to forget, but the music was always just what you needed.* I knew all of the words, and I barely needed the music to keep the song going. As the song ended, I giggled, and Gabe leaned his head on my shoulder.

"I can always tell when you like these songs, Janie. You have such a connection with some of them." He smiled, and stroked the tops of my knuckles.

"Yeah, some of them have been branded into my brain forever." I sat up to take a drink, and adjust my seating. Setting my drink back down, I laid back down next to Gabe on the couch. Our bodies pointed in different directions on the couch, but our heads met in the middle. His hand instinctively stroked my cheek, and I instantly sighed. I closed my eyes, and relished in the quiet. I felt his lips on my forehead, gently kissing away the bad thoughts.

I opened my eyes to find him staring directly into them, and his eyes were on fire. I could tell what he wanted in a second, and I was more than willing to oblige. He slowly rolled off of the couch, and swung around to lay even with my body. He was so warm, and furnace like, no extra blankets were needed when we cuddled. His arms found their way around me again, and I nuzzled my face into his neck. He smelled so good, just like always. When I inhaled deeply, I could feel the thousands of little lights flicker on in my abdomen. My legs began slowly, shyly rubbing together, writhing for him to get closer.

He immediately pulled his shirt over his head, and smiled coyly when he wrapped me in his arms again, and our lips met. It was the same electricity that we have always had together. The electricity that tells me I'm home. Our tongues danced in our hot, breathless mouths. Our hands pushed, pulled, and grabbed around our bodies. At times, catching on to breasts, cocks, and hair. *Oh fuck... I love it when he pulls the hair!!*

My pants slid off rather easily after he managed to figure out the buttons, revealing the lace suit to him. I couldn't help but stare in awe when his pants fell to the floor. That, by far, was my favorite package, ever. Gabe noticed my intense, lustful stares at his package, and caught my eye. He half-smiled, looking all geared up like a horny porn star. *MMMmmm… I want to eat him.* He palmed himself, wrapping his large hands around his thick girth, throwing it around in circles. I couldn't hold in my giggle.

"Baby," he leaned in and kissed my mouth. "I know you want to…" he whispered in my ear. I nodded, smiled, and pulled him back to my mouth. I nibbled on his ear lobe, and gently flicked it with my tongue. He moaned into my ear, and my crotch was immediately responsive. His hands began to wander down my abdomen, around my belly button, and in between my legs. His fingers circles around my clit, and dove inside. I couldn't control the moans escaping my lips. "Oh, I think you're ready for me." He growled.

He pulled me over the side of the couch, and I rested my feet on the coffee table near the couch. I held on to the back of the couch, and opened myself to him. His hands trailed from my knees up to the apex of my thighs. A thousand butterflies danced in my stomach. His smiled at me rather deviously, and teased me with his tip. I was too revved up for too much excitement, and I just wanted him to fill me up.

"Hold on, Janes." He managed to get out between his tightly closed lips. I clung tightly to the back of the couch, and smiled at him when I was ready. Without a beat, he thrust straight into my depths, going deeper than ever before. His balls smacked my ass with every thrust, and his moans grew louder, and longer. His fingers squeezed into my hips, as he clung to have the tightest grip possible.

"Ahh," his head tipped to the side, and his eyes rolled around. "You feel soo good." I couldn't help but smile at him, and when he saw me, he quickly came down and our lips crashed into each other. His hands quickly moved to my breasts, and as he built up to climax, his grasp on me tightened. His fingers closed around my nipples, and squeezed them as he hit his peak. "Ohh... Fuck!" He stilled, and I could feel him emptying himself into me. We laid together for a few moments, before readjusting ourselves on the couch.

"I love you, Gabe." I quietly said, as we lay in the dark, in the quiet, together. He pulled a blanket over both of us, and his hand slowly touched my forehead. I nuzzled into his chest again, this time closing my eyes in the comfort and warmth.

"Oh Janie," he ran his hands through my hair slowly. "I love you beyond everything." His lips planted a kiss on my forehead, and we drifted off to dreamland together.

~

Waking up in the morning proved nothing to

109

me but I needed to go back to sleep. It had been a restless night, and I had terrible dreams. *I hate that he's still in my dreams.* But I had hated even more, that now in my dreams, he was trying to protect me. I rolled around on the bed, and tried to pull the covers back over my face. I heard my cell buzz after I stopped fidgeting. I picked it up to see that it was Donovan, and a few other missed messages.

> *J- Tuesday and Thursday next week have your name on them. Please? D*

I couldn't help but smile, I quickly responded in favor for his scheduling ideas. I had another message from my mom, going over the details of the weekend they had planned for us. Reading over her itinerary, I knew that the kids would be very pleased with what they had picked out. The kids were spending the day doing errands with Jean, and getting ready for Grandma and Grandpa Taylor's arrival.

I cleaned the house, and relaxed in the quiet, trying to get ahold of my swirling thoughts. *Who is this Visitor?* Over and over, I tried to put all the pieces together. But I couldn't. I sat down to my lap top, and shot off a few emails to Liz Malloy about the Tribex Estate event coming up. Everything was going off without a hitch for this one, and I was beyond pleased.

Suddenly, the decibel level in my house skyrocketed. Kids were squealing, running crazy, and screaming for Grandma. I could hear my parents' voices beaming with happiness to see their grandbabies. I stood, and turned towards the noise, and Gabe's open arms. All my people had arrived at the same time. *Let the weekend begin.*

~18~

I wasn't sure how I had managed, but when I rolled out of bed this morning, I felt awake and ready to go. The weekend was amazing, and we had no intrusions from the Visitor. The kids were back into their school routine, and with Jean. Gabriel was already at work, but expected home early tonight. I was off today. I took the opportunity to turn on the radio, and send out some emails. It dawned on me that this weekend was to be our party, and realized I needed to touch base with Sean, and everyone.

I sent out a mass email to our closest friends inviting them all to the cookout and hot tub party this Saturday. I picked up the phone while I typed, and dialed Sean. It only rang once before he answered.

"Ah, hello?" he answered in a sarcastic sounding voice.

"Hey buddy, how you doing?" I heard the radio turn down in the background, and things shuffling around.

"I'm good, driving right now. Heading home a few days early!" He sounded excited. "I'm glad you called. Did you and G ever get anything figured out for party time?"

"Yes! That's why I was calling. We're set for Saturday, if you are." I waited.

"Oh, I would NOT miss seeing you, Janes!" *Somehow I was not surprised.*

"Well, good. Bring your usual party items, please." I giggled, and heard him chuckle, too. "And your bathing suit. And your wife!"

"We'll see if she comes or not. She's not

been in a great mood still. She says that pregnancy is not her thing." *Aww...* I felt for her, and not having someone to do it all with must've been even harder. "But definitely plan for me."

"Okay, I'm excited! I'll see you in a few days! I'd better-" He cut me off mid-sentence.

"Janes?" he questioned.

"Yeah?" I cautiously waited.

"How's it going with Donovan?" The question rolled off his tongue smoothly, and hit my ears like a cement breaker. *What did he say?!* "Hello?" He said again.

"Oh, it's going very well. Business is booming!" Surely he couldn't have known.

"I figured he'd like you just as I do." I felt my eyebrow raise higher than ever, and my breath got caught in my throat.

"Well, thank you for the referral. I really appreciate it."

"You're welcome. Alright, back to highway driving for me. See you soon, babe." He hung up quickly, which relieved me from having to figure out an awkward goodbye. I checked the time, and it was only 2:32pm. I had a few hours left to finish up my emails, and work before Gabe would be home. I shot off my last few confirmation emails for the Tribex event coming up on Wednesday.

I looked up immediately when I heard the doorknob click, and was momentarily confused. My head snapped back to the clock, and I noticed that it was now 6:48pm. *What the hell??* Turning back around, I was met by Gabe's big smile.

"Hey baby," he threw his stuff on to the bench, and moved towards me. "How was your day?" He wrapped his arms around me, and I fell into his warmth.

"It was good. Got work things wrapped up, and the party invites all out for Saturday." He kissed my lips gently, and his fingers gently surrounded my neck.

"I can't wait for Saturday. It will be good to have everyone together for once." He smiled, and moved to eating his dinner plate that I had left in the microwave. "Thanks for the chicken, too. I'm starving." I smiled at him.

"My pleasure." I closed my lap top, and stood to clean up my mess. "Sounds like everyone's coming Saturday, except maybe Laney. Sean said she isn't doing so well with the pregnancy." I must've wrinkled my face, Gabe giggled.

"Of course she's not. Pregnancy's hard, and she's sort of a wimp." He shrugged his shoulders, and I shook my head.

"I'm going to sit on the deck. I need a brief chill before bed, if you catch my drift." I smiled, and headed out to the patio. With my tin, I sat myself on the big patio couch, and lit the lamp on the side table. Everything was so quiet, and sort of chilly.

For October, the weather was holding up nicely, but the brisk evenings definitely needed more covering now. I reached over to the outdoor box, and pulled a blanket out of it. Readjusting, I opened my tin, and filled my pipe with smoke. While I stared at the stars, my fingers reached for the radio remote, and I turned it on. It always seemed that just the right songs came on the radio, right when I needed them to. *There you go, falling into songs again.* I sang aloud…*So, don't ask me no questions, and I'll tell you no lies*…

Half-way through my smoke, Gabe emerged, freshly showered. He smiled and quickly joined me on the couch, underneath the blanket.

"Jesus Janie," his teeth chattered. "Sort of chilly out here without the fire lit." I scooted closer to him to share my warmth.

"I wasn't planning on staying out here too long. Just needed to be illegal for a few moments." I inhaled again, blew it in his direction, and turned off the radio. He rifled around in the tin until he found his half-smoked joint, and quickly lit it up. We both sat quietly, enjoying listening to the silence of nature, in the dark. I finished, and dumped out my ashes. I laid back down next to time while he finished.

His hand slowly landed on my thigh, and trailed up the blanket a bit. He leaned over me, intentionally putting his weight on me, to use the ashtray that was on my side of the couch. I couldn't contain my laughter.

"Really, Gabe?" I giggled. I reached farther, squishing me even more.

"What? A problem? Come on," he swiftly stood up, and pulled the blanket off of us. "Time for bed. I've got a big day tomorrow." He extended his hand to me, and I took it. He pulled me into a half-hug, and together we headed in to bed.

I curled up in bed, and his body formed next to mine. I could hear his breath slowing, and falling to sleep. My mind was still running wild, with thoughts I couldn't even understand. I turned my thoughts to Donovan's tomorrow, and I felt a smile sneak across my lips.

Walking through the trees, I heard the voice coming behind me. I sped up trying to walk faster, and faster. The trees were rustling, and the footsteps were coming closer. I began to run, and turned back to see the shadow gaining ground. My chest felt heavy, but I still ran. There was a building ahead, and I hoped it had people in it. I ran, and ran, and kept running. The shadow was closing in, and tears began streaming down my face. "Please! No! Please!" I screamed at the no-faced shadow. "Who are you?!" I yelled, and ran. I reached the building, and banged loudly on the door. I had to run around the side to get away from the shadow, and began screaming for help. "Anyone! Please! He's going to kill me!" As I rounded the corner of the building, a terrible buzzing noise made me turn around suddenly. There he was, ready to grab my throat. I began to scream...

"Janie! Wake up!" His hands were on my chest, holding me on the mattress. I managed to pull open my tired eyes, to see Gabe staring at me, confused and bewildered. "It's okay, honey. Just a dream." He loosened his grip, and pulled me closer to him. I could feel the tears on my face, and knew I must have been crying. In my sleepy haze, I tried to remember the events of the dream, but I couldn't.

"I'm sorry," I managed to mutter from under his chin. His arms squeezed tighter. He had gotten so good at dealing with my nightmares that it barely phased him anymore. Thankfully, they only seemed to reappear when I was stressed. I rolled away from him to check the clock. It was already 5:45am. *Damn, almost time to get up.* I sighed, and rolled back into his warmth.

"I guess it's good you've woken us... I need to get up and get ready for work." I nodded at him, and pouted at the same time. He smiled, and punched my arm, lovingly. I rolled out of bed, too, and headed in to make some breakfast for the kids.

115

~19~

I was able to get Gabe off to work on time, and both Jean and the kids' breakfast before they all ran off to the daily grind. That left me to get ready for work, which today, included going to Donovan's. *What happened to the 'Mr. James,' Janie? Now it's just 'Donovan.'* Peering into the bathroom mirror, the shook the devious smile that had overtaken my lips.

"It's just a job." I chanted in the mirror, while putting on my mascara. I slipped into the deep purple thong and bra set, and poured myself into an old white hippie skirt I had kept for years. I put on a black tank top, and a sweater. I turned to check the mirror, to make sure that my wardrobe selection was again a little confusing. I smiled at my reflection. "Nailed it." I giggled, as I headed to grab my bag, and towards the door.

The drive to Donovan's house was getting easier, and my Jeep seemed to know the way. She was like new again, with all her windows fixed. *Let's hope that nothing gets too smashed this time around...*

I pulled in, and punched in my newly made code. He had reset all his gates, locks, passwords, and some security staff members since the incident with my Jeep the previous week. As I drove around to the parking area, I saw the bright red car, and knew we were not alone. Smirking again, I straightened my floor length, fully covering skirt as I exited the Jeep. I left my shades on, and continued to the door. I rang the bell, and waited. I could hear the commotion coming towards the door, and what sounded like yelling. The door opened hastily.

"Oh Janie," his face looked pained, but eased when he said my name. His idle smile told me enough, and I smiled back. "Come in," he motioned me in, and closed the door.

"God damn you!" I heard her scream from the upstairs loft area. I looked towards the voice, and then back to Donovan, who was rubbing his forehead. He sighed.

"Allison," he yelled back, and headed back into the fire. I heard his heavy footsteps head up the stairs, and doors slam. I could only make out certain parts of the argument, but I did pick up that she was not happy. "You're insane! I don't know why I fucking bother with you anymore!" Another door slam. *Shit! Should I hide?* I heard his steps getting closer, and coming back down the stairs. Then I heard small footsteps, in heels, loudly stomping behind.

"Fuck you, Donovan James! I am so done with you." I watched her storm out of the house with a wheeled suitcase almost as big as she was. I quietly lingered cleaning up the kitchen trying to see what was going on.

"You're such a money whore. You couldn't be more done than I am!" As the front door slammed, and Donovan swore and kicked at the walls, I started to feel bad for him. His business was involved with so many charities, and he helped out so many local schools and children, I couldn't understand what his wife's problem was. *Suck it up, lady. He's a decent guy.* The things that I had heard about her seem to be true. *I'll have to remember to ask Sean about her.* I tried to register the thought for later. He pulled out his cell phone, and stopped pacing for a second. "It's Don," he paused. "I need all the locks changed, passcodes reset- everything."

Oh, this sounds bad. Did I just watch the end?
"Don't let her back on the property unless I give the authority. Understand?" He nodded. "Thanks."

He was moving so swiftly, from one important thing to the next. His fingers moved furiously, and his phone was to his ear again. "Hey, Donald, this is Donovan James. I need to immediately remove Allison from my accounts. Yes, exactly. Please issue her an account, with half of what the checking account she was on has in it. Got it?" He walked to his desk, and emptied his pockets. "Okay, send the papers by courier. Great, Thanks." He put his phone down on the stand, and headed towards the kitchen, rubbing his temples the whole way. I quickly turned away from him.

"Janie," he started. I slowly turned to face him, and his eyes were full of tears. My heart fell out of my feet, and without thinking, I instantly ran to hug him. My arms were around him, hugging him tightly, before my brain realized what was happening. His arms fell around my lower back, and he lowered his chin to my shoulder. *Whoa.* The electric impulses surged through us both, and I instantly stepped away from him, trying to catch my breath.

"I'm sorry..." I stuttered. He squinted his eyes a bit, then looked down. I heard a small laugh escape his lips, and when he looked at me again, his eyes were burning.

"Don't apologize. I'm pretty sure what you witnessed was far worse than giving an emotional friend a hug." He smiled, reassuringly. "Allison won't be joining us today, so it seems." He nodded, and adjusted his shirt.

"Well, I'm sorry about all of that. Surely she just needs a little bit of perspective..." I caught myself before the rest slipped out, and found Donovan still smirking at me. "Thankfully, I managed to finish the kitchen while all….that, was happening." I smiled at him. He returned the smile.

"Let me go turn on your music for you, okay?" He left the kitchen, and I tidied the dining room. I heard him clinking around in his study, most likely at the bar. Cautiously, I entered the study, to find him shirtless, and downing a glass of scotch. He met my gaze, and swallowed his last gulp. The smile that broke out across his face was greedy, and I knew what he wanted. My heart started to beat faster, and I felt my unhinged self, take over. *Janie…come on. What are you thinking?!*

"Would you like a drink?" I nodded. Slowly he poured me a shot of scotch, never taking his eyes off of me. He stood from his desk, and sauntered over to me, putting the glass into my hand. "Here." He took a few steps back, and refilled his own glass. Slowly, I put the glass to my lips, and downed the contents. I set the glass down on the table, and slipped the sweater off onto the chair. He stumbled to his couch, and silently fell down, watching my every movement.

I turned away from him, and slipped my skirt down to my ankles, revealing my deep purple lingerie for today's session. A moan escaped his lips. I turned around towards him, and picked up my glass again.

"I'll take this, and get back to cleaning." I smiled, and left the room. Out of the corner of my eye, I caught his smirk. I quickly bolted upstairs to attempt to get some cleaning done, before I was completely derailed by my new voyeuristic pleasures. I finished the master bedroom, and couldn't help run my hand across the silk bedspread. I loved silk, but not enough to own it. *You only like to get fucked on it, girl. Don't lie.* I raised my eyebrow at the thought.

As I walked back into the loft, I finally saw that he had joined me. He looked like a drunk mess, but sexy as ever. Still shirtless, and now his belt undone, his eyes looked so heavy and hurt. *No, Janie. You can't save him!* I just wanted to help him out.

"I don't mean to interrupt you, Janie." I smiled at him, and silently dusted the tables near him. I could smell the scotch oozing out of his pores, and I knew this was going to get interesting.

"You're not interrupting Donovan. What do you need?" My emphasis hung a little too long on "need," but it was too late to take it back. His eyes burned into mine.

"I think you know what I need." His hand landed on my shoulder, and fell down the outline of my side to my waist. I blushed. "See, you do know what I need…" he trailed off. He was right. I did know what he wanted, and needed. But giving it to him? I ground my teeth together. *Business is business, but…*

Before I could blink, he had spun around to the chairs, and taken seat in his own. He quickly swung his chair to face mine, as we had set up before. He smiled, devilishly.

"See, I can follow the rules." He laughed deeply in his throat. "Or, at least try, but I think that I may be drunk, Janes." *Oh no.* My inner devil grinned, and it just got bigger.

I sat down in my chair, facing Donovan. His eyes hungrily scanned me up and down, and over again. I could see his hands grasping at the arms of his chair tighter and tighter, and his eyes were getting darker.

With little warning, he slid his pants and boxers down to his ankles. My eyes settled on his hard-on, and I felt my breath change. Watching his massive member throb feet in front of me was enough to heat me up. I spread my legs, and hung one over each chair arm. His eyes immediately focused on my core, and his fingers wrapped around his cock, tightly.

My hands wandered all over my body, stopping to pull on my nipples, and refocusing on sliding down to my hot center. Gently, I slid my panties asides, and slipped a finger inside. I heard his breath hitch, but I did not open my eyes to see. My fingers sped up, digging, probing, and poking into all my secret places. When I opened my eyes, he was hovering over me, feverishly jerking himself off. I could tell by the look on his face that he wouldn't need too much longer today. Suddenly he stopped pumping away, and kneeled on the floor in front of me.

"Can I touch you?" He held up his right hand, and my crotch throbbed. I swallowed hard, and tried to focus. *Janie! Are you sure about this?*

~20~

Without a second thought, I nodded, and his hand dove straight into my panties. He rubbed my slick folds, and groaned deep in his throat. His eyes rolled back into his head, and his breathing stopped. His fist pumped his still growing cock, when suddenly, he stuck his little finger in my ass, as well. I instantly clamped and clenched around his fingers, that were now tightly in all of me.

"Oh, oh God…" I managed to get out. As I squeezed him, he withdrew his fingers, and stopped

121

momentarily on my clit. A second later, his tongue was lapping into my hot core, and my body was writhing and shaking everywhere. I fisted his hair while he devoured me, still pumping away on himself. I couldn't help the moans that were escaping my lips.

"You're so fucking perfect..." he spoke as he poked his tongue into my holes again. I groaned, and clamped on him again. This time he stood above me, and shot his load all over my legs and chest. He moaned loudly as he came, and it echoed through the house. He fell into his chair, and I got up to get a towel, and head into the bathroom to wash off. *How's that for you? You let him blow all over you? What the hell Janie?*

I turned to find him smiling at me, but still very drunk. I smiled back, and headed downstairs to dress. I found my skirt quickly, and my tank top. I stopped in the study, and poured myself another shot of scotch. What the hell had I just done? What had *he* done? *Oh, right. Twist it like it was all him. You Okayed it all, honey. Ugh.* I downed the shot, and shook the thoughts out of my head.

"Hey, hotness!" He yelled from behind me, stumbling all over the place. "You're so perfect that I'm gonna pay you DOUBLE when you let me touch you." He smacked his hand on his forehead, "Oh!" He stopped dead in his tracks. "What do you want for me to taste you? You taste so wonderful... in fact..." I saw his eyes turn dark again. Parts of me heated instantly with the thought of him ravishing me for hours, and hours. But at the same time, my heart was pulling me home. *Thankfully, your heart is keeping you safe.*

"Oh, no...no more today. I've got to get home." I started to pack my bag, and head for the door. I felt myself start to shake, and my head was foggy with confusion. Suddenly, he was there, holding the door closed. I didn't look up at him, but instead stayed focused on the door. I inhaled deeply.

"Look," he sounded focused. "Are you okay?"

"I think so. I just need to go for now. Think this over…as it sort of veered from our original agreement. I'll be back on Thursday, okay?" I tried to smile reassuringly. He smiled, and stepped out of my way.

"Thank you Janie. You saved my shitty day." He winked as I got into my Jeep, and drove away. While I drove, I thought of what had just happened. *Paying you double doesn't make it right. Worth it? Maybe. But definitely not right.* It's so easy. *Too easy? None of that even matters though, does it?* I couldn't hold in my smile. *Exactly, because you're having fun.* And it *was* completely safe with Donovan. He surely wasn't going to spill the beans. When I arrived home, I hit the shower, and texted Jean to tend to the children tonight. I just wanted to chill by myself.

After a quick shower, I cozied myself into the bed, and emailed my last few contacts for the Tribex event tomorrow. It would monopolize most of my time, and I wanted to have everything set for Gabe to deal with at home. So far, everything was going well. I pushed the events of the day away, and focused on the next. As I lay down in bed, my cell buzzed. It was a text from Gabe.

Sorry, love. There in 15.

I smiled, and felt my eyes drift closed while the radio lightly played in the background.

~

"Thank you, Liz. I'm so glad that you had such a wonderful time tonight, and that it was such a great turn-out!" Liz patted my shoulder, and leaned in to my ear. It was still very loud with the DJs playing, and all of the chatter from the guests.

"You're fabulous Janie. You've picked the perfect business for yourself. I'd be happy to give you our major event account, as well as referrals whenever you need them." I was beaming. I finished up my paperwork, and headed for the door of the party. Not paying attention, I ran smack into him. When I looked up, my mouth fell open. *Shit! Donovan.*

"I had a feeling you would be here." His smile was ravenous, and I felt myself instantly blush. His eyes darted around, and his fingers brushed against mine. "Can we talk for a minute? Please?" He locked his finger with mine. I couldn't find the harm in it.

"Okay, sure. Here?" He looked around again, and shook his head no. He pulled me down a hallway, and into a back office room. He closed the distance between us suddenly, placing our bodies only inches apart. Searching his face, I could see and feel his longing. *What the fuck are you doing Janie?! You're going to be so sorry.*

In that split second, a million thoughts smashed through my head. Thoughts of Gabe, and the loves of my life. My parents. All the years of turmoil. Michael. *All the pain and nightmares.* And then, right then, I needed it. *No one will understand this. You barely do.* It didn't matter. I needed this for me. Just then, something shifted in my head. Looking up into Donovan's deep, lust filled eyes…I wanted him. I had no control over my body. My arms slowly slid onto his forearms, and my eyes met his. In a second, his mouth covered mine in a deep, probing kiss.

We fell against the cabinets that were lining the walls in the break room, loudly banging the doors around. He probed my mouth deeply, fisting the back of my hair. His hands trailed down the front of my shirt, and he squeezed my breast. Down lower he went, and his fingers slid across my panties. My breath hitched, and I pulled away from our kiss. Checking the door to make sure it was closed, I sighed a little.

"Donovan," he stepped towards me. "This cannot work like this. Please don't risk us both." I placed my hand on his chest when he stepped forward again. I smiled slightly at him, and he nodded.

"I'm sorry, you're irresistible." He ran his hand through his hair, and adjusted his pants and shirt. He took a step back, and his eyes met mine, though this time they were more relaxed, and not as needy. "Please don't hold it against me. I've been trying not to do that for over a week." I smiled sheepishly.

"I feel it, too," I said, fixing my shirt from being groped. "It just can't be here, and I need to get home." I smiled at him, and patted his chest. I'll see you in the morning though. I believe I have an appointment set." I smiled coyly, and raised an eyebrow. His beaming beacon of shiny whites told me he was looking forward to it.

"Janie," he stuck his hand out to shake my own. I laughed, and accepted the friendly hand shake. We both smiled, and shook out heads as if having the same thought.

"Time to go. I'll see you in the morning." I started to dash by him, and he quickly grabbed my hand. I turned towards him, and he was an inch from my face.

"I'll pick up here tomorrow." There was a hushed, heavy silence that rushed over us both. "Unless you stop me, of course." I had no intentions of doing that.

"Until then, Mr. James," I nodded, and left the room. As I walked out of the building, my cheeks flushed yet again, and my crotched throbbed for relief. I had high hopes that Gabe was home, and possibly not exhausted from his day. I rifled through my purse, looking for my cell phone. Once I found it, I quickly dialed Gabe's line. It rang three times, and I almost hung up figuring he was asleep.

"Hello?" he answered with a husky, sleepy voice.

"Hey Gabe," I said lightly. "I'm sorry to wake you. I'm almost home." I heard the sheets and blankets shift in the background.

"Oh, good. I can't wait until you're home." I smiled, he sounded so cute. I wanted to touch him. *Everywhere.*

"Alright, I'll be in soon. Hang up now." I giggled, and turned into the driveway. I pulled into my spot, and jumped out of the Jeep. I opened the garage door, and slipped into the house, closing the garage door behind me. The house was quiet, and checking on the kids quickly showed me that they were out. I slammed a quick drink of water, and headed into my bedroom.

There he was, sprawled out on the entire bed. Shirtless, wearing only his boxer briefs. I couldn't help drop my skirt to the floor, and toss my shirt into the chair. I climbed into bed slowly, and

126

he stirred a bit. I straddled his back, and began kissing his neck and shoulders. He groaned a bit, and shifted underneath me. I let my teeth grind across his shoulder blades, and he inhaled sharply. He was awake. My fingers found their way down his arms, and intertwined with his own.

He flipped over, and pushed our bodies into each other. My breasts were flattened with his chest, and my hips thrust into him with need and desire. His eyes opened slowly, shaking off the sleep. I traced his cheekbones, and smiled at him. His mouth covered my own, without hesitation, and sunk deeply into the depths. His fingers dove immediately into my hot core, and pushed deeply. I inhaled sharply, pushing against his fingers. His mouth skimmed over my skin, biting everywhere it could. In second, he had shifted again, and was now slammed into my core over and over again.

The friction was wonderful, and so needed. I could feel the climax coming, as all the thoughts in my head were finally ceasing, and calming. My fingers clenched into his back, and I could feel myself start to tighten around him.

"Oh Gabe," I breathlessly spoke. I clawed at him to enter me more, to close the space between us. He drove into me deeper, and his fingers tightened on my hips. He poured himself into me, and our bodies flowed against each other effortlessly, perfectly in-sync. Our eyes closed, and we enjoyed the climax together.

Falling asleep again was no trouble, as his arms were around me and I was sated. *Janie, you are one fucked up girl. You know that?* I tried to shake the voice, and shut her up. My thoughts were scattered as I fell asleep, jumped back and forth from the evenings events. Tomorrow was a new day, and my brain settled into dreaming.

~21~

I awoke in the morning with a note from
Gabe, and a buzzing phone. My head felt heavy, as
if I didn't sleep quite as well the night before. I tried
to squint through reading his note.

"Love,
Had work early. Hopefully
home earlier tonight. Need help with party?
I love you.

G. X"

I reached for my cell phone before I rolled
back over, and unlocked it with my fingers. I lift the
notification bar, and saw my check in texts from the
girls, and one from Donovan. Curiosity killed the
cat, and I opened his first.

*J- Ready to have you over to work.
It's a disaster. D-*

If I didn't tell you about the smile that
busted across my face, I'd be lying. I sprinted out of
bed, and into the shower. It was so nice to be
desired in that new way. I quickly washed,
scrubbed, and picked my outfit for the day. The
lacey thigh highs, and see through camisole were
perfect. *Your energy sure is flowing, for doing
something so shady.* I connected the cords of the
thigh highs, raising an eyebrow catching myself in
the mirror, and put on black dress pants over them. I
wore a basic white blouse over the camisole, and

128

headed for the kitchen.

When I got there, there was another note from Gabe. I smiled at his sentiment, and opened it quickly.

"Have I told you lately that you're beautiful?" Love. Always. Gabe"

My heart lurched into my throat. Had he noticed the distance between us? Oh, I hoped so. I headed out to the Jeep, and jumped in. I cranked the radio, and *1, 2, 3, 4* was on. I couldn't help get lost in the song, and started to sing it aloud. *"Give me more loving than I've ever had, make it all better when I'm feeling sad. Tell me I'm special even when I know I'm not..."*

Pulling into the gated drive gave me promise. I'd had a have a few hours to squish this burning need to relieve a bit of energy. Parking next to his Beamer, I smirked knowing without a doubt that we were alone. I all but ran up to the steps, and opened the door myself, without knocking. I walked into the house, where everything was quiet, except the radio blared my CD. I smiled at his thought. I set my purse down on the table, and headed in to the kitchen.

He instantly turned to me, and smiled very big. He reached for the wine glass that had been poured, and motioned me to sit on the bar stool. I smiled back, and took the seat. And the drink. *Maybe slam that? I'm terrified of your poor decision making.* I knocked back the wine quickly, and he smiled while refilling my glass.

"I'm so glad you're here." He gently ran his finger across my shoulder.

"So am I," I slammed the second glass. When I looked up, I smiled at him through heavy lashes.

"Guess you were thirsty." His voice was low, and getting huskier. I stood to tidy up the kitchen. Suddenly his hands were on me, lifting me up onto the counter. His eyes met mine, and almost as if asking permission, I nodded in acceptance.

His hands dipped into my blouse, pulling at my nipples hardening them instantly. My breath ended heavily into his ear. I held on to his shoulder, and pressed my lips against his, allowing my tongue to dance with his. *You shouldn't do this, Janie. But he tastes so good...* I was hungry for the danger and deceit he offered, and took it more than eagerly.

I slowly backed away, unbuttoning the buttons on my blouse, and tossing it to the floor. He matched my motions, and threw his own shirt on to the floor. I slowly thumbed the top of my pants, and latched my fingers around the button, unsnapping them. The motion quickly dropped them to the floor, and I stood bare, in my thigh highs and camisole. He grabbed his chest, and inhaled sharply.

"God, Janie," he took a step forward. "You're so beautiful." He mouth over took my own, and I found myself lost in his kiss. It was so wrong, but burned so hot in my head. He lifted me onto the desk, and spread my legs widely. "I can't wait to taste you..." His fingers rubbed my wet slit, and dove into the core. My mouth suddenly felt dry, so I collected myself to focus, and get a drink. I put my hand on his chest, and pushed him away. Filling the glass, the cool water felt amazing flowing down my throat. I noticed how hard my heart was beating, and how heated my libido was.

"Care to follow me upstairs, Mr. James?" I

asked causally, and headed for the stairs.

"Yes, Mrs. Lazarus," he inhaled. "Please show me the way." He trailed behind me, shedding his pants along the route.

"Oh, those chairs look lovely." I said, motioning to our normal chairs. Turning around, his boxers were stretched to the max, and he throbbed for release. I approached my chair, and bent over it instantly exposing my rear end to him, and the thong. In a sudden second, he was pressed against me, kneading his fingers into my sides. He bent, and lowered himself to me, biting at my back. I seized, and clenched with each movement with his mouth.

"Please..." he groaned. I couldn't stop him, I was enjoying it too much. His fingers slid into me, and suddenly, the doorbell rang. He pulled me into a deep kiss that left me longing for more. On his way down stairs, and pulled a robe out of what seemed like the side of the wall. I heard his steps trail down to the door.

I sat down hard in the chair, and caught my breath. I was way too turned on to stop now. I was determined for release. I threw my leg over the chair, and sunk my fingers into my tight hole. I reached deeply, and felt my walls begin to shake. I fell into the thoughts of Donovan's eyes burning into my body, and I was instantly too hot to handle.

Then I heard them, two inhales. Two breaths hitching, close to me. *What the fuck?* I opened my eyes, mid-orgasm, to find two sets of eyes staring at me. Donovan's robe, half open, exposing his still engorged and blood filled penis. And...Sean. *Oh sweet Jesus!* I sat up instantly, blinking, and tears filling my eyes.

"Janie!" He held out his hand in protest. "Please!! Please don't stop! Don't let this weird you out! You *know* how I've felt for years! I know that you've known..." his voice trailed off. It was true, I did know. He hesitantly stepped towards me, still extending his hand, and my breathing sped up. He threw his coat on the floor, and took off his shirt. I couldn't catch my breath in the fury of the moment. *Take him.* Taking his shirt off revealed the tight abs that the military training had left, and I ran my hands down them instantly. "Janie..." he moaned into my ear. My mouth instinctively clung to his, and our hands desperately grabbed at each other. Our tongues intermingled, and the room went silent. There was nothing other than this, and this was a powerful thing. It was electricity that had flown between us for years, and often been forcibly turned off. *Not now. Oh Janie… he's so hot for you.*

His hands fisted my hair, and our bodies crashed together like waves. My breasts crashed into his warm skin, and he ran his hands across my nipples. I couldn't get enough of him, and my tongue drove deeper and deeper inside. However wrong it was, we would face it later. *This is just too much… both of them? One comes with many emotions, don't forget that.* It was too late, I had let the emotions flow. Now, it was only those immense amounts of emotion and pleasure that made me unable to stop doing what I was doing.

"Sean," I moaned into his mouth, and his hands over took my face. He clawed at my breasts, pulling each nipple into his mouth to suckle. Each time making a low moaning noise that I could feel humming in my body. His fingers searched, and abruptly pushed into me, causing me to cry out and cling to him.

"Hold on Janie," he huffed. "I've been waiting for this ride for years." His fingers dug into my ass, and I was losing control of myself. My body was allowing it all, and enjoying every dripping moment of intimate contact. *Of desire.* I dug my fingers into his shoulders, and he positioned his mouth under my core. His tongue dug into me, and my head fell back in enjoyment.

When I opened my eyes, I found Donovan standing next to me, smiling widely, and pumping away. My hand fell to him, and grasped his length. *I don't know who you are anymore...* I shook my head, and quieted the voice. Pumping Donovan, and watching Sean's eyes meet my own while he dove into my soul, all I could do was moan. My body thrashed around, writhing for touch of anyone. Both men responded, revealing their massive erections. I continued to hold Donovan in my hand, while Sean spread my legs open wide. My heart sped instantly, and the voice was louder than ever. *I don't know about this! I can tell you're thoroughly enjoying yourself, but...*

He looked at me intently, and pushed against me slightly, declaring his intentions. I nodded, and smiled. Using my free hand, I pulled him into me, allowing him to sink into my tight, hot hole. His breath instantly hitched, and his fingers dug into my hips.

"Oh, fuck!" he hissed through his barely opened teeth. I pulled myself down onto him, taking his whole length inside. *Is it all in there? Can you even feel it? I guess they're all made differently...* His head pulled back, and a loud moan escaped his lips. His eyes re-joined my own, and his hand drove into my breasts. Squeezing each, he let out a roar of pleasure, thrusting into me harder than before. He slid out of me, and fell back a bit to the corner, trying not to let the whole situation over power him.

Without a chance to catch my breath, Donovan appeared at my chair. Now that I was sitting again, he kneeled before me, and pushed my legs open. My heavy breathing told him he had the go ahead, and I threw each leg over the arms of the chair. I knew what he wanted. An instant thought of Delany flew into my head, my throat closed, and I had to close my eyes tightly to shake it out. I took a long cleansing breath, and tried to focus on finishing with Donovan.

When I opened my eyes again, Sean was in front of me fisting himself fast and hard. His eyes were dead set on me, and the look on his face told me that I may have just screwed up our friendship. There was a new connection between Sean and I, and it just suffocated the past fifteen years. This has been waiting for years to take place, and on some level, I was glad it had happened. *Then on another level, well, I don't think you're ready to deal with what that's going to cause.* Donovan's head plunged into my crotch, lapping up the aftermath of Sean's destruction, and my head fell back in orgasm.

Internally, I felt wanton. Devious. Devilish. Hot. Desired. And I needed more. I pushed into Donovan's mouth, and his forced his fingers into me. I moaned loudly, while starring Sean in the eyes, watching him come to the brink of climax. He closed the gap between us, and fiercely pumped his cock. He was close, and so was Donovan. Both men pulled away from me, and stood on either side of me, spewing their hot loads onto the floor around them. They then proceeded to fall into spent heaps on the floor. Swallowing hard, it took a moment to move on from what had just happened.

Slumping in the chair, I was exhausted, as

well. What an afternoon this had turned into. I took in the surroundings, wishing that I had some green to smoke. Repositioning in the chair, I sat up, and fixed my hair. I rose out of my chair, and I could feel their eyes burning into my half naked self. As I walked to the stairs, I turned and smirked at them.

"Meet me downstairs." I got out as I continued to get my clothes on. As I slid it all back on, I checked my phone. It was already 3:30? *Fuck. You caught, Janie?* Hell no. I unlocked my phone, and saw Gabe's text.

Kids at mom's tomorrow night. I'm going to be late again. So sorry. Love you.

I slid it back into my purse as both Sean and Donovan entered the room. The both looked traumatized. Thankfully, more than I did. Donovan hit the bar, and poured three glasses of scotch. He handed Sean his, and slowly walked over to me. He smiled, and sheepishly looked at the ground.

"Alright," I started. "This obviously was not in our contract," I glanced at Donovan. I sighed, and opened my throat for the scotch. It burned my throat, and I coughed a little as it rolled down. "If anyone ever asks me, this never happened." I smiled as wide as I could. Donovan raised his glass, nodded, and swallowed the contents. I turned towards Sean's stare, and raised my eyebrow. "Well?"

~22~

Friday morning, finally. I woke up early, quietly sneaking out of bed to hit the showers.

135

Again. As I washed my body, I couldn't help think of yesterday's intense afternoon. I kept falling back to the things that Sean said, and trying to read between the lines. *"Janes, 15 years. That's how long I've waited. You're beautiful. The best thing I've ever had. Thank you. Thank you. Don't worry, everything will be fine. Secrets are safe. Who would've thought, my best friend?"* It was all running together in my mind.

I heard the doorknob shift, and the door creak open. I shook the thoughts from my head, and finished rinsing my hair.

"Morning, baby," he said as he had his nice long morning pee. Raising an eyebrow at his boldness, I responded and smirked at his nonsense.

"Morning, sleep well?" I waited for his response, but was instead greeted in the shower. His arms surrounded me, and he pressed our bodies together.

"Once I was next to you, I slept just fine." He turned me around, and kissed me deeply. "Now the bad news," he frowned. "I've got to go in for a bit this morning." He turned and grabbed the shampoo, and I poured it into my hands.

"Oh, well, I'll run to the store, and get my errands done. Later we can just pre-make party stuff. Or do nothing. Or maybe do something else…" my voice trailed off, as my eyes trailed down his happy trail. His finger quickly caught my chin, and brought me back to his level.

"Don't you dare start that now, or I'll never get to work, to get back home to ravish you again." *Very valid point. See, Janie? Why do you need anything else?* It was true, he was perfect. Everything about him was perfect. Maybe that was it. I watched him clean in the shower, and ready himself in the mirror after.

From day one, it's always been about protecting me. *And you've appreciated that.* But parts of me miss the chaos, and the unpredictability. *And now you're seeking it?* I slowly dressed, just simple sweats and a sweatshirt today. He scooted around quickly, grabbing an apple for breakfast, and crunching on it while he repacked his briefcase. Maybe all of this was just one of those midlife crisis times that everyone talks about. *Hopefully this one doesn't lose your husband, or your business.* I smiled at him when I saw him gazing at me.

"You okay, baby?" I nodded, and frowned a bit. "There's that 'v'," he was instantly thumbing my forehead. "I won't be gone long today, and tonight we can do some just us stuff." He hugged me tightly, and I couldn't help breathe in his fresh, working man smell.

"Okay, I'll meet you here later. You said the kids were good today and tonight?" He picked up his briefcase, and slid on his coat.

"Yes, my mom's taking them to the museum this weekend. She's got a plan, bridge night, and movie night planned. We'll see them again, maybe, Sunday night." He smiled, and kissed my cheek.

"Wow, I'll have to thank her today. Work well. Love you." He smiled, and exited through the garage door. I sat at the bar for a little while, reading my email and getting caught up on business things.

Mylah's email check-in was rather hilarious, and made mention of wishing she could just clean naked, and make millions. I chuckled hardily. *Until you end up doing the clients...* Oh, voice. Always ruining everything. Caty and Kiara were doing fabulous, and all of the customer's feedback was great. I emailed to set our meeting date for the last time at the pavilion at the end of the month. Quickly my email pinged back with a response. I giggled, until I opened the email.

> "To: Janie Lazarus, At Your Service, LLC.
>
> From: unknown sender
> October 16, 2008 11:58pm
>
> I prefer the black. I think it makes your skin tone really shine.
>
> See YOU Soon."

My hands grasped my throat when the attachment opened. It was a picture of Donovan and I, from what appeared to be in his loft. We were both obviously in the throes of passion, but separate from each other. *Oh, for fuck's sake. At least it wasn't purple, and more than two people...* My heart fell out of my body. There were no words, and no breath. I needed help with this. *This is not something that can get out. This will RUIN you.*

With shaking hands, I pulled out my cell phone, and called Donovan. It rang only once before he picked up.

"Hey, beautiful." He answered sinfully.

"Donovan," my voice was shaking.

"Janie? What's wrong?" his emotion turned from passionate and friendly, to sheer panic.

"I've gotten an email, and it's got a picture in it of us. In your loft, from a few weeks ago, I think." I was breathing heavily, almost to the point of hyperventilating, I thought.

"Okay, can you forward it to me? I can have

my security team track it, and see what comes up."
He paused, and I could hear him rifling through
things in the background.

"I don't know what else to do..." escaped
my lips before I could stop it.

"Try not to worry. I'll do everything I can to
keep this all under wraps." There was a pause, and a
poignant silence. "I'll take the fall for any of this,
okay? No questions." *Are you kidding me? Are you
THAT good?* Although I was shocked, I accepted
readily.

"Okay, I need to get back to work. I'm sorry
to have bothered you."

"You're never a bother. I'll still see you
Tuesday?" he sounded hopeful.

"Of course, D. Until then." I hung up the
phone, still lost in my own thought. I had enough of
the computer today, but quickly forwarded the
email to Donovan. It was almost 2pm now, and
Gabe was due home soon. I needed to recoil my
thoughts, and calm down a bit before that happened.
There was only one way to do that. I headed for the
wine cabinet, and pulled out a bottle of red.

~

When the headlights pulled in the driveway
at seven o'clock, I knew it was Gabe. I shifted
myself around in the hot tub to face him, and waved
him onto the deck.

"Ooover here!" I yelled, obviously on my
sixth or seventh glass of wine. I could hear him
chuckling as he climbed the deck stairs. I sloshed
the water all over, leaning towards him in the tub.
"Lookie here!" I motioned at the hot tub. "All
cleaned, and the ch-chemichals are all super!" I fell

back into my seat, and grabbed my glass, finishing off the little bit of wine left. *Yes, Gabe, come on over and experience this disaster for yourself...sheesh.*

"Oh my, you are a hot mess. Let me go change real quick." He turned around to walk away, and stopped abruptly. "One thing, head above water. Okay?" He winked, and I laughed loudly. I relaxed in my chair, and let the jets knead my back skin. He returned a short time later with the tin, and a bottle of water. He smiled, and dipped his feet in the hot tub.

"Here, drink this." He handed me the water bottle, pre-opened. I wrinkled my face at him. "Seriously, you'll want to be fresh tomorrow night. And I'm sure we'll all be hammered." *Tomorrow night? Hammered? Shit....Sean.* "Am I right?" He nudged my shoulder, and I started to down the water. It was cold and refreshing, and tasted great while in the hot water.

"Thanks," I wasn't thinking. He handed me his pipe, and encouraged a hit. I inhaled quickly, and relaxed again in the tub. My breasts bounced in and out of the water.

"You're a real distraction, you know that?" He said, as his head bounced in unison with my breasts. "A beautiful distraction." He inhaled, still only dipping his legs into the tub. "You excited for tomorrow?" he asked. I shrugged.

"Yeah, I think so." I was hesitant for unspeakable reasons. "It will be good to see everyone, and I think that most everyone is attending." As if the spark went off in my head, I sat up suddenly. "Hey! Did I tell you I got the Tribex account?" It has been a busy, over-stimulated few days, and I had forgotten to tell him

140

the big news. His smile told me all I needed to know. He quickly pulled me out of the tub, and into an embrace.

"That is so wonderful, baby." His fingers caressed my neck and hair line, sending electric impulses all around my body. Sitting back a bit, and our eyes meeting, set off the biggest sparks yet. I smiled, and our mouths crashed together like the never-ending waves in the sea.

He pulled away long enough to grab my towel, and wrap me in it. He put the smoke back into the tin, and put it in his pocket. He picked me up, and carried me into our bedroom. The tin hit the dresser, and his pants hit the ground in mere seconds. His hands clung to my body, and followed the curves up and down. His mouth devoured my own, probing for anything he could find.

We fell into the bed, clawing at each other for closeness. Our bodies intertwined on their own. We didn't have to do much extra. Our mouths were unbreakable. Only unsealing to take gasps for air. *This is the way it should be. This is love.* I fisted his hair more with that thought. It was true. All I needed.

Rolling me over, and pinning me to the bed, he pressed his chest against mine.

"Take this off, please." He gently tugged at the hem of my shirt. I smiled, and pulled the shirt over my head. Once my bare breasts were exposed, he began to suck at them fiercely. The pulling and heavy feeling went straight to my core, and made the juices start to flow. Before I could stop it, my body was grinding against him hard. Showing him exactly what it needed.

"Gabe…" I moaned loudly into his ear. He pulled back, and took account of my expressions and the situation. He smirked, and bent to bite my earlobe. I convulsed at the mere touch, and when his fingers enclosed my nipple, I screamed with delight. "More... Please..." I begged.

His hands made quick removal of my bikini bottoms I had worn in the hot tub. Slightly drunk made me forget I even had them on. His fingers slowly entered my hot core, and he gasped at the heat. His mouth crashed against mine again, and his erection rubbed ready on my thigh. I needed him. *Please.* I spread myself to him, and hoped he would take the bait.

His shaft was hard, and throbbing when he slid into me. My breath completely left until he hit the bottom, and pressed even further with his hard cock. I couldn't hold the moans in, and he bit at my neck with each thrust. *Home.* The comfort I felt with him shown through, and I felt myself start to climax. There was nothing I could do to turn him away from me.

Clenching around him, I took him in deeper than I knew possible. His moans showed me the difference, and the welcome acceptance. Our eyes locked, and our lips met. He drove his cock into me, and my loins exploded. I could feel the constant pulsing, and he gritted his teeth, and drove through it. Pushing, moaning, and digging his fingers in, soon brought on his own last hard thrust, and explosion.

He collapsed on to me, and then the bed, smiling the whole way. There was no denying that the sex was insatiable with my knight-in-shining armor. His eyes closed while he caught his breath, and I took in every detail. The way his head laid on his arm, right next to my exposed breast. How young he looked with his eyes closed, and hair all crazy and astray. How warm his body was lying next to my own. *And you're risking it.* No, I wasn't trying to. It was for business. *And pleasure.* True. But I loved it, and it did solidify customers. The slip with Sean wouldn't happen again. That was pure... *sex. Oozing, gooey sex. Stop lying to yourself.* It was necessary, and just how it was going to be. I closed my eyes, and threw my arm over my eyes.

"I love you Janie." His mouth closed on my lips, and I felt the tension in his body release with our kiss. I felt myself smile into his mouth. Suddenly remembering the email, I swallowed the build of tension forming in my gut. He slid out of bed to head for the bathroom, and I turned on my side, and curled into a ball. He was back in bed in mere moments, I was still feeling...*terrible.*

"I love you, too, Gabe." I said, curling my body into his. His arms draped over me so naturally. As my eyes drifted closed for the night, heavy with off thoughts and worry, I suddenly wondered if I was making terrible decisions. *It's too late now...*

~23~

The sunlight bit my eyelids when it hit, and I squinted, even in my sleep. Waking up slowly, I turned to feel the bed next to me, and he was gone. I turned back over slowly, opening one eye to check the time on the clock. It read 10:36am. *What the hell?!* Ugh, I groaned and moaned, and turned over the bed. My head throbbed, and I knew it was from the red wine the night before. I forced myself to sit up, and try to get moving. We were expecting company in a few hours, and I wanted to at least be presentable.

As I finished pulling my black dress over

my new green bikini, Gabe whisked by me in the bedroom.

"Hey love!" His fingers gently tapped my ass as he went by. "You look fabulous." I blushed, and turned back to the mirror. *Hopefully not too fabulous. Don't want to start anything tonight.* I thought of Sean, and the way he squeezed my ass...*NO!* I shook the thought out quickly, and finished pulled my hair up.

After taking my time to get ready, and Gabe watching a movie, it was now 3:30pm, and our guests were due in a mere 30 minutes. I waded through the kitchen, making sure that all of our dishes and entrees were ready. *Everything looks fabulous.* I smiled with pride, and caught Gabe's eye. He sauntered over to me slowly, and collected me in his arms.

"Thanks for this," he began. "I'm so excited." He kissed me deeply, and broke the kiss with an obvious thought. "Shit! I need to get the playlists going!!" He darted into the living room to set the hours and hours of songs. I went into Lilah's room, and tidied up. Closing both of the kid's doors, I knew their rooms would be safe. I couldn't help hum the song on the radio, *Wild Horses. You cannot be that lost in the irony, Janie.*

I headed out to the deck, and stoked the fire that Gabe must have started. The hot tub was warmed up, and at last check, the chemicals were perfect. Gabe appeared with a drink in his hand, and it tasted of pink lemonade.

"This is really good, G." I smiled at him, and down half the glass. *You nervous?* For mid-October evening, the weather was beautiful. It had been in the upper 60's most of the day, and hovered there now. I took another drink, and felt the warmth flow through my middle. I dinged my glass on the side of the deck, and smiled once he looked. "What's a chick have to do to get a refill in this place?"

"Oh baby, all you have to do is ask!" He came over, and dipped his tongue between my lips. He moaned, rather loudly. "You're right. I am a genius. I think I'll have some too." He trailed into the house, and I closed up the grill from all the cooking we had done that morning. Just as I was finishing, I heard a vehicle coming down the driveway. I turned to see the bright green Mustang, and knew Greg and Heather had arrived.

I met them at the car, and was greeted by my old friend with a hug.

"Janie!" She pulled back, and checked me over. "You're looking very well!" I hugged her again. It had been too long in between visits this time. "Greg told me about your Visitor…any new news?" She wrinkled her face. I shook my head.

"No, thankfully. Nothing for a few days." I sighed. "It is really, really good to see you. I'm so happy you guys could make it!" It had been a few months since Heather had been able to come over and visit, with or without their kids. "How are Beckett and Rylee doing? The kids miss them, and want a playdate." She smiled, and filled me in on the kid's activities. Greg got everything out of the car, and headed in to the house. We followed behind him.

When we got into the kitchen, we heard the boisterous voice of Aaron coming through the front.

"Hey hoes!" he yelled loudly, as he entered. Without delay, everyone yelled, "Give me an A!" at the same time. Laughter flowed out of everywhere. "That's right. Aaron has arrived." I shook my head,

145

and hugged him.

"Hey buddy," I patted his back. "How's everything going?" I raised my eyebrow, and looked over his shoulder at the tiny black haired beauty behind him. He caught my look, and handed me some booze.

"Her name is Stacy. Please be nice, she's new here." He whispered into my ear. I nodded, and motioned him into find Gabe. I heard their loud yells once they connected in the kitchen, and it was obvious we needed to do this more often.

Everyone conversed, and grabbed food. Drinks were flying, and I was on my... *third? Fourth? Uh oh...* I examined my glass, and wrinkled my forehead. Without a question, Gabe's hand went around my waist, and his mouth met my ear.

"It's your fourth, you lush." He spanked my ass, as he walked out onto the deck with Greg and Aaron. I poured a refill, *your fifth,* and called for Stacy and Heather to join us in the tub. As we exited the house, I turned up the radio, drowning out all other sounds but our laughter, and good vibes.

When I set my drink down on my chair's holder, I turned and was blinded by headlights. My breath left me for a moment, as I figure I knew who it was. I finished laying my towel on the chair, and slid my sandals off. I heard the sound of glass banging together, and turned to see Sean carrying ten or more bottles of alcohol.

"The party has arrived!" he yelled towards Gabe, barely paying any attention to me. I shrugged it off as part of his play. *Sure, that's right. Tell yourself that.* He headed into the house to deposit his cargo box of booze on the counter, and I turned around and slid my dress off. Heather took the seat

146

next to mine, and took a long drink of the cocktail.

"Damn girl," she started. "You look fabulous. Seriously." She drank more, and took her shirt off. I watched her eyes look me up and down, and felt myself blush. "I'm sort of jealous." I chuckled, and then we both laughed heartily. When I turned to enter the hot tub, Sean was inches behind me. I took a step back, and almost tripped and fell into my chair. Of course, he was there to catch me. *God damn. Of course he is.*

Patting his arms, I attempted to stand back up again. Heather was laughing hysterically at me, and I was flushed for other reasons. Our eyes met, and his breath instantly hitched. I stood, and moved out of his grasp. His eyes trailed my body up and down, and I noticed the twitching in his pants.

"Janie!" he yelled. "So great to see you!" My eyebrows raised high, and I had to hold back a smile as he engulfed me in a hug. "Where's the booze?!" he joked, releasing me, and heading to get a drink. I shook it off, and slid into the hot tub.

Immediately, Heather tapped my shoulder.

"Hey, you want this?" she held up my phone. "Someone just texted you." I nodded, and took it from her. Unlocking the phone, I saw it was a text from Donovan. I quickly opened it, and tried to keep my composure.

The IP traces to the downtown library. It's hard to track from there, but I am on it. Trust me.

I closed my phone, and handed it back to Heather. She put it back on my table.

"Hey, Heath, while you're up, can I have my drink?" I pointed to the same table. She nodded, and came to the side of the tub to sit. As she handed me my drink, Sean returned with all of the guys. Gabe walked around the tub, and threw his clothes on my chair. He bent to kiss me, and he tasted of weed and beer. "I see how it is." I quietly said into his ear.

He slid into the tub, and slid his arms around me, pulling me onto his lap. He slid his hands around to my rear, and slid his fingers underneath my bathing suit. An excited, slightly drunk giggle escaped my lips, and everyone laughed.

"Now, now, Gabe…go get a room!" Aaron teased. And unfortunately continued. "I remember living with you two… it was like it never ended." Gabe's eyes burned into mine, and everyone's eyes bore into the both of us. "Just when you thought they had exhausted each other, nope. There it started again." He laughed loudly, and drank more of Gabe's concoction.

"God, Aaron… can you blame me?!" he bounced me on his knee, and all of me bounced in return. His lips landed on mine, and his tongue dug inside me. I fisted his hair, and we emerged seconds later. *Oh, God. Now the throbbing...* I noticed Stacy, Aaron's new flame, sitting back away from the crowd. She did have a beer, so I gave her that much. *Poor thing.*

"Ohh, Aaron… don't get me started my memories of living with you..." I warned and winked. Everyone laughed. Gabe was fumbling with something behind the tub, and I needed to pee. I moved to get out, and his hand caught my rear.

"Where are you going, love?" he looked worried. I smiled.

"Just need the bathroom. I'll be right back." I exited quickly, hitting the kitchen, and downing a glass of water, too. I grabbed a few pretzels, and

148

munched on them as I headed to the bathroom. I finished quickly, and when I opened the bathroom door, was met by Sean.

He put his hand on my shoulder, and pushed me back into the bathroom. I was instantly annoyed with his choice of antics, and shook my head. Crossing my arms over my chest, he overtook me, and smothered my lips with his own. The kiss was breathless, and desperate. He was lost, and searching for the answers on what to do. His hand pressed my back awkwardly into his chest, and his other hand crashed to my breast. I pulled away, and tried to push him back.

"Whoa, Sean," I stepped back.

"I can't stay away from you." I shook my head again, and held up my hands. *Get it out. Fix it.* I hoped he wasn't too drunk yet.

"Listen, what happened…," it felt like my throat was closing on itself. "That can't happen again. Ever. Not that it couldn't happen in a different pretense, but…" I stumbled over myself, and my thoughts. He frowned.

"So it was nothing to you?" I shook my head again, seeing this had upset him. His breathing became heavier, and he put his hand on his chest. *Whoa, he had way more riding emotionally on this, obviously.*

"No, please understand." I held his hand in my own. "It was an amazing afternoon, and I had fun with you. It was comfortable, and I felt that. I know you did, too." My words were heavy, and my belly was grumbly. "That's just not what I want to happen right now. You're a great friend, Sean. You always have been." I patted his hand, but it didn't seem like it was working.

"I don't want you to rule it out. I mean,

happening again. Just maybe? You know, if the circumstances are right?" he looked strained. Pained, maybe.

"Well, we'll see, I guess. How's that?" I checked his face. He smiled, and nodded idly. "But understand this, no means no. Cross me there, and everyone will know." I pointed at his face, and he stopped smiling to agree. "Now get out of this bathroom, before you're hung in the yard." I joked. *That's an old Michael joke we'd both never forget, for sure.* He laughed, and exited the bathroom.

As I climbed back into the hot tub, with the pitcher of frozen, cold goodness, everyone held their glasses high. I filled them all, and put the pitcher behind me. I sat back down by Gabe, and Sean returned to the tub, climbing in on my other side. *Oh for fuck's sake…*

Alcohol pumped through our veins, and the radio blared loudly. We all sang together… *I said Hey! What's going on? And I said, hey-ey-ey-ey, I said hey! What's going on?* Leaning into Gabe, while I was up refilling my drink, he began nibbling on my sides. Facing away from everyone, I felt myself get lost in his bite. Throbbing in all of the right places, lost in his touch, I opened my eyes to find Sean deeply staring at me. Obviously getting off on the moment. I quickly repositioned in the tub, and shot him a nasty glare.

"Janie!" Heather yelled. "We should've done the Jell-O pits so we could wrestle! Remember when we wrestled?!" she was giddy. I nodded, and couldn't stop laughing.

"That was the best night ever! I think everyone else loved when our bathing suits slipped off…" I trailed off, and we both covered our faces. We all bounced, shouted, and drank more and more while we stayed warm in the hot tub. *This night is going very well…*

~24~

I got out to refill the pitcher again, and noticed that Aaron was tongue deep in his new flame, and Heather and Greg were whispering in the corner. *Here's where this gets awkward.* Like every other party we ever had, they always ended up with drunken sex. Everyone did it. No one cared. But who would he partner up with now?

I returned to find Aaron now moved to one of the chairs, and removing Stacy's lovely top. I couldn't help but check out her pert little nipples. *Cute, but not enough.* I smirked, and thought of my own more-than-a-handful size breasts. I found Gabe, holding out his glass, gazing only at me. I felt my mouth raise, as I filled his glass. I climbed in to his lap, ignoring all else, and downed my pink lemonade slushy.

"You know what is next, correct?" I questioned. My hands felt his chest, squeezing his shoulders and arms. His breathing was heavy, and his hands came up to my back. He gently rested them on my shoulder blades. He shook his head.

"I vaguely remember, but I'm not positive." He shifted, and I felt his erection. I smiled, and raised my eyebrow. "Maybe you'd like to refresh my memory?" I giggled, and looked around. Aaron and Stacy were in it deeply, moaning and groaning away. Greg and Heather had gone to the porch swing, and were connected at the mouth. I couldn't find Sean… *but I could feel him watching me.* I turned back to Gabe, and he was ready. His fingers snuck up my sides, and pulled the string on the back of my bikini.

"Let's stay in the warm water…" his mouth crashed into mine, and his fingers dug into my bottoms. Suddenly, Sean appeared. I watched the exchange of glances between Gabe and Sean, and swore I saw a nod. *What the fuck?*

Sean climbed into the hot tub, and took position across the tub from us, saying nothing. Gabe continued to assault my body by poking into hidden places, and moaning into my ear. He shifted, and slid his swim trunks down his legs. He pulled my top over my head, and laid it on the side of the hot tub. I glanced over my shoulder, and clearly saw Sean jerking himself off.

"Gabe?" I questioned gently, as his finger slipped inside me. I gasped, and fell into him. His lips were so soft on mine, there was no denying my lust towards him.

"You're okay, baby," his fingers twisted, and pressed into me deeper. Our eyes met, inches apart. His blue eyes told me pleasure was coming. Lots of it. *That's what I'm talking about. That's what I need.* I smiled, and fell into his kiss. Moments later, he shed my bottoms, and I focused solely on him. I knew what was going on behind me, but no way would I even allow him the thought that this bit of voyeurism was… *MMMmmm…..* I throbbed. That it was really getting to me.

I felt Gabe's hands circle my stomach, and flip me on to my stomach. *MMmm, all fours.* I felt him tease me with the head of his massive hard flesh, and I braced on the tub. Within seconds, he filled me, hard. His fingers found my ass, and began to tease me there, too. I could hear Sean's breathing behind us.

Refocusing, every inch of Gabe slid in and

out of me, making my insides boil and melt. The fullness he created was enough to send me over the edge, and an endless tantric orgasm took me over. It was only him, and me, just like always…taking me to the brink, and beyond. His rhythm changed, and I adjusted my hold on the hot tub. The jets suddenly restarted, and I knew who had done it.

His hands drove into my crotch, and his finger drove into my ass. I cried out with pleasure, screaming his name.

"Gabe!" There were no other noticeable words, only moans and screams. He held my shoulder, driving deeper for his own release. My head fell backwards, and I was lost in his orgasm. His moans, his tight grip on my flesh… I wanted to go and go and go. I collapsed on the side of the tub, and Gabe slid out of me. Once he did, I heard Sean's breath hitch, and tense. *He had climaxed.* I kept my eyes closed, and focused on myself. *Oh come on Janie, you know you loved that. Everyone watching, and with your true love.* For once I agreed with my thoughts.

Moments later, I stood up, and found my robe. I headed towards the fire, and Gabe headed towards our room to get our tin. I could read his mind, and I smiled at him. I stoked the fire, and added some wood. Checking the deck, Greg and Heather were passed out, and Aaron and Stacy were still fucking, now on the kid's swing set. *Whatever works!* I chuckled. Sean exited to the bathroom, and Gabe rejoined me with a lit joint. He passed it to me, and I inhaled quickly.

It flowed down my throat, and we relaxed on the couch together. Sean appeared moments later, and I felt better knowing that I was now covered. He smiled at us both, and joined us on our couch. He turned to Gabe, and smiled.

"Thanks," he looked down, and pulled his flask out of his pocket. He took a long drink, and closed it again. "You're amazing," he looked at me adoringly. I shook my head, and covered my face. "I'm hungry, going to get some chips. You want some?" I nodded. I was parched and starving.

"And some water, please?" Why not ask. He offered. He nodded, and disappeared into the kitchen. I relaxed my body into Gabe's, and passed the joint to him. It was nearly 3am, and we were all blitzed out of our minds. He turned to me suddenly, and clasped his hands around my cheeks.

"Tonight was awesome. Thank you, so, so much." His lips told me how true his statement was. "Reconnecting with everyone was so necessary." I knew exactly what he meant. Life was getting away from us, and we needed to reach out more often. Gazing into the fire with my best friends, with no cares in the world.

~

Something off in the trees woke me up suddenly, and my eyes opened quickly. I could still hear the noises, and they didn't sound too far away. Cautiously, I looked around without moving much. Everyone was still in place, Gabe passed out next to me, and Sean across the now dwindling fire. *Crack.* There it was again, branches breaking under footsteps. I stopped breathing to listen closely. *Oh for fuck's sake! You have got to be kidding me...* I could hear the footsteps, and I couldn't control my loud gasp.

I sat straight up, and stood immediately. I dove for the wall of the house, and turned on the outdoor lights. I could see the shadow running through the yard, and I knew something had to be done.

"WAKE UP!" I yelled, and took off after the suspect. I didn't realize how fast they were running, or that our yard was so big. "GABE!" I yelled. Behind me I heard them all waking up, coming to life, and Greg was at my side in seconds. He continued to run past me, tapping me on the back as he went. No words, only the sound of his legs pumping fast, and feet hitting the dry, crisp forest floor.

There was a commotion in the trees, and yelling from two people. Without warning, something exploded from behind me. I froze, turning quickly. *OH my God!* I turned to see a small fire ball rolling into the sky, and Gabe, Heather, and Stacy were now dumping water behind our shed. I was distracted by the sound of punches, and grunts. *Greg.*

Breaking the tree line, I saw the shadowy figure wrestling with Greg. Punches were being thrown by both parties, and Greg was trying to keep the Visitor from his car, which was now only inches away from his hands. My head started to spin, so many details to remember. My eyes froze when the Visitor's met my own. Time seemed to stand still.

His left hand was squeezing Greg's throat, as he tried relentlessly to punch and kick at the Visitor. He only wore a stocking cap, and smiled at me widely when he saw me. I could see his eyes were gleaming, and he tightened his grip on Greg.

"Janie," he cooed deeply. I braced myself with the tree I was hugging, and was ready to run in an instant. I took a small side step to better my view of this mystery Visitor. Greg saw my movement,

155

and tried to speak.

"No! Jan-" He squeezed his throat again, and his words were lost. Tears pricked my eyes for my dear friend, and I just wanted this to end. Looking behind me, I saw the group still fighting the fire. Their chaos seemed easier. The panic was coming.

"I-I" cleaning my throat, I stepped out again. "I don't know you. Who are you?" His face never changed, the smile remained. *Oh, that's fucked up.* I could see the Visitor was breathing heavily, and Greg was barely moving.

"You do know me. Now I know how much you truly cared." His voice was bitter, almost burnt. "Soon," he turned for his car, and threw Greg into a tree. He collapsed to the ground, and the Visitor closed his car door. The window was down, and he turned to me again. "Soon. I'll see you again *real* soon." He laughed, and floored it, kicking up all sorts of debris from the forest ground.

Silent, I rushed to Greg. He was bleeding, and had a huge knot on his head. He was breathing regularly, and seemed to have no other physical damage. *Soon. I'll see you again real soon.* I heard the sirens in the distance, and knew it was almost over. Again. *For now.*

I pulled Greg up to a sitting position, leaned on a tree. I stopped the first police car at the mouth of our drive way, and that's when Gabe and I made eye contact from a mile across the yard. Other officers and cars pulled down the drive to the group of my panicked friends, and Gabe took off in a dead sprint towards me. I turned back to Greg, and stood protectively over him.

Moments later, the ambulance pulled up directly next to us on the main road by our

156

driveway. The EMTs surrounded him, and I backed away, thankfully into the arms of Gabe. I turned into his hug, and the shakes began. I looked at him stone cold, and my lips twitching. His hands brushed over my cheeks, making sure I was okay.

"Oh God," he pulled me closer, pulling my head into his neck. "Just breathe baby." He rocked me like a child, and I gasped for air. I clawed at his chest, desperately seeking the calm I needed to breathe. The panic was back. *Oh fuck.* The shaking finally stopped, and I looked at his face, wide eyed.

~24~

When I woke up, I was on the couch in our house. There were police officers everywhere, and my heart fell out of my feet. *Greg! The fire!* I was breathing too heavy. *The Visitor!* I jumped off of the couch, and straight up. Looking around, Gabe stood before me, hands out in defense.

"Calm down, love." I steadied myself, and cleared my throat.

"Where's Greg? Everyone okay?" I could feel that my angry face was on, but I wasn't sure why. He nodded, and I saw Stacy and Aaron in the corner. "Where's Heather?" My eyes searched everywhere for my dear friend. Gabe approached me slowly, and I grasped his hand. He sighed.

"Heather's with Greg at the hospital. He's okay, just banged up. There for evidence collection more than anything." He rubbed my forehead. "Are you okay? You've been out for a few hours." His hand brushed my forehead, as if feeling for a fever. I squinted, and closed my eyes. It all came flowing back to me.

"Is the shed okay?" I sat down on the couch

again, fearing that some of this news was going to make my stomach churn.

"Yes, the bomb didn't go as planned, and only caught the weeds around the shed on fire." Gabe laughed, and the police officer chuckled. "Good for me, less yard work!" He rubbed his forehead with his palm, obviously beyond stressed. *Who laughs about a bomb?! I don't care if it didn't go off correctly! What are we going to do here?* I turned and checked the time, 5:36am. The officer approached me on the couch, and she sat down next to me. She smiled, and offered her hand. I took it, and we shook.

"Hello, Mrs. Lazarus." She seemed so small, and I couldn't help wonder how she was a police officer at all.

"Janie, please." I smiled back. "Could I have someone get me some water before we do this?" She nodded, and I motioned to Gabe. He was off in a flash.

"Okay, well before we start, let me introduce myself. I'm Officer Zaidi. You can call me Salma." She pulled out her note pad and pencil, and I could tell she was ready for my statement.

"Well, I was on my back porch with my husband and friends, sleeping off the alcohol we had drank the night before, when rustling, or a noise woke me up." I turned my head a bit, because I saw someone move behind me. *Sean.* I cleared my throat, and turned back to Salma. "I listened before I sat up, and was sure that I heard someone or something moving. Once I was startled enough, I stood up instantly. I saw the shadow of someone running through our yard towards the tree line, and I took off after them." Gabe had just returned with my beverage, and was frowning.

I took a large gulp of the cold water, and it tasted so good. Burning off the alcohol, because I was sure that I was still hammered, and that this was all a terrible dream.

"I yelled as I took off to make sure that someone heard me, and a few moments later, our friend Greg came running after him, too. He passed me, as he is much faster, and caught up with the Visitor in the trees." I swallowed hard, and grabbed my throat. "They fought for what seemed like forever, and finally, he hit Greg so hard that he looked to have passed out for a few minutes. He held his throat, and stared at me." My fingers writhed in my hands, and my nerves stepped in. Gabe sat next to me, and slowly rubbed my shoulder blades.

"You're doing great, love. Greg's going to be fine, remember that." His voice was low, almost monotone. Calming to my ever heightening sense of crazy. His hand rested on my knee, and I sat up straight to try and continue.

"I'm sorry." I paused. "He only wore a stocking cap, but I could not see his features or face clearly thought the trees. His teeth weren't perfect, but they were bright in the dark when he smiled at me. He spoke to me, too." I swallowed hard. Gabe's hand tightened on my leg, and he scooted even closer to me.

"I asked him who he was, and I said that I didn't know him. He said that I did know him, and that this showed him how much I truly cared." My heart was beating very fast. "I immediately thought of Michael." It fell from my lips, and Sean stood to his feet.
I shook my head. "I know it wasn't him. But I don't know who else it could be." Everyone sat in silence,

159

and Officer Zaidi took her notes. My head fell into my lap. "And then he said he would see me soon." Tears stung my eyes, and steamed down my face. *You're doing an excellent job keeping you cool. Especially under the influence. I always knew you were talented.*

"Ok, Janie," Officer Zaidi began. "I've got the description, and the description from Mr. Hartley. If you think of anything at all, you call this number, and let us know." She smiled, and handed over the card. Gabe stood up, and rifled through his phone.

"We work with Detective Gustovson on this case, I believe. Will he be notified of this immediately?" She nodded.

"Yes, Sir. He'll get my report in about fifteen minutes." She smiled at him reassuringly.

"Wonderful. Thank You, Officer." He extended his hand, and they shook. *Always so polite.*

"Also, from what we can tell, the fire was started with gasoline, and some sort of yard pellets. No pieces of the bomb itself were discovered at this point. Please avoid the area, if you can though, just in case." We both nodded. She stood, and headed towards the door. "We'll be in touch," she nodded. "Mr. Lazarus, Mrs. Lazarus." And off she went.

I stood, leaning against the house, unsure of what to do. It was now almost 6am, and I was exhausted. Gabe came over to me, and kissed my hair. He pulled my hand, and headed back out to the deck.

"Come on, Sean." He called behind him.

The sun was just coming up, and it was a bright pink, purple and red horizon. There were so many smells in the air. The crisp coolness of the fall morning. The burnt wood smoldering in our fire pit. *Thankfully, the coals are warm…it's cold out here.* The hint of gasoline in the air, and I wondered if that's what the Visitor has used. Sean joined us on the couch, and Gabe pulled the tin out from underneath the cushion. I smirked at him, and he smiled.

"Didn't think I'd lose this in the may-lay, did you?" He pulled out one of the joints, and we sat down at the table to smoke it. The silence that fell around the table spoke so much. We were all a little shocked, and unsure of what was next. After a few moments, he spoke. "I just wish I knew who it was." And if Sean was on cue…

"Yeah, then we could beat the fucking hell out of them for this." He shook his head, and reached for a beer. He cracked the can, and guzzled the entire can. As he finished his phone rang, and he answered. "Oh, hey…" his voice trailed off. Gabe passed the joint back, and I quickly huffed it in. "No, no we're alright. On the scanner?" He looked up at us in shock. "They read our names?!" his head shook back and forth. "I promise we're okay. After we all calm down a bit, I'm heading home." He paused, and took out another beer. "Ok. Ok. Yes, I agree. I know. Ok," he rolled his eyes. I frowned. "Alright, you too." *So cold towards her. It's hard to not feel terrible for her right now.*

"Was that Delaney?" I felt my eyebrow raise. *Just because you survived torture with us, doesn't mean I've forgotten you're turning into a stalker.* He nodded, and smiled. "How's she doing?"

"She's alright. Scared to death that we were hurt, but I told her it was Greg." I nodded, and couldn't help but hope Greg was alright. My heart hurt that I had again pulled the people I loved into some sort of trouble. I just wish I could figure out where the trouble was coming from, and why. My head was spinning, and I needed sleep. I stood up, and rocked to the side. Two sets of hands were on me in and instant, and I looked wide eyed at both of them.

Quickly, Sean released his grip, and Gabe steadied me to my feet. *This is so fucked up, Janie.* He helped me to the bedroom door, and I closed it behind him. I watched him rejoin Sean, and stoke the fire again. I was too tired to care. I stripped my clothes off, and climbed into bed. How could such a great evening turn into such a god awful morning? My mouth tasted of old lemons. *Gabe's pink lemonade.* My mind raced through the evenings memories. Stopping slowly on the fantastic cocktail, and then to the laughter, and finally on to the hot tub. I shook my head, and smiled.

I heard my footsteps echoing down the hall. When I turned the corner, I held my breath, because I wasn't sure of what to expect. I couldn't believe what I saw when I turned...caged at the end of the hall, screaming my name. "Janie! Janie!" his voice sounded broken. Panicked. "NO! Janie!" he yelled, even more terrorized than before. Cocking my head to the side, I squinted at him. Is this real? Closer I crept, and his screams got louder. Finally I was close enough to see his eyes, and he was truly frightened. Michael, frightened? No. That's not possible. Looking in his eyes again, I noticed his stares was over my shoulder. Slowly, I turned around. The Visitor. "Janie! No! He'll kill you!" Michael screamed into my ears. I pressed my back against Michael as the Visitor stepped towards me. He reached out his hand for my throat, and I slammed my eyes closed to look away...

~25~

I sat straight up in beg, gasping for air. Gabe's hands were quickly on my back, gently stroking me back to reality. I felt so panicked, and frightened. The dream. It had to be showing me something. *Is the Visitor worse than Michael? Oh God...* I felt myself pale, and stood and ran into the bathroom. I purged into the toilet, and felt immediate relief. I brushed my teeth, and returned quietly to bed, and Gabe.

"Are you okay, baby?" His forehead looked wrinkled. I nodded, and nuzzled into his chest.

"I'm so sorry about all of this." I started, and his fingers cut me off. He rolled his eyes.

"Janie, you know this isn't all your fault. Somehow, the weirdoes just really flock to you." He smirked, and nudged my arm. "I'm so glad you weren't hurt last night." His eyes closed, and he put his head in his hand. He sighed heavily.

"I've thought and thought, and I can't figure out who it could be." I paused, re-running the words of the Visitor through my head. "I don't know what man I hurt in the past. He seemed hurt..." I stared into the distance. Reality smacked me in the face, and I sat straight up again. "Where are the kids?!" I panicked.

"Shhh," he shook his head. "There you go again. They are fine. Wonderful. Your parents were in town last night, so the kids have been at a hotel for the past 36 hours." He pulled out his cell phone, and opened it to a picture of their beautiful little faces, playing in the pool.

"I miss them right now. A lot." He nodded,

and kissed my forehead. I know he felt the same. I collected myself, and sat up a bit on the pillows. "Seriously though, I've thought about the past, and I can really only think of my old friends back in the day, or someone from the Phoenix." He nodded, and sat up a bit with me. He reached for his notepad, and a pencil. "I know that many of Michael's friends are married now, and have moved on. Walter's married with kids, and lives out of state. Sean's, well, Sean, and always around us. All of the others…I just can't imagine they'd ever give three shit's about us like that. You know?" He nodded, and jotted what I said down.

"I thought about people from the Phoenix, too. And I've worked there so long…I mean, it could be one of two hundred people…" his eyes got big, and he closed them tightly. "How about anyone we haven't seen for years?" We both sat against the pillows, in deep thought. Suddenly, his phone rang, and he pulled it out to answer.

"Hello?" he paused. "Yes, Detective, Hello. Have you been updated about the past twelve hours?" he nodded, and smirked. "Yes, my wife has that effect on men." He laughed loudly. "Okay, that sounds fine. We'll see you in a bit." He nodded. "Thanks, Brian." He turned towards me, and picked his pen back up.

"What's going on?" I waited.

"The Detective is coming in an hour, to review everything, and discuss the plans." We exchanged glances, and went back to thinking of the past. "Want to smoke one before he gets here? Sort of make me feel like a criminal." He giggled. I nodded.

"What about Bill?" he instantly turned and scowled at me. "Just a thought…I didn't really think so." I paused. "Not really his build or smile, either." I had a random idea, and remembered that I had old photo albums with my friends over the years. I jumped out of bed, and ran to the closet. Gabe lit the pipe, and smiled at my obvious light bulb moment. I reached for the high boxes, and a pile of sweatshirts fell on my head. Gabe laughed loudly at me, and coughed through his hit.

I scampered back to the bed, taking the pipe from his hands, and taking my own, long draw. Handing it back, I turned back towards the box. Opening it, I was hit in the face with memories. Things from my past. Pictures. Memories. *Michael.* I drew in my breath, and held it. I dug for the photo album, and closed the box. My hands brushed over so many photos, some I wasn't even sure why I had kept. Pictures of Michael, Sean and I together, and all other the sneaky memories that still popped in sometimes. Opening the album, there were all sorts of faces looking back at us. Pictures of Nichole and me from our teenage years; of friends from the swim team, and of working at the Phoenix. Turning through one page, Gabe pointed to an old stock boy. I wrinkled my nose.

"I don't even remember his name. And I only worked there a month or so before I quit when I was pregnant with Lilah." I flipped the page, and there was a picture of Gabe, Simon, Bill, and myself. *If it's not Bill....what if it's....* "Simon." My breath stopped, and my forehead wrinkled. I looked closer at the picture. "Have you heard from him, ever, in all these years?" I squinted my eyes.

"No, not at all. Last I heard, he was out of state working at another franchise." He shrugged, and drew another hit. He leaned into the picture, and stared.

"Do you think it could be him?" I was so confused. "I can't really remember his smile, or his eyes. I never really looked at him in such a way though." I winced, and handed the pipe back to Gabe.

"I can't say that it wouldn't be him. Let's bring it up to the Detective when he gets here. Bring the album. Let's move to the living room." He pulled me off the bed, and to my feet.

By the time I had everything transferred into the living room, and gotten myself a drink, I heard the knock on the door. Gabe was there quickly, and I heard them greet each other. When I returned to the sitting area, I was greeted with two smiles.

"Hello, Detective." I said.

"Mrs. Lazarus." He nodded. "Well, let's get down to business. I don't ever like to overstay my welcome." He smirked, and Gabe roared. *Why do I feel like I'm missing something with these two?* "Okay, so basically you had an outdoor party with a small group of friends, and then it was crashed by this mystery man. Is that correct?" We both nodded.

"Except that he also tried to blow up my shed, and beat the shit out of my best friend." Gabe said, matter of fact like. The Detective nodded.

"Yes, and the arson. Absolutely." We nodded. "We've got the description with a medium build, and bulky. Wearing a stocking cap this time. Crooked teeth." We nodded again. "I've also got that he spoke to you, and said that you did know him, and that he would see you soon? Correct?" I nodded, and swallowed. "Okay, have you given any thought as to who this could be?" It was like the air was getting heavier by the minute. I nodded, and held out the album.

"Going through this album a bit ago, I found

166

this picture of Simon. I'm not even positive of his last name. Maybe Knight? But I'm not sure of the spelling." The Detective wrote frantically in his notebook, as did Gabe.

"Tell me about Simon." He sat back on the couch, and relaxed a bit.

"Okay, well..." I scratched my forehead. "We were good friends back in the day. I had trouble back then with Michael Comaro, who is now in jail for my attempted murder. He worked with me at the Phoenix when I worked there, and we often hung out. He was a good friend." I replayed many of our interactions while the Detective took his notes. I remembered my birthday, and going back to his house. He was driving in his car, after antagonizing Michael. I winced, thinking hard.

"You okay over there, Janes?" Gabe asked, gently. I nodded.

"Just thinking. Trying to remember." The more I thought, the more memories flooded back. Trouble was, bringing up one thing with Simon usually brought up one attached with Michael. The memories burned, and made me feel sick. It was so long ago, but the memories made it feel like just yesterday. Suddenly, there it was. He smiled at me in the car, and his teeth were indeed crooked. Very bright white, almost as if they were professionally whitened. I swallowed hard, and it was loud.

"What is it, Janie?" the Detective asked.

"His teeth are crooked." My body began to shake. His eyes bored into my head, and he could see I was deteriorating at these thoughts.

"Okay. We'll be done for today. I want to call this one in. Your reaction to him..." he paused, and stood. "It's very intriguing. So, please stay

167

away from the arson area until further notice." He turned to Gabe. "I'll call you in a few hours, once I've got a name, and more information." They shook, and he nodded in my direction. "Janie."

"Thank you, Brian." Gabe said to him frankly. He waved as he left the driveway. Gabe smiled, and patted my shoulder as we came back into the house. I checked the time as I walked through the kitchen, and it was already 5:12pm.

"Hey, are the kids staying with your mom, or what? I don't know if I want them in this house with the Visitor around." I couldn't help but be frank. There didn't seem to be time for anything else. "Maybe they could stay with your mom? Or my mom?" I was rambling.

"I talked to my mom, and she's going to keep them at her place for a while. She's never noticed anyone back that far, and her security alarm is way more extravagant than ours is." I nodded, and smiled.

"I want to visit them tomorrow." I reached for the radio remote. Melissa Etheridge blared through the speakers, *I want to Come Over...* Gabe's arms embraced me suddenly, and I couldn't help but fall into his warmth. "But that's tomorrow..." my hand trailed up his back, underneath his shirt. I clawed at his muscle, unsure of if he was feeling the groove like I was.

His mouth fell onto my neck, and nibbled lightly along my hair line. That immediately rose the hair on my arms, and his hand slid underneath my shirt. His thumb and finger squeezed around my nipple, and I gasped. Resting my forehead on his chest, I looked up into his eyes, and they were darkened with lust. My core instantly heated, and throbbed for him.

168

He pulled my hair back, and our mouths met. Our tongues danced around with each other, with no hesitations whatsoever. He worked my panties down my legs, and my shirt over my head. Pushing me back into our bed, I collapsed under his weight. He pressed into me, and I could feel every part of him on me. *MMMmmm, how it should be…always. Your life saver.*

He slid his pants off, and pushed himself between my legs. He was ready to take me instantly, but instead taunted me with only the tip. In and out, in and out. My hips flailed frantically around, writhing for his touch. The fullness. *Him.* I ran my hand down his face, and over his cheeks. I needed him.

As if he knew my internal monologue, he drove himself into me, probing deeply. He held my arms over my head, and pushed into me fiercely. I groaned with pleasure, and his eyes grew hotter with desire.

"Oh, MMMmmm" I moaned loudly. I drove my hips into him, as hard as I could. His hips bone poked into my thighs as he drove into me. His teeth were clenched and grinding, and he held me firmly down.

"Janie," he said in a hushed whisper. He put his hands on both of my shoulders, pushing me even farther down on his shaft. With every thrust, I felt his balls smack my ass. *This is intense. Hold on, girl.* He adjusted his grip, and rhythm, and really picked up the pace. I felt myself instantly cling to him, a tantric orgasm, I wasn't letting go. I began to moan, and whimper, and my muscles began to seize over and over.

In a flurry, his hand fell to my breast, and squeezed as he thrust as deep as he could. Moaning and screaming out his aggression into the air. My head fell off the bed, and I was lost in oblivion. I felt him give final thrust, and felt the throbs and warm shoot through my abdomen. Every muscle in my body clenched, throbbed, or froze in place. This was ecstasy. Perfect.

Collapsing on my stomach, we both lay together. I grabbed a blanket with my toe, and pulled it up enough to grab with my hand. I covered us the best I could, and turned to close my eyes. Finally, everything was quiet. For this moment, I just needed sleep.

~26~

By the time Tuesday morning came around, I had finally felt like I was rested. Gabe and I finished our coffee in the kitchen before our day started. *Tuesday. You've got this. I think.* My thoughts had been so scatter brained, and all over the place. I knew that I couldn't rearrange my life to fit this sonofabitch, but I also knew my level of vigilance must be raised. I lifted my eyes off of the counter, to find him smiling at me from across the bar.

"Baby, don't let this get to you. You've been through so much worse." I snuggled into his hug, and didn't really want to let go. "Day by day, and one of these days, he'll slip up. We both know it, because we've both lived it." I knew he was right, but hearing the heavy words still made tears sting to my eyes. I felt him crane to check the clock, and he instantly broke our hug. "Sorry, I'm going to be late. I need to go." He smiled, a big flashy Gabe smile. "Call me whenever you need to." He kissed my fingers, mouthed 'I love you,' and was gone in a flash.

I finished cleaning up the kitchen from our breakfast with Jean and the kids, and it was so wonderful to be around their bright spirits for a while. Considering all that has happened, and is happening, Jean agreed with Gabe, and the kids will be staying in her guest house while this gets sorted out. Kills me, but if they're safe... *that's all that matters.*

Heading into the closet, I managed to duck from under the cloud of gloom, and try to find something appropriate to wear to Donovan's today. *Is that really safe?* I winced. Is anywhere really safe? Digging through the closet, I found a newer white lace corset, and bikini briefs. I liked the clean look, and buckled myself into it. I checked the full length mirror as I was leaving the room, and I couldn't help but stop and stare.

My long blonde hair was curled perfectly at the bottom, hanging around my shoulders and chest. My dress hung effortlessly over my chest, and didn't cling. My makeup was done well, but nothing could hide the stress. *You've got some heavy purples, there honey.* My eyes looked so tired. So stressed. Gazing at myself, I could see the fear hiding behind my hazel eyes.

I shook off the thought, and headed for the door. Surely I just needed a quick pick me up. I jumped into the Jeep, and locked the doors behind me. I cranked up the music, and thankfully, Duffy's Mercy was blaring. Within moments, I was lost in the song, dancing with my hands while I drove. *You got me beggin' you for mercy...why won't you release me? You got me beggin' you for mercy...*

As I parked next to his Beamer, I finished belting out the last bits of the song. I felt my phone buzz, and it was Caty.

Janie, I'm sick. Can't do tonight's EazE Stop. Can someone cover for me?

Without hesitation I texted back that I could help, and I threw my phone back into my bag. When I got closer to the front door, I saw that he was already there to meet me.

"Hello, Mr. James." I said, nervously. He smiled, and closed the door behind me. Once the door closed, his hand came down on my shoulder, and he spun me to face him. His hands were shaky, and he stepped closer to me.

"Are you okay? I heard about everything." I wrinkled my forehead at him. *How the fuck did he know?* "I've been thinking about you nonstop. Wondering if there's any way I can help." He hand brushed the tendril of hair from my face.

"No, Donovan." I grabbed his hand, and lowered it. "I'm fine." I turned and put my bag on the desk. "Could you put on some music, please?" He nodded. My phone buzzed again, and thinking it was Caty, I looked. Nope. *Sean.*

Can we talk? Want to make sure we're okay.

Then I knew how Donovan had gotten all the details, and I couldn't help but wonder if they'd been discussing me as well. Frustrated, I slammed my fist on the desk, and bolted for the bar. I quickly poured myself some rum…*tasted like piss. You sure that was rum?* It didn't matter. I slammed another.

172

There was no way I was going to let my outrageous thoughts kill my clientele. I need this job, and the money. I slammed another, and my legs heated up. *Whoa, there, lady. It's getting a little fuzzy up here…*

I turned to find Donovan staring at me, mouth open to the floor. I slammed my fifth drink while he watched, and being the lady that I am, used my arm to wipe my mouth when I was done.

"I'm going to clean your fucking house now, Mr. James." I said rather sardonically. I stormed off through the double doors to the kitchen, turned up the sound system, and dove into making his house shine. I started a load of dishes in the dish washer, and headed up stairs to clean the loft and bedroom. *Where the fuck is he?* I didn't hear any footsteps. This time must be different. I was slightly under the influence, and at the moment, didn't really care. I finished the cleaning upstairs, and headed back down to the kitchen to finish up. The song changed as I turned the corner, to one not on my playlist. *Eagle-Eye Cherry? What the fuck?* I turned the corner to find Donovan sitting on the bar, two drinks poured. He smiled.

"Here," handing me a drink. "Seems like you might need it today." I took it, and downed it without thought. *Jesus, Janie…you still have to drive.* I smiled at him, and continued my work. "You seem…off today. I'm not sure how to handle you." His eyes stared into his hands, and to the counter. I watched him, and his fingers swirled the rim of his glass of scotch.

Without much hesitation, *or good thought…* I stood, and reached behind me to my zipper. His eyes were still in thought staring down, blankly. Undoing the zipper, and sliding it down, the dress exposed my shoulders before falling to the floor completely. I stepped out of the dress, and kicked it towards his feet. Slowly, his head turned up to look at me, and I watched his eyes steadily go up my legs, to my abdomen, to my breasts, to my face.

I stepped towards him, and bent over to put a plate away. I could feel his eyes boring into my ass, and knowing that, I wiggled a little bit more. *Is this some kind of cathartic release?* He stood near his stool, and lifted his shirt over his head. His body was tight, and muscular. For someone of his age, he was definitely a prize to be had. He stepped towards me, and ran his hand down the front of the corset.

"I love these things," he trailed off, eyes burning. "You don't have to do this Janie, I know you've been-" I put my finger over his mouth. I ran my hand down his stubble-covered cheek, and smacked it. He smiled, coyly. I turned my back to him.

"Unhook them," I paused, and inhaled. "All of them." His hands raised to the top of my corset, and I felt a few hooks loosen. "I don't know what I need Donovan," I felt his hands move, and unhook more. "I just want my privacy. *My* choice." He nodded, eyes wide watching me. Once the last hook was undone, I spun to face him, standing in white pumps, and white bikini undies.

I could see his pants tightening, and without hesitation, he let them fall to the floor. His hard length bounced up and down before my eyes, and my thoughts turned hideously sexual. Without care, I wanted him. I needed him more than I had ever felt before. The intense need of relief, of less stress, just overwhelmed me. I stripped off my undies, and hopped on the counter.

I laid on the hard, cold counter top, feeling

my naked body with my hands up and back down again. Donovan pulled the bar stool over, and sat next to me, watching intently. My hands stopped and focused on my erect nipples. They were crying out for pleasure, for anyone to love them. Up and down they went again, this time lingering around my slickened, wet folds. I dropped one leg off of the counter, and dipped my hand into my hot hole. I needed release, and my thoughts jogged to Gabe. Closing my eyes, I could feel every move he made on my body. *MMMmmm, Gabe…*

His perfect dark hair, and his deep blue eyes. His strong, forceful hands… *the spanking.* Oh, I couldn't think of that much, or I would need so much more. I glanced to my side, and Donovan was there, pumping away. He lingered directly over my pussy, looking as if he would do anything for just a piece. My fingers pulled forward, hitting the spot directly, and I felt myself started to tighten.

I knew Donovan was close, and I knew how to get this over with. *That's better, Janie. Much more businesslike of you. Just get it over with.* I reached for his free hand, and pulled it to me. Taking his finger, I first put it on my clit, and then I pushed his finger inside me. Fully knowing he would feel my clenching, and shoot his load on the counter. His fingers slid in, and his breath hitched.

"Jesus…FUCK!" he yelled, and blew all over the floor. *Wrong. Counter top, and floor.* Coming over my own mountain, I watched his body tremble, and convulse. His breathing slowed, and started to regulate, and he sat back on the stool. I smiled at him, and swung myself around on the counter. He picked up my undies, and handed them to me.

"You never cease to amaze me." He shook

his head, and cleaned up his mess. "All this shit you've got going on, and this." He chuckled, but very pleased.

"It's our deal. We have a contract." I smiled, and shrugged. His eyes focused on my nipples, I could tell. I hopped off the counter, and grabbed my dress. *To hell with that corset, I'll just be free.* He nodded.

"Janie, I also wanted to apologize." I spun around, and wrinkled my face at him. "For last week." He pulled his pants on. "For Sean." The breath slid out of my body, and the thoughts started to roll. *Do I tell him now that my own husband had me on display for him? Unknowing?* I zipped up my dress. "When he knocked on the door, and knew your car was out front, he wouldn't leave. He knew I was up to no good due to the robe, and he barged in. I wasn't using my brain…" he shook his head.

"Its fine, Donovan. It was my choice to…proceed." I shrugged again. I approached him, getting a bit too close. "I feel safe in here." I looked around. "And I don't mind our contract. Not one bit. Today, it's helped me calm down." I looked back to him, and smiled. "But, please don't put me in any awkward positions, as I've about had my fill. If you want something special, ask me first. Please. I'm done with surprises." I grabbed his collar, and pulled him into a deep kiss. *What the fuck Janie!!!!*

The kiss lasted mere seconds, because there was nothing behind it. No sparks. No fireworks. Nothing. It was just a kiss, and that answered all of my unspeakable questions about him. He was a business friend, and also a client. I pulled away, and smiled even bigger. He smirked, and stumbled over his words.

"God, why can't all women be more like

you? The world would be so much better." He snickered, and walked me to the door. "I suppose I'll get to see you on Thursday, right?" I nodded.

"It's in our contract." I winked at him, and headed to the Jeep. Turning her on, she blared some old Alanis at me, and I instantly felt empowered. I cranked the speakers to a deafening level, and headed out. I felt my phone vibrate in my jacket pocket, and I pulled it out. Two missed text messages, one from Caty.

Thanks, J.

Oh shit! I forgot about EazE Stop. I turned on my GPS, and headed to the mart to clean it quickly. At a red light, I opened my phone again to find another text. I didn't recognize the number, but opened it to read.

I am interested in your services for my business. Please text 555.6983 to set up time to set up services. Thank you.

Awesome! A new client. Although our load was already full, I was eager to grow and expand after all of this drama was done. I quickly responded with our plans and fees, and sent the text. I pulled into the parking lot, and parked on the side. The store was just closing, and I was early.

"Hi, I'm Janie Lazarus, from At Your Service, LLC. I'm covering for your regular, so I'm here a bit early." I told the beautiful golden blonde behind the desk. She had fabulous tattoos covering her collar bone and shoulder, and her eyes were deep forest green. Her eyes were the kind you could get lost in. I could tell that she most likely had a real

177

good life story, and I wished I had time to hear it. *A tattoo. Now that would be something exciting to think about.* She nodded, smiled, and sent me on through security.

It only took about an hour to finish up, and as I packed up, my phone buzzed again. I closed my bag, and sat on the bench for a moment before I left. The same number had texted me again.

This is perfect. Plan two. Can we sign the contracts tonight? I am out and about.

Tonight? I checked my watch, and it was already 5:45pm. Gabe would be home soon, and I really needed some time with my man. I decided against it, and answered offering Thursday afternoon to sign the contracts.

Thursday is great. Meet at the park at 4?

That was more like it. I accepted the meeting time, and wrote it in my planner. I stood up, and left the building, entering my cleaning code as I left. I opened my back hatch, to put my cleaning things away, and I had the feeling hit my gut. *Someone's watching you.* I quickly packed my things inside, and slammed the door. I was in a strip mall plaza, and all the stores were open still, except the EazE Stop.

As I walked back around to the driver's side door, I skimmed the area silently. As my hand reached the handle, my eyes looked over my hood. I stopped breathing immediately. Leaning against the side of the wall of the building was a black clothed

178

man. He didn't react to my instant stopping, only slowly turned his head in my direction. I blinked repeatedly, hoping I was losing my mind. *Nope.* I opened them, and he was still there. Jumping into the Jeep, and locking the doors faster than ever, I sped out of the parking lot barely looking in my rearview mirror.

I was surprised to find Gabe's car in the driveway already when I got home. I all but sprinted into the house, to find him cleaning up the dinner that he had just finished with his mom and the kids. I smiled at him, out of breath and nervous. I was overtaken, suddenly, by two small angels, both clamoring for my affection.

After I tucked them in to bed, I went searching for him. I needed him. I needed the closeness and love more than anything. *And obviously, you're willing to get that from about anywhere.* When I turned into our bedroom, I saw him lying on the bed, smoking a joint. He patted the bed next to him, and it was all I could do not to jump out of my skin, and into bed with him to relax.

~27~

I threw my purse down to the floor, and smiled widely at him. He looked so relaxed, smoking and reading.

"Hi," I said quietly, and kicked off my shoes. I rifled through my purse, and put my planner on the desk that I desperately needed to clean. I slid my jacket off, and hung it on my chair. I walked into the bathroom, and sat to pee. I was still smiling about my hot husband, sitting there so vulnerably, when I looked down and saw my thigh high white stockings peeking out, I caught my breath. *Oh, come on…you know what to do.*

I slowly opened the bathroom door, to hear the Gin Blossoms playing in the background. I stepped out of the door, and leaned on my desk. He slowly looked over at me, and stalked me with his eyes. Reaching behind me, I grabbed my zipper and undid it. Opening my side drawer, I pulled out my secret bottle of vodka. Watching him the entire time, I untwisted the cap, and put the bottle to my lips. The cool glass was welcome, to the rush of warmth that then rushed into my chest, every time that I swallowed. A few swallows later, my body was burning, raging hot. *And hungry…look at him…*

"You going to join me over here at all tonight, Janes?" he lowered his reading glasses on his nose. *If you don't eat him, I'm going to.* I shook my head no, and walked over to his black light, and turned it on. Dancing back to the door, I closed it, and turned off the bedroom light. Everything lit up with a purple haze effect. Now Everclear blared loudly, and I cranked it louder. Pressing the cool glass to my lips for one last rush of heat… I set the bottle down, and my eyes met his. "Did you say no?" His voice went flat, and my crotch throbbed hard.

"Yes, Gabe. I said no." Wiggling my shoulders, I let them pop out of my already unzipped dress. His eyes moved to each shoulder, and he swallowed hard. I shimmied more, never taking my eyes off of his, knowing my dress would fall to the floor any moment, exposing my secrets to him. *He's going to wonder why you wore that today… hopefully he's so taken with you that he forgets to notice.* He blinked, and when his eyes opened again, they were dark and greedy. My dress hit the floor, and his mouth fell open at the white corset, which now glowed a pretty, luminated purple in the light. I smiled at him innocently, and did a slow turn in front of him.

"Oh my God…" his breathing was so slow and heavy. "So beautiful…" His eyes wide, watching the show. Taking all of me in. I walked over to him on the bed, and bent over towards him, revealing the low cut top, as well. I could see him melting before me, as always. *Mine.* I turned my back to him, and sat slowly onto the bed in front of him. I pulled my hair off to the side, and slightly turned my head to look at him.

"I was wondering," I cleared my throat. "Could you help me get this off?" Without a moment's notice, his hands were on me, and flipping me under him on the bed. He pulled me closer to him, and ran his hands up and down my entire body, watching each thing they touched on their journey. He rolled me on to my stomach again, and carefully moved my hair from my eyes.

He got up from the bed for a moment, but I knew better than to move. I could hear him moving around, and I heard his pants hit the floor. I kept my face buried in the pillows, hoping to get what I needed so badly. In the next flash, his hand came crashing down on to my ass. I groaned. His hands caressed my legs and thighs, and slowly he began pulling off my right thigh high. As I lay there, he nibbled the back of my leg as the hose came off. *MMMmmm…*

His hand came crashing down again, this time making me jump slightly. The moan escaped my lips before I could stop it. His fingers traced the top of the thigh highs, and slowly pulled them down, just as the other, nibbling all the way. Every part of my body was throbbing. Every part of me was calling out for him. *Jesus Janie, why can't this be enough?* I tried to focus only on the sheer pleasure I was partaking in right now. Another spank.

"MMMmmm, Gaaaabe." I cried out, and writhed on the bed. His hands started on my backside, and worked their way up to my back, beginning to unhook each tiny clasp. Three clasps in, his hand struck me again. More clasps, more spankings. I was so close to coming, just from his touch. My moaning and groaning was uncontrollable. He rolled me over, and in the deep, heated pleasure of being spanked, I hadn't even noticed that I was now corset free. I was also down to a small pair of bikini undies, too. Gabe made easy work of those, pulling them straight off of me, ripping the seams.

"I can tell how badly you want me, Janie." His voice was dark. I nodded fiercely, licking my lips. He nodded, "it's the same for me baby." He gritted his teeth together, and rubbed his palm over his rock hard cock. "Carte blanche?" I smiled widely, and nodded. His head fell into my crotch, and his tongue began the fine dance of circling, sucking and licking my clit. I ran my hands through his hair, urging him on for more. *Feel how comfortable you are right now? He is your panacea. Stop threatening that...* This was a terrible time for the voice to start yapping.

"Gabe," I said, breathless. "Can I have a drink?" I pointed to my vodka bottle, and he willingly grabbed it for me.

"Open up," he said matter of fact like. I listened, and opened slightly. I knew this trick, as being the klutz that I am, have almost choked on this same trick in the past. He slowly poured a drink

182

into my mouth, and I swallowed and opened for more. He shook his head, and took a drink himself. Sliding back down my body, he sat and spread my legs around him. His eyes stared deeply into my core, making me feel so many emotions at once.

Never would I ever allow anyone to blankly stare at my lady parts…it's just so invasive. I felt so self-conscious, that I was sure I was blushing. But here I was, spread eagle, hoping that I would be the lucky recipient of this man's undying love. Hoping I hadn't screwed everything up, yet again. His fingers pushed into me suddenly, and he smiled.

"Hold the bars, Janie." He said flatly. His fingers probed, and poked around inside me, until they found the spot. Once they found it, they were relentless. I could feel myself clenching, and my body was writhing around wildly. My fists were clenched tightly around the headboard bars, and I was thankful for this. His assault was brutal, and he knew I would come forever. My muscles started to stiffen, and his drive only grew stronger. "I feel you baby… so fucking tight."

My head fell back, enjoying the moment, I was lost. I felt myself release on him, and saw him fall back a bit, and catch his breath. He slid his fingers out of me and sat back on the bed. After catching my breath, I looked to find him. I smiled when I did, and he returned my gaze.

"Another drink, please?" He nodded, and reached for a water bottle. I frowned at his drink selection, but accepted it anyway.

"You can let go now, baby." I took the water, and smiled. It was reasonably cold, and went down nicely. After a few gulps, I was refreshed, and ready. Looking over, the first thing I saw was Gabe's enormous cock. Throbbing against his belly, floating up past his belly button. I quickly spun up on my knees, and took him before he had the chance to move.

The velvety softness of his head slid into my mouth with ease, and his taste was perfect. I let him fall to the back of my throat easily, and back out again. His head fell back after a few repetitions, and quiet moans escaped his lips. I wrapped my fingers around his girth while I pumped his head feverishly with my mouth. One of his hands grabbed my breast, and on to my nipple. I moaned while he was deep in my mouth, and his body vibrated under my touch.

He broke my suction on him, and pulled out of my mouth. I wiped my mouth of with my arm, and in a flash, his mouth covered mine. The kiss was deep, almost claiming ownership. I pulled him into me more, and his thigh pushed in between my legs. I felt his head rounding my entrance, and his hands squeezed into my flesh. Palming his length, he rubbed himself all over my opening.

"You want this, baby?" he rolled around more over my slicked folds.

"Yes, please." I nodded, and tried to scoot down to impale myself upon his massive rod. His hands stopped me, and he shook his finger in my face. I smirked, and writhed under him. "Still, now. I have a favor to ask…" he trailed off, while constantly teasing me. I met his gaze, and felt him start to enter. "I want you to come all over my dick." I lost my breath, and his words shot straight to my core. I instantly tightened, longing to be filled with his hard man muscle.

Pushing into me, he gasped through his semi-opened lips. He dove into me again, seeking to be in the depths. I opened myself further to him,

184

allowing for him to fall in entirely. His head fell back, and I could feel his abdomen hitting my thighs. He clawed at my skin and hips, and held me tightly. When I clenched on him, it held, and got tighter and tighter as he pushed on.

Suddenly withdrawing, and flipping me on to my knees, he quickly reentered me, and I held on to the bed for leverage. Deeper than before, I pushed myself against his every thrust. I turned to re-grasp the bed and sheets, and his fingers entered me. Now he filled me entirely with his cock, and his fingers. I was losing touch with reality, and I was losing control of my body.

He twisted his thumb in my ass, as he drove into my pussy with such force. I came all over him, and I could feel the extra wetness on us both. His breath hitched, and he pressed into me harder in both places. Again, I squeezed and soaked him with myself. Pulling his thumb out as I squirted him, only caused it to go on longer. He knew my body so well, and how to make it do what he wanted.

"Hang on," he muttered. I let my head fall to the bed, and pushed my ass into him more. He moaned loudly, and pulled my hips into his. I could feel his cock swell, and every vein pulsating with his blood pressure. His load shot deep into me, and warmed my entire belly. He collapsed on my back, gently stroking my side. I couldn't help but hold in my giggle, and I wiggled a little. "Easy, baby…or I may die." He chuckled, and rolled on to the bed.

We lay together in a heap of hot breath, and the smell of sex was heavy in the air. The radio played behind us, and his arms wrapped around me tightly. I felt him adjust behind me, and pull the sheet over us both. His head laid in my mass of hair, and his mouth was close to my ear.

"I love you so much baby," his voice was a husky, sleepy whisper. "Together, we're unstoppable." He kissed the back of my ear lightly, and I relaxed in his arms. As my eyes began to get heavy, the voice started to jabber. *How will you fix all of this? What if the Visitor does something terrible?* I tried hard to push the thoughts out, and drifted away to sleep.

~

I met the family in the kitchen around 8am, and everyone was ready to go start their days. Lilah was bubbly, and ready for school.

"Morning, Mom! I miss you!" her little arms wrapped around me tightly.

"Aww, baby. I miss you too! We're not far though, you know." I patted her head, and she rambled on about school. She was loving the extra time with Grandma, and I was pleased that she seemed clueless about everything else that was happening. Galen ate his breakfast quietly, and I sat down on the bar stool next to his.

"Hi, buddy. How're you?" I nudged his arm. He frowned, and ate another bite of cereal.

"Ohh, I see..." I started. "You're angry with me for something? Could you tell me what?" He frowned again.

"I miss you and Daddy too!!! I'm tired of Gwamma's house, an I want MY bed!" he all but shouted. I nodded, and patted his tiny head. He just wasn't quite old enough to fully understand what all was happening.

"Aww," I wrapped my arms around him. "I'm sorry little man. We're never far, and we're just getting some stuff fixed up around the house.

186

No need for you to have to worry about your toys getting dirty!" I tried to spin it so he could relax a bit. Jean arrived while I was hugging Galen, and he scowled at her. She smiled at us both, and shook her head.

"Oh, Galen boy," She joked. "I know we're having our rough times, but you're the cutest boy I know!" She poked him as she walked by, and he tried to hold in his grin. I glanced over my shoulder to find Gabe's eyes watching Galen and I, almost in awe. I smiled at him, almost as if I was reading his mind.

At this moment, everything seemed normal. We were just "that" family doing our daily thing. Daddy goes to work, and Mommy does now too. Both kids go to school, and Grandma helps to take care of them. *Well, parts of that are indeed true.* But not all of it. There's a psychopath stalking me. I clean a rich man's house naked for extra money. *And pleasure.* I've crossed too many lines lately with friends. I've put my family into a pile of shit, yet again. I sighed, and kissed my little man's head.

"Alright, you two. Your school bus leaves in five!" Jean yelled as she ran out the door waving. Lilah quickly put her bowl in the sink, hugged Gabe, and then came to me.

"Mom, I love you." She said so seriously. I pulled her into a hug, and breathed her in.

"I love you too, princess." I wiped a tear off of her cheek, and looked into her eyes. "This will all be over with soon, I promise you. Everything I can do to fix this, I will." I kissed her forehead, and she headed out the door, waving behind her. Galen was a little slower, and Gabe was helping him get his backpack zipped up. He was getting angry with it, and his temper was starting to show.

"This is a stupid bag, Ma!" I held in my laughter, as he was definitely our child. Gabe got him zipped up, hugged and kissed, and he came over to me. Arms big and wide, I sucked him up, and carried him out to Jean's car.

"You try to relax a little, and have a good day, okay?" he smiled. "Remember, one of these days you'll get to come to work with me. You've got to get all of your work done first though, okay?" I raised my eyebrows, and he got serious.

"Okay, Ma. Because I'm gonna have a lot of work in school today. Ya know?!" He kissed my cheek, and jumped out of my arms to get in the car. Closing the door, he waved as they left the driveway. I sighed loudly, and rubbed my forehead in the driveway. I turned to go in the house, and Gabe stood before me outside.

"I've got to go too, love." Embracing me in his arms, he kissed my hair. "Thank you for last night. I feel so revived." I smiled at him, and noticed his eyes were a bit brighter today.

"I'm glad. I love you too," I breathed him in. "Always. Will you be late tonight?" I asked quietly, secretly hoping he'd be on time.

"Yeah, I've got a meeting with a new company rep tonight at 8. As fast as I can after that…" he paused, and pulled my mouth to his. His kiss was romantic, and gentle. I smiled, and released him to work.

"Go then," I giggled. "Leave me to work from home, in my pajamas all day." I smirked, and headed for the house.

"Set the codes, baby." He waved, and climbed in his car. "Love you!" he yelled again, as I threw up my mind to wave back. Still smiling when I got inside, I locked the door behind me, and set the alarm code. I set up my lap top at the bar, and cranked up the living room stereo system. Matchbox 20 was on the radio, and I couldn't help but reminisce about the concerts that Gabe and I had gone to. Until I opened my email…

~28~

The house was quiet while I got ready to go to work this morning. The day yesterday sailed by quite smoothly, minus having to call in Donovan's favors again. *Hopefully now the emails will stop…as he's managed to block the IP addresses.* Rifling through the closet, I stood in my robe and pondered today's wardrobe. Not only did I have Donovan's this morning, I was also signing a new client this evening. I needed tasteful, yet bossy. I came across a chocolate brown set, with tiny lace bows and buttons. I hadn't tried it on for years, but thought I should give it a go, as it was a little 1950s-ish.

Looking the mirror, I almost didn't recognize myself. There was a pin-up looking blonde staring back at me in the mirror. *Oh yes, this will do.* I found a pencil skirt, and nice sleeveless blouse. My black sweater made it perfect, and gave me pockets. I slid on my flats, and reapplied my lip stick. Whatever this day would have in store, I was ready. *Ready to deal with Donovan, my client. Ready to deal with new customers to further business. Ready to move forward again.* I nodded at my thoughts, and headed for the door.

I swung by the coffee mart's drive through, and got myself an iced latte. I just needed a bit of caffeine to jolt the sleepy out of me. I sat in the parking lot for a moment, and opened my phone. I

189

quickly wrote an email to my staff, reminding them of our upcoming meeting.

"To: Mylah, Kiara, Caty
CC: Janie Lazarus

Re: October 29 meeting

Hey Girls! Just reminding you we'll have a meeting in the afternoon on the 29th. I'll update locations as soon as I've chosen!
Work reports and customer comments are fabulous for all of you. I'm very happy that you're all on my team!
Caty, I do hope you're feeling better! EazE Mart was handled last night, no problem!
Thank You! Talk Soon!

Janie~"

I scrolled through my texts, and found the number of the client I was to meet this evening. I opened my planner, and wrote the number in the date. Typing quickly, as I noted it was nearly 10am, I shot off the text.

Morning! Looking forward to setting up your accounts this evening. For our computer systems, I'll need your name, the Company's name, and telephone number ASAP. Thank You!

As I pulled into his gated drive, I entered my code, and smirked. Donovan was out in the driveway, dusting off his new ride. He smiled when he saw me pull into the drive, and waved me over to park by his new toy. I hopped out, and skimmed the sleek deep blue color. I walked around the car, and took in its deep tinted windows, and bold silver accents.

"It's custom." His voice was heavy. I nodded, and grinned.

"I can see how much you love her…" I giggled. "May we go for a ride in the Bentley, darling?" I joked, and he laughed. "I'm heading in to get started, you can keep oogling that, if you'd like." I turned on my heel, and went into the house. Today I needed new music. I went to his system, and opened the CD tray. Putting my CD into my purse, I then turned back to make a music station for myself on his internet radio. I laid my sweater down on the desk, and slid off my flats. *Do you even need to disrobe if he's going to be outside all morning?* I laughed at the voice. Yes, yes I do. Because even though it was dirty, it was beyond stimulating. *Sticking to the contracts, at least?* Without a doubt.

I slowly took off my blouse, and laid in next to my sweater. I let the skirt hit the floor, and headed upstairs to clean. An hour later, I returned down stairs to head to the kitchen, but I wanted to check my cell phone. Heading into the study, I opened the doors and bolted in without thinking. I was met by two sets of eyes, wide eyed, and piles of drugs on Donovan's desk. Sitting across from him sat Sean, who now stood abruptly.

"Oh, shit. I'm sorry." I said, awkwardly. They both relaxed a bit, and I walked around the perimeter of the room to the back desk and opened my purse. I turned my back to them, and opened my phone. They began chattering behind me, and I assumed all was well. I had a text from the new client, and I needed to respond. I turned slightly, and said, "Just need to respond to this new client, guys. I'll be out of here in a second." Reading the response, I took note.

*Bare Luck is our new company. In the Industrial Plaza, 341-B. Name is Shy. 555.3692. *

I thought momentarily about Simon, my old friend. And remembered my past fond memories of him when he use to work with us at the Phoenix. His family ran into some rough times, and ended up splitting up in a few different states. He had kept in touch for a while, but I hadn't heard from him in years. *Could he be the Visitor?* Shrugging off the thoughts, I quickly responded.

Thank you. Is 4pm okay?

I opened my planner, and jotted down the address and name of the company. *Bare Luck.* I noted that the address wasn't far from Donovan's, in a plaza strip mall that was expanding and under construction. Quickly sending off the info to the security company for verification, I expected nothing bad to come in return. As I finished writing the contact information, I shifted which hip I was leaning on as I was bent over. I thought I heard someone lose their breath.

I turned slowly to find them both staring at my barely covered ass, eyes dark with lust. *Oh great. Sean too?* I frowned. It was time to set some boundaries. I approached the boys, and they looked me up and down. I stopped in front of them, and motioned their eyes up to my own.

"Alright. Donovan," I turned towards him. "We have a contract. I will stick to that contract, regardless. As will *you*." I said, raising an eyebrow. He nodded, and folded his hands. I could tell he knew where I was going with this. I turned towards Sean, and he was almost drooling. "No way," I started, as his eyes settled in on my core. "I was wrong to let it go so far when you were at Donovan's last week." I looked at the floor. "Like you said, it was a long time coming, I guess. But now it's happened, and it's done. Not something I want." I looked at him, and he looked frustrated. "That said, no touching, boys. Unless it's been preapproved." I smiled at both of them, and fell to the couch.

Sitting up, I leaned over my knees, exposing the top of my breasts to them. Donovan's eyes lit up instantly, and he relaxed in his big boss chair. I heard his zipper release, and his pants his the floor. I turned to Sean, and sat back against the chair, slowly opening my legs. I put my hands on my knees. As my legs spread, my hands rose up my thighs. He kept looking away, almost if pained that I had just said those words. My fingers danced around the silky material of the chocolate brown lingerie, and I loved it.

I dipped my fingers into my panties, leaving myself fully covered. Tossing my head back against the couch, my eyes met Sean's. *Awkward!* Hideously. I withdrew from myself, and slowly turned over on the leather couch. Now my ass was facing them, and they were both now manually stimulating themselves. The voice in my head smiled, and I smacked my ass hard. I moaned at my own abuse, and that alone almost brought them to the brink.

I spread my legs a little wider, and spanked myself again, this time directly on my core. It sent nerve impulses up to my belly, and made me needy. Shaking the thought, it was time to seal the deal. Wider my legs went, and again, I spanked my slit. Grinding my hand, I heard Donovan's breath hitch, and he tensed behind his desk. Looking towards Sean, he had beads of sweat on his face. He was close. One last spank sent him over the edge, and his cum shot across the room feet away from him.

"Jesus Christ…" he mumbled under his breath. He quickly pulled up his pants, and began cleaning his mess. I smiled at Donovan, and he nodded and returned the smile. I stood, and began to get dressed in the corner of the room. I was buttoning my blouse, when he approached behind me. I didn't want to deal with him now. I just wanted to move on with my day. "Janie," he started. I crossed my arms, and listened. "I'm sorry, I know I shouldn't have stayed." I shook my head.

"Let's be honest about it, at least. I can't say much about your watching, as Gabe apparently feels comfortable sharing me in that way, too. I'm not going to dwell on it, and you'll be back on the road soon." His mouth fell open.

"I don't want it to be awkward Janes…," almost pleading. I put my sweater on, and pulled it closed. I grabbed my cell phone, and sighed at him.

"It won't be awkward. Stop feeling bad about it. It's amazing it never happened in the last 15 years, I guess." I shrugged, and unlocked my phone. "Anyway, you two better get back to discussing all those drugs on your table." I winked, and their mouths fell open.

"Uhm, about that Janie," Donovan stood. I held out my hand to him, and shook my head.

"Discretion, and our contracts are in place. You have no worry with me, as I am a user, as well." I smiled, a nodded. Sean left rather suddenly, and Donovan lingered, putting his stash away while I read my text.

4pm fine. Use front door.

I checked my watch, and noticed it was only 1:04pm. Picking up my phone, I noticed the security company had responded. Reading it quickly, they gave the all clear. Instantly, thoughts of Gabe pushed through my mind. I met Donovan at his desk, and he handed me a thick envelope.

"Here's your bonus, plus some extra for your extra guests this past week." He cleared his throat, and I took the envelope without hesitation. *Another bonus? Fabulous! Now how about some green?* My eyes fell to his desk, and the biggest buds I had ever seen. *Oh stop salivating, you addict!* "Do you want some of that?" he asked. I smiled, and raised my eyebrow.

"We do love to smoke, so, anytime to need testers…." I giggled. He broke off half of the giant piece, and stuff it into a shoe box. He smiled, and passed the box to me, my eyes wide.

"For you. Sell it. Smoke it. It's yours. Need more?" He put his hand on my shoulder. "Just ask." I exited Donovan's house feeling powerful, and on a mission. I wanted my husband more than ever, and had enough time to go meet him at work. I hopped in the car, and hid the shoe box underneath my seats. There was a sudden knock on the window, and Sean stood outside. I rolled it down half-way.

"I'm back on the road for a bit, and I leave tomorrow night. Gabe wanted to have Delaney and me over for dinner tomorrow. I understand if you don't." I smiled at him.

"Stop. Of course we'll do dinner. Sounds great. I'll see you then, fully clothed." I winked, and backed out of the driveway. I loved the convenience of my jobs, as they were all quite close together. When I pulled into the Phoenix's parking lot, I took the front spot. The lot was pretty full, and it was good to see that business was flowing again.

Walking in to the store, you were always hit with a smell of chemicals, paints, varnishes, and flowers. It was the strangest, most welcome smell I'd ever remembered. Just stepping through the doors sent off a flood of emotions and thoughts. I walked through the isles, getting blankly smiled at by new employees. Some brunette smiled extra wide at me, and I noticed her polo was unbuttoned past her cleavage line. *Oh hell no she doesn't...* I walked into the back, and Gabe was sitting in his office. He looked up slowly when the doors crashed together, and his face lit up when he saw me.

He quickly came over to me, beaming the entire way. I hadn't surprised him at work for quite some time, and I knew that he already knew what I needed. His arms around me in a second, and his mouth dropped to meet mine in a passionate kiss. When I opened my eyes, that brunette was staring at us, mouth wide open. *She may actually be glaring, there Janes.*

"This is my wife, Janie," he motioned to me. "This is Audrey Schwartz. She started here a few days ago as my secretary, essentially." He smiled, and raised an eyebrow at me so she couldn't see.

196

Fully understanding his quiet message, I turned to her, and extended my hand.

"Hello, Audrey. It's nice to meet you." I glared into her eyes, as if staking my undying claim to this man. "I'm here to pick up my husband for a surprise sex- oh, I mean surprise date." I turned towards Gabe, who was now holding in laughter at my behavior.

"Sounds lovely, baby." His voice grew hoarse. "Let me get my coat." I nodded, and turned away from her. I could read all over her face what she had hoped would happen with him. Seeing how he reacted to her eased my mind. *Not in this lifetime, skanky bitch.*

He climbed into my Jeep, and I locked the doors behind him. I smiled big, and bent over the backseat. I purposefully shoved my ass into his face while I pulled out the shoe box. He looked confused.

"I got you a present." I handed him the box, then pretended to take it back. "Now, some people may be offended by a gift like this. But, I know that you, or I, would indeed love it." I giggled, and he pulled the box from me, all but ripping the lid off. His eyes grew huge, and his head snapped back to me.

"Where in the hell?!" he was almost breathless. "How much was this?!" close to panicking. My eyebrows raised high, and I quickly leaned over and covered his babbling lips with my own. Taking his breath away, I dipped my tongue in a few times.

"Relax, Gabe. It's from Donovan, for us both." I smirked at him, and he laughed. "You should've seen the choices..." my eyes grew to pancake size.

197

"Okay then. That's fucking awesome." He pulled me into a kiss, and closed the box. "Put this away now please." I took the box, and bent backward over the seat again to hide the box. His hand slid under my skirt, to the silky material covering my ass. I slowly slid back into my seat, and our heated eyes met. "How long do we have here, love?" his voice was dark. Checking the time, it was now 1:46pm.

"We've got 2 hours." I said breathlessly, looking to him for what he wanted to do.

"Ok, I've got an idea… if you're up for something… old." I raised an eyebrow at him, and nodded. He programmed my GPS quickly without speaking, and turned on the radio. "Alright, let's go." He smiled, and I left the Phoenix's parking lot.

~29~

When I turned down the road, I instantly recognized where we were going. It had been, maybe, five years since we had even driven down here for memories. My belly turned, and the butterflies flew rampant. *And now you're here for pleasure…* I closed in on the small parking lot, where everybody and their brother always went to screw, and found my old hidden spot. When I was a teenager, I had found a secret, more hidden place between some groups of trees. Although it was now a tad overgrown, it was nothing the Jeep couldn't handle. I pulled past, threw it in reverse, and backed into the tree branched cave.

Turning it off, and turning on the radio, we sat back in our seats for a moment, taking it all in. I eyed him over my sunglasses, and he unfastened his seatbelt. I popped the arm rests up to the middle, giving us free reign of the front seats. I climbed into his lap, and left my feet in the driver's side seat. My fingers trailed down his sideburns, and his cheek.

"Good idea," I whispered. "Brings back some good memories." His eyes traced my face, searching everywhere, and he nodded. I wondered what he was looking for, because I was right here, more than ready. I covered his lips with mine, stealing his breath away. His hands and arms surrounded me, and wrapped me safely. I unbuttoned my blouse while leaning back on the dashboard, and he hungrily slid his pants down. I pulled the skirt up around my waist, revealing the deep color of my lingerie, and cute little bows. His hands trailed around the lingerie, stopping to feel some of the tiny bows.

"Best lunch I've had in week's, baby," he chuckled, and grasped my breasts tightly through the silky fabric. He pushed his hardening crotch into my now soaking panties. Sliding my panties to the side, he probed into me with his fingers, and I moaned. I wrapped my arms around his neck, and held on while he pushed and pulled his fingers around inside me, hitting nearly every nerve.

My legs were spread apart, and I couldn't close them the way we were sitting, forcing me to take in all the pleasure, constantly. My body started to clench, and I could feel the rush of wetness.

"Oh baby," his fingers dug deeper into me, causing even deeper, darker moans. He slid his fingers out, and I panted, hoping he would take me without thought. Wrapping his fingers around himself, he pushed himself up to my entrance, and I dropped on to his thick shaft. I held his shoulders as I pushed myself up and down on him, relishing in every throb, pulse, and inch. *MMMmmm...because*

199

he offers so many... My head fell back, and he drove into me deeply.

His palm splayed out on my chest, in between my bouncing breasts. I sat down hard on to him, creating the deepest, skin to skin contact we had yet today. I swore I could feel him pressing into my rib cage. I compressed around him again, this time forcing the orgasm to stay. I could feel my muscles squeezing his thickness, making it harder for him to push through, and instead taking all of the feeling of each hot hug. I leaned back into his neck, and nibbled on his earlobe. His thrusts into me turned ravenous, and greedy. I let go of him, and leaned my elbows back on the dash. This provided a perfect view of him taking complete advantage of me. *Of his wife.*

The look in his eyes changed, and the beads of sweat appeared. His fingers constricted my flesh even tighter, only making my clenching even stronger around his cock. His thrusting slowed, so I picked up the pace. Grinding down his shaft until his breath stopped, and his hips began pumping into me, releasing his hot load. I could feel each pulse, and subsequent eruption.

Leaning back to his chest, I rested my head on his shoulder, riding out the waves of pleasure pulsating through him. I checked the clock over his shoulder. It was 3:26. I used his shoulders to help slide myself off of him, and he helped me sit back down in the driver's seat. Glancing at him, I saw the smirk on his lips. I leaned into him, and smothered him in a passionate kiss. *Get him, girl.*

"Jesus," he sighed. "I love you so fucking much. My dreams have come true!" he fanned his forehead with his hand jokingly, and squeezed my hand. I smiled, and fastened the last buttons on my blouse. Turning the ignition key, the Jeep roared to life.

"I love you too, baby." I threw it into drive, and stomped on the gas. Bouncing out of the trees and over-brush, she steadied, and rolled down the road smoothly. I put my hand on his knee, and cranked up the music. We both rode in the silence, and heavy love of the moment. When I pulled into the Phoenix's lot, the cars had emptied a bit. He leaned towards my face, and I met him in the middle.

"You're back to work safely, sir." I smiled, and kissed his lips. His blue eyes peered deeply into my own, and I took a mental picture of those beautiful things for my permanent brain file.

"Thank you, baby." His kissed me back. "I"ll call you this evening once I'm finished with the rep." He smiled into my lips, and kissed them again. He was out of the car before I knew it, and I was heading towards Bare Luck, to meet my new client. I couldn't help the thoughts through my head. *What a day this has been. Feeling good? I feel like you've reestablished your boundaries today. I'm happy to see you're back.* I giggled at myself as I pulled into the lot, and parked.

I took note of the new blue Ford 350 also parked outside of Bare Luck. I grabbed my planner, and left my folders in my briefcase. I texted Gabe before I went in, because I couldn't get him off of my mind.

Minutes after dropping you off, I've arrived at Bare Luck. I cannot wait until later. I love you so much… XO

I smiled, and locked my car. Opening the

201

door of the establishment, I was hit with a rush of potpourri, incense, and a heavy construction smell. The store was basic with, a small waiting area, chairs for clients, display cases, and what looked like hallways with small rooms attached. Seemed pretty close to the cosmetic surgical and massage store the security team had researched about. The walls had some artwork on them, and there were lights on in the back. I peeked around the doors, and saw a lot of boxes and inventory.

"Hello?" I yelled through the back stock room. I didn't see any movement, but moments later, I voice came from nowhere.

"Back here!" the voice yelled. *This must be Shy.* As I stepped into the back, my phone buzzed. I pulled it out, and stopped to check it. *Gabe.*

You are my life. Rep's here now. Won't be so late.

I checked around me, and no one was there. I quickly typed my response, and hit send.
Meeting Shy to sign papers now. Should be literally twenty minutes. Meet you in bed.

"Hello?" I asked again, as I stepped through the curtain door. My eyes flashed around me when I saw what I had walked into. There was a medical chair in the middle, and cuffs hanging from the walls. There was a table full of... *tools?* I tried to look more closely, and now they looked more sexual. Looking around, this looked like an insane set up. I heard a creek, and turned around. Suddenly, I couldn't breathe.

The Visitor. He was standing feet away from

202

me, across the room. His arms were crossed, and his head tipped slowly to the side.

"Janie…" his voice made me feel ill. He lurked around the other side of the room in the dark corners. I moved away from him with each step he took towards me. We walked around the medical chair a few times, almost in a slow, stalking dance. I couldn't breathe, and I just wanted Gabe. "You can't get away from me now. And I think you know that." A tear fell down my cheek. *Holy shit. I'm dead.*

"Who-who are you?" I stumbled over a cord. I quickly looked up, and met his darkened face. "Why are you doing this?" I waited, and tried to collect myself. The mere thought of being trapped with a man, again, brought everything right back. I swallowed hard, trying to stay calm.

"I can't believe you haven't figured it out yet. Christ, Janie. I've all but told you. Showed you, even." His voice sounded frustrated, and angry. *Just keep him talking. Remember? Michael would just talk and talk and talk..* He paced back and forth, but stayed on the opposite side of the room. "All these years, you know, and you're still making shit choices. For someone so beautiful," he paused. *He thinks you're beautiful? What the hell?* "You're just plain stupid sometimes. For instance," he stepped half into the light, and threw a handful of pictures onto the medical chair. He stepped away once they landed, and I cautiously stepped to look at them. *Oh my God.*

There were dozens of pictures of me. *Everywhere.* Pictures of me and the kids. Of Gabe and I. Of all of our friends sitting around our bonfire… *the hot tub party! What the fuck?!* I looked up to see his bright smile, again outlined by firelight. I couldn't take my eyes away from the pictures, and pushed more off of the chair. I lost my breath now seeing myself splayed over Donovan's counter, and in my own bed, spread for my husband. My heart sank into my heels, and tears sprung to my eyes.

"You've been following me? I don't understand." I stepped away from the chair, and back towards some large tool storage bins. He strolled back and forth again in the darkness. I could see him putting his hands to his face, and back to his sides frantically. He suddenly stopped, and I could see his feet turn towards me in the half light. He stepped forward one small step at a time, coming to the medical chair in the middle.

"I've been desperate for you for almost ten years. I've waited," he took another step. "And I've waited. I'm done waiting." He stopped, with the light revealing him up to his chest. My heart was beating out of control, and I couldn't breathe. "I've watched you give yourself freely to these… these…" his voice became enraged. "Strangers!!!" He slammed his fist on to the chair, and I instinctively turned my face away. "I've helped you, been there for you. And what have you done for me? Tell me, Janes." I swallowed, and froze. *Tell me, Janes. Tell me, Janes. Oh my God…* I turned my head slowly, still cowering in a defensive position. Tears fell freely from my eyes, and I could make no sound. I was right.

Simon. In the blink of an eye, our entire friendship flashed before my eyes. Were the things that he said true? Had I taken advantage of him? My hand clasped over my mouth, and I gasped for air.

"Yeah, it hit me like that when I realized all of it, too." He chuckled. And stepped towards me. I couldn't breathe. I couldn't move. My old friend. My confidant. *Now what? What does he want?* He grabbed my arm, and I did little to fight him. I couldn't wrap my head around this. "It's my turn now." He said idly, as he pushed his gun barrel into my hip.

I looked down, confirming that his Colt was pressed into me. A sob escaped my lips. I quickly sucked it in, and looked him dead in his eyes. There was nothing. No friend. No past. Only something terrible, and hungry. My stomach began to heave, and I couldn't control the gagging. The thoughts of the inevitable were setting in, and I wasn't sure I could go through all of it again. I wasn't sure he would let me live.

"Simon," I sucked in a breath for control. Clearing my throat, I pressed on. "Please, please help me understand this. I think that's fair to ask." I swallowed hard, and he watched the lump roll down my throat. He leaned into me, smelling my hair. Reflexively, I pulled away.

"That. Your reaction, that's exactly what. The thought me of disgusts you… like that." He looked at his hands. "I'm tired of not being good enough." The voice almost jumped out of my body. *WHAT?!*

"Simon! It's not that way between us! I didn't ever find you attractive because you were my best friend! My brother!" I screamed in his face, with tears streaming down my face. I was angry, because this was not fair. "You left me! You moved away, and stopped talking to both Gabe and I." I tried to pull away from him, and he only clung tighter. His jaw clenched, and his eyes squinted, and then pierced into me.

"None of that matters. Not now." He

smirked, and I heard another noise behind me. I turned suddenly, to be thrown into the arms of another man. And I knew him. *Cain Comaro.*

"What the fuck?! Get away from me!" I screamed, and clawed at his face. In a moment, everything went black. Nothing was everywhere around me, and it was heavy. I could feel pulling, but couldn't hear or see anything but black. I gave up, and fell into the blackness.

~

I heard their voices, and I was instantly afraid to open my eyes. Parting my lips to take a breath, I could taste the iron on my lips. *Blood. Oh, fuck.* I dare not move, as they were close. Cain and I had only ever met once or twice, and that was early on in Michael and I's relationship. He was his younger brother, by quite a few years. He was always a sweet kid. And Simon… oh my God if I survive this.

My head instantly flashed of Gabe. Then Lilah, and Galen. My parents. My friends. Greg, and his beating to protect us. *Don't give up Janie.* Just hold on a bit longer.
Maybe if I just do what they want me to do. Or pay them? I didn't know what to do. Listening to them talk, they didn't either.

"Look at her, I'm going to take her first." There was laughter, but I couldn't tell who was saying what. Shuffling, and banging around.

"You'd better get on it then. You're not going to have long. The Detectives will be all over this." *See? Even they know they won't have long. You can do this. Breathe.* I tried to lay calmly, but suddenly had to cough. Uncontrollably, unstoppable. Both men appeared at my sides, and I noted that I was tied and restrained in the medical chair. Both stood and watched me choking on my cough, gasping for air. Moments later, I regained control of my heaving chest, and quieted my cough.

"Well, now that you're awake, and with us," Simon started. "I should fill you in on a few things about our little arrangement here." I nodded, and swallowed. "Those pictures you saw earlier? I've delivered those to your husband, your best friend, and your top client, Mr. James, by courier, this evening." My mouth fell open, and tears poured from my eyes. My lips quivered, and I wanted to curl up and die. I looked at Simon's face, and his smile told me what I needed to know.

"Lift your ass," Cain commanded next to my right side. I didn't move, and looked at him with tears pouring from my eyes. "I said, lift your ass, bitch." I swallowed, and stayed still. In a second, his hand crashed across the side of my face, knocking my head to my shoulder. The pain was immense, and my head instantly ached. "Now, do I need to do that again? Or will you lift your mother fucking ass?" his voice stern.

I lifted myself up as much as I could, and he slid my skirt down to my cuffed ankles. He slid a knife down the front of my blouse, popping all the buttons off. He slid one side open at a time, and inhaled with the reveal of what was underneath. Oh how I wished I had not worn this lingerie today. He trailed his knife down my chest, stopping just under my belly button. "If you fail to listen to me, I'll cut you," he pushed the knife in a bit, and my breath stopped. "Here, first." I nodded, and stared into his cold eyes.

He grabbed at my panties with his hand, and

pulled them straight off. The rubber band caught my skin, and tore it a little. Blood dripped down my hip. He stood before me, and unbuttoned his pants. I swallowed, fully knowing what was going to happen. *I just hope this is all he's planning to do...* He and Michael had different fathers, from his mother's indiscretion, so the resemblance was not too familiar. His temper, however, was exactly as I remembered Michael's to be.

"Spread open, now." He stood before me, pumping his thin, smallish looking penis. "This is for Michael." He smiled, and stepped up to force it in. And force it in he did. My body wanted nothing to do with him, but forced to be spread open in an old gyno chair did not help the cause. I refused to let myself focus on what was happening, and instead tried to focus on the outcome. I felt him push into me, but not much other than that. I was numb. I could not feel this, any of it. *Motherfucker, you can't break me.* I stared directly at his face while he raped me.

His moans and disgusting grunts told me it was almost over, and I was excited about that. I turned away from him, and stared blankly at the floor next to me. His pumps grew forceful, although I could not feel his miniscule dick.

"Look at me bitch! Know who's fucking you right now!" I shook my head, and laughed. When I met his eye, he was angry. He punched the side of my eye, knocking me into my shoulder again. I felt his release, and he quickly made it known. "See, that's for my brother, you dumb bitch. I promised him I'd give it to you, and make you remember him." I laughed again.

"You're so stupid, and you have a tiny dick." He screamed in my face, and punched my stomach. I absorbed the entire punch, and being strapped down, I couldn't protect myself.

"Fuck you! Simon! Get your bitch!" he motioned to the corner, and Simon stepped out, laughing to himself. He stepped towards me, and stood in between my spread legs. Looking around, he wrinkled his face.

"I had no idea you'd be so... messy...Cain." He groaned, and reached for a box of baby wipes.

"I'll go watch the doors." Cain said, as he took off to the front of the store. Simon came back to me, and began wiping me off with the wipes. *Cleaning Cain off of you.* I watched him cautiously, as his face told me of his unpredictability. A few wipes later, he stepped back to admire his handy work.

"Now you're ready for me." He smiled, and looked back to my eyes. I hadn't seen a look like that for 8 years, and I had wished that I'd never see it again. I was looking into the eyes of the devil now, and I knew I was going to pay for whatever I had done. I knew I only had this one last chance to even attempt to save myself. Over his shoulder, I saw a digital clock. It was already 9pm. Surely Gabe had figured out something wasn't right. *But those pictures...* Someone would still care...they had to.

~30~

"Simon," I shifted in the chair. "Please talk to me. I don't understand why you're doing this. I never knew you had feelings like that back in the day." He paused, and shook his head. "You were friends with both of us, and you never seemed to have a problem with it." Blood dripped into my eye,

209

and it burned a bit. I squinted my eyes together, to try and prevent the blood from flowing in again. His hands were on me suddenly, wiping the blood off of my face. I pulled away from him.

"Well, you want the blood in your eye?" He made a tsk-tsk sound with his mouth. His hand dropped to my chest, and he ran his finger over my breast. My breath hitched. "What do you think all your friends think of your photos right now?" Horrified. I wanted to scream, and kill this man.

~

The phone rang at 8:30, while Gabe paced the house, waiting to hear from her. He had dinner with his mom and the kids, and had planned to surprise her when she got home. Trouble was, she never came home, and it was now hours later.

"Hello?" his voice was heavy, and full of anxiety.

"Mr. Lazarus, this is Donovan James." There was a long pause on the phone, and Gabe instantly knew who it was.

"Hello, Mr. James. What can I do for you? Janie's not here-" Donovan cut him off.

"No time for small talk. Have you checked your porch? Found the envelope yet?" His breath was lost, and suddenly it felt like someone was squeezing his chest. "I can tell that's a no. Listen, you're going to find one of these envelopes. I know because both Sean and I got one, too." He sighed into the receiver, and Gabe found it impossible to move. He couldn't speak, he could only listen. "You're going to find out some terrible things in these pictures, and we will deal with that. But now..."

"Where's my wife?" he said blankly. He heard Donovan swallowed hard, and his heart froze.

"Someone's got her. The note says, "Time for the truth to come out. It's my turn." I don't know what to do. I'm heading to your place now, and Sean is out combing the area." Gabe's heart started beating frantically, but he knew what to do.

"I'll see you when you get here. No one is going to hurt her." He hung up the phone, and raced to the front porch. Opening the door and racing out, he instantly saw the manila envelope placed perfectly on the porch chair. He snatched it, and ripped it open. Pulling out the contents, he was perplexed.

The first were of his family at their house, doing random things. Flipping through, he found some were of himself and Janie in the throes of passion. Seeing they were taken through the windows of their own home made his blood boil. Turning them again, he now found a picture of Janie and Donovan. He studied this picture, and the one after. One of her straddling a chair, and him masturbating in a nearby chair. One of her on the counter, with him feet away again. Bile rose in his throat, and he pulled out his cell phone.

"Detective, it's Gabe Lazarus." He steadily controlled his breathing. "Someone's got my wife." He looked down again to the pictures, turning the pile once again. Now there was a picture of the backyard party. A close up of he and Janie in the hot tub, with Sean feet behind. The look on his face caught Gabe's eye, and he closed his eyes as if in pain. "Yes, I'm here. Okay. Her last known whereabouts?" His head rushed with thoughts of the afternoon. Suddenly, he remembered. She had texted him and said where she was. "One second

Brian, I've got a text."

"Okay, Gabe. Calmly, brother. She's a feisty one."

Flipping it open, and to her text, he read it aloud.

"She's at the Bare Luck, meeting someone named "Shy," to sign new client paperwork." He paused, and rifled through the photos. "You should know, whoever has her left photos with myself, Donovan James, and Sean Westing. The photos are…very bad." He cleared his throat.

"Ok, brother. Have you been in contact with any of those men tonight?" he could hear the Detective typing frantically.

"Yes, Donovan is on his way here, and he said Sean is out searching for my wife." He heard a noise behind him, and found Donovan tapping on the window glass. He motioned for him to come in. "He is here now."

"Ok, I'll come and pick you up. I'm dispatching units to the location she last texted you at, and I'll ping her cell phone. Keep breathing, I'll see you soon." He hung up, and turned towards Donovan. He stormed towards him, stopping mere inches from his face.

"What the fuck is going on? These pictures?!" His blood pressure sky rocketed, and he envisioned himself killing James, and hiding the body. James swallowed, and looked at the pictures he held. Tears welded in his eyes, and he lowered his head.

"Fuck, Gabe, I'm so sorry." He looked back up to him, and Gabe saw the sheer emotion on his face. He took a step back from him. "Janie's been cleaning my house nude. For weeks. Sean's known about it, and was there twice." He put his hands up as if giving up. "Nothing like this should've happened. Our deal is a hands off, eyes only sort of thing. I don't know who's doing this." His lips twitched.

"You were fucking my wife?" his voice hitched, and cracked. He thought of the past, and everything they had been through. Now she wasn't even here to explain herself, and she may never be again. James' head shook frantically in front of him.

"No, I can one hundred percent tell you we have never had sex." There was no question or hesitation in his voice, and Gabe was satisfied. He swallowed, flipping through the pictures again, and focusing his thoughts.

"Why would Sean get an envelope?" He clenched his jaws together.

"Sean and Janie…" he motioned for him to hurry up with his hands. "They've got an odd history." Growing exasperated with Donovan's explanation, Gabe stepped forward, invading his personal space again.

"Just be honest. I want her back. Alive." He spoke in an angry whisper. Donovan swallowed.

"Sean came over once while she was cleaning, and doing her thing. He couldn't take his eyes off of her, or his hands. This was before your backyard party, and then this morning at my house, she told him it was a huge mistake." Gabe closed his eyes, and sat on the couch for a moment, collecting himself. He couldn't help but think of how he put her on display that night…after that had happened. Donovan sat next to him, slowly. "Listen, she's a wonderful woman. I am truly sorry about my part in this." As they both turned to see the headlights pull into the driveway, they both rushed outside.

~

"I don't care about the photos, Simon. I just want to go be with my kids, and my husband." The tears were streaming down my cheeks. Nothing was helping. He started to walk away, to the small counter near the wall. He turned around, and had what looked like nipple clamps in his hands. *What the fuck?* "What are you doing?" I asked flatly.

"Oh, you know. I've got a small list." He smiled widely, and stepped in between my legs. His hands came close to my throat, and I gasped and turned away. They stopped on the top of my lingerie, and quickly ripped it apart. Now I lay spread, completely naked, shriving from the stress and cold.

His eyes lit up with fire, as he gazed down my naked body. He rubbed his belly, and down the front of his pants. I could see the front fabric twitching, with the blood rushing to his weapon. His hand touched my shoulder, and then down to my breasts. Lingering for moments, he quickly grasped my right breast, and slammed the clamp onto my nipple. The electric pulses it sent through my body were confusing, and painful.

"Please stop this," my thoughts were lost. *Think of something!* His hand grasped my left breast, and he repeated the same torturous procedure. The metal bit into my nipple, and I was sure they were going to come off. Wincing, I remembered the times that Gabe has used the clamps on me. Sniffling through the tears, I tried to focus my thoughts on him. *"Easy baby, just be calm. If you're tense, it's going to burn."* God, how right was he! My nipples are on fire! I wanted to

214

scream.

He didn't stop, only continued what appeared to be a long, drawn out torture setup. He walked back to the counter, now humming a tune. I tried to focus on what the tune was, but I couldn't place it. He turned back to me, and had a Wattenberg's wheel in his hand. This was not something I was familiar with, and I'm not sure I wanted to try it out. Approaching me slowly, he again stepped in between my legs. He held up the wheel, and spun the tiny sharp points around. My eyes grew large, and his hand began to low to my abdomen.

The wheel pressed into my flesh, and it stung. He drove the wheel around on my flesh, leaving a trail of red scratches and blood dots on my chest. Parts almost tickled on my abdomen, and my chest was numb from the clamps. *Suddenly thankful for those, I think.* I gritted my eyes closed again, and tried to look away. His hand came up to my face, and forced me to face him again.

"Don't look away from me. I want to know how I affect you." Every time he spoke, I lost a little of our good past. He turned away from me, yet again, and returned with another odd sexual device. Now it was a large plug. *Oh fuck no.*

"Please don't...Simon..." I begged. There was that flicker of flame in his eyes that seemed to reignite with my every whimper, and cry of pain. *Turn off the emotion! It's only making him do it more!* How could I do that? So simply? God, I just wanted my husband. *Where is everyone?* Inside my head, I started to panic.

~

215

Climbing into The Detective's 4x4, Gabe could only hope. He was upset that she didn't tell him just how she was serving her clients, but he hadn't want her to hurt, or suffer for the poor choices. He just wanted her back, so he could talk it out with her. He was disgusted with Sean, and knew there had to be more to the story with him. Looking up, the scenery flashed by them, as the Detective drove fast with lights and sirens blaring.

"Gabriel, I'll do anything I can to help you. To help her." He nodded, and gave a stern look back to Donovan.

"I appreciate it. It's hard to be angry about all of this, when now my reason for living is in trouble." He paused. "Thank you for the explanation of the photos. It helps to know that you were never closer than the pictures showed." He turned away from Donovan, and looked out the window. Donovan put his head in his hands, momentarily, knowing he has just told half-truths to Gabe. He sighed heavily, and leaned his head against the window.

"Gabe, we're almost to the location. We've discovered that there are two unidentified subjects vehicles parked outside the establishment." He paused, and looked in the rearview towards Gabe. "This building is under construction, and will soon be a speedy medical service. So, whoever this is, has lead her on from the beginning." Pulling into the parking lot, Gabe saw Janie's Jeep parked in front, next to a large truck.

"Ok, what's the plan?" Gabe asked the Detective. Simultaneously, 10 more police cars and the SWAT vehicles pulled silently into the lot. Surrounding the entire building, showing their force. His hand instantly covered his mouth. The

Detective turned in his seat, unlocking the doors.

"Please follow me to the safe zone, and we'll go over the plan there." They nodded at each other, and carefully exited the vehicle. Gabe turned around slightly as he passed, and noticed two SWAT officers approaching the Jeep, and opening the back hatch. They climbed in, and he craned his head to look further. Detective Gustovson's arm was suddenly around him, guiding him into the safe zone.

"I know this has to be hard," he kept him walking. "They're pulling out some of what the robot showed was inside the Jeep. They're just being cautious, as they found another car in the back of the building." His forehead wrinkled, and he looked back to the Detective with confusion.

~31~

He placed the plug directly outside my rear, and let it dance around the area. There was nothing I could do. I had no other way to cover or protect myself from this happening. I swallowed hard, and silently stared him in the eye.

"Why're you being so quiet?" he poked me in the gut with his finger. I didn't react as he would like, so he changed tactics. "How about this, then?" He paused, and pressed the plug hard into me.

"NOOOO!" I screamed. The plug was huge, and my body was not anywhere near ready for an intrusion like this. I tried to wiggle, desperately pulling at the straps holding me to the chair.

"Ahh, I knew you were still paying attention. Hard not to, huh?" He smiled, and leaned in to kiss my breast. He trailed his tongue around my entire abdomen, never stopping. Suddenly, Cain came barging back into the room. He was frenzied and angry.

"Mother fuckers! The police are outside, and it's like they brought fucking reinforcements! What the fuck should I do?!" he was screaming at Simon. Calmly, Simon smiled, and winked at me.

"Calm down, now. It's going to take them quite a while to form a plan, as they have no idea where Janie is inside of this building. You've had your fun, now let me have mine. We'll stick to the plan, alright?" Cain ground his lips together, and clenched his fists. "Just go back and hold your post. Let me know if they move to the doors." He smiled, and motioned for Cain to leave.

Turning back towards me, he leaned in towards my face. I stopped breathing, and pulled my head back as far as I could. *There's just no escaping.*

"Where was I?" He tapped his chin, as if thinking, and then thrust his fingers inside of me. The sheer force felt like it had ripped me apart. He moaned in his throat, and leaned into me again. "I'm going to have you over and over and over… But…" he trailed off, and kneeled between my legs. "Let's make things slide easier for all of us, okay?" he smiled deviously, and dipped his head into my core.

His tongue was hard, and forceful. My body was defying me, and responding in all the wrong ways. I couldn't get away from him, and had to absorb all of the feelings. Lapping at my folds, probing inside of me, he was rubbing himself all over me. He stood suddenly, and his hands dove for the button on his pants.

My heart stopped as I watched the scenario

218

unfold before my eyes. As if it were in slow motion, his pants fell to the floor, exposing his very hard weapon. I swallowed hard, knowing he was not going to be taking gentle care of me. *Jesus Christ...* Within seconds, he had sunken into me, and was hammering away. My body rejected every inch of him, and I hated that I couldn't fight anywhere near fairly.

I cried out in pain, and anger, as he pushed into me over and over. I turned my head away, and closed my eyes. His hands surround my head, and turned me back to look at him.

"I don't want to fucking look at you, you piece of shit!" I screamed, and spit in his face. He pulled back a bit, and cocked a crooked smile at me. Raring back, his right hand struck my head, and the room went black.

~

"Who the fuck is it?" Gabe stopped dead in his tracks, and demanded the answer. Donovan came to his side. The Detective swallowed hard, and ran his hand through his hair. Officer Zaidi appeared by his side with a roll of blue prints. She nodded at Gabe, and continued to the safe zone. Brian put his hand out, motioning Gabe to stay calm, and Gabe released a cleansing breath.

"It's registered to Cain Comaro." He said flatly, as Gabe's faced immediately turned eighty seven shades of red. "I know. I think you'll appreciate this one even more though." He looked up from the folder that the Officer had just delivered. "This truck is registered to a Simon Knight." His memory instantly jogged back to the old days of the Phoenix, and working closely with

Simon.

"I use to work with a Simon at the Phoenix, but I'm not sure of what his last name was. Do you have a picture of him?" He wore his worry on his face now, and anyone could see it. The Detective nodded, and pulled out a piece of paper.

"This is him, in a recent mug shot." He held up the paper, and Gabe fell back a few steps. Donovan quickly threw out his arms, and caught him mid-stumble. Swallowing hard, and snatching the picture, he looked even closer. While he looked, the Detective and Donovan pulled him to the safe zone, to begin the discussion on the plan.

His hair was still blonde, and he looked a little chubbier than he had been. His teeth were crooked, and his eyes were piercing. Tears sprung to his eyes, and he nodded at the Detective.

"That's definitely him. We worked with him. He was one of her best friends." He shook his head, and started heaving. Steadying himself on his knees, he breathed in and out slowly. Slowly pulling himself to stand, Gabe crossed his arms tightly over his chest. "And now he's working with Michael's brother." The Detective nodded.

"Pretty disgusting." He said, opening up the blueprints of the building for the group to see. "Here's the blue prints. From what they've seen with the window cameras, no one is in the front area, or the very rear of the place. That leaves here, to here." He paused, and pointed out the area in the middle, near some of the office rooms. A big, burly officer with a vest marked 'SWAT' approached the table, and put down his weapon.

"I'd like to create a diversion in the front, and sneak in through the back. Or the roof, if there's an entry point." He bent, and checked the blue prints. "Ah, yeah, here." He pointed to a large vent on the roof.

"That will do just fine, except what if it's rigged? Or if there's a bomb?" Everyone froze. "I don't mean to alarm anyone, but at the Lazarus home days ago, this same person attempted to blow up their outdoor shed." The Detective spoke the truth, and everyone did need to be cautious. "We don't want her in any extra danger." Gabe felt his phone buzz.

Pulling it out of his pocket, he looked down to find a text from Sean. Reading it, he decided he should be reading it a loud. He raised his hand, and the group turned to him.

G, I'm coming to the Cove Plaza. I've got Michael's mom with me, hoping to talk her son out of this. Gabe, they want to kill her. Michael told his mother this at their weekly jail visit, and she didn't believe it. There in 10.

He swallowed, and coughed. Choking on a dry cough, he stopped and thought of Janie, and all the coughing she's done over the years since Michael first hurt her years ago. He closed his eyes, and rested his arms on his head. Walking away from the group, he needed a minute to compose himself. Facing the mother of the devil that first broke his wife would take patience. Not killing the motherfuckers inside this building after this was now next to impossible to promise. He turned around again to see the headlights of Sean's Hummer pull into the lot.

"That's Sean Westing, Detective." He nodded in the direction of the car. Everyone motioned for the car to park, and went to meet the new bodies.

~

I woke up slowly, to the feeling of extreme warmth all over my body. Once I could muster opening my eyes, I ripped them open to find hot wax all over my body. Still being poured on. *Oh my God...just breathe through the pain, Janie. You can do this.* I looked at his face, and it was devilish. He poured it on my shoulders, and it was scalding hot. I could smell the hairs and parts of my skin burning off my body. Looking down at my legs, I could see the hardened wax all over, and the intense red and peeling blisters underneath. I was thankful that my body was going more and more numb by the minute.

"Took forever to wake you up. I thought you had left us." He joked. Still dripping the wax on me. Now on to my legs.

"Please stop, Simon." I shook my head weakly. "This is so stupid. You think you're not surrounded right now? That's a joke." I swallowed hard, and rolled my head around to hold up in front of him. "See, those pictures are just going to infuriate all the men in my life. And as you can see, and have pointed out...there are a few." I coughed, and blood came out of my mouth.

"Settle down, you're getting all worked up." He stood up, and picked up his bucket of wax, returning it to the warmer it had been on. "Now that you're awake, I'll resume." He stepped in between my legs, and dropped his pants once again. He palmed his weapon harshly, and smacked my core with it. He pushed through me again, searching for something that he wasn't going to find.

I lay limp on the medical chair, numb to every feeling. My mind reeling with thoughts of the past, and of the future. I turned to stare at him. *God, what is the fucking point of this? What's he going to gain?* I tried to search his eyes, or his face for something. This was not the Simon that had been there for me. This was not the man that stood up for me, and by me as my friend. I looked him up and down. *Disgusting.*

His body smelled of pine, and his hair was blonde. *Just like Michael.* His words were filling, caring, and supportive. But his plans were devious, and he resented the good. His body was larger, even more so than when we worked together. His attitude seemed to tell that he felt everyone owed him something. I could indeed see why his life had gone the way it had, and why no one wanted anything to do with him. *Keep your head about you Janie. Gabe will save you one way or another.*

Another thrust inside me, and I thought I'd kill him with my scream. Suddenly, Cain reappeared in the doorway, out of breath.

"Uh, Simon? They're everywhere. They've taken their places around the building, and SWAT has moved in. It's not going to be long now until they make a move. What should I do?" He paced around, looking behind him, and all around him. Simon pulled out again, and looked down to me angrily.

"This had better be for real. Every time I try and get my turn in, some shit happens." He grunted and groaned, and followed Cain out to the front area. I quickly looked around to get a better sense of my surroundings. The first time I had been alone, awake, and ready to be out of this fuck hole. There was no way I could get out of the straps I was in. I would need another person, without a doubt. Frowning, I sat back in the chair, discouraged.

I heard something loud above my head, and looked up to find a large register vent of some sort. I could feel the air pumping out of it, and figured it must have been the heater kicking on. I sighed again, wishing for a miracle. I heard them coming back, quickly towards me.

"Just leave me be. I'm finishing my turn before we act. They'll get a phone in here to us soon…I can feel it." He turned, and Cain opened his mouth to speak. Instantly, Simon's hand covered his mouth. "No! I've waited for eight fucking years for this, and I'm fucking taking what I want. That was the WHOLE point!" He pointed Cain out of the room, and Cain eerily grinned at me as he left. I swallowed hard, as Simon turned back to me.

"Ah, now we're alone again." His pants dropped on the floor, and he stepped up to me. Looking intensely at my core, I felt so vulnerable. His hands clamped down on my breast, and he sunk back into the pounding of my insides. Forgetting what was happening was impossible. There was no other noise in the room but that of the sounds of sex, my crying, and his heavy breathing. No solace. No love. No help. *Oh, Janie…keep going, girl. Think of everyone who needs you… Hold on…*

I toyed around with passing out again, but stopped when I heard the noise again above me. This time I could not turn and look, or Simon would know something was up. Instead I closed my eyes, and focused on every detail of the sounds I heard above me. Through the vent, I heard a rubbing sound. *Oh, God please let this be my help. I don't think I can take this much longer.*

224

~

Sean approached the safe zone slowly, hands in the air. Michael's mother, Martha Comaro, walked closely behind him. She was wiping her eyes, and looked like she was very upset. They both approached Gabe, Donovan, and the Detective. Sean took an extra step towards Gabe, and Gabe shook his head.

"I'm sorrier than you know right now. I know I fucked things up." He gritted his teeth, and Gabe nodded. "I seriously over-stepped the boundaries, and I know I've hurt people. You're both two of my best friends-" Gabe cut him off.

"We'll talk after this is done. I just want my wife right now." He looked over Sean's shoulder, to Martha. She stepped up to Gabe, and smiled, extending her hand slightly. Gabe shook his head, and gently shook her hand.

"What do you have to offer us, Mrs. Comaro?" The Detective asked bluntly. She swallowed, and wiped her nose with her Kleenex.

"I saw Michael this week, and he was upset. I asked him why, and he told me that Cain was getting mixed up into trouble. He told me he tried to talk him out of it, but he didn't think that it worked." She cleared her throat, and blew her nose. "He was really worried about Janie." Gabe couldn't help his outburst of laughter.

"Oh, Jesus. Please not the "pity Michael" routine. Not now, lady." He shook his head. Her forehead frowned, and she shook her head.

"I know. I know how it sounds. I couldn't believe what he did to her. It took me years to accept what happened, and understand that he was a sick person. Is a sick person. I think that's somehow rubbed off on Cain." She sniffled. "Anyway, I tried to talk to him, Cain I mean, and he almost hit me. I knew it was serious." She turned to Sean. "When he showed up, I knew he had done something." The Detective finished writing, and asked his last questions.

"Do you know Simon Knight?" She shook her head, and shrugged.

"Not at all. Never even heard his name mentioned." She wiped her nose, and steadied herself on a nearby police car.

"Does your family have ill will towards the Lazarus family?" he looked at her blankly.

"Years ago, after this first happened... Yes," she hesitated, and looked at Gabe. He wasn't going to stand idly and listen to a bunch of bullshit, and crossed his arms over his chest. "But now, eight years later, and hearing Michael's confessions... No, I don't wish them any harm. They've honestly not been discussed much except between Michael and myself during our private visits." She turned towards Gabe, who was now disgusted, and his face told her so. "Believe it or not, he just wants everyone to be happy." Gabe shook his head, and turned back to the Detective.

"Ok, the plan. Let's do this. The longer she stays in there..." he voice grew hoarse suddenly. The Detective nodded, and pulled him to the blue prints.

"We're surrounding the building now. Taking the precise aim in certain places to have a chance to take them out, if we can. We'll have a team go up to the roof, and enter through the vent to get a better view, and drop a communication line in." He turned on his walkie-talkie, and raised the volume so everyone could hear.

"Delta-9, we are in the vent and proceeding towards the center of the establishment. No sign of the package yet. Over." Came the voice of the lead officer crawling through the building. Gabe swallowed hard, and took a seat on the car's hood, burying his head in his hands. "Delta 9- I am approaching the vent. Officer Grady, flank, silent. Oh my God-" The man's voice cut off. The Detective turned to look at Gabe, his faced was pained.

"What's happening?!" Donovan spoke in a panic, as if reading Gabe's mind. The Detective shook his head, clueless of what was happening.

"Delta 9- the situation is grave. We have eyes on the package. Over." The Detective picked up the walkie-talkie, and quickly responded.

"Is the package intact? Alive?" His pen ready in hand to take note of anything that came back.

"Sir, the package is currently being... assaulted. I cannot blow our cover yet, and can only see them through the vent. This is horrid." Silence over took the safe zone, and the men's faces all changed. "This is hard to watch, over." All of the faces in the area went limp, and faces began to pale.

"Oh my God..." escaped Gabe's lips. "They're killing my wife!" Donovan quickly came to his side, and helped steady him. His eyes were pained, and his face was white as snow. He swallowed hard. "We have to do something. *Now.*" He stood suddenly. "Can I just go in and risk it?!" He was desperate. The Detective turned from him, and spoke into his walkie-talkie.

"No more waiting. Blow the phone through the front window NOW." Gabe heard the buzz on the walkie-talkie, and moments later, the sound of an explosion, and glass shattering all over the ground. He turned to see the building, and there was smoke coming out of the window.

"Delta 9- Good job. There is commotion. Over." They all exchanged glances, and looked back to the store for movement. Suddenly, there was brief movement from behind the smoke and broken window.

"Oh, no! Cain!" Mrs. Comaro screamed. The Detective quickly radioed that the phone had been picked up, and subject one identity confirmed. Everyone stood in silence, for what seemed like forever. Minutes were taking hours, and seconds were taking years. He just wanted Janie back in his arms.

~32~

Suddenly, an explosion. There was glass shattering everywhere, and Cain was yelling. Simon's reaction was strange. He slowly pulled out of me, as if he wasn't panicked in the slightest. He pulled up his pants, and turned and left our little room. I could hear both of them arguing, intensely about something. Looking above me, I squinted as if trying to look through the grates of the vent.

The light came from nowhere, and shined in my eyes three times. I blinked up, and tears flowed from my eyes. My whole body began to shake, and I didn't want to take my eyes off of the light. I looked around, and found my captors direction. Using my head, I showed the vent people where they were. The lights shined again. There was Simon, barging in the room holding a phone. He smiled eerily, and as if on cue, it rang. He answered it on the third ring.

"I've been waiting for you to call me." He tapped his fingers on the desk. There were long pauses in between his words, and I wondered what on earth they were discussing. "Well, that would be simple enough. I will be hidden though. Throw a bull horn in here, and we can talk that way then. I need to talk to Mr. Lazarus." He closed the phone, and there was another loud noise in the front of the store.

"What the fuck are these mother fuckers doing? They're throwing shit at me!" Cain was panicking, and uncontrollable.

"You dolt. I asked for the bull horn to communicate with them." He shook his head, and pushed past him to pick up the bull horn. He turned the nob, and squawked the alarm button. It rang through the building. He pushed it again, and it loudly pushed his voice out into the crowd.

I checked the clock, because I felt so exhausted. It read 3:36am. Rolling my head back, I looked up into the vent again, and cried. The light turned on to my face again, and stayed on. *That's the hope, right there, Janes. That's the love… just focus on that. Listen to the disorder and chaos… it's going to end.* I sniffled, and rested my head on my shoulder, listening to the exchanges.

"HELLO!" Simon spoke through the bullhorn. I could hear Cain whispering to him, but not what was being said.

"Simon Knight. This is Detective Brian Gustovson. We seem to have a problem, being that, you have Janie Lazarus in there against her will. You need to release her immediately, and we can talk." I couldn't help but slump in my seat a bit. One way or another, I would be out of here soon. *Right?* There was a cackle of laughter, and another button squawked.

"That's a joke. I want to talk to Gabriel. And Donovan. And Sean. And if they're all together, I can do that now." There was a pause, and Cain returned to the little room. His presence made the hair on my body rise. He came close to me, and circled me cupping each breast. My eyes met his own, and he suddenly smacked my core so hard that it brought tears to my eyes.

"They are all here, and listening to what you have to say. If they wish to respond, I will tell you when you are done." I could hear each bullhorn clicking on and off in the distance.

"Gabe, what do you think of the pictures I've provided you? Disgusted with your little bitch of a wife?" He laughed and strolled back into the little room with me. Turning directly in to my ear, he added, "That one's for you. So you can know just how you make people feel." He laughed again.

"I could care less about your pictures, Simon. I know what Janie's been up to, because as you can see, I was in those pictures too. What are you trying to prove? What's your point?" The silence in the air between their conversations were heavy, almost palpable.

Simon approached me again, looking at me like he was disgusted. He shook his head, and grabbed the plug. He centered it right on my ass, and began to push in. I begged, and I pleaded. But this time he didn't stop. He pushed the squawk button as I screamed and pleaded for him to stop. There was pain of ripping, or tearing, and an intense burning sensation. And then it all went numb, and my screams subsided.

"That was your lovely wife, giving it to me." Simon spoke into the bullhorn. Tears pooled in my

230

eyes. I could only imagine what Gabe was going through out there exposed to all of this, and still sticking by me. "So you're not at all upset that she's getting other men off? I find this odd." He walked out of the room again.

"No, I don't like what happened with Sean. I don't mind what she does with Donovan, actually. And she's paid very well, and safe. Why are you so worried about my business anyway? You were our friend." I heard Simon sigh loudly.

"I was tired of never getting my turn! My turn was past due, so I took it! Why don't you care about this more? GOD DAMNIT!" he yelled suddenly into the bullhorn. I swallowed hard, figuring he would show up in the room again in a minute.

~

Everyone watched in suspense, while the SWAT team screamed and threatened the moving person in the window. Time was frozen, and everyone seemed to have the same worried expression. Looking around, Gabe saw distress everywhere. His eyes turned back towards the front store window, and he could see the red sensors pointing in one direction.

"We're not comin' out!" A voice yelled from inside the building. The Detective's walkie-talkie began to beep again.

"Delta, Updates." As if nothing was moving, and even the air stood still, the response was terrible.

"Delta 9- 207, package is losing consciousness, multiple 261's. 240, 219, and repeat 245. Over." The Detective's brow furrowed, and his body language told Gabe things were not well. Codes asides, he knew it wasn't going to be good.

"Delta, can we get her out without killing these assholes?" He waited, and everyone's head snapped and turned, looking towards the yelling. Just then, the bullhorn from inside the building squawked.

"Don't come in here, or shoot in here… you'll hit Mrs. Lazarus." Simon's voice mocked to the crowd. He clenched his teeth, wanting nothing other than to beat the shit out of Simon. And then kill Cain. Turning towards the Detective, Gabe's eyes brightened.

"Okay, we're smarter than these dipshits. You've got eyes on her in the vent. Can we just take her through the vent? I can distract him in the front of the store, and Sean can help me." He turned around, and fiercely looked at Sean.

"I like that, except that if they were tipped off, and turned on her, I'd hate to think of what would happen." Gabe shook his head.

"I don't think they have the balls for that. I'm willing to risk it, and if they moved, just shoot them for Christ's sake." The Detective nodded.

"Are you sure about this?" He questioned, and put his hand on Gabe's arm. As he did, the bullhorn squawked again, and everyone turned to listen.

"I just tore your wife apart again, Gabriel! She's so good at being unwilling." He said sardonic manner, antagonizing them as much as he could. "I found it much more exciting to watch through your windows when you were all doing her. Although," he paused, and Gabe's head twisted towards the Detective. They nodded at each other, and immediately he spoke the new plans into the walkie-talkie's to get everyone's okay. He turned back to the building, and the words just kept flowing. "She wasn't quite as giving with Sean. Was she Sean?" Gabe took a steadying breath, and glanced at Sean, who was now hanging his head.

"Gabe, the Delta team in the vent thinks that with five minutes of time, they can get her out. Can you hold them for five minutes?" His voice was to the point, and very serious. He nodded, and looked again at Sean.

"Think you can keep your dick in your pants to save my wife?" He raised his eyebrow at his friend. Sean swallowed hard, and nodded. Turning back to the Detective, Gabe smiled, and nodded. "Let's fucking do this."

Sean and Gabe both were fitted with bullet proof vests, and above the waist body armor. They were unsure of the weaponry that was being held inside, or aimed at Janie. They wanted to take no chances.

~

I sat listening to Simon taunt everyone outside, trying to shock them with accusations and disgust. I had again caused all of these problems, and all of this turmoil with everyone. None of this is what I wanted to happen. All I was ever trying to do was be myself... *whoever that may be.* Closing my eyes again, I just wished for calm.

After hearing him now pull Sean into the conversation, I opened my eyes, to find him standing before me. Still smiling, just as he had been the entire day. *What the fuck is it with evil and smiling all the time? Note to self.* I swallowed, refusing to utter a sound. I watched him pace back and forth, and rub his forehead.

"Well, our time may be coming to an end. I'm so glad I was able to see you again all these years later, Janes." He turned away from me for a moment, and I was confused. Hoping that it all meant this was almost over, I still feared the worst. When he turned around again, he was holding a knife in his hand. Coming towards my chest, he slowly leaned into me. He put the knife to my shoulder blade, and dug in, pushing and twisting in all directions. My teeth instantly clenched as the metal dug into bone. Sheer pain feel over my body, and the scream that came out was murderous. I could feel things tearing, and blood rushing over my side. He finally backed away, and tipped his head to one side, as if checking his handy work.

"There," he giggled. "Now I'll always be on you." Leaning in again, he kissed my tightly closed lips. Pulling away, and shaking his head, he spoke. "You still can't stand me, can you?" I squinted, and shook my head. *What a fucking moron.* Cain walked through the room again, and roughly smacked the area that had just been carved. Making my blood pressure skyrocket, the blackness surrounded me again.

~

"Delta 9, Move on this now. Package is not well." The call came over the radios, and Gabe adjusted his vest. Sean stepped up behind him, and sighed loudly. Both had been fully briefed, and prepped on the situation, and what to do. Detective Gustovson approached both men, before they stepped into hell.

"You're doing a very commendable thing,

234

but I know you've done this before for her. True love is always worth saving…" he nodded, and Gabe wiped a tear from his eye. They stood, ready. The Detective picked up the bullhorn, and began to speak. The earpieces in their ears allowed both Gabe and Sean to hear what was happening all of the time. Everyone took a steadying, collective breath.

"Simon! This is Detective Gustovson again. You've requested to speak to Mr. Lazarus, and his friend, Sean. Both are willing to talk, and are approaching the store front broken window now. They are UNARMED, and come only to talk." The button clicked off the bullhorn, and Gabe started to approach the building, raising his arms to show he had nothing on him. Slowly, Sean followed him, staying a few feet back.

As he approached the building, he could see two figured in the window. He was breathing very heavy, walking very slowly, concentrating on the exact orders. In his headpiece, he heard the mission begin. "Delta 9- opening vent now." It was time. Now, or never.

"Hey!" he shouted over all of the shouting and banging around. Slowly, both figures turned towards him, and as the police shown the large spot light in, his eyes met with Simon's. Gabe crossed his arms quickly, as he didn't want to be seen clenching his fists. "Well, what do you have to say?"

"Gabriel," Simon cooed. "It's been so long. Really, how have you been?" Simon took a few steps closer to the open window. "Well?" he asked again.

"Up until a few weeks ago, and your antics. We were fine." He spoke with his emphasis on the "fine." Simon smiled at him.

"Yes, I do have something that belongs to you. I couldn't let her get away with what she was doing to you. I just couldn't bear to see you hurt like that, Gabe." Gabe felt his forehead crease, and he was confused.

"Why would you worry about my safety? I can assure you, I'm fine. She's fine. Even all of the discretions that you've been trying to point out…they don't really amount to much." In his ear, he heard another update. "Delta 9- lowering Delta 1 down to her now." His teeth gritted.

"You're all so dense. I couldn't let her ruin your life, not like I watched her ruin Michael's." Cain stepped up next to Simon, and smiled at Gabe. "Once I found out what she was up to, I figured this would be a lot easier." He scooted some broken chairs around inside the building. Almost panicking, and fearing that one of them would turn around and see the SWAT team recuing Janie, he couldn't risk it. He took three steps closer to the building.

"I don't understand Simon. I thought we were friends… If nothing else, I thought you and I had really-" Simon interrupted him.

"Bonded? Yes, so did I. I had hoped that what I felt for you years ago would be returned. But instead, you've remained my unrequited love." Gabe's mouth fell open, and he was sure that everyone that was listening just keeled over.

"What?!" Gabe asked, panicked and now angry. "So, let me understand this." Simon nodded, and stepped closer to the window. While he moved towards Gabe, he saw the butt of a gun in Cain's waistband, but could see nothing on Simon. "You've kidnapped my wife, to try to break up our marriage, tried to *ruin* my family, so you could have me for yourself?" His eyebrows were high in disbelief.

"Yes, quite precisely. Normally, men don't want a woman who is willing to give it to his friends and strangers." He shuffled around, and sat down on a chair in the window. Cain kneeled, peering out from the broken glass occasionally. "You seem to be abnormal though, as you've said you don't mind. Can you tell me now that we're feet apart? So I can see your face... You don't care that she's fucked your friends? And now Cain? And myself?" Gabe cocked his head to the side, and smirked at Simon. Slowly sliding his hand behind his back so it was out of Simon's view, he formed his fingers into a gun, as to alert them that there was a gun in the building.

"Oh, yeah. You've obviously got it all figured out. Are you just that stupid? Did you not see your own photos?" Gabe shook his head, hoping for an update.

"What do you mean, Gabe?" Simon now looked frustrated, as if accused of something terrible.

"I myself put her into half of these situations. I put her on display, and my friends," he turned to Sean, and pointed at him. "I let him watch us for years, never really thinking there was any motive behind it but to see a terribly beautiful woman in the throes of passion, and for release." He turned back to Simon. "So yes, you've shown me that what I didn't prevent, happened."

"Once." Sean said adamantly behind them both. "Delta 9- Cuffs are off. Lifting her out of the chair and into the vent. Over." Gabe shot Sean a devious smile, and Sean nodded. Stepping towards Simon again, Gabe got even closer.

"Oh, isn't that nice that he wants to apologize now? How ironic. Well, she didn't do much of anything for me." Gabe laughed aloud, almost taunting him.

"Simon, seriously?" Gabe turned towards Sean, winked, and faced Simon again. "Dude, you said it yourself: you prefer Gabe. Males. And just because you prefer males, doesn't mean that you have to go fucking psychotic on everyone else." He stood, and met Gabe's gaze. "You know, I want to fucking rip you apart right now." He leaned in towards the window, and glared in Simon's face. Sean stepped up to his side, to back his every move.

"Oh Gabe, you're so pitiful!" He laughed, and sat back in his half broken chair. Sean didn't appreciate the emotionless ass, and stepped to the window, in front of Gabe.

"You're such a sorry excuse for a human being, you know that?" His fists clenched, and his jaw wired tight. "Gay or straight, no one would ever want your ugly, fat ass." Sean smiled in at Simon, who was now scowling. He stood up again, now pushing himself to stand nose to nose with Simon. Gabe's thoughts spun out of control, and he just needed word that Janie was out. Sean took another step towards Simon, and the voices in their heads instantly spoke up. "Stand down! Stand down!" The Detective spoke into their ears. Sean seemed too enraged to listen. Turning towards Gabe, he nodded, and turned and dove at Simon through the window.

Simultaneously, the voice in his head said the best thing ever. "Delta 9- package in ambulance, safe. Over." As he turned to step away, he heard the gun cock, and Sean scream out in pain. He turned around, and tried to assist, but was forced out of the way by the SWAT team, who now pushed into the

238

building as if they owned the place.

Pushing his way through the crowd, and back through the safe zone, he ran into Detective Gustovson. He put his hand on Gabe's shoulder, and shook his other hand. Without a word, he pointed Gabe in the direction of the ambulance, and nodded. Gabe took off in a slow run at first, and sped up once he could see her outline in the back of the ambulance.

~33~

The gurney they wheeled me out to the ambulance on was rickety, and bumpy. I was afraid of falling off of it as fast as they were running to get me safely put inside. Once inside, they quickly gave me pain meds, and I was insanely grateful for those right now. My whole body was numb, and throbbing everywhere. I listened to the EMTs talk before we were leaving, and kept hearing of the bloodshed happening in the building. *Oh God, please don't let it be any of my people.* I closed my eyes, and laid my head back on the pillow, drifting off.

I was awoken suddenly, by a siren driving by where we were parked. I opened my eyes slowly, and everything was hazy. I shook my head a bit, and squinted hard. It looked like someone was running towards the ambulance. My breath stopped, and I tried to shift backwards in the bed. The female EMT quickly saw what was happening, and jumped out of the back of the ambulance, radioing for back-up to the back of the bus.

"Stop there, sir!" I heard her yell. I could faintly see the outline stop moving, and put their hands in the air. Squinting more, I couldn't make anything out. My head was spinning and I was dizzy from all of the pain meds.

"Whoa, Its okay." I heard his voice, and my heart screamed for him. "I'm Gabriel Lazarus. I'm her husband. Please, please let me see her." He was pleading. *Tell them he's no danger. Let him in!*

"Gabe!" I half shouted, out of breath. The EMT stood steadily by, never letting Gabe out of her sight. He climbed in the back of the ambulance, and grabbed my hand. I gave up opening my eyes, due to the medicine fog, but I squeezed his hand hard. Smiling, I let myself fall into dream land. I was just so tired.

~

Opening my eyes felt like pulling bricks out of dried cement. Before I could really wake up, all my thoughts came pounding back into my head. I could feel my heart beating faster. I tried moving, but couldn't pick up my arm. *Shit! Trapped again!* I started to panic, trying to sit up and run. Hands were on me suddenly, and they were big, and warm. I swallowed hard.

"Baby, calm down. It's just you and me here." *Gabe.* I pulled one eye open just a bit, to verify I wasn't going insane. His beautiful face was right in front of mine. I smiled, and his hand caressed my cheek.

"It's you..." I mustered. Even though it sounded like I had drank a gallon of Jack by myself. "I love you..." He smiled, and kissed my forehead.

"Can you understand me?" I nodded, keeping my eyes closed again. *Closed is just easier after a certain point of morphine.* "You've got a

240

few broken ribs, some stitches and cuts, and quite a few burns. Nothing permanent. Sleep off the drugs now, love. I won't be leaving your side." I smiled, and nuzzled into his hand and my pillow again.

Drifting off, I tried to remember the moments that I realized who the Visitor was. I couldn't believe that it had been Simon, my Si, that whole time. All that heartache, worry, and hurt... the threats and torture, and for what? *Maybe you'll never know. Get some rest, Janie. You'll feel more alert in a little while.* Drifting off, I hoped for a peaceful nap.

~

I could hear the commotion in the hallway, and it awoke me from my nap. Opening my eyes was much easier now, and I could actually see what I was looking at. Scanning the room, it was empty except for me. The couch-bed looked laid in, so I figured Gabe was close by. Then I heard him louder than anyone in the hallway.

"No, get his mother fucking ass out of this hospital. Now, or I'll sue for endangerment." He stormed in the room, closing the door ever so quietly, not realizing I was already awake. His face looked so stress, and so upset, but so determined. This was what I loved about him.

"Hi," I roughly mumbled, and I pulled myself up to sit in bed. He turned quickly, as if he was shocked I was awake, and rushed to my side. I smiled at him, wide.

"Janie! Oh thank God, you look more refreshed already!" His arms wrapped around me, and he hugged me gently. Pulling away, he kissed my hair. "What can I do for you?" I pointed immediately to the bathroom.

"I need a shower. Scalding. Boiling. Now." He nodded, and ran out to the nurse's station. He returned with my nurse, and she was a very smiley blonde. She checked my vital signs, and checked out my shoulder. I wrinkled my face, and Gabe noticed immediately.

"I'll fill you in in the shower, unless you'd like the nurse to explain." I shook my head quickly.

"No, no one explain right now please. Just want a shower." They all nodded. I just wasn't ready to go there quite yet. "What time is it? What day is it?" The nurse turned quickly, as if stunned and worried I had forgotten who I was. I quickly attempted to fix it. "Oh, I mean, I know it's the weekend. I was just… tied up for so long." I shook my head and laughed a bit. Out of the corner of my eye, I caught Gabe's smile, too.

"Mrs. Lazarus, you're free to take a shower. We've already completed your rape kits, your open burns are covered, so please enjoy a good, long hot one." She set some scrubs down on the bed with some socks, and put her arm on mine. Her eyes were filled with silent emotion, and I smiled back at her. "The doctor and police will be in for your statement soon, and then you can go home." I nodded, and sat up slowly.

"Thank you. We're pros at this unfortunately, so I won't be of much trouble. My husband on the other hand…" I smiled, and stood slowly to my feet. Nurse Jackie stepped aside, and let Gabe slide in to assist my walk to the bathroom. Once inside, I stripped the gown, and Gabe turned away to turn on the shower. Trying to keep his eyes averted, he opened the door so I could slide into the water spray.

It instantly wasn't hot enough, and I cranked the hot to the maximum setting. The steam poured out of the shower, and parts of my skin that still had feeling didn't appreciate the intense temperatures. I could hear Gabe shuffling around the bathroom, pacing the minutes away.

"Thank you for saving me," I said idly. His head peeked into the shower, although through the steam he could barely see me. Waving his hand around to move the steam, I finally found his eyes. I couldn't help smile at him. He smiled back, and it was the fully in love smile that I only got to see on special occasions. *Maybe it's not broken with him? Fingers crossed, baby girl.*

"Janie," he stuck his arm into the shower to reach my cheek. "Understand that I'd do it again in a heartbeat." I looked to the floor, feeling hideous despair for causing all of this to happen.

"I'm sorry I lied to you." It rolled off my tongue before I could think, or stop it. I swallowed hard, and tears welded up in my eyes, pouring down my cheeks. "Hurting you was *never* on my list." I blinked, and they poured down my cheeks.

"Aww, baby, stop it. Please. You know, I'm not blameless in this. I've put you on display too many times before." I couldn't believe his words. He truly wasn't angry with me, but I couldn't help but wonder if he didn't know all of the truth. "I've talked with Donovan quite a bit the past 72 hours, and he's a good guy." My mouth fell open, and I gazed at his goofy grin. "Can I blame him that he thinks you're the hottest thing around?" He laughed a loud, and pinched my chin. I smiled, and turned back to washing. My skin was turning beet red, and I was getting wrinkly.

Stepping out of the shower, Gabe helped me

into the scrubs. They fit well, and were soft enough not to pull or push on any of my sore spots. Heading back to bed, I was met with a room full of people. The Doctor had come, as well as Detective Gustovson, and a new, female Detective. They all smiled at me, as I hobbled back to bed. Sitting slowly, I sat back down on the bed. He sat on the bed next to me, and held my hand.

"Mrs. Lazarus," The Detective began. "I'm so glad that you're safe. I need to take your statement of the events, and I'll be out of your hair. This is Aimee Barber. She's a Detective from our Special Victims Unit." I nodded, and smiled.

"Hello, Mrs. Lazarus." She smiled, and took out her pen and paper.

"Thank you for saving me," I added quietly. He stopped digging in his pocket, and looked up and nodded. I wondered about his family, and if he had a wife or kids. He seemed very down to earth, and was always very helpful. Looking at Gabe, I smiled. "Gabe, could you have them get me some ice water?" He nodded, and headed to the nurses station.

"Okay, Janie. If we record this now, you most likely won't have to appear in court. I'm very confident that there is enough evidence to put both of these losers away for a long time." I squinted, thinking about what he was saying carefully. *Do you want to face these two again? In court, faced with hundreds of questions?* "Is it okay to tape this interview, Janie?" He asked, hesitantly. I nodded immediately.

"Yes, it's no problem." He nodded, and pressed record. Mrs. Barber was already writing everything down.

"Okay, a few questions first." I nodded, and

Gabe took his seat back at my side. Thankfully, his phone was the communication hub for my family, so he was looking down more than at me. "How do you know your kidnappers?" My eyebrows raised at his choice of words.

"I know Simon from years ago, working at the Phoenix together." I swallowed hard. "And Cain, I only met a few times when I was a teenager and involved with his brother, Michael Comaro." My fingers twisted around themselves nervously.

"Okay. Now, did you know the identity of who has been stalking you and your family for the past few months?" I shook my head quickly.

"No, I had no idea." That was honest, because the only person I would have ever even thought could do that was already in the pen. Gabe looked at me, and smiled, wiggling his phone in his hand.

"Please now tell me what happened on the evening of October 23rd, 2008. If you can, please tell us the order in which things happened." I yawned, and collected my thoughts.

"Okay. I had received texts from a person that wanted my business cleaning services, and to meet at that location to get the contracts signed. Once I got there, someone in the back room called, and I headed back. Walking in, I thought nothing of it, honestly. It wasn't until I saw the medical chair, and devices all around that I knew there was trouble." I paused, and closed my eyes for a moment. *If this isn't just like 8 years ago, I don't know what is. It's like the crazy just smells you, and is instantly attracted for life.* Shaking the thoughts, I continued.

"Once I was in the room, I saw Simon. Before I knew it, I was knocked out, and waking up to Cain. It's hard to remember every detail, because honestly I was trying not to think about any of it. I was completely strapped in to the chair, with thick leather. Cain went first. Beating me, and raping me. He disappeared after, and I was in and out of consciousness from getting hit in the eye." I pointed to my eye, and took a quick drink.

"After, Simon kept leaving and coming back. All the while raping me, but stopping for moments here and there. He dripped scalding wax over me, and..." I paused, and looked around. All eyes intently on me, and Gabe's poor, drained face.

"He forced a large item into my ass. Hit me many times, and screamed in my face. Towards the end I remember a scalpel. But he never finished. Never solidified the rape." Wrinkling my nose, I shook my head. "I saw the lights in the vent above me, and then I knew help had arrived, so I kind of zoned out even more." He nodded, and scribbled on his notepad.

"Did either say anything to you that you can remember?" I thought back through the hours, and remembered Cain's words.

"Cain told me that he was doing this to me for his brother. To show me that Michael can still get to me while he's in jail." I shook my head. "I tried to talk to Simon quite a few times, but he never really gave me any answers. I asked why he was doing it, and he basically said 'just because.'" I shrugged. Gabe's laugh rolled over the room, and I turned to him, frowning.

"I'm sorry," he held his hand up. "I know why he didn't finish Janie. Detective Brian knows, too." Both men met eyes, and tried not to smile. "Simon told me why he did all of this, but I'm not sure you heard." He turned to me, asking with his

246

eyes. I shook my head, obliviously. "Simon was going to hurt you, to break us up. He wanted *me*." My mouth fell open to the ground. Not that this was funny, by any means, but so fucked up and backwards.

"Why would he think that you were-?" I couldn't finish. Now I was baffled. "And how could he want to hurt me because of this?!" The Detective paused the tape, so everyone could calm down.

"Listen, everyone. Let's calm down, and then we can discuss this, off record. We need to wrap up this interview, and I only have a few last questions. Okay?" I nodded, and sighed. He pushed the button, and began.

"Janie, did you at any time set this up, or work with the two suspects?" he said flatly.

"Absolutely not." I responded, even more flat line than his question.

"Lastly, would you like to press charges against both Simon Knight and Cain Comaro for kidnapping, rape, attempted murder, false imprisonment, and anything else the District Attorney may charge them with?" I nodded.

"Yes, absolutely." I waited, and he pushed the buttoning, turning off the recording function. Turning towards Gabe, and squeezing his hands, I smiled. "Let's hope this is the last police interview, in a hospital, that I ever have to do in my life. I'm so done with all of these crazy bastards." I leaned into his shoulder, and inhaled him deeply inside me.

"Thanks, Janie." Detective Brian said. "You have any questions for me? Your husband can answer most of them, if you'd like. We've already gotten all other statements, so you're free to go after you meet with the doctor." I nodded, and extended my hand to him. He shook it, and began to leave the room. Turning only once to add, "If you need anything, call me."

~34~

Sitting back in the bed, I watched as the Detectives left. I just wanted to be home. It was like I was reliving every moment of the past, down to ending up here. I stretched my arms a little, and my shoulder pulled, and stung a bit. I winced, and the Doctor approached the bed.

"Hello, Mrs. Lazarus," he extended his hand to me, and I took it in a hand shake. "I'm Doctor Verma, and I took care of you when you came in. For the most part, your wounds were superficial, except for the shoulder." Motioning to my shoulder, and gently peeling down the bandage, and pulled a mirror out of his pocket so I could see. Angling it just right, I lost it. Tears streamed down my face seeing what had happened to my shoulder.

No one spoke, and I took in the fact that I now had chunks of flesh missing, and re-sewn together, and they were in the shape of 'SK.' *What in the fucking hell? He branded you?!* Tears streamed from my eyes, and I saw Gabe in the corner, covering his face with his hands.

"Janie, this should heal well, and then the letters won't be so prominent. Once it's healed more, we can fix it, if necessary. Don't worry about this, okay?" he patted my shoulder, and looked for the nurse. He pushed the call button, and she appeared quite readily.

"Yes, Doc?" she smiled politely.

"Please prepare Mrs. Lazarus' discharge papers, and let's get her home." Turning back

248

towards me, he continued. "Pain meds, if you need them. Use gentle soap cleaning the wounds, and the bandage can come off in three days. The ribs may be sore. The fractured ribs were re-fractures from years past." He paused, and flipped through my chart. *The past? Michael.* "Oh, and sitting may be uncomfortable for a few days, but nothing some rest won't fix." He added, looking me in the eye as to make sure I knew what he was talking about.

"Okay, I think I've got it." He turned to leave, and stopped to shake Gabe's hand. I could hear them both mumbling, but not what they were saying. *Typical.* The doctor patted him on the shoulder, and left. Instantly turning his head towards me, he flashed a half smile.

"You ready to get out of here? Go home and see the kids?" Surprisingly, I shook my head. He frowned, and took cautious steps towards me. "You don't want to go home?" I shook my head again.

"I don't want the kids to see me like this. Can we wait a few more days until they're back in our house?" He nodded, and patted my thigh.

"I'm sorry baby, I didn't think. You're right, as always." I smiled, and moved to stand. Gabe grabbed my few personal items I arrived with, *which weren't many, as you were stark naked...* and we headed for the door.

As we walked out of the hospital this Sunday afternoon, I turned and looked at the grand entrance behind us. I couldn't help but hope that I never ended up back here. *I'm still not sure how you've ended up here so much to begin with...* Gabe pulled the car up, and ran around to open my door. Climbing in the car, I was ready to be in my own bed. He turned on the radio, and *Boston* was on. *"You don't know me, you don't wear my chains... I*

249

think I need a new town, to leave this all behind..."
I swallowed hard at the similarities, and buckled up.
Just like every time before, Gabe was saving me,
and taking me out of the darkness.

~

      I was silent the entire ride home. So much to
take in, so many thoughts to process. Walking in the
house, I headed straight for the couch. Flopping into
it, the leather warmed and molded to my skin.
Gabe's phone was ringing constantly, making it
impossible to rest.

      "Who's calling you so much?" I sat up
slowly, trying to not move too quickly. The
soreness was setting in. *Muscles. Why do they
always have to hurt more, before they feel better?*
Appearing next to me with a glass of water, he sat
down.

      "It's everyone. Your family I spoke to last
night, as well as my own. Now it's just people
finding out from the news reports, and newspapers."
I frowned. *In the headlines again, huh?* "I know, I
tried. So did Donovan. It was too big of an event to
hide from the media, however, he was able to work
his magic and keep all the details out of it." I
nodded, and looked at my fingers.

      "I never imaged this. Ever since Michael,
I've always tried to foresee what was coming at me.
You know?" He nodded, and pulled the corner of
his mouth back. "But this," I inhaled. "How could I
not see this coming?" I turned quickly to him, trying
to suck in the tears. "But he wanted you?" I shook
my head again. I just couldn't wrap my mind
around all of this.

      "Do you want to talk about any of it?" his

voice was calm, and gentle. He knew better than to push. I shrugged. *What is there to say?*

"I don't really know…" I drummed my fingers on the couch. "You know what happened. I know what happened. I think I just need a little while to recuperate." He leaned over, and pulled a bottle of pills out of his pocket.

"Doc said to take these if you had pain, but I know they make you tired, too. Want to sleep?" I smirked, nodded, and held out my hand. After capping the bottle, he put it back in his pocket, and promptly scooped me up to carry me to bed. I laid my head on his shoulder, and wrapped my arms around his neck. *Home.*

~

When I woke up, it was dark outside. Stretching out my stiff body, I searched the room. Gabe wasn't in it, but I thought I saw the TV light on the living room. I veered into the bathroom to pee, and then headed out to find him. I found him curled up on the couch, watching our wedding video. My heart sank. This poor man had just been through the ringer, yet again, at my expense. In the end, risking himself for me. *Again.* Now he needed me, like I needed him. Tip toeing up to the back of the couch, I leaned over so he could see me.

"Hey, love. What're you doing out of bed?" He smiled at me, and his hand gently ran down the side of my face. I grabbed his hand, and held it to my cheek.

"I just woke up finally. Slept enough, I guess." I smiled, turning back towards the kitchen, thinking of what I could devour. "I'm so hungry…going to go calorie load now." Slowly, I

251

made it back to the fridge, and opened it up. Oh, thank you mother in law! Jean had filled the refrigerator with her delicious food. Multiple Tupperware containers to choose from, so I went with what was on top. Cracking the lid cautiously, it was a turkey dinner. *MMMmmm....*

I sat at the bar, and shoveled the food into my mouth. Sitting there, I checked the clock. It was 10:46pm on Sunday night...*when was the last time you have even eaten?* Gabe watched as I crammed the food into my face, and I almost started to laugh.

"I haven't eaten for days. Literally." He covered his smile. "Be nice, Mister!" I shouted, with food falling from my lips. He patted my back, and grabbed the cookies.

"You want to sit with me for a few moments?" he asked, winking at me. I nodded, and finished up eating my delicious dinner. Joining him on the couch, I saw what he meant.

"I know this isn't as perfect as yours, but..." he smiled, and handed me the joint. Just what I needed, and I couldn't wait. He lit, I sucked, and it roared to life. Leaning into his side, his arm draped around me perfectly. Each inhale relaxed me, and it was then I knew how truly tense I had been. My muscles were relaxing, and I could finally take a full breath of air.

"You okay, baby?" he asked, while he flipped stations on TV. I nuzzled into his side.

"Yeah, pretty good. Finally relaxed." I inhaled again.

"I can tell, I think you just melted into me a minute ago." He smelled my hair, and twisted his hand around my fingers. "I am so glad you're back with me." His arms got a little tighter, and we polished off the joint. Felling mellow and calm, we

252

lay on the couch together, falling asleep watching Armageddon.

After what seemed to be only five minutes, we were both startled awake by the phone ringing. Gabe sat up quickly, and recovered me with the blanket. He answered pretty quickly, still half asleep.

"Hello?" He stretched, and listened. "Oh, its fine, Detective. What's going on?" His face changed a bit, and he strolled away from me, and into the kitchen. "I see. That's when?" He got himself some water, and took a sip. "Yeah, she's rested a little bit. Pretty sore." Another loud gulp of water. "Okay, I'll talk to her, and let you know in a bit, okay? Alright. Talk soon." He set the glass down, and I could feel him coming back to me. *Oh God, what's he going to say?*

Sitting gently next to me, pulling pieces of hair from my eyes, he rubbed my back slowly to let me wake up. Once my eyes opened a little more, he cautiously began.

"That was the Detective, and he's got a huge favor for you." He paused, and swallowed. "The case is moving quickly, and going before the arraignment tomorrow morning to hear their formal charges. He would like to know if you are comfortable enough to sit in court for this. With me, of course." His face was blank, and kind of pale. I could tell he didn't want to ask me this, but knew it was important. I closed my eyes, and fell back into the pillow.

Swirling thoughts, jumping everywhere around my mind. So many questions that I needed answers to before I could commit. *Can you get the answers you need in time?*

"I think I can," I began. "I need to know a

few things first. Will they both be in the court room? And..." I hesitated, and Gabe listened intently. "How close will I be to them?" I asked in a whisper voice, suddenly feeling so small.

"Good questions, love. Let me go call him back and ask. But," he turned back to face me. "You don't have to do this, Janie. You know that, right?" I nodded, and smiled. "But let me guess… You have to?" He smirked, shook his head, and disappeared into the darkness. I tried to keep myself awake, but kept losing the battle.

He returned awhile later, and stroked my arm again so I could rejoin the living. It was even harder to pull my lids open this time around, but I managed. Reaching my hand out for his, I used him to help sit me up. Rubbing my eyes, I yawned big.

"Make it quick, I'm tired." He laughed.

"Okay. Tomorrow 1pm. It will be in an open court room, and you will be sitting in the crowd of people. He says there will be people, barriers, and police in between you and them, so zero chance of trouble." I nodded, and cocked my head in thought. "He said they will stare at you, and try to break you. That part is up to me, which he and I talked about." He put his hand on my leg. "I promise you, I won't leave your side, move away from you, or move without you." I wrapped my arm around his neck, and hugged him.

"I know you won't." I smiled, and released him. "Can you help me up?" He wrinkled his face at me, confused about my plans. Grabbing my hands, he pulled me to standing. "I'm going to my bed. If I've got to put them in jail tomorrow, I've got to not have eye bags." I winked at him, and yawned again.

"God, you're so beautiful Janie. So strong." He kissed my hair, and walked me into the bedroom. I quickly fell into the bed, and sighed as I breathed in my pillow. "I'm going to call him back, and join you. You need anything?" I moaned a little.

"No, but I don't want to see anyone but you until after court tomorrow. Okay?" I opened my eye to verify he got the message, and he smiled at me. Closing my eyes, I drifted away quickly. Right into dreaming, in the hot tub with Gabe. *MMMmmm....*

~35~

I woke up early on Monday morning, unable to sleep anymore knowing what was coming for me today. Trying not to think about it, instead I spent the morning cleaning up the house, and the kids rooms. Staying away from the bathrooms, I figured I could just handle those later. *Or, maybe you don't want to see yourself.* Whichever it was, right then all I knew is that vacuuming was sort of relaxing.

After I was satisfied with the house, I turned towards the clock. 8:23AM. *Ugh.* This day was going to take forever to finish. I grabbed my lap top, and headed to the couch. I turned on the radio, and set up my couch office space. Pushing the on button, the computer quickly sprang to life. I had quite a few emails to go through, so I figured now was as good a time as any.

The first few were the cleaning girls checking in, and reporting on their jobs. It was really refreshing to know that even when I was down, my business still went on. I typed up a quick mass message email to my employees, moving our Wednesday meeting to my house, instead of a public place. I briefly wrote that my ordeal was coming to an end, and that I would be back in the swing of things soon. Sending that one off, I felt a little better about the business idling without me, for now.

The next email I opened was from my Mom, and it made me smile.

"To: Janie Lazarus
From: Samantha Taylor
October 26, 2008 10:34pm

Janie, I'm so glad to hear you're back at home. Honey, I'm so sorry that this seems to be a repeat event in your life. Please know that these are completely unrelated incidents, and neither are your fault. There is just no way that you could have predicted these people's behavior, or choices they would make. I am so grateful for Gabe, and your friends Donovan and Sean. Gabe has said nothing but wonderful things about both of them, and that they both helped with your rescue.

I wish I could be there with you now, and hug you tight. We'll be visiting for a bit longer next time, and already have it worked out to stay in the guest house with Jean, your wonderful mother in law. Keep your head held high today, baby. Know that I'm with you always, and only a phone call away. Be strong for yourself, and your life. Your babies need you.

Love You,

Mom"

She's right, you know? I did know. She was always right about these things, and how I managed to turn it around to blame on myself. I couldn't respond to her right then. My emotions were too off the wall. Distracting myself a bit, I opened an old photo album, and flipped through the pictures of year past. Hundreds of pictures, and most all of my kids. I rested my head in my hands thinking of how close I came, yet again.

There was no sense in loafing. *Focus on work, it's only 9:45.* Closing the album, I flipped back to email, to see that I now had two emails, and had just gotten a new one from Donovan. I opened the other email first. It was a prospective client, and instantly the hair on my neck stood up. *How do you know if this is a real company? Call.* In time, I would just call. For now, I emailed Joyce from Toys4Less back with our prices, schedules, and package deals.

Sitting there, it dawned on me that I was going to need to change my security procedures, and take more precaution about all of the girls' security on jobs. I quickly jotted down the note, and instantly knew who to talk to about all of this. After taking all my notes for Toys4Less, I hesitantly opened up his email.

"To: Janie Lazarus
From: Donovan James
October 27, 2008 11:11am

Hey Janie,
  Glad you're safe at home. Wondering how you're doing, and if there's anything you or Gabriel need. I'm a phone call away, and only a few minutes down the

257

road. I hope this doesn't turn you against me, but... I miss you. Get better soon.   D"

I caught myself smiling a bit that he missed me. It did feel like it had been forever since I had been in my routine, even though it had only been three days. My stomach was rumbling, and I needed to eat. I got up and grabbed a banana off of the counter. Peeling it slowly, I sat back on the bar stool, and ate all I could. I just wasn't that hungry. My nerves were starting to hum in my body.

Focusing back on the email, I hit the respond button to Donovan's email.

"To: Donovan James
From: Janie Lazarus
October 27, 2008 12:36pm

Thanks... I need help with security for myself and the girls' while they're out at jobs. Can you help? We'll talk more after today. J"

Clicking send, I felt a bit better that we'd all be a little safer. The house phone rang suddenly, and I didn't want it to wake Gabe up. Speed tip-toeing across the room, I answered by the second ring.

"Hello?" I said in a hurried whisper.

"Janie! Hello, sweetheart. How are you?" Jean. Her voice was so calm, and I could hear the kids in the background.

"Hi Jean, it's so good to hear your voice." Tears welded up in my eyes, but did not fall. "I miss all of you...so much." She sighed.

"I know honey. You just worry about

healing up, and they'll be back home before you know it. They're doing wonderfully. Would you like to talk to them?" I swallowed hard. I hadn't thought of that, but I really, really wanted to.

"Do they know about what happened? I couldn't help to ask, and I truly hoped that they knew nothing.

"No way. We haven't watched TV, and I threw all my papers away." She paused. "But, I did tell them you got into an accident. I thought they were going to see you banged up, and I thought that was minor. I'm sorry if-" I cut her off, smiling.

"No, it's perfect. Thank you. I appreciate it." I sighed.

"If you're not ready, honey, don't let me force you." I nodded, fully knowing she could not see my motion over the telephone.

"Yes, I'd like to talk to them." My hands were shaking, and I wasn't sure why. These weren't strangers. Just my babies. It wasn't that I didn't want to talk to them. I just didn't want to poison them with all of this bullshit. I heard the phone, and some heavy pant breathing into the receiver.

"Mommy?!" Galen's tiny voice screamed into the phone. "Is it weally you?" This made it hard to control the tears at all.

"Yes, baby. It's me. How are you? How has your week been?" There was more shuffling in the background, and I figured he was playing with toys while trying to chat.

"Gwamma's house is awesome, and I get jewwy beans!" He laughed a little. "Uhm, Ma?" now he sounded perplexed.

"Yes, Galen?" I cautiously asked.

"When do I get to come home?" A very honest question. I knew he missed his room, and the

259

routine. *And his Mom, Janie.*

"Soon baby, just a day or two more. Okay?" That may have been harder for me to say, than for him to hear. He giggled, and things fell in the background.

"Okay, here's my sister." I smiled, and listened as the phone changed hands.

"Hello? Mom?" She sounded twenty years older. I caught myself holding my breath.

"Hey princess. How are you?" I glanced at the clock on the wall. *11:25Am.* Shit. It was almost time. I felt the lump in my throat start to rise, and swallowed it quickly.

"I miss you. A lot. When can we come home? Are you okay?" She was full of questions, and I was running low on time.

"Soon Lilah, maybe a day or two more. I'm okay, but I did get a black eye from the accident. I miss you, too. And your stinky brother." She giggled.

"A black eye?!!?" she exclaimed. "Can you take a picture?! That sounds neat." I shook my head.

"Can you put your Grandma back on the phone, please? I've got an appointment to get ready for. Lilah," I paused. "I'm really proud of you. You're being a great big sister, and helper to Grandma. I love you soo much."

"I know Mommy. I love you, too. I'll get Grandma." I could hear her running around trying to find Jean.

"There. Did that help a little bit?" she asked cautiously.

"Yes Jean, thank you. I've got to go now though... Gabe will call later." We said our goodbyes, and I headed to the bedroom to wake

Gabe. I sat down on the bed, carefully as to not shake it too much and startle him. Rubbing his arm slowly, I laced my fingers in his, and his eyes instantly opened. Smiling at me, he stretched out before me. All of him, and my libido suddenly throbbed.

"Hey Gabe, it's time to get up. We need to head to court soon." He nodded, and I headed for the closet. *What are you supposed to wear when you're sentencing your kidnappers to life in prison, I wonder?* Pushing through the hangers, I came to a sleek black knee skirt, blouse, and jacket set. That was it. I headed into the bathroom, and put it all on, carefully sliding my sore shoulder into the jacket. Wetting my hair slightly, I was able to pull most of it up in a bun, and hairspray the rest down. The full length showed me looking professional, and ready for business. However, my personal mirror showed the bags under my eyes, the worry on my face, and the panic running right below my surface, through my blood.

I turned around to find Gabe's eyes staring at me intently, up and down. I frowned a little, and he put his hands up in defense.

"No sneak attacks, Mrs. Lazarus." He stepped towards me slowly. "You look fabulous. Elegant. Business like." He looked directly into my eyes. "I'm really proud of you." Leaning into him, I smelled him in. I just wanted these next few hours to go by quickly, and without turmoil. My eyes met his, and he frowned.

"I'm just really scared." I whispered. He sighed, and looked at me with the saddest, most emotion filled look. His hug got a little tighter, and I felt him pressed against me. While it didn't make me melt right then, somehow after all of this, I wanted nothing more than to be with my man. Alone. Just us.

"I won't leave your side." I nodded, and he hopped over to his sink, and finished freshening up. I watched him in the reflection of my mirror to his, lathering his face, and shaving the spots in between his beard. "According to Gustovson," he started. "This should take an hour or less." I nodded, and headed out to the kitchen. Quickly opening the bottle of rum, I quickly downed a few drinks. *Easy there nerves. See? I'm trying to help you.*

Gabe met me in the kitchen, and I could feel that I was oozing with tension. *He can tell, too.* Handling me with gloves, as if I was breakable, he helped me get into the car. The radio turned on, and Staind came on, playing *True Colors.* Time tripping to the past, the scenery seemed to fly by. Seeing everyone for what they were was really hard to grasp. I mumbled the song to myself while Gabe got in the car. Internally, I knew he wasn't speeding, or taking any short cuts. But the rest of me wanted to climb into his chair, and push the brake pedal.

I could see the court house as we pulled in to the lot, and was quickly confused when Gabe pulled into the locked lot. He stopped at the sign, and a little old man came out of the shelter.

"Hello, Sir." He said to Gabe. Gabe fumbled with his wallet, and pulled out a paper with a code on it.

"Hello. We're here for the District Attorney, password is Package nine." He turned and looked at the old man, who promptly nodded, and smiled at us both.

"They are expecting you. Door 2." He motioned us on our way, and we pulled in to the gated lot to park. I already felt a bit safer, being away from the public lot, and possible scrutiny of anyone else. I closed my eyes, and tried to do some deep breathing. I felt him park the car, but kept my eyes clenched instead. I heard his door open, felt the car shift, and his door close. *Oh God. Oh God. Oh God.* My door opened, and I peeled my eyes open to face him. His hand extended to me, and I took it tightly.

I needed him now more than ever. He supported my weight as we walked in, silently. *He's got you, Janie. You need to do this.* Tears filled my eyes, and he opened the doors, and we walked into the Green Valley Court House.

~36~

We were instantly met with crowds, cameras, and flash bulbs. Instinctively covering my face, suddenly there was a man in front of me. He wore a blue suit, and grabbed my free hand. Gabe's hands around my waist, and this blue suited man were leading me to quiet and peace. *I hoped.* Once we reached the security point, it was like the place was empty. I let out a cleansing breath, and turned to this new man.

"I'm Jack Austens," he escorted me through security, and motioned both Gabe and I to door 2. "I'm on Donovan's security team, and was assigned to you and your husband as long as you need." I smiled at him, and turned to Gabe.

"Hello, Mr. Austens," Gabe extended his hand. "Thank you for helping us." They nodded at each other.

"Mam," he looked at me pitifully. "It's time to go in. I'll be sitting on your other side, and between your husband and I, you will stay safe." I swallowed, and nodded idly. I felt Gabe's hand at the small of my back, reassuringly stroking side to side. Glancing at my watch, I noticed it was 12:40, and the court room seemed empty.

Rushing over to us came Detective Gustovson, and the DA Mitchell Dallard. They both nodded to us, but their faces looked stressed.

"Mrs. Lazarus, it's nice to meet you. However, I am sorry for the circumstances. Please, let me thank you on behalf of the State for your presence today in the court room." I shook his hand gently, and quickly stole my hand back.

"You're welcome." I said quietly. This room felt too big for me. It made me feel so small. My eyes darted around the room, and to the Defendant's table, where a man was sitting alone.

"That's the public defender, David Dvorkan. He's their lawyer." He paused, turning back to me. "Your presence alone will shatter their case, at any angle. You'll not be forced to speak today, so don't be afraid. You're here to stand up and up and say you're not going to take it, and they need to pay. I plan to ask the judge for no bail, and for them both to be held in jail, as they did admit to stalking you previously. I see no issues here, Mr. and Mrs. Lazarus." Turning back towards the Detective, he smiled a bit. "Yes, Brian, I do feel a plea deal coming on." He turned, and went back to his seat in the front of the court room.

The Detective escorted us to the third row, far off to one side. He motioned us to sit, and just as promised, Jack came to my other side. He climbed over the seats in front of us, and took seat himself right there.

"The court room is going to start to fill up.

Just remain calm. Both of the defendants are going to be brought in any minute." His eyes met my own, and he turned in his chair. Gabe's arm was around my shoulder, and his hand squeezed my own. I quietly sat, watching the people stroll in and sit down. I didn't recognize anyone, nor did I see any cameras. *Thank God.* And then I saw Mrs. Comaro, and my heart sped up a bit. Oddly, she smiled at me, and Gabe nodded in her direction. My head all but snapped off turning to look at Gabe with confusion.

"She was there that night. She came willingly, with Sean." My mouth fell open. "Took her a few years, but she knows her sons are worthless." I understood completely, and nodded as such. Turning back to the front, I saw the side door of the court room open, and I knew what that meant. I felt my muscles tighten, and my nerves start misfiring all through my body. Swallowing hard didn't help, and I started to feel feverish. Without hesitation, Jack handed me a cold water bottle, and some Dramamine.

Readily accepting, and swallowing the cold liquid cooled me internally, and relaxed me somewhat. It was still as if time was standing still, and I saw Cain round the corner. My teeth clenched, and gritted together. My head floated back to him hitting me, punching me, and raping me. *And his brother.* I never did anything to either of them, and now they both hold something terrible in my past. *I bet they'll compare notes in jail. Ugh.*

He sat down, and I stared into the back of his head. Seeing more commotion by the wall, I looked up to be met with his psychotic glare. *Simon.* He smiled widely at me, never looking away. He moved quickly to the defendant's table, and leaned to whisper into Cain's ear. Suddenly, they both turned and stared at me. My jaw clenched, and I sat up a bit straighter in my chair.

Glancing back over at them, Cain flapped his tongue in his lips, making an obvious sexual reference in my direction. Simon laughed loudly enough to echo a bit in the court room, and everyone turned to look at him. His lawyer silenced him multiple times, and each time he turned back to look at me. I tried to look away, but it wouldn't end.

Suddenly, Detective Gustovson shot out of his chair, and raced up to the DA's side. He gave him his cell phone, and whispered in his ear. They both stared at the phone for a moment, and then I saw DA Dallard shake his head. The Detective came back and sat down, turning only to smile at us. The judge stepped in, and everyone stood. My legs shook, and my hands were sweaty. I listened as the bailiff asked everyone to rise.

"All rise." The judge took his seat. "Case number 4545-33 State against Simon Knight and Cain Comaro." The DA stood, as did the defendant's lawyer. They met at the stands in the middle, and talked with the judge.

"What are the charges?" Judge Alvin asked the District Attorney.

"Okay judge, I'll give you the list." The judge nodded, and readied his pen. "Arson, Aggravated Battery, Computer Crime, Kidnapping, Sexual Assault separately by both defendants, Harassment, and Conspiracy. Not to mention, Mr. Comaro has multiple probation violations." The judge nodded, and turned to the defendant's lawyer.

"What do your clients plea?" he asked, with eyebrows raised high.

"They plead not guilty, and feel they are being set up." He said with little force, or belief.

The judge turned back to the District Attorney, and sighed.

"What are you asking for, Mr. Dallard?"

"That the defendant's be remanded into the custody of the state, in the prison system. If they are free, they will surely torture the victims even more. As I have proof of that already, from them being in court for a mere five minutes before you arrived, your honor." The judge frowned, and hesitantly asked.

"What do you mean, Mr. Dallard? Has there been a farce in my court room?" The District Attorney approached the bench, with the Detectives cell phone in hand. Judge Alvin motioned for Mr. Dvorkan to come to the bench, also. "Mr. Dallard, what must you show us?" He pressed play, and turned the phone to the judge and lawyer to watch.

"This is a video that the Detective sitting by the victim's in court today took as the defendant's came into court." The judge gasped at the behavior, and their lawyer turned and eyeballed them, astounded and angry. "Please note their intimidating behavior, and their inability to look away from her." Without any hesitation, he added, "They need to be remanded, as you can see." The judge nodded, and jotted notes on his pad.

"Due to the immense amount of evidence in this case, and behavior in my court room today, they are both remanded until trial or plea deal is reached." He turned towards the public defender, who looked no more than twenty years old. "You'd better talk your clients into a deal, if the District Attorney is nice enough to offer." His gavel slammed onto the wood, and echoed through the room.

"Next case," the bailiff began, and the room

267

cleared a bit. I glanced over long enough to see his eyes boring into mine again, and I shook my head. At this point, I'd of given anything to have answers for his behavior. I still don't understand why he did this to me. *He would've done it to anyone, Janie. You were just the easier target. Less work to do, because of your past...* Gabe's hand clasped around mine, and he pulled me into a hug.

"Great job, baby." He kissed my hair. Pulling away, his smile was brighter than ever. "Let's get out of here." Kissing my forehead, he nodded towards Mr. Austens. Jack promptly cleared a path, and pulled us through it.

Stepping through the court house doors, and on to the pavement, I couldn't help but breathe a little deeper. They weren't being released, and the DA was sure that this wouldn't ever even see the court room. I sighed loudly.

~

Climbing into the Jeep, I could feel the tension and unspoken nervousness flowing through the air. It was heavy. I closed my eyes for a moment, and leaned against the head rest. Focusing on the calm, I tried to still my thoughts. *They'll be in jail for a while. It's time to breathe, Janie. Calm down, and get back in your groove.* Breathing in and out, I slowly opened my eyes. I was surprised to find Gabe staring at me, silently waiting for me to talk.

"Hi," I whispered, and put my hand on his thigh. He wrinkled his brow, and I knew he was wondering what I was thinking. "Just getting my bearings. Want to go for a drink?" I smiled, and he nodded.

"Anywhere special?" he asked, his voice still very monotone and nervous. I shrugged, and wrinkled my nose.

"Close to home, maybe? So we don't have to drive far?" I smirked at him, and added, "I feel quite a few drinks coming my way." He nodded, and headed towards the local bar. When we pulled into the lot, I giggled at the sign, announcing it was 80's night inside. I glanced at Gabe out of the corner of my eye, and he was holding back his laughter.

"Well, I know they have drinks…but that's about all I can say for now." We both laughed loudly, and hopped out of the car. I checked my cell as we walked in, and it was already after 4pm. Gabe pulled the door open, and we walked into what seemed like a bad eighties movie. The hair, the high waist jeans…it was fabulous! He led me over to a quiet corner in the back, and he motioned for the waitress to come over.

"Hi, I'm Melissa. What can I get for you?" she asked, and set some napkins on the table.

"I'll have four shots of vodka, please. And Cherry Pepsi." I smiled, and she turned to Gabe.

"I'll have what she's having, but a Budweiser instead of pop." She nodded at us both, and skittered off into the bar. Turning back towards Gabe, I noticed he was intently staring at me. Feeling awkward, I frowned at him.

"I'm sorry, baby. I don't mean to stare at you." He paused, as the waitress came and deposited our drinks on the table. We both smiled, automatically.

"Just get my attention when you need me, or you're ready to order." We nodded, and he turned back to me.

"I'm just trying to figure out where your head is. Today was such a big day, and you..." his hand fell to mine on the table, and I smiled. "You were so strong. Through all of it, this whole past week. I'm just wondering what you're thinking." *Ahh, there it is. He wants to talk.* I pulled my hand from his, and reached for my first shot. Grasping it firmly, I put the cold glass to my lips, and slung it back. Without hesitation, I picked up the second shot, and slammed it as well. The burn crept up my chest, and I sighed.

"Today was difficult." I began, and eyed the two shot left on the table. "I'm so sick of facing people down. I don't want to deal with this stuff anymore." I grabbed the third shot glass, and opened my throat to the liquid heat. Wincing at the burn, I slammed the glass back to the table. Gabe chuckled, and shook his head. "It's hard to think straight, with the constant thoughts of violation..."

I had to stop thinking about this. The mere thought made me relive the past day's events, and then the past years. I didn't want to let this make me into what I wasn't. I didn't need to dwell in the past, or in the hours I spent tied down days ago. I just needed to get things back on track, so my family could get back to living. I squinted, and picked up the last shot. Meeting Gabe's eyes across the table, I couldn't hold in my smile.

"You know, G," I started. "None of it matters. Just another part of my fabulous past. I just want to concentrate on the future. The business, and the kids. And you..." The songs were shifting on the jukebox, and people began shifting around.

"Janie, are you sure you're okay?" I nodded, and smiled. As if on cue, a song came on the radio I hadn't heard in years. Downing the last shot, I stood up, and started to dance by my chair. The Pointer Sister's sang '*I'm so excited!*' loudly through the speakers, and I could feel the alcohol burning through my veins.

"I'm fine Gabe. I'm just ready to get back to life. To work." I sat back down as the song ended, and the next began. I laughed aloud, hearing it was Manic Monday. *How true is that?!* He raised his eyebrows, and looked away while he drank. "What's that about?" I asked, hesitantly.

"You want to rush back to everything, and pretend nothing happened. I don't know if I can do that." I shook my head.

"Which part, exactly?" I waited a moment, and met his stare. "The person who has been screwing with us for months is in jail. There were no other accomplices, I am sure of it after being with them both for hours." I shook my head, remembering the memories of Cain. And Simon. The waitress appeared out of nowhere with two more shots for me. I smiled at her, and took them willingly.

"Thought it looked like time," she joked, also dropping a beer off for Gabe. I quickly downed another shot, and shook my head violently to push the heat back into my belly.

"Anyway, I don't want them to win. I don't want them to ruin everything." I paused, to drink my sixth shot. It went down much easier, and I could feel my limbs start to get heavier. *Finally.* He smiled at me, and chuckled at my current state. "I'll go back to work at Donovan's, and the kids can come home. All will be well, and we will live on ever so peacefully." He shook his head, and his mouth was in a small line.

"I don't know if that's a good idea, Janes."

271

He said flatly.

"What? Working at Donovan's?" He nodded, and suddenly, I understood. I smiled at him, widely. And picked up my water that she had brought. The coolness flowed right into the hot fire that was burning within, and put out the flames. "Look, I'll never be able to apologize enough for not being completely honest with you about Donovan's, and just what I was doing there." I paused, and he sat up straighter in his chair.

"Janie, it's not my-" I cut him off, holding my hand over his mouth. I couldn't help but giggle, as normally he was the one cutting me off with this method.

"I'm planning a few changes with Mr. James that will benefit us both. I'll need to go to discuss the changes, but I think everyone will be very pleased." I smiled widely, and he returned the same big, drunk, cheesy smile. It was true. I had these epiphanies while I was in the shower, and I knew it was what I had to do. But right now, my numb body only wanted one thing, and it was becoming focused on attaining it.

The songs changed again on the bar jukebox, and now the Notorious B.I.G. played, and I stood quickly again to dance. Circling Gabe in his chair, I rubbed into him every chance I could. Grinding away to the thumping of the beat of the music. Finally, after a few moments, I felt the tension he carried fall away. Smiling at me, he stood, and finished his beer. Pushing himself into my back, he moved his body along with mine. Matching me, groove for groove. He arms circled around my chest, and his hips pressed into mine. I let my head fall back on his shoulder, and closed my eyes to savor the moment.

I opened my eyes again, sleepily, in Gabe's arms being carried into the house. The cold air woke me up completely, and I checked the time. It was about 9pm. Gabe noticed I had woken, and slowed to set me down on the counter.

"Welcome back, sleepy head." He smiled, and filled a glass with water and drank it. He refilled it quickly, and handed it to me to drink. "Better?" he smiled.

"Yes, thank you." I hopped off the counter, and his arms surrounded me quickly. "I'm okay, I promise." I patted his shoulder, but he didn't loosen his grip. Instead, my eyes met his, and they were dark and needy. I knew what he wanted, and I fought the voices in my head. Swallowing hard, I put my hand on his chest, and pulled him into me. Cautiously close, and breathing into his throat, I tipped my head up slightly to meet his mouth.

His lips met mine hesitantly at first, but growing hungrier by the second. I felt my walls falling down, and I knew that "normal" was definitely within reach. With quick movements, he scooped me into his arms, and carried me quickly to the couch. Dramatically taking of his shirt, he turned away to turn the radio on. Hushed, slow music played over the speakers, and he knelt by me at the couch.

I sat up off of the couch, and pressed my lips into his again. While we were locked at the mouth, I took the opportunity to wrap my legs around his waist. He readily accepted by pushing me back into the couch to slide off my skirt. I frantically unbuttoned my top, and threw it to the floor. He pulled away to drop his pants, but never broke the stare. I felt myself blush, and he smiled wider. Bending back down to my side, now our chests were close to crashing into each other, skin on skin. *Oh, please. Please, Gabe.* I pulled him back down to me, and his tongue dove into my depths.

His hands began to travel, and left a trail of tingling warmth behind them. My body yearned for him to touch every square inch, and to linger on certain places of pleasure. As if reading my mind, I opened my eyes to find him trailing his fingers into the band of my underwear. I could feel the shift within me, from the mental processes, to the automatic. My body was giving itself over, relinquishing all control. There was nothing I could do to stop it, and I really didn't want to.

His fingers poked around underneath my panties, to which he moaned loudly. His head falling back threw me over the edge more, and I pulled myself up to a sitting position. I thumbed his boxer briefs, and pushed them to his knees. He instantly sprung towards me, with his warm, silky soft skin. There was no time for games, I wanted what I wanted. *Take him.* One last look at his beautiful face, and I closed my mouth around his hard, soft length. I was hungry for him. Hungrier than I had ever been.

When his head fell back, and he clung to me for support, I knew I had him. He slowly sat next to me on the couch, making sure not to break the seal between my lips, and his massive cock. His hands trailed down my back, reaching in between my folds for my core. Once he found them, I could tell, because he swelled even more inside of my mouth. I could feel every vein, and every throb. *He's yours.*

Make him remember it, always. Now. Turning my head slightly, I met his eyes with my own. Biting into him ever so gently, I pulled my teeth lightly along his shaft. His breath hitched, and he instantly pulled me off of him.

"No more, I want to come inside you." Pushing me back into the couch, he spread my legs open wide. Grasping my undies, he pulled them off in one swift tug. His cheeks were painted with color, and I watched him lick his fingers. Leaning down to me, his mouth only inches from my own, I felt him push into me. I closed my eyes, trying to stay in the moment.

Every thought I'd had in days was suddenly trying to push in, and I found myself clinging to the image of Gabe burned into my eyes. *It's not Simon. It's not Cain. It's not Michael. It's just your husband. Your knight-in-shining-armor. It's safe to let him in.* I repeated to myself over and over, until I finally felt my body relax, and welcome his fingers inside me. He felt the shift, too, and smiled down at me.

"You okay, love?" he delicately swirled his fingers inside of me, and my body responded by tightening around him. I nodded, and caught my breath. My head thrashed around on the couch cushion, and again I found the calm inside my head. He pressed into my sensitive spots, and my hips responded my gyrating into him. He withdrew his fingers, and licked them off. "God, Janie, I've missed you so much." He mouth flew to mine, and crashed into my lips.

Pulling back enough to palm himself, and aimed straight for the core. With momentum, he dove inside of me, loudly moaning when he hit the bottom. Opening my eyes, I could feel my body burning for him. Grabbing my legs, he held one in each hand, straight into the air. Diving in again, he hit something deep inside, setting off my own deep, snarly moan.

"MMmm," I moaned in acceptance. I met his gaze, and he was hungry. I reached for his chest, and ran my hand down the parts I could reach. "I've missed you, too." I whispered to him. His face instantly changed, and his smile turned wicked. His fingers tightened around my shins, and he dove deeper inside of me. I could feel him hitting what seemed like my stomach, and my whole body was tensing up around him. His hands trailed up and down my legs, squeezing the muscles, trying to confuse my body.

There was no denying that I was coming. I felt my body squeeze one final time, and I caught Gabe's expression change to a strained push. Suddenly, I could feel every inch of him sliding in and out of me. His hands settled on my shoulder, and he pushed me even farther down on his length. I could feel him losing himself in me, and I loved that feeling of normalness. *Now, Janie. No more fucking with fate, got it?* I smiled at his beautiful face, and pulled him back into a kiss.

His thrusts grew more forceful, pushing deeper and deeper into my soul. I clung to him, and clawed into his skin. Finally, I felt him freeze, and explode inside of me. The pumping went on forever, and I could feel the completion of the moment. Staying inside me, he circled me in his arms in a loose hug.

"I love you, Janie." His lips found mine, and our kiss brought on more throbs shared between our connected loins.

"God knows how much I love you, Gabe. I

276

always have," I patted his cheek, as we both dealt with more throbbing. "I always will." His smile, and kiss told me all I needed to know. He eased out of me, and threw me a towel. Not feeling like cleaning up, I stayed naked on the couch, listening to the music play. I covered myself up with a blanket, and relaxed.

Moments later, Gabe returned wearing some low hanging warm up pants. *God, he is so amazing.* My eyes followed his abs down to the lines around his hip bones that then lead into his pants. All over again, I was ready for him. Taking a slow, calming breath, I tried to refocus on relaxing. I felt the couch shift, and looked to my left. Gabe sat smiling, with a lit joint, passing it over to me.

"Here, love." He was beaming, as if his cares had been washed away. I smiled back at him, and nodded.

"Your smile," I inhaled. "It's contagious." He nodded, and put his arm around my shoulder. I took another hit before handing it back, and I cuddled into his side. I rubbed his thigh with my free hand, and laid my head back on his shoulder. "Thank you for being patient with me." His hand patted my shoulder, and I heard him inhale.

"I'll do anything I can for you, always. Which includes not sharing you, I think." I sat up quickly, and winced at him. "Oh, no. What's that face, Janie?" He was instantly on defense, but I understood where this was all coming from.

"Well, remember I mentioned an idea about Donovan's..." I began, and he nodded, raising an eyebrow. "I need you to come with me this next time. I want to show you what I'm doing, so you clearly know. Just one time, and then I am done." I smiled at him, and waited.

"Done? Like done with Donovan?" he wrinkled his face, and I nodded.

"Well, not the company's relationship with him. But myself, yes." I took the joint from him, while he sat there befuddled by my announcement. Inhaling, I couldn't help but giggle at the faces he was making. "Just trust me, okay?" He smiled, and nodded.

"Donovan said that he wanted to talk to me about some business things at some point. So, maybe if I went with you, we could chat for a bit, too." I nodded.

"I'm sure of it. You'd love his study…its very man-cave like." I giggled. Leaning back into Gabe, listening to Lisa Loeb on the radio, I felt like things were falling back into place. *Calmly, even, it seems.* Oddly enough, I was quiet awake for 11:30pm. After such a long day, I had no energy to move, but my mind was running a mile a minute. "I know this may be weird, but I'm going to send out a few emails." I pulled the laptop on to my blanketed lap. Gabe shook his head in disagreement.

"I know. But I'm wide awake." I handed him the now miniscule joint, and turned back to my email, which pinged with new emails. "This will only take a few minutes anyways." I stuck my tongue out at him. He shifted around, and brought some beverages out for us. He turned the radio up a little bit, and sank into the couch with a book.

This seemed so normal, the only thing that was missing was the kids being home. It had been so long since I'd seen them, I wondered if I would even recognize them. *Oh, stop it! Of course you will! It's only been a few days since you've seen them, honey. It just feels like longer.* That was the truth, but again, I was so thankful to Jean. I checked the clock, and it was almost midnight. I opened the first email to find Mylah's weekly update. I smiled internally, and opened her email.

"To: Janie Lazarus
From: Mylah Bush
October 28, 2008 7:32pm

Hey Janie, the week has gone well. I'm wondering if you had any other clients to give me? I could really use an income boost, so I could get out of the area I'm in. I hope you're doing okay…I've thought about you so much, and wanted to stop by. But I know Gabe said soon. Just know that I'm thinking of you.

Mylah"

This was the chance I was waiting for. I thought even more how perfect it would be for her and Donovan to connect. With his strong desire to watch beauty, there should be no problem between him and this brown haired beauty. *It will all be in how you handle it.* I clicked respond, and began to type her reply.

"To: Mylah Bush
From: Janie Lazarus
October 29, 2008 12:12Am

Hey Mylah. Wonderful to hear about your great week! Actually, I do have a client that I'd like to talk to you more about. I've been working with this customer since we

279

began, and he is wonderful. The pay is huge, and I think you will like it. Let's plan to meet at my place on Friday. Let me know if you can!

                        Thanks,
                                Janie"

Hitting the send button, I felt a sense of business empowerment. My next email on the list was from Donovan. I stretched my fingers a bit, and turned towards Gabe. I couldn't resist reaching out to him, and rubbing his shoulder gently while he read. He looked up at me, and rested his head on the back of the couch.

"How's it going over there?" I smiled back.

"Very well, getting my emails done now means I can sleep all day tomorrow." He nodded, and I squinted. "You know, maybe you could roll us another? I mean, you're home, and I'm home… I miss all our evenings together." I shrugged, and he tossed his book to the side, and sank to the floor to the secret box under the couch.

"Great idea. I'm pretty awake, too. So, we'd better take advantage. You almost done on there?" he pointed to the computer.

"Yeah, setting up a few meetings with Donovan, and verifying details about his event that's coming up next weekend. Give me just a moment." I turned back to my keyboard, and quickly pushed out the email.

"To: Donovan James
From: Janie Lazarus
October 29, 2008 12:42Am

Thanks for the email, and words. You've been so eloquent with your words to me, and I appreciate it. Thanks for being so great to Gabe, too. Tomorrow still okay for cleaning? I'd like to bring Gabe with me, and show him our set-up. Considering your past guests, I thought this wouldn't be a problem. Gabe also mentioned that you wanted to talk business with him. Do that then?

Your event is completely set, and has been for weeks. Most all of the RSVPs have come in already, and it's looking like around 300 people. I sent out invites to all of your business contacts, and solidified the menu and drink list last week, before the bullshit. Are you sure you want me at the event? With you? No, I don't think Gabe would have a problem with coming along. He knows you're legit. Okay…text me once you get this so I know what's up.

Going to go play with my husband now. See you tomorrow, Boss.   J"

~38~

I hit send, and quickly shut down my computer, just as Gabe returned to his seat on the couch. Handing me the joint, I leaned forward to grab it, and the blanket slipped. His eyes fell to my chest, and I quickly retreated with my now lit joint. He shifted again, now pressed against my left side. I took another long draw off of the smoke, and watched him dance to *Possum Kingdom* that had

281

come on to the radio. *Oh, his lip singing is impeccable!* My phone buzzed, and I dug for it under the blanket.

Gabe took the smoke, and I opened my phone. It was Donovan, already responding to my email.

Bring Gabe. Can't wait. You're the best planner ever. Seriously. D

I closed my phone, and tossed it to the end of the couch. *To be found at a later time, I hope? Now, maybe some more time with that amazing man over there...* Turning back towards him, he held the joint to my lips. My hand instinctively came to his wrist, and I drew in slowly, as to not burn my lips, or throat. Watching him while I inhaled, he intently watched the smoke go into my mouth. Our eyes met, and he reached to set the smoke down in the ashtray.

Rejoining our face-to-face seating, he brushed the hair out of my face, and I sank into the palm of his hand. My body was ready for him again, so much that I almost wanted to jump him on the couch. I opened my eyes to find his staring, hungrily, at me. In a rush, our lips crashed together in the middle, our teeth clanking a time or two. Our tongues were furious, and wrestling to the sound of Everlong on the radio. I broke our kiss to stand, and the blanket dropped in front of him. His eyes followed my body down, and back to my face. I reached out my hand for his, and pulled him into our bedroom.

He fell on top of me on the bed, and his hands ran the course of my body over and over. His lips stopped only momentarily on each nipple, biting and nibbling at my skin down my sides. My hips thrust at him without push, and my legs spread willingly. I urged him into me, and could feel his hard length pushing against me.

"You want this baby?" he palmed his length, and circled his head around my core. I nodded frantically, out of breath, and too turned on to speak. He pulled my legs to the side of the bed, and kneeled on the floor in front of me. Looking up, I found him staring into my core, licking his lips, ready to dive in. My head fell back, and my eyes closed, bracing to feel his hot mouth on me. In no time at all, I lost my breath with the touch of his tongue.

"MMMmmm..." the moan escaped, and I didn't even try to stop it. My fists clenched the sheets around me, and my legs failed around him. The mere feeling of his tongue pushing in and out of my hole tightened muscles I didn't even know I had. It wasn't until he stuck his fingers inside me, and his tongue pressed into my clit that I jumped out of my skin. "Oh Christ!" I yelled, holding tightly to the sheets while the waves of orgasm rolled through my body.

He pulled away from me for a moment, and reached for something at a distance. *Ah, the pillow.* He was back in between my legs, pushing into my core moments later. The feeling of him slowly filling me up was almost more than I could handle. With every inch, I could feel myself tighten more around him. His eyes grew darker, and darker.

"God, you're so fucking tight." He grunted in my ear, and he nibbled down my neck to my breasts. He pushed into me, over and over. Clinging to my shoulders, he pushed in farther and farther, deeper than ever before. Suddenly pulling out of me, he walked across the room to get a drink of water. I sat up a bit, and smiled at him, lost in a cloud of love and extreme sexual need.

He stalked back across the bedroom, and pushed me back to the bed. Grabbing both of my hips, he suddenly flipped me to my stomach. I pushed my hair out of my face, but dared not turn back to look at him. I felt his hands circle my rear end, and his fingers fell between my crack. My breath hitched, and suddenly, I knew what was coming. He circled his head around my core again, and slowly sank back inside.

His moans told me how pleased he was, and the way his fingers dug into me, pulling me closer, filled me with exploding love. I felt myself tighten around him again, my body now uncontrollable. His hands fell to my rear, and his fingers began fumbling around my ass. I felt him thumb my hole, and push into me slightly. The pressure that came after made me go numb. *Focus Janie…it's only Gabe. You use to like this sort of thing. Just let yourself go. Trust him.* The activity in both my core, and ass pushed me over the edge. I couldn't control the clamping that I was doing around his cock, or now his finger.

"Jesus Christ Janie, you're so fucking ready." He pulled out of me suddenly, and I felt his thumb replaced with the head of his penis. My ass was a little resistant at first, but once his other hand found its way back to my clit, he slid right in. "Oh my God," he lost his breath, and pushed farther inside of me.

The orgasms that followed from the double stimulation was more than I had ever felt in my life. Bliss, and then some. Once our rhythm was established, I pushed back into him, and met his every thrust. *MMmm, this is nice...* Even my subconscious was pleased. I pushed back into him again, and heard a moan like no other.

"Oh fuck!" he grunted, as he squeezed into my hips with his fingers. I could feel him throbbing hard inside me. He fell onto my back after catching his breath, and we both lay in a heap of sweat and fluids. *Fucking perfect.* He pulled out of me slowly, and rolled over on the bed, making room for him to fall down. He landed close to me, and I kissed his cheek.

I got up and used the facilities, and crawled back into bed. Turning the radio down, I set it on low, and turned on my black-lit nightlight. Wincing, I could sort of make out the time. *3:47 Am.* I felt the bed bounce a bit, and Gabe rolled over to his pillow, pulling me back with him. His arms fell around me, and he spooned my back skin to skin.

"Sleep now, baby. All day. You need the rest." God was that ever the truth. I would need the rest to put on my final show for Donovan...and Gabe. I knew they would both never forget it. I shook my head, trying to quiet the thoughts. Focusing on the warmth of Gabe's arms wrapped around me, I slowly fell into dreamland, where everything seemed so real.

~

When we finally got out of bed on Thursday morning, we were both almost bouncing off of the walls. Only getting out of bed Wednesday to grab dinner, and drinks...we slept the day away. I felt so much more rested, that getting up with the alarm was really no trouble at all. Gabe seemed extra happy today as well, bouncing out of bed to juice himself a smoothie first thing. He appeared in the bathroom as I dried off from my shower.

"MMMmmm," he moaned as he walked by me to his side of the bathroom. "That's a sight to see, right there." He teased. I shook my head, and walked over to the closet. "So, you're getting ready for work then, like you normally do?" I nodded, and smiled. I rifled through the clothes, and came across a newer lingerie set, and held it up next to me. Gabe's eyebrows wrinkled, and he whistled across the room. Looking down at his pants, and meeting my eyes again, he added, "Yep, that's pretty fucking hot." I couldn't hold in my laughter.

Sliding into the thong, and hooking the hooks on the top I stepped in front of the mirror. The satin material had a beautiful shimmer in the light, and I knew it was the perfect outfit. *Don't look now, but your husband is drooling over you. Don't act shocked. You know what you do to him.* The deep midnight blue color was brought out more by the shimmer of my blonde hair. I frowned when my eyes stopped at my shoulder.

"You can barely even see it, don't worry." He said idly, without ever taking his eyes off of me. I shrugged, and slowly reached up with my hand to feel the rough patch of skin. It was starting to scab over to heal, but it felt disgusting. Turning away from the mirror, I had to walk away or face reliving every memory tied to my shoulder. Gabe's eyes followed me closely as I bolted around the bedroom to escape being in the mirror's reflection. "Baby?" I slid my dress over the lingerie ensemble, quickly covering up my tainted shoulder.

"Its fine, I just don't want to see it. I don't want to go there." I headed back into the bathroom, and saw Gabe put his jeans on. Leaning into the mirror, I had to still my shaking hands to put on my mascara. *Don't poke yourself in the damn eye, Janie. Jesus Christ.* I blinked a few times, to make sure that no clumps had been left. Reapplying my foundation, I looked up, and nodded. That was as good as it was going to get. Period.

I grabbed my sweater, and headed for the kitchen. Gabe was waiting for me, having a drink at the bar. I smirked at him, and nudged him with my rear.

"You nervous or something?" I chuckled under my breath, and saw him turn his head to the side.

"Yeah, actually. Even though I've heard from you both about this, and even though I'm not threatened by it… I'm still sort of freaking out thinking I'm going to be watching this." I shrugged, and wrapped my arms around his back.

"Don't worry, it's nothing that you're not use to already." I winked, and grabbed my purse. "Come on, Jeep's waiting!" As I stepped out of the house, my cell phone rang, playing *Almost Lover.* Pulling it out of my pocket, I stopped to see who it was. *Shit, Sean.* I looked up at Gabe, and motioned for him to hold on a second. This needed to be over. I walked down the path, towards the pond, and answered the phone.

"Hello Sean," I said, trying to not sound as petrified as I was to have this conversation.

"Janie," his voice sounded quiet, and forlorn. "I just needed to hear your voice…and make sure that you were still talking to me." I shook my head, this wasn't a game.

"Of course I'm still talking to you, and I will continue to." I cleared my throat, and pushed on. "I

287

just can't ever let it get like that again. It will surely ruin everything." I waited for his response. He was breathing heavily, but the background was silent. "And anyway, I don't want to hurt your pregnant wife like that. That's not me."

"I understand that. I'm just all over the place emotionally. We were here, and then we were…there. The images of you burn my mind every day, and some times, you're all I think about." My mouth fell open, and I heard him catch his breath. "I know it's wrong, and I know it shouldn't happen. But it did… and it was everything I've dreamed of you. If only…" I shook my head again. *I wonder if this conversation was a good idea at this point…*

"Maybe it will just take a little time, you know? Memories will fade, and we can all go back to being great friends." After all these years, it almost hurt thinking that I may have to step away from his friendship. I wanted to prevent that, if possible.

"I don't know, Janes…" he paused. "Anyway, I just wanted to hear your voice. I'm glad that things are calming down for you guys now. I'm going back out on the road for a little while for work, so I gave Delaney your number if she had questions. I hope that's okay." *WHAT?! Seriously… that's not strange or awkward at all there, buddy.*

"Oh, sure, but Sean, isn't she due soon?" I couldn't understand him, running away when she'd need him the most. "Shouldn't you be home with her?"

"I just can't right now." His voice was suddenly stern, and cold. "Don't worry about it, okay?" I didn't like his tone, at all. Looking up, Gabe was leaning on the car, smiling. I smiled back, it was time to move on with the day.

"Wow, okay. I'll be here if she needs me." There was silence, and it was heavy. I hated this. Walking back on the path, listening to each other breathing on the phone... I knew it would never be the same again. *Guess this is your awkward conversation, Janes.* "Alright, when you're ready...just send me an email or something." I swallowed hard, and I know he could hear it.

"I'm sorry Janie. I messed everything up." The phone clicked, and I sighed. Sliding my phone back into my bag, I cheerfully climbed in my now open door, winking at the love of my life. *Goodbye, drama.*

"How was that, love?" Gabe questioned as I sat down. I shrugged, unable to put words to the odd feelings.

"It was Sean. Delaney needed my number." I nodded, and Gabe seemed to quickly understand. He closed my door, and walked around to get in. His hand rested on my thigh as we drove to the James Estate together. *It sure is nice making this trip together...*

As we pulled in, I watched the expression on Gabe's face change a few times. First, at the hugeness of the house, which I was still taken aback from whenever I pulled in. I punched in my code, and the large gates opened immediately. I turned to smile at Gabe, and his mouth still hung open. I laughed out loud. Pulling into my spot next to Donovan's Bentley, I was sure that I had lost Gabe forever.

"Oh Jesus...look at that car!" He all but jumped out of the Jeep's window to get a closer look. *Now, this is the Gabe I've missed.* I got out, and headed towards the door. Gabe ran around the

Bentley one last time, and joined me at the door. I rang the bell, and heard the footsteps coming on the other side. Opening the door, Donovan smiled very widely.

"Janie!" his arms were around me in a flash. "Thank God." He shook his head, and released me to turn towards Gabe. "Gabriel," he extended his hand, and they shook firmly.

"Hello, Donovan. Your Bentley is amazing, Sir." He said jokingly, and they both laughed.

"Okay, okay. I'm going to get started. Maybe I'll see you both around in there…" I tip toed past them both, and threw my sweater into the corner chair, barely inside the door. I could feel both sets of eyes on me, and I could hear their muffled whispers following my flow through the house. Before I entered the kitchen, I turned around to see them both giggling, as if telling each other great secrets. I smiled, and went in the kitchen.

Moments later, I heard the radio turn on very loudly, and heard the security system get armed. I sighed, knowing that here, I'd be safer than anywhere else. Protected by the best, I giggled. The kitchen wasn't really lived in, and only took me mere moments to clean up. I kicked off my shoes, and began dust mopping the halls. When I got to the stairs, I began heading up, and stopped when I heard their laughter. *I love this for him. A real friend, one that's solid in business, and a truly decent individual. I hope that Donovan is as receptive about your proposed changes as you think he will be. He did only want you for this, you remember.* Approaching the top of the stairs, I could clearly see our two chairs at the top. Ironically both still facing each other, sloppily out of symmetry with the rest of the furniture set up.

I quietly began to clean the upstairs, and I heard two voices approaching. I finished tidying the room, and headed for the stairs. "Here's where Allison stayed," I heard Donovan tell Gabe. I lingered to try to hear what they were saying, but I couldn't make much out.

While the boys were upstairs, I decided to haul ass down to the study, and prepare for them there. I took two stairs at once on the way down, and jumped off the staircase with six stairs to go. Their voices were getting closer, so I knew his tour of the upstairs was almost over. Racing through the study, I closed and locked the main doors. Smiling at myself, I had just given myself a few extra minutes to breath. *To hell with breathing, drink girl! Drink!*

My eye brows raised, and I headed over to the bar. I poured myself a quick double shot of vodka, and downed the fire liquid as fast as I could. Shuttering, I almost couldn't hold it in. Breathing deeply, I heard the main door knob shake. I smirked, and finished pouring to the double shot line.

"Janie??" Donovan asked through the door. I listened, and turned up the music. "Oh, she's in there. Let's use the side door." Downing the second double, my chest was on fire, and as if on cue, my limbs started to throb appropriately. I took my hair out of the clip it was in, and let it roughly fall around my face. Reaching around, I grabbed the zipper on the back of my dress, and pulled almost all of the way down.

The door burst open moments later. Their faces went from worried, to very intrigued in seconds. It may have been the loud music. It may have been the wild look in my eyes, or the ornery smile that fell across my lips. Regardless of what it was, they both strolled around the room, tapping out the beat of Zeppelin's Communication Breakdown. Reaching the couch, Gabe fell into it. Donovan headed towards the bar, and poured two drinks. *Looks like scotch...*

I moved to the table, and climbed it. Very deliberately bending every chance I got, and running my hands down the lengths of my body as often as I could. The songs shifted, and I turned to face them.

"Ready for this?" I smiled, and kept moving. I looked at Donovan, and turned towards Gabe. I let my eyes intentionally meet his, and lock on deeply. Lightfoot came over the radio, and *Sundown* made me time trip. I spun around, and pulled my shoulders out of the dress. With one slight shimmy, it fell around my ankles, and I heard them both shift.

Moving with the beat of the music, I let my hands fall to my hips, circling them around and around. I couldn't help but hum the music while I moved. Turning back to them, I faced them, slinking around on a table, wearing the midnight blue lingerie. Donovan had moved to the sitting area, and was sitting near Gabe. Both of their mouths were parted slightly, and I could see their tongues falling around inside their lips. I smiled, and sat on the table, spread eagle.

"So, Gabe, here's where it gets interesting. Donovan likes to watch, very, very intently." I shifted, and laid flat on the table. Pulling my knees up, rolling over to my side, causing one nipple to peak out of my bra accidentally. I looked down at my breast, raised an eyebrow, and looked back up to both sets of eyes. "Gabe, you can do what you'd like. I'm sure Donovan wouldn't mind." I looked at Donovan, and he cleared his throat roughly.

"Not at all, by all means…forget I'm here." Gabe turned to look at him, and they nodded at each other. I shifted on the table again, throwing my body around with the beat of the music. I closed my eyes, and let my hands wander from my lips, down to my chest. They lingered around my breasts, spending an extra moment on each nipple, pulling and tugging a bit.

Continuing down my abdomen, I let my fingers trail a path from my belly button, into the brim of my thong. Suddenly, I felt hands on my feet, climbing up my legs. I opened my eyes to find my beautiful husbands blue eyes staring into mine, and his mouth slowly dipped in to kiss my own. He took my hand, and pulled me to the side of the table. I hung my legs over the side, and his thighs pushed my legs open wide. I watched him intently, never breaking the stare.

His breathing was ragged, and his face told me he wanted me badly. I was ready, and glancing over his shoulder, my client was very happy with this. *Back to your husband... Turn it up now.* Pulling myself up, I locked lips with my man again. Our tongues danced around, and our lips connected with little effort. His hands moved to my head, and held my face in place. His mouth then assaulted my own, leaving me breathless, and longing for more.

Pushing me away, and flipping me over on the table, he put one hand firmly on my back, and held me down. *Oh, hell yes! You know what's coming!* His hand crashed into my backside, and I gasped for a breath. Again, and again. The stinging was perfect, and the internal throbbing was growing. I spread my legs wider, hoping he'd

293

understand. His hand smacked into my ass again, and this time his finger dove in between my legs. Dipping in and out of me, I could hear his breathing change.

Looking to my side, I caught sight of Donovan. His pants around his ankles, and pumping feverishly. He held a huge grin, and watched us like a movie. I smirked at him, and he winked at me. Focusing back on Gabe, I felt him push all his fingers inside of me. My body writhed under his touch, and made me needy for more. Wrapping his fingers around the sides of my thong, he quickly pulled them off of me. They ripped the seams, and he tossed them over to Donovan. *Ha! Did you see that Janie?!* I tried to stifle any giggles.

I climbed off of the table, and fell in front of Gabe. Fumbling with his buttons, I finally got his pants to fall, exposing my favorite thing ever. I greedily grabbed his shaft, and pulled him into my mouth. His silky soft head ran over my tongue, and I swirled it around the tip. Taking him to the back of my throat was easy, and doing so, he lost his breath. I loved causing that to happen. Reaching my hands around his waist, I pulled him into my mouth deeply. His teeth ground together, and his head fell back.

"Jesus Janie!" he hissed through clenched teeth. Grabbing my shoulders, he pulled me upwards, breaking the seal I had created around his shaft. Putting me back on the table, I sat on the edge, and waited for him. He pushed forward, and pressed straight into my core. My body instantly tightened, my nipples so hard and perky. My abdomen absorbed each thrust, and my hips were perfect grips for his fingers.

"MMMmmm," I moaned, reaching out to

touch him. My hands landed on his biceps, and I squeezed into his flesh. He thrusts grew harder, and his grip tightened. I wrapped my legs around him, and squeezed into him, feeling as much of him as I could. His eyes locked with mine, and his mouth was closed tightly. I felt his balls tighten, and the hot ooze flowing into my insides. His body gyrated with each pulse, while he drained into me. My body convulsed around his throbbing, rock hard shaft.

Carefully, he laid us both back on the table. His head rested against my chest, and he closed his eyes. Breathing slowly, he cleared his throat, and steadied his footing.

"You okay, baby?" I nodded, and smile. Peering around him, I look towards Donovan, who was cleaning up his own mess, and now oblivious to us. Gabe turned to see what had happened, and turned back to me and nodded. "I get it now." He leaned down to kiss me, and slowly pulled out. He gave me a hand to sit, and picked up my dress and gave it back to me.

Smiling at this entire situation, I slid my dress back on. Falling over on the couch, Donovan brought over two drinks, and placed them on the table next to me. He cleared his throat loudly, and lit a cigar.

"As always, you never disappoint, Janie." He turned towards Gabe. "Your wife is… amazing." He gestured with his hands, and Gabe agreed with him.

"You're very correct. She's more than amazing, and I'm pretty fucking lucky." He tilted his head, and drank back the glass of scotch. I shook my head, and sipped at the beverage Donovan had brought to me. Watching the two of them, both of their ornery smiles made me laugh.

"What's so funny, Mrs. Lazarus?" Donovan asked jokingly.

"Oh, nothing." I smirked, and met Donovan's gaze. "I need to ask you something." He nodded, and I sat up a bit on the couch. "I'd like to introduce you to one of my employees tomorrow. Her name is Mylah." He frowned, and thought deeply for a moment. Taking another drink, he walked over to his desk, and pushed a button on his phone.

"Jack, let yourself in with the code."

"Yes, sir." A male's voice replied through the microphone. I sat back, wondering what was going on. Donovan smiled, and raised his hand to ease us both.

"Thank you, Jack." He sat at his desk, and swiveled his chair towards me. "Janie, I will NOT let you leave me as a planner, and I do hope that you'll hear out my plans. Both of you," he turned back towards Gabe, and cleared his throat. Gabe's eyes met mine, and turned back to listen. "But, I do understand your need for change, after everything that's happened. I've grown to know you, and your wonderful business ethic in these past many weeks." He smiled widely at me.

"Thank you Donovan," I said brightly. "I really think you'll like her. She's beautiful, really." I giggled quietly. "And she's single." I raised my eyebrows at him, and he shook his head and laughed.

"Gabriel," he stood, motioning Gabe to his desk. He stood slowly, and hesitantly. "I've got a business offer for you. One that can make you both very wealthy." He smiled, devilishly, and opened a large cabinet. I couldn't see what was happening, but I did hear Gabe's breath stop abruptly. I stood

296

quickly, and moved to where they were standing. *Oh my God! Look at that…*

~39~

I'd never heard Gabe so excitedly giggly, but I could tell he was genuinely happy with the offers that Donovan made. As we pulled in the driveway, I watched the black car park at the end of our driveway, officially blocking it from entry. Our new security gates were being installed soon, and our safety was now at the top of Donovan's list. We headed down the driveway, past our own house, back to Jean's. It was time to pick up my babies. Gabe parked the car, and turned to me and smiled. I hopped out of the car at a full sprint pace, and didn't even bother ringing the doorbell.

Turning the corner, I was met with squeals, gasps, and laughter. I lost my breath when their arms wrapped around me, and finally, those tears I couldn't find were flowing out of me. *See? Everything's going to be okay. Adjustments are to be expected. Just breathe.*

"Mommy!" Galen screamed. "Can we come home now?" I nodded, unable to speak through my tears of joy.

"I'm soo glad about that! I left my Goosebumps book in my room, and Grandma wouldn't let me get it!" Lilah crossed her arms.

"Well, let's go get in the car then, and go home." I turned to Gabe, who was sitting down at the kitchen table.

"I'd like to fill mom in on the updates, and the security. You drive home, and put the kids to bed. I'll walk in a bit." He smiled, and for the first time, I didn't feel uneasy about being alone. *Because you're not.* Jean walked over to me, her face full of every emotion.

"Oh honey, I'm so happy for you. And for them." The tears trickled down her cheeks, and I hugged her tighter than I had before.

"You're such a lifesaver, Jean. I love you." She kissed my cheek, and moved to sit down with Gabe. "I'll see you in a bit." I winked at him. "Goodnight, Jean." I turned to find the kids already in the back seat, smiling brightly. I climbed in, and couldn't help but look at them in the rearview. *Those are the reasons, right there. The reasons for change. The reasons for risk.* I smiled at myself in the mirror.

"Mommy?" Lilah asked quietly.

"Yeah, princess?"

"Are we really safe now?" Her voice shook a bit, and I pulled into the garage. Parking, and closing the garage door, I turned to her in the back seat. I reached for her, and for Galen, putting my hands on both of them.

"Yes, we've got a new security man. His name is Jack, and he's very nice. I'll introduce you tomorrow. Let's go inside, and I'll tell you more, okay?" They nodded, and instantly ran into the house, putting their bags and coats on their hooks. "Hey, put your pajamas on, too. Then come out here by the front door." I grabbed my cell phone, and quickly opened it to send Jack a quick text.

Two minutes, flash the headlights. Showing the kids it's safe. You can meet them tomorrow. Thank you, Jack, for everything.

I sent the text, and looked up to find them both staring at me. I smiled, and motioned them over to the window.

"Look towards the end of the driveway. In a few days, we'll have a new locked gate there. It won't let anyone in, unless they have a special code." I checked, and they were both straining to see. "For now, we have Jack." As if on cue, the headlights flashed toward the house three times. "That's him, saying hello." They gasped, and laughed out loud.

"Cool! We've got our own ninja!" Galen yelled, and jumped up and down. Lilah smiled at him, and nodded at me. She reached for a hug, and I quickly embraced her.

"That makes me feel a little better," she admitted.

"It should. We're all going to be fine." I hugged her, and patted her soft dark hair. "Alright guys, let's head to bed. It is a school day tomorrow, and we'll be back to regular schedules." Without the typical bedtime hesitation, they both went to their rooms, and happily hopped in bed. Heading into Lilah's room first, I turned on her radio, and nightlight. Sitting on the edge of the bed, I pulled the covers up around her, and she smiled.

"I love you, mom." She said sweetly.

"Love you too, princess. I'm very proud of you for being such a helpful, big girl this past week." I kissed her head, and stood to leave her room. "Goodnight," I said, and closed the door behind me. Walking into Galen's room, he was sitting up reading to his dinosaur.

"He wanted to hear a book. Look!" he motioned for me to sit, which I speedily did. "I can read now!" And he began pointing at the words, making up his very own story about a dinosaur.

"That's super, honey! But now it's bed time. Will you read to me more tomorrow?" I tucked him in, and he smiled very big. Nodding, he was now pretending he was a mute dinosaur. "Okay, good, dinosaur Galen. I'll see you in the morning." I got now human answer, only a short, "Rawrrr..." as I closed the door. I shook my head, and leaned on the wall in between their bedrooms. *Normalcy. It's finally coming back, and you're getting nervous. Don't panic, Janes. Everything's going to be alright.*

I sighed, and headed for the bedroom. I heard my phone buzz, and stopped by my desk to check it. It was a text from Mylah.

Tomorrow morning okay? 9ish?

I quickly responded, as I needed to get some sleep. 9am would be perfect, and leave me enough time to take her to meet Donovan, too. I sent the text, and turned to find Gabe leaning in the doorway. I smiled at him, and pulled my clothes off. I grabbed one of his big shirts, and slid it over my head. He smiled, coyly.

"It's starting to feel normal again." He paused. "That shit makes me nervous." Instantly, I felt closer to him than ever, and I patted the bed next to me. He sat down, and rested his head on my shoulder.

"Me too, I feel like it's going to fall apart at any second. I'm trying so hard to think of the future." I felt him inhale deeply, and heard his exhale.

"Same here." He sat up, and pulled his shirt off. Kicking his shoes off, he wrapped his arms around me, and pulled me down to the bed. We lay in the silence, and darkness, breathing the same pace. *Quite possibly, thinking the same thoughts.* Planning for the future would soon be much easier, and the kids would want for nothing. Irresistible deals brokered, and accepted.

"Love you, baby," he said in a whispered sleep. I nuzzled into his body, and his arms tightened around me. At Your Service, LLC would be even bigger six months from now, and the business detail would be so much different. I tried to relax knowing that I had two of the best businessmen I knew on my side, helping with every step. *Everything will be fine.* I tried to repeat to myself, but my eyes were finally getting heavy.

~

I woke up to my phone buzzing, and a note next to me in the bed. I turned over, and rubbed the sleep out of my eyes. The sun was shining, and I had hoped the day would be perfect. Checking the time, it was already 8:15am. I grabbed my phone, and checked the messages. I smiled. *Gabe.*

Love, just waking you up. You were so peaceful, and I needed some Daddy time. Checking in with the Phoenix, and heading over to Donovan's. See you soon.

I closed the phone, and ran into the bathroom to get ready. I pulled on my jeans, grey vintage t-shirt, and boots. My hair was a disaster, but that didn't really matter today. I put on some thin layers of makeup, and hit the kitchen for a banana. As always, Mylah was early. My phone rang, and it was Jack.

"Hello, Jack."

"Mrs. Lazarus, Miss Bush is here if you're ready for her." He was very business professional.

"Yes, please let her through."

"Thank you, mam." I chuckled, and hung up the phone. Opening the front door, I waited for her to run in from the chilly weather. She got out of the car quickly, and trotted quickly to the door.

"Hey Mylah!" Her arms instantly engulfed me, and she hugged me tightly.

"I was so worried about you, and I'm so glad that you're okay." I smiled, and nodded.

"Thank you. It's good to be feeling better." I motioned her over to the bar. "How're you doing these days? Other job going okay?" She shook her head.

"Things are okay, but I did quit the other job. It was too much pressure, and the clientele was not very friendly." I nodded, and wrinkled my nose. "I'm really happy working for you, and I'm so happy you care to give me more work." She smiled, being as truthful as she could. *It's time to sell this deal.*

"Mylah, this deal I'm about to offer you," I paused, and squinted at her. "It's only for you, and must remain very secret." Her brow wrinkled, and she sat forward in her chair.

"Do tell me more," her smile turned slightly crooked.

"Okay. Since we began cleaning and taking clients, I have been servicing the James Estate. Not only am I his main event planner, I have also been cleaning for him." She nodded, as if understanding the big dollar amounts. "But I wasn't just cleaning for him." Her mouth fell open, and she tried to stifle a giggle.

"Were you screwing him?!" it fell out of her mouth before she could stop it, and her hand instinctively covered her mouth, and her three shades of red cheeks. "I'm so sorry," I held up my hand.

"Don't be sorry. No, I wasn't doing him. I was carrying out his fantasies of voyeurism. We participated in dual masturbation, as well." Her mouth hung open, and I waited for something to come out. *Something? Anything?* I cleared my throat, hoping that would get something to fall out of her mouth. "He doesn't touch, he only looks. He's respectful, very safe, and the pay is ridiculous." Her eyes met mine.

"How much are we talking about here?" I smiled at her, and leaned over the bar towards her.

"You'd get six thousand dollars a month." Her mouth fell open again, and she began nodding her head. "Does that mean you'd like to meet him?" She nodded again, and I suddenly remembered Gabe would be there, too. "Oh, one other thing.." I walked around the bar, and laid a new contract out for her. "My husband, Gabriel, knew about the entire set up between Donovan, ah, Mr. James, and I. He will now be working with Mr. James frequently, and may be in and out of the residence while you're there." Her eyes grew wide, and I knew her mind was racing. "Don't worry, Mylah. It's not something I'm worried about, as I'll be in and out of there, too." She smiled, and looked back at her hands. *She's stunned. That was kind of a lot to take in. Don't you think?*

"Is this for real?" she asked, almost shocked.

"Yes, it's very real." I grabbed my keys. "You can ride with me over to Donovan's. It's not

303

far from here." I smiled, and held out my hand to her. She took it, and we hopped into the Jeep.

She was silent on the way over, and stuck to reading the new contract. I saw her nod a few times as she read, and I hoped she had realized how much she was truly getting.

"Janie, this seems like a dream. I mean," she paused, and finally spoke as I pulled in to enter my code. "I could move with this!" I smiled, and punched the buttons. "Oh my God..." her mouth fell open again, seeing the size of the Estate.

"It's a lot to take in. Uhm, so is he, by the way." I winked at her. "He's in the process of a divorce, too. Just food for thought." I giggled, and parked next to the Bentley. I noticed another newer looking car, and loved the color. It was a deep blue, and almost shimmered in the sun light. "That's beautiful."

~40~

"You're right," his voice came behind us suddenly. I turned to see Donovan walking towards us, opening his arms to me. I embraced him, and deep down, really liked his hugs. *He feels like safety.* "I'm looking at two very beautiful things now. Janie." He pulled back. "Introduce me to this exquisite lady, please." I smiled, and Mylah blushed.

"Donovan James, please meet Mylah Bush. She'll be taking over my lead for you," I giggled, and motioned Mylah up the stairs. Their hands met with a firm hand shake, and their eyes locked instantly. *Uh oh... do you see what I see?* Smiling again, I opened the front door. Clearing my throat, I

304

spoke up a bit. "Let's go discuss the details then." They turned to walk in the house.

"Janie," Donovan turned towards me. "Don't set the codes yet, Gabe's almost here." I nodded, and took Mylah into the study. Donovan scurried into another room, and left me to handle the details with Mylah.

"Put down your stuff, and I'll show you around." She nodded, and we headed upstairs. The loft was still as we had left it, disheveled, and everything out of place. I chuckled a bit. "You'll find the upstairs to be quite eventful, once you're comfortable. These rooms here, and this bathroom. Plus the loft." I motioned around, and she took it all in.

Following me downstairs, we went into the kitchen, where Gabe was now standing with Donovan, in a deep discussion.

"Hey baby," he walked towards me, looking over my shoulder. "Hi, I'm Gabe Lazarus. Janie's husband." He extended his hand towards Mylah to shake it, and she accepted."

"Hello Gabe. It's nice to meet you. It sounds like we may be seeing each other here soon." The room fell silent, and little bursts of laughter emerged from just about everyone.

"Yeah, I guess you could say that." He chuckled, and Mylah's cheeks turned red.

"Oh, okay. I see how you all are! Give me a few weeks to adjust, and I'll be joking right there with you!" she crossed her arms, and tried to look fierce. We all laughed harder.

"See, Donovan?" I turned towards him. "She's going to fit in perfectly here." Mylah smiled very wide, and you could feel the flow in the room. I turned back towards Mylah, "Now, you want to start today?" Her eyebrows instantly went up.

"Does that mean I get paid today?"

"Hell yes!" Donovan's voice rang out over all else. "Cash, if you'd like." Her mouth fell open. "You do understand the deal, and have signed all of the proper paperwork?"

"Yes, sir." She said flatly.

"Oh now, none of that "sir" shit. Just call me Donovan, please." He smiled at her, and extended his hand to her. "Friends?" he asked gently. She nodded, and I walked her back to the study.

"All of the cleaning supplies are in the hall closet, and you can use the hall desk to hold your things while you are here. He'll get you your own code for the gates, too. Are you good with this? You're sure?" Without hesitation, she nodded.

"Yes. I promise. This is an amazing deal, and he does seem like a genuinely nice guy." I smiled. *Oh, he is. He's handsome, and has a huge package, too. Ahh, memories.* Swallowing, I shook the thought from my head.

"Well, okay then. I'm going to go find out what the deal is with my husband, and let Donovan know you'll get started. Last bit of advice?" She listened eagerly. "Turn on some music, and just dance." I left the room, and headed back to the kitchen. Gabe was at the counter with Donovan, and they both turned to smile at me when I entered. He was closing the box on the counter, and taping it up. I lifted my eyebrows at them, unsure of exactly what was going down.

"No worries, baby, Don and I were just working out some future plans, and he wanted to make sure certain things weren't completely ruled out." *Did he really just call him 'Don'?* Gabe's mouth met mine for a quick kissed, and he turned to

306

pick up the box. Still just as confounded as before, I turned back towards Donovan.

"Donovan, she's getting started now." His eyes lit up. "What are the plans with the rest of today?" I turned to Gabe, and he shrugged.

"I'm done after this already. Want to go home for a bit before the kids get home?" I smiled, devilishly.

"Yes." I headed for the side door, stopping only briefly to say goodbyes. "See you, Donovan. Have fun with my Mylah, and treat her well." My head was twirling around again, and the first steps in our future plans were off without delay. Mylah was very happy, and I could now focus on growing the business, and helping Gabe in the latest ventures with Donovan. *I told you everything was going to be okay.* I turned up the radio, and *Stand by Me* rang into my ears.

I knew he'd be close behind me, so I got into the house quickly, and closed all of the curtains. I quickly kicked off my shoes, and threw my jeans on the floor on my way to the bathroom. I left a path of clothes so he would know exactly where to go. The jets were calling my name. I turned on the tub, as hot as I could stand it, and climbed in. As I did, I could hear the garage door open, and close. *He's home.*

I felt positively giddy, and the butterflies floated in my stomach. The tub reached the fill level, and I pushed the on button. The jets sprung to life, and instantly pushed into my still sore muscles. I rested my head on the pillow, and waited to be joined by my love. My thoughts spun on the past few months, and everything that had happened. *You have to stop going there, Janie. It's in the past, and there's nothing you could've done to fix it. Lucky you, no more lies, no more secrets. Now you're an open book, and your life is pointing in a good direction. I can't say your choices are the ones I'd make, but I understand your thoughts. Gabe's, too, for that matter. Relax, honey. You've earned a little bit of peace.* I heard the door click, and I opened my eyes to find his deep ocean blues staring back at me.

"Now this looks like fun," he gently poked at my breast through the water jets. "Would you like some company?" I smiled, and nodded. I laid my head back again on the headrest, watching the most beautiful man I've ever met strip in front of me. *God, just look at him. So real, and so perfect.* I was sure I was drooling, and as he sat in the tub, I sat up and our lips locked together. Clinging to his shoulders, I just needed him to feel my complete and utter love for him. He broke our kiss, and stared deeply into my eyes, whispering only, "Janie..."

Lost in his kiss, and the feel of his exquisite touch, I was home. *Safe at home.* Who knew what the future was going to bring to us with all of this, but we were definitely going big places. He slowly slid into me, and I clung to his shoulders to stabilize myself. Every inch of him fit into every inch of me, and molded us together. My head fell back again, taking in all of his pleasure, and I caught myself in the mirrors above the tub.

I almost didn't recognize the devious grin that spread across my face, but it told me that I was ready to deal with anything. Clenching around him, my lips fell open, as a moan escaped my lips. *This is your life Janie. It's time to start really living, and taking those important risks. Don't you think?* Oh, yes. I couldn't agree more. ~

Here Comes More!!

~

*Book 3 of the Probed Saga coming SOON!

*Gluten Free for Me cook book coming in 2014!

*A short story collection of the Hilarity that has ensued around me in my 10+ years in the adult industry! Little bit of the lighter side of funny. ☺

~

Thanks for the Support!!!